SEPARATED BY A DREAM

"Fay, tell me about your dream—is it all just money and applause? They're nothing but trappings."

"I need them," she said. "They're important to me."

He was shaken. "But surely they aren't enough!"

"What else is there?" she cried. "For me, I mean. Oh, sure, you can become the great engineer. And so you build monuments—lasting monuments out of wood or iron and mortar. And for a hundred years, your work will stand for all to see and praise. When *I* perform there is *nothing* left for tomorrow. When the applause dies, it's over until the next time."

She stepped back, her eyes glinting with fire and fury. "Know this, Glenn. I'm in it exactly for those 'trappings,' as you so arrogantly put it."

Glenn took a deep, ragged breath. "I'm sorry to hear that. I thought we were both aiming for something higher."

She slapped him. Hard. And there were tears running down her cheeks when she sobbed a good-bye and ran.

SILVER WINDS

Gary McCarthy

BANTAM BOOKS
TORONTO · NEW YORK · LONDON · SYDNEY

SILVER WINDS
A Bantam Book / February 1983

For information address: Bantam Books, Inc.

ISBN 0-553-23127-8

Published simultaneously in the United States and Canada

Bantam Books are published by Bantam Books, Inc. Its trademark, consisting of the words "Bantam Books" and the portrayal of a rooster, is Registered in U.S. Patent and Trademark Office and in other countries. Marca Registrada. Bantam Books, Inc., 666 Fifth Avenue, New York, New York 10103.

PRINTED IN THE UNITED STATES OF AMERICA

H 0 9 8 7 6 5 4 3 2 1

SILVER WINDS

1

Julia Matson felt sick again this morning as she bought the Wells Fargo ticket, but it didn't matter. Nothing physical could compare with the pain she felt remembering. She closed her eyes; his face appeared and his touch seared her skin like a crimson brand that all others would recognize and, in the seeing, despise.

Julia stood by the stagecoach door and prayed the driver would soon tell her that she could climb aboard and leave San Francisco forever. Had she been able to afford ship's passage, she would have fled across the world in exile, but that was impossible. What little money she had left would have to suffice until . . . Until what? Julia bit her lower lip and knew she wasn't going to cry with people watching.

She was going to run before they learned the truth, which was even now being whispered among the city's most influential. How they would snicker, Julia thought. It would feed their gossipy tongues for weeks.

"Ma'am?"

Julia looked up, and something in the expression of the stage driver said she'd not been keeping her thoughts well-hidden.

"You all right, ma'am?"

"Of course," she said, far too quickly. "I'm concerned about the schedule, that's all. If I can't leave at once, I'll have to make other arrangements. Please. I want to go."

"I've talked to the man who hired this special run I'm making. He knows the passes may be closed but he's offered the company a thousand-dollar bonus if I can get it through. And I will, because I get a third if we make it. The gentleman must be rich and in a powerful hurry to become even richer. Name's

Bevis York, and he's bringing his daughter, Miss Holly. I told 'em what you said and Mr. York agreed to let you come. Mostly, though, it was on account of his daughter."

"Thank you," she whispered, almost sagging with relief.

He nodded hesitantly, acted shy for such a powerful-looking man. Then he turned and limped away to climb up onto the driver's seat. For the first time she noticed he was dressed in buckskin clothes.

"Julia, wait!"

She pivoted, feeling her stomach twist up as if there was a knife inside. Then she saw him, racing across the street, dodging wagons and yelling her name. A low moan escaped her lips and she wrenched open the stage door, knowing they couldn't leave without the Yorks being aboard. She threw herself inside, falling hard.

"Julia!"

"Go away!" she cried. "Leave me alone!"

"No! We've got to talk this thing out!"

She tried to speak, tried to say something and couldn't as she felt him lift her to the seat.

"Julia, I'm sorry. I didn't know they were coming. My wife swore she'd never leave Philadelphia."

She whirled, raking at him with her fingernails, wanting to tear and ruin his handsome face. She screamed at him, "William, you never told me about her. You used me with lies!"

"Stop it!" he yelled. And when she didn't, he slapped her hard. "I did love you!"

"I hate you. You're just like all men. Vicious and conniving and a liar."

An arm, thick and heavily muscled, encased in soft leather, blurred inside the coach and clamped down on the wrist that was drawing back to strike her again.

There was a cry of pain and then she felt William Allison lifted and saw him pitched out into the dirt. The driver roared something in a language she did not know, and when the derringer suddenly appeared in William's hand, the roar ended as bone cracked.

William Allison, who had probably never felt so much as the hurt of a blister, screamed in agony and rolled and roared with hurt as Julia gaped in shock.

"My name is Clayton James," the stage driver told her as he gently closed the door. "I can't abide a man who hits a lady."

Clayton James glanced back at the writhing figure and his face was taut and cold. "I apologize for not stopping him quicker, ma'am. You're in my coach and you're my responsibility. Won't happen again."

She nodded mutely, felt herself being steadied by his simple, uncluttered statement of fact.

"Can we go now?" she breathed.

"Yes, ma'am. I'll tell Mr. York we can't wait any longer. I'll make him know I've a timetable to keep. A stage to handle."

He turned, then changed his mind. "Ma'am. I didn't hear anything and . . . and your lip is bleeding some. Shame to see on one so beautiful as you."

Julia watched him limp over to the man she'd loved and drag him erect, then propel him away with a hard shove. Several minutes later, an angry Bevis York clambered heavily aboard, threatening to insist on a new driver.

But it was too late, and as the stage jumped forward and gathered momentum, Julia's glistening eyes saw William Allison as he disappeared from her life forever.

Somewhere ahead lay the mighty Sierra Nevada Mountains they'd have to cross, and maybe the snows would block them. But nothing could stop the hurting she felt and the seed of William's which multiplied deep inside her like a terrible reminder of her sin.

More than a hundred and thirty miles to the west, Glenn Donovan's eyes stung with grit as he rounded the mountain and faced the blasting, icy wind which raged downward from the Sierra peaks. The wagon tracks he followed were blown dirt-clean of wheel marks until only the rocks underneath could hold. The blizzard waited, seemed to beckon him with gray, twisted fingers of cloud toward a fate which had made the Donner party a name to be remembered for its frozen depravities.

Glenn twisted around until his back was to the wind. His numb fingers scrubbed the tears from his eyes and he pulled his collar higher. Behind him, the gale moaned off the peaks. Soft it was, a pleading. Come higher, it called. Higher!

He shivered at its sound and peered down into the treacherous gorge of the American River, a river which plunged its way back to Placerville, the town he'd left two days earlier, then erupted itself into the broad San Joaquin valleys below. Down in that protected womb of grass and rolling hills, the American would merge with the Sacramento and grow warm and languid under the sun as its temper softened and it rolled out to San Francisco and the ocean beyond.

Maybe he should turn around now. Go back and wait until the blizzards slept for another year and made their peace with the mountains. He could return to San Francisco and work for the engineer he'd grown to admire deeply this past winter. Work for Philip Deidesheimer for a couple more months until the passes were safe.

But could he? Beyond the mountains was a new strike that he'd heard whispered as being rich beyond description. A mountain of silver! Solid information on its true wealth was difficult to obtain because, like all new strikes, the discoverers had tried to keep it a secret from the world. But, with California teeming with the played-out and hungry forty-niners, such a find could not be hidden for long. Even now, San Francisco and the gold camps were girding themselves for an onslaught over the Sierras after the first spring thaw. In another two months or less, there would be a wave of miners crashing eastward. Glenn knew from hard experience that no matter how vast the wealth, the mountain of silver would already be claimed.

To wait was to lose all chance of making a stake. He'd reached California too late to find gold. Years too late. But now, now he had the opportunity to reach this new discovery before the hordes. And he would, if these mountains didn't kill him first.

Glenn swallowed as his pale blue eyes stretched out toward the San Joaquin. Yes, there was life and warmth. Food and protection. He wanted to go back and knew he should, but could not because he had a dream that was even stronger than fear of the Sierra blizzard. Comstock wages would buy that dream; he'd go away to become an engineer. Then he'd return and build a railroad over these towering mountains and help to unite a continent and tame a frontier.

Glenn faced back into the wind, and lowering his head, he plunged on, a lonely figure bent halfway forward and sometimes staggering as the gusts played their tricks and jerked him from side to side.

Ever higher he crept. The air was thin and he concentrated on moving one boot in front of the other and not thinking of the cold. Up on top, they said the snow was like a shivering, bottomless cloud where you might step off the trail and just disappear. Drifts a hundred feet deep, they swore, and some never melted, just grew mean and dirty in the summer with their bleeding and sulked in the darker valleys until winter came again.

By late afternoon, the feet were dragging, the legs unfeeling, and he knew he could go no longer. Rest. Make the blizzard wait until tomorrow or blow itself away in the night. He looked for shelter and found it almost at once in the rocks close by. It was a cave with a flat rock overhang and a dry floor. Granite walls framed three sides, and far back he saw a blackened fire ring where others had cooked and huddled for protection.

He unslung his heavy pack and let it drop to the ground. Then he exited the shelter, moving quickly while there was still light. With the threat of new snow on his mind, Glenn hunted firewood and carried an armload of damp branches, then stacked them neatly out of the weather. Only one task remained, and that was to get water that he could boil for warmth. In his pack he found a battered coffeepot and debated whether or not to go down to the river. It all depended on whether or not it snowed. He shook his canteen. Almost empty.

Outside, the wind had strengthened and he wasted no time crossing the stage road and descending toward the river, following a game trail through the rocks and trees.

He moved well, his eyes instinctively judging the best path, the surest step. Glenn didn't hesitate to admire the scenery, the tortured river which squeezed through rapids below. He'd seen it before, and always as a prospector down on his luck, searching for a trace of gold in the quicksilver western rivers of the Sierras. Except for this past winter, he'd spent two years trudging the worked-over goldfields, all the way from Rich Bar to Chinese Camp down on the Tuolumne River.

A rattle of gunfire jerked his attention upriver and he froze when he saw a buckskin break from the trees across the water and pound along a narrow river trail. The horse seemed to falter with each stride, as though it was exhausted and about to fold, which wasn't surprising since it was carrying double.

Seconds later he saw the pursuers, and the gunfire grew in intensity. The trail ended at the water. Glenn watched as the rider swung the horse around, and the smaller figure behind hung on tightly. Then the man in the saddle reined back and spurred the buckskin into the river. It landed with a splash, and slowly the current seemed to grab hold and the horse began a slow spin.

Glenn began running down the slope. There didn't seem like much chance anything could survive the rapids, but if they did, he wanted to try to save them. Especially the smaller one, who must be a boy.

At the water, he found a high rock and scrambled on top as he saw them coming. The man was a dozen yards out in front, but he was drowning and his strokes were feeble, his head barely above water. And he was far out in the river as he swept by. For a moment their eyes locked; then the struggling figure seemed to strike something submerged and rolled under the foaming current. But in that last second, Glenn hadn't seen fear, only anger.

He looked upriver and saw the horse and rider, and all at once he realized it was a girl fighting for her life in the water. Then the horse rolled, and for a heart-stopping moment its legs waved like broken tent poles. After what seemed like an eternity, the thrashing buckskin righted itself, with the girl dangling, her fist wrapped in the animal's mane.

Glenn peeled off his coat and boots as he watched the two careening down toward him. He waited until they were just above the rock, then dived into the water. The impact was stunning and the water ripped the breath from his lungs and drove icy needles through his chest until he thought his heart would rupture. Cold terror possessed his brain and he drove fighting to the surface, swimming frantically. The girl saw him, and when his fingers gripped the stirrups, she threw an arm out as the horse struck his legs and churned him back underwater. He tried to grab the animal, but it was thrashing so wildly he became entangled in the reins, and the harder he fought, the more they seemed to wrap, until he couldn't breathe.

The girl surged forward, tore at his neck, and pulled him close to the saddle. Then the horse's body jolted and he felt it scrabbling for footing. They clung to each other as it pulled them out of the American River.

For several moments he lay facedown on the gravel. Then he began to shake. He made himself push up from the rocks, and he saw the girl only a few yards away. Quickly he crawled to her side and rolled her onto her back.

"Are you all right! Miss, answer me!"

Her lips moved but made no sound except for a ragged breathing. Glenn knew she was probably very near dying, and that if he didn't get her warm and dry, she stood no chance of surviving the night—nor did he.

He tried to lift her but she stiffened with pain and he placed her down quickly.

"Miss, we can't last down here. It's almost dark, and in wet clothes we'll freeze to death."

She opened her eyes, and even though they were pain-glazed, he saw they were beautiful. Deep blue and exceptionally large, with long, tapering lashes.

"Did you hear me?" he asked, bending close.

She nodded. "What... what about my brother? Dade. Where's Dade?"

"I'm sorry. He's gone."

"Dead?"

He nodded and saw her bite her lips. Lips purple with cold. After a moment, she opened her eyes again and looked into his face. "My leg is broken."

Again he tried to lift her, saying, "I'll look at it up above."

Her fingernails bit into his shoulder. "No," she whispered, "you've got to do it here! Set it straight before I move."

"I've never done it before. Anyway, there's no time!"

She was crazy. Out of her head with the cold and pain. He pushed away, intent on getting the horse and packing her into the saddle. She didn't realize they were in danger of freezing.

He started to get up, but she wouldn't let go. "Please!" she begged. "All my life I've wanted to be a stage dancer. If you take me out of here like this, I might become a cripple! Don't be afraid of setting the leg. I'll tell you how. I've seen it done before."

"All right. All right," he soothed, trying to knock down her rising hysteria.

Glenn scooted down and grabbed her ankle; he was shivering so badly he squeezed it tightly in order to keep his grip steady.

"What now?"

"Grab my knee."

He was staring at the purple mass of distended tissue and wanting to look away.

"Grab my knee!"

He grabbed it hard.

"Now pull!"

He tried. Tried twice, and each time she cried out in anguish.

"Dammit," he swore, "it ain't working! My hands keep slipping. I don't want to hurt you anymore."

She raised up on her elbows, breathing fast. For several moments she studied the leg. Then she pulled her dress up and bunched it between her legs and pointed at the spot. "Place your foot *here*."

"Miss, I can't—"

"You have to! Do it. Put your foot there and grab my ankle. Throw your back to it! Hurry!"

He placed the broken leg between his own, knowing she was right and he had to do it the way she said or it wouldn't get done at all.

"Ready?" he whispered.

She nodded, her eyes round with fear yet bright with resolution. There was a trembling in her voice when she said, "Mister, no matter what I say when you do it, keep pulling until it's straight. Maybe you'll have to . . ."

Glenn couldn't bear to see her wait. He felt shamed by his own fear and so he threw his weight backward in one violent lunge, and when he did, her scream was like a blade plunging into his heart. Then it broke off inside him as she lost consciousness. The bone snapped back into position; he felt it almost pop into line.

Very gently his fingers smoothed along the broken place until he was satisfied. She couldn't hear him, but Glenn talked to her anyway.

"I'm sorry. But it's straight now, honest it is, and I'm getting us out of this gorge alive. You're too brave and young and pretty to die. I'm getting you outta here, and someday I'll watch you dance on that leg. I *mean* it."

He caught the buckskin. It hobbled painfully, but that couldn't be helped. If the animal died trying to pack the girl, then that was the way it must be.

Glenn bent to lift her, then caught himself in time. Maybe he hadn't known how to set a fractured bone, but he did know enough to splint one. If they survived, this girl was going to walk straight and dance. She'd paid the price and deserved to.

He sliced a rein off the bit and found two pieces of flat driftwood by the river's edge. Then he splinted the leg and hoisted the girl across the saddle and tied her with the saddle strings. Glenn hoped she didn't revive until after they reached camp. It was going to be a nightmarish climb in poor light—if he got out fast enough. He pushed out the fear that maybe she'd never regain consciousness and die from the shock and cold.

"Come on, horse! Move!"

The animal balked. It looked half-dead itself. "Come on!" he shouted, yanking on the rein.

It hobbled forward, and Glenn's eyes began to trace the steep mountainside. He had to find the fastest way up. Already the canyon was dark in shadow. To be caught on this tangled mountain in the dark was a sure death sentence.

It seemed to take hours, but somehow he managed to find the rock shelter as the blizzard raged in on them. Glenn tied the buckskin in a thick stand of ponderosa pine which he hoped would give the animal some protection.

Then he carried the girl to shelter, lurching wearily through the deepening snow.

It was almost totally dark underneath the rocks and his hands felt like chunks of ice as he fumbled in his pack for matches. The first one snapped in two and he hurled it out into the wind.

"Steady," he said through clattering teeth.

The second match spluttered into life but died when he touched it to the moist firewood. Three more extinguished themselves in the same fashion.

Glenn expelled a cloud of breath and shivered violently, as much out of fear as the cold. Two matches left—two chances at survival. He bent very close to the firewood, rubbed his hands together furiously, trying to bring some life to them, as though it might somehow alter the final outcome. He tried again. The match flared boldly and he touched it to a small branch, then blew softly on it. For a few seconds it seemed to take life, to bite at the wood and spark. Then it failed.

Glenn shuddered and heard the girl behind him moan. He reached for the last match, and a silent prayer echoed inside. As he started to pull it against the matchbox, he hesitated, then froze, knowing it wasn't any good. For a moment he rocked with indecision; then he whirled to his pack until his fingers located the books. He worked blindly now, totally without light. Each of his books was a beloved friend; each had a separate voice, a different and familiar touch, and represented a vision of what he hoped to be. Glenn deftly pulled out the volume he knew was entitled *Structural Evolution of European Bridges*, by Arthur Kurzweil, a German and one of the most brilliant structural and stress engineers in the world. Glenn had studied the man's drawings and equations until he knew them intimately, even though many were beyond his scope of understanding.

He began to tear out the pages. One by one, he shredded, then crumpled them into a pile between his legs—it was like bleeding a drop at a time. When he finished, he took the match between his numb fingers and scratched it to flame. This time the fire seemed hungry as it ate the paper. Glenn fed it slowly, watched it grow stronger and the light rise to illuminate the shelter, until he couldn't give it enough nourishment and began to tear out entire chapters at once. The flames were ravenous now, and he gave them the precious leather cover and watched the fire devour the binding as he started to wean it onto the pile of branches. For a moment the fire seemed to resist the change; then it attacked the wood until it roared with hungry satisfaction. As though it were a child, he banked its cradle with rocks, and it snapped with hungry contentment.

Glenn quickly unpacked his heavy woolen blankets and spread them as close to the fire as he dared.

"Where are we?" she breathed.

He twisted around quickly, relief flooding him. "You're alive."

"Of course," she whispered. "It's only my leg that's hurt, and . . . and I don't feel anything now. Only I'm so tired."

"You can't sleep! Not yet."

"I must."

"No!"

He grabbed her and realized her clothes were frozen solid. "We've got to get you undressed."

She didn't answer.

"Miss! Do you hear me?" When she still didn't respond, he began to pull off her dress. Where buttons resisted, he tore them away. Dress, underclothes, everything was icy, and her skin was blue. He rolled her onto the blankets and wound them around her body, then scooted her close to the fire.

"Miss, you've got to stay awake!"

Her eyes opened slowly. "Too hot," she moaned. "My face. It's burning."

She began to struggle against him and he drew back the flat of his hand and slapped her on one cheek and then the other, hard and stinging blows that brought cries to her throat and color where there had been none.

"Stop it! Stop it!"

Twice more he slapped her, until she was trying to fight him and he knew she was alert.

"Let go of me!"

"I'm sorry. I had to do it."

A slow trickle of blood ran from the corner of her lips and he was filled with relief, knowing the body chills from the outside inward. A freezing person wouldn't bleed from a cut like that.

Glenn wiped the crimson smear away with his fingers and brushed it onto his stiff shirt.

"Your hands . . . they're so cold."

He tried to smile, but his face was so stiff he couldn't tell if he succeeded. "I'll put them closer to the fire," he told her.

Outside the ring of firelight, Glenn could see the snow slanting with the wind. It seemed to mesmerize him, and his eyelids grew very heavy.

He must have dozed for a moment, because he heard her yelling into his face—shouting something about his hands burning. She was crazy, he thought, as though from a great distance. Now, with the fire, it was time to sleep, to gather strength, to rest.

His head and body were being rocked, and he had the sensation of standing on the deck of a ship, rolling with the seas, content with their motion. Then . . . then he was suddenly falling toward the water, knowing it was going to be cold and dreading the chill. He was wrong. The water felt incredibly warm, it caressed him, seemed to rub and pull at his skin.

He blinked, then realized it wasn't water that kneaded heat into his body, it was the girl. Glenn put his arms around her and smiled drowsily.

"I thought I was swimming in the tropics. Like I did on the ship to California. I liked the feel of it then. I like the feel of you even better."

She pulled away. "You're waking up, Mister, and I'm getting nervous. Do you have any more blankets?"

"No." He grinned happily.

"How about some dry clothes I can wear?"

"Sorry," he replied, reaching toward her.

She placed her hands on his chest and pushed him up against the fire ring. A patch of skin on his back touched rock, and he yelped.

"I'm sorry!" She closed her eyes, and when she opened them, he saw they were glistening.

"Mister, I'm only seventeen and my brother just died and I've no one left. But . . . but I've never slept with a man and . . ."

Glenn touched the scorched place on his back. It hurt like hell, but at least he was feeling something now. "What's your name?"

"Fay Taylor. I'm only seventeen, and Dade, he was ten years older."

"What about your parents?"

"Died of the fever in San Francisco four years ago. My brother has taken care of me since. He wouldn't like us together this way. He'd go crazy if he saw us now."

Glenn remained silent. The brother was dead.

"What's your name?"

"Glenn Donovan."

"How old are you?"

"Nineteen."

She drew back. "That's old enough. I've got to get out of here."

He grabbed her wrist. "You can't, Miss Taylor. There's only one way we'll keep warm, and that's together."

"No!" Her eyes fell to his grip. "I didn't mean to shout. But . . . but I know how men think. Dade told me."

Glenn released his hold. She *was* scared. More even than down by the river when he'd set her leg. "All men aren't the same," he said.

She stiffened. "That's one of the things he told me you'd say. But he said it was a lie, and when I heard a man say that, I should run or call him."

"Fay, listen to me. You've got a broken leg and we're going to have our hands full keeping from freezing if the temperature goes lower. Besides, your brother isn't here now and that means you've got to trust me."

"I know. I know. But I don't. You saved my life and everything, but . . . but all of a sudden things are all adrift and I'm scared."

"Of those men who were shooting at you?"

"No. They were hunting Dade, not me."

"Why?"

She seemed to debate whether or not to answer.

"Well, come on," he said, "if they're going to be searching up here tomorrow, I've got a right to know."

"They won't. They'll be satisfied now."

"Satisfied. Satisfied with what! Killing a man and a girl? What kind of business were you and that brother of yours up to?"

She couldn't meet his eyes. "Dade was no saint, I'll admit that, but he was hell on a deck of cards."

He saw it now. During his rambling, Glenn had come across plenty of drifting gamblers. It was a most dangerous occupation. "What about you?"

She faced him squarely. "I sang and danced," she said defiantly. "I earned money fairly given."

"Fine. But what's the tie-in? I want to know what your brother was doing while you entertained around the campfire."

Her long eyelashes dropped a fraction and he saw sparks glitter angrily. "You're a hard man, Glenn Donovan. But I'll tell you. While I was singing, Dade would be gathering what he called the price of a ticket."

"The price of a ticket! He was picking pockets, wasn't he? A cardsharp and a thief."

She slapped him—hard. And he saw pain fill her eyes as she tried to hold back tears. "He took me when no one else would. And he was good to me, though I was a burden at first. He didn't rob unless he had to, and then only from men who were well-fixed. And he was my brother, mister. So don't you say such things!"

Glenn turned around and began to replenish the fire. She was right. The man had been her brother, and he had no call to accuse a dead man. Besides, he'd done a few things in his own time that he wasn't so almighty proud of. Like when he'd left his family back in New York and come west. His father had begged him to stay and promised him part of the saloon they'd owned.

Glenn said no because he realized what his father really wanted was for his son to become a bare-knuckles prizefighter, as he'd been himself once. Glenn was sick of fighting and always having his father matching him against some other kid to stir up drinking and betting. And because he'd always won, it got so he was fighting men heavier and stronger than himself. It became ugly and he'd hurt and been hurt, then sorry. Like when he'd almost blinded Jake Muldoon and made him cry in front of his friends. No, Glenn thought miserably, I've no right to cast stones.

"I'm sorry, Fay," he said quietly. "It's a hard world we're facing. So never mind what I said."

"Fair enough. Glenn?"

"Yeah?"

"Do you think my leg will heal straight? It's got to, for, you see, I mean to become as famous as Lola Montez."

Glenn said nothing, but felt disappointed. He'd never seen Lola Montez, but there were men in San Francisco who remembered her performances well. She'd been beautiful and wicked as hell, marrying and leaving husbands as fast as she could spend their money. They said she couldn't sing and her dancing was awful, yet she was so notorious and beautiful men packed the houses to see her do things like her famous Spider Dance. She would have them panting in the aisle as she shook her skirts, letting black spiders fall around on the stage.

"Maybe you'll be even better," Glenn said. "You're pretty enough, and I think you'll do about whatever you want."

"I mean to," she vowed. "Nothing will stop me if this leg mends straight." She looked over at him. "What about you?"

"Oh, I've got big plans, too," he said with a sheepish grin.

She perked up. "I like men with ambition. Dade had that, and so do I. So, if we're going to be friends, I want you to tell me what you'd most like to do."

"Be an engineer—that's easy enough."

She frowned thoughtfully. "I don't know much about them."

"Well, I don't either, really," he admitted, "but I'm trying to learn from books that I have. But engineers build things, Fay. They get an idea for something big and draw it all out, nice and clean, so they can look at it and test it and see if it will stand or fall."

"You mean like a barn or a ship?"

He stared into the fire and tried to put it into words. "Could be, but I think more like bridges and tunnels and roadways. Things this country needs to grow. When I look at the road I followed, for instance, there's places where they did it all wrong. Oh, I'm not saying I could have laid it out a whole lot better, yet I know where they should have cut deeper and I see places where a bridge should have gone."

"But bridges are just for going across rivers."

He smiled. "Before I came out west, they were talking about building a railroad across this whole country."

"I don't think they can do it, Glenn. Too many mountains."

He poked at the fire. "Oh, they'll do it, all right. And they'll have to put in bridges across these gorges and dig tunnels clear through rock. That'll take engineers and surveyors, too. I can survey."

"You can?"

"Sure. Learned it this past winter. Nothing to it, really, except peering through a transit and figuring lines and angles, using the basic principles of geometry and trigonometry."

She wrinkled her nose at the words. "Sounds like a couple of diseases."

"Oh, it's not hard. I could have stayed in San Francisco and done it for the man I worked for."

"Why didn't you? I mean, you sound as if you liked it."

"I did. But . . . well, maybe that's where that ambition you were talking about takes over. I just knew I'd get tired of being a surveyor in a few years. I'd want to design things for myself, but I couldn't, you see, because I wouldn't know how. I need to get schooling to become an engineer. Then I'd be as good as any of them."

"Yes, you would. Neither one of us wants to just get along. We've got to be the best."

He looked up at her and nodded. "I never thought about being the best. Not yet, anyway. One thing at a time. Just becoming an engineer seems pretty far away."

"Phooey! You can do it. But I didn't know there were schools in Nevada."

"There aren't. Fay, there's a new discovery across these mountains that I mean to make a claim on before anyone in California joins in. They say . . . they say it's richer than King Solomon's mines!"

"Who says?"

"I heard about it in San Francisco while I was working for an engineer named Deidesheimer. He told me because he knew how bad I wanted the money so I could go to school and become an engineer."

"Glenn, maybe it's just another rumor. You know how they are. Someone says something about maybe this looks like gold country and then another man hears it and the story gets bigger. By the time a dozen men pass it along, it's being called another strike and thousands are heading for the place. It happens that way."

"Not this time," he said stubbornly. "Mr. Deidesheimer himself saw an assay report on some ore that was packed out by snowshoes just before the passes closed this winter. Seems that for more than a month these fellas named Comstock, O'Riley, and McLaughlin had been washing a funny-looking kind of heavy blue sand in their rockers. They hated it because it clogged up their equipment and had to be thrown away. You see, they were after gold. It never occurred to them until later that the blue stuff was silver. Finally, an assayer in Grass Valley tested it. You know how rich it was?"

She shook her head.

"A ton of that blue stuff they'd been cursing is worth three thousand in silver and almost nine hundred in gold!"

Fay smiled. "That's good, huh?"

"Good! It's rich! The reason I know the story is that a friend of that engineer named Mr. Hearst went over last fall and bought an interest in a mine called the Ophir. He and a couple of friends, working day and night, managed to extract thirty-eight tons, and as winter closed in, they loaded every mule they could buy or steal and came through as the first blizzards struck."

He looked at her closely. "That thirty-eight tons, even given all the expenses, made Hearst and his partners a profit of more than ninety thousand dollars."

"That's a lot of money!" Fay swore. "If you made that much, I doubt you'd quit to become an engineer."

"Yes I would." Glenn smiled. "That silver and gold could last another twenty years or twenty days. There's no telling, because it's down deep in that mountain. But engineering's different. With luck, I'll earn enough in six months to go back to New York. They've got a school there Mr. Deidesheimer says he can help me get into."

"Sounds like a good friend."

"He is."

"Well," Fay said, "I hope you strike it rich and it all comes true. But right now, I'm cold!"

"The temperature is falling." He piled more wood to the blaze. "This fire has got to last the night. Even so, I don't know if it'll keep us from freezing. There's only enough blankets for one. I wasn't expecting company."

"You're trying to tell me we can't divide them."

Glenn looked down at his hands. "The blankets are thin, Fay, and our clothes are wet. I can't find dry wood outside and I've got to keep the fire alive through the night. There just isn't enough to keep us warm."

She nodded, then looked at him squarely. "Glenn, can I trust you not to . . . to take advantage? You could if you wanted. We both know you could."

"I don't want to," he heard himself tell her.

She smiled, and it was nice. "Really?"

He felt embarrassed. "I know it sounds crazy. You're beautiful, Fay, and the softest thing I ever held. But it wouldn't be right, would it?"

Her lower lip trembled and she shook her head vigorously.

He could tell she was frightened, wanting to believe him but not sure she dared. "Look, I was raised by God-fearing parents, and though I tote engineering books instead of a Bible, I know . . . well, I'd have no respect for myself in the morning."

She nodded shyly. "Glenn, my leg hurts bad, yet I'd hurt inside a lot more if you was lying."

"I'm not lying, Fay. It's just that I can almost feel you up against me and . . . and I know what I said, but I'm still worried."

"Maybe you should try and read one of your books tonight."

"Might be better if I put them edgewise between us. Like a bundling board. That way we could keep our warmth but not, well, you know."

"You're smart, Glenn. Honest, that's a good idea. Pile them up between us!"

"All right."

She closed her eyes and he watched the firelight play off the golden wisps of her hair. She looked like an angel fallen out of heaven. Glenn swallowed and grabbed the books. Self-consciously, he fumbled, trying to line them up at her side. His fingers brushed her body, and he swore she trembled.

Fay pulled the blankets tight around them and Glenn lay rigid with self-control. She nestled in close, the books pressing into their skin. "Glenn," she sighed, "wouldn't this make a great, really great Shakesperean tragedy?"

"What do you mean?" he asked huskily.

She spoke into his ear. "Think about it. If we freeze tonight, I mean."

"I'd rather not."

"But, if we do." Suddenly she chuckled. "I just had a

thought. Can you imagine, if they found us like this with all these old books in between, side by side, without a stitch on either of us! Can you imagine their faces?''

Glenn didn't laugh. They'd probably be as disgusted as he was. Tragedy? More like a farce or a joke. Right now he could feel her warmth seeping through the books, making the blood pound in his ears. Until this afternoon the dream had been enough. Up to now, he'd never slept with a woman. Kissed a few back home, but that wasn't so much, and they hadn't looked or felt like this at all. His fingers clenched and unclenched in the wanting of her. Dammit! Things weren't going to be quite the same after this.

Her breathing became soft and regular on his cheek and he began going over and over the equations and principles he remembered in Kurzweil's *Structural Evolution of European Bridges*. Brilliant mind. But then, the engineer hadn't had the distraction of Fay Taylor lying warm and undressed beside him.

Daylight came without sun, and outside, Glenn watched the pregnant, lumbering storm clouds pushing west. Snow lay on the ground but there was none falling.

He twisted around to look at the girl. In sleep, there was the contradiction of child and woman all in one person. A beautiful combination he did not want to disturb. She would be waking soon, and the moment of discovering her wrapped in his arms would vanish forever. Then he'd have to think about their survival and decide the best course of action. Let it wait. Wait until he'd studied every line of her face and pressed it into his memory. Someday he'd become an engineer, because nothing would stop him. By then, Fay might be famous and only remembered like a fairy tale. It saddened him to realize he would never sleep beside Fay Taylor again and probably never possess such a special feeling.

So pretty, and when he remembered the courage she'd exhibited down on the riverbank, it made his throat tighten with the sudden desire to protect her from hurt again.

An impulse to kiss her had kept him awake half the night, and finally he couldn't stand it any longer. His lips brushed hers, not wanting to wake her, only to remember. Fay's eyes jumped open and stared in wild fright. She pushed back quickly and fumbled between them to make certain the books were in place.

"What are you doing!"

"Kissing you," he said to her. "Kissing you good-bye."

"Are you leaving?"

"No."

"Then . . ." Her question hung between them and the silence grew.

"Our clothes are dry," he said. "I'd better get up and hunt wood before the fire goes out."

She reached out and took his arm. "Glenn, wait. I think I know why you did that just now. It . . . it wasn't very easy on you, was it?"

"Hardest night I ever spent," he said honestly.

"I know. Do you always talk about bridges and such nonsense in your sleep? Really, I could barely understand a word of it."

He began to laugh as she watched with a half-smile. "I couldn't either. Not last night, anyway."

"Get your clothes on."

"Don't peek," he teased.

She snorted with disgust and pulled the covers over her head. "Not much to see anyway, Glenn Donovan. You're all bones."

He dressed quickly, pulling on the clothes he'd left hanging on a branch poked in the rocks near the fire. When he was done, he knelt beside her and tugged the covers down to her neck.

"How's the leg?"

A cloud passed over her expression. "You look at it. I'm afraid to. Just feeling it has me worried."

He pulled up the blanket and stifled his reaction. The leg was dark and swollen, but no more than he should have expected.

"Glenn?" she whispered, anxiety riding over her voice.

"It's fine," he said, trying to sound confident.

"Tell me, honest. You wouldn't lie to me?"

He pitched the blanket back down and scooted up beside her. "You'll see it yourself. It's about what you'd expect. Fay, there's no sense trying to kid you, it'll be a while before you can move."

"Can we stay here?"

He nodded. "We'll have to until the stage comes along. I can hunt and keep us in wood so we don't freeze. You'll have to stay here alone while I'm gone, and nurse the fire."

"I'll be fine. Glenn?"

"Yeah."

"I'm lucky you found me. There isn't one in a thousand who wouldn't have used me during the night."

He didn't know what to say and was afraid of saying anything, because once he opened his mouth, everything he felt inside would come spilling out and he'd be sorry. Sorry because they both had plans and knew, when the stage came by, this would all be over.

Perhaps she read his feelings through her eyes, because her arms reached out for him. And then he tasted her lips, felt her hands slip around his shoulders and pull him down to her. When Glenn felt his passion reaching up to strip away all self-control, he broke free and unsteadily rose to his feet.

"Someday . . ." he rasped brokenly, then staggered out into the snow and walked until the heat from his body died in the cold wind.

2

As Glenn Donovan crunched through the snow, it occurred to him that the mountain was toying with their fates.

Today the sun was so bright and warm its glare burned the eyes and turned snow to slush. Tomorrow, the blizzard above might descend as it had in days past. The mountain gave warmth and hope, then snatched it away, as if to prove that it cared nothing for man or wildlife.

Glenn didn't care. Being snowbound with Fay Taylor could go on indefinitely, provided he could get wood that burned and shoot enough rabbits and squirrels to keep them from starving. So far, he'd been lucky on both counts. He was just average with a pistol, but the mountainside had an abundance of animal life. There were a dozen or so bullets left, and they'd last until the blizzard grew weary of its sport.

Firewood remained his primary concern. Without matches, they had to keep the campfire going at all times, and that took a lot of wood. Every day, his tracks went deeper and deeper into the forest in search of new supplies. Most of what he found was green, wet, and hard to burn. Sometimes Fay had to hold the pieces of wood over the flames and turn them to dry before they'd burn. He enjoyed watching her do things and dreaded the clear skies which would end what he thought was a beautiful closeness between them. Having someone to protect and care for brought more real satisfaction and happiness than he could ever remember.

Like now, for instance. Though still a mile from camp, he felt a growing excitement as he trudged along with a rope-tied bundle of wood slung across his back and the carved staff in his hand. He'd whittled it special for her this very afternoon and knew with satisfaction that it would match Fay's length just right. She was taller than most women; five and a half feet at least.

Glenn came to a rise over their camp and studied the land beyond. He could see the Wells Fargo stage road twisting like a sectioned snake as it dipped and slithered out of the valley. Today it was warm and the snow seemed to melt faster on the roadway. It looked as though some giant had tied a pair of knives together and slashed parallel furrows through the trees. If the weather held, there'd be a stage coming up before long and he'd see she was on it and safe.

They hadn't talked about that much, but there was no doubt she was as determined to become an actress as he was an engineer. Their paths, he thought grimly, were just like the road ruts. Both going higher but never joining. He'd decided he was going to ask her to go with him to Virginia City. And why not? Fay needed him until her leg mended. One thing sure, he had no intention of using her as she'd been used until now.

Behind him, a branch snapped, and at the same moment he heard the unmistakable cocking of a gun.

"Don't move!"

Glenn froze in his tracks. The staff dropped and his lungs seemed to compress, expecting a bullet to rip into their mass.

"Raise your hands, then turn around. Slow and easy."

He released the rope-slung firewood and it fell into the snow as he pivoted.

A blur entered the corner of his vision and he tried to duck as pain exploded like a sunburst across his eyes. He dropped heavily and felt ice fill his nostrils.

The man eased back a step, then squatted on his haunches, pointing a leveled gun at Glenn's face. "I discovered your tracks down by the river this morning. Knew if I circled up the road, I'd find you before dark. You're a horse thief, mister. I can kill you legal. Only, first, I want to know what you did with my sister."

Glenn twisted sideways until he could see the man. One side of his head was numb, and where it had rested was a streak of blood on the snow. He blinked and remembered the face he now saw. Only then it hadn't been composed and hard with purpose. Not in the grips of the American River, it hadn't.

He pointed downhill. "She's in camp. Broke her leg in the rapids. I've been taking care of her."

"Yeah, I bet you have!"

There was no missing the twisted passion in that voice. Dade Taylor's lips curled into a tight smile and the man's eyes went as flat and cold as an ice-covered pond. Handsome, yes, but Glenn saw neither relief nor gratitude at learning of Fay's condition. Only murderous accusation.

"You've been with her four days. What do you take me for, an idiot? It's my sister we're talking about. You telling me you didn't notice she's a woman?"

"I noticed," he said. "And I know what you're thinking, but I'm telling you the truth."

Dade motioned with the gun. "You'd better be, friend. I'll talk with her alone, and she doesn't know how to lie. But, if you do, there's nothing either of you can say to make me let you go. Now, start walking."

He picked up the wood and the present he'd made for Fay. The good feeling inside he'd nursed about giving it to her was all gone.

Glenn stood down by the roadbed and waited. He could hear them talking, Dade's voice angry and Fay's soothing. After a while their conversation grew quieter. Off to the west the sun dipped into the horizon and glowed up toward the high mountains where he stood. An owl glided silently through the dusk and into the shadow of forest. The pine trees lost their shapes, seemed to pull in tight as the coldness deepened. Far below, the river surged with monotonous intensity.

He tried to figure Dade Taylor out, imagine how he'd have

reacted if it had been the other way around. Maybe he'd have done the same. Maybe.

She called to him and he saw her hobbling down to meet him as he started back. They stopped, apart from each other.

"Well, what's the verdict?" he asked.

"I told him the truth. He had no choice but to believe me."

"And?"

"And I told him I was tired of traveling from one gold camp to the next. Always wondering if he'd get shot or we'd have enough money for food the next day."

Glenn stepped forward. "Then what are you going to do?"

"Well," she mused pensively, "I don't know how you're going to take this, Mr. Donovan, but I'm afraid you've got a couple of traveling partners."

He began to laugh. With relief and happiness, he laughed until his voice echoed across the gorge.

"How?" he cried. "How did you get him to do it?"

She smiled into his eyes. "I let him yell a little until he calmed down. He's got a quick temper but it goes away fast. Dade is smart. Smart enough to listen when I reminded him those men who chased us into the river think we're dead. If we go back, they'll hear about it and come hunting. He doesn't want that either. There's nowhere else to go."

"And that's it?" He couldn't believe it was so easy.

"Just about. He's managed to wear out our welcome in California. Besides, I repeated all your stories about the Comstock, that blue stuff and how they'd found a mountain of silver and gold."

She frowned. "There was one other thing."

He waited.

"I had to show him how we used your books under our blankets."

Glenn shook his head, a wry smile crossing his lips. "If he believed you, I'll be surprised. Come on, let's go back and see what he has to say to me. Ought to be interesting."

As it turned out, Dade had surprisingly little to offer except a grudging apology and a bone-crunching handshake. Glenn was relieved, because Dade Taylor had the look of a dangerous opponent in any kind of fight. They stood eye to eye, but Dade carried an extra fifty pounds of muscle. He was the kind of man that people looked at and wished they could be. Handsome, with a strong jawline, straw-colored hair brushed over the ears, a broad sloping pair of shoulders tapering down over a flat stomach. Even his teeth seemed whiter than cream, stronger than bone had a right to be, and so perfectly matched they looked to be carved ivory.

"First thing in the morning," he said, "I've decided we have to leave for the Comstock. Fay can ride my buckskin."

"It's still lame."

"I know, but that can't be helped." He produced a pocketknife and carefully cleaned his fingernails. The fingers were long and tapered, almost feminine except for their strength. "You can't ever sit still in life. One thing I've learned, Glenn. A man can't sit in one place worrying about which direction to jump. If he does, he'll find that anything worth jumping on is already occupied. That means fighting, taking something someone else thinks they've got a right to keep."

Glenn studied the man. He had the feeling Dade wasn't one to worry much about taking things. "That's one way of looking at it, I guess. But some of us don't 'jump' at things just to move."

"What do you mean?" Dade asked sharply.

"I mean my pa always told me a person got out of life about as much as he put into it."

Dade scoffed, grinned with mirth. "Don't you believe it. I've seen enough of things to know the hardworking people of this world are the poorest. Dirt farmers, prospectors, cowboys, and sailors all work like dogs and never get anything for their trouble but stooped shoulders pointing to an early grave. Open your eyes, Glenn! Rich men got the hands of babies."

"Yes, but . . ."

The knife snapped shut with finality. "By the way, I pushed your blanket over a little. Hope you don't mind my sleeping in between you and little sister."

Glenn flushed and was grateful for the poor light. He hadn't missed the implication and knew that Fay hadn't either. One thing certain, with Dade Taylor, a handshake didn't change anything.

Dade reached into his pants and turned up a heavy gold pocket watch with a busted chain, then held it close to the firelight. "Hell," he chuckled, "it's only eight-thirty! I can't go to bed yet."

"Where'd you get the watch?" Fay was standing close, with a troubled look in her eyes.

He shoved it back into his pocket and said nothing.

"Dade?"

"Traded for it. That's all. I busted mine in the river." He looked over at her. "Some fellas that pulled me out of the water was happy enough to trade for the gold in my pockets. Why, I even bought a flask of whiskey from them. It's in my pack. Glenn, you can have a drink, can't you? We can toast to good weather, pretty girls, and the fortune we'll soon claim."

"No, thanks," Glenn said, "I'm going to turn in for the night."

"Fine with me. Guess I'll step outside and watch the stars roll around. I'll be *just* outside. Sleep well."

Glenn threw a couple of pieces of wood on the fire and eased onto his blankets. He felt the girl watching him and rolled to look at her.

"What are you thinking, Glenn?"

"Oh, nothing much, I guess. Seems kind of empty in these blankets."

When she didn't smile, he dropped the banter and said, "I never met anyone like him, Fay. Can't say as I hope to again."

"He's at war with the entire world. Maybe he was born that way. I don't know, 'cause he's ten years older than me and he left home early. I've seen him do good and bad and sometimes both. It's like watching something balanced in the wind and being pushed from side to side. He could go either way."

"At least you're both going my way tomorrow."

"Yes." She smiled. "Let's think about that as we go to sleep."

He nodded and watched her until his eyes became heavy.

Dade had tried to distinguish their conversation, but the wind had broken up their words, and he couldn't follow their meaning. It wasn't important; he'd seen the way Fay had fought to defend Glenn, and it was plenty clear she'd formed an attachment that wasn't in anyone's best interests. He was angered and disappointed to think that the first time she'd gotten out of sight, she'd become emotionally involved. And to a worthless prospecting dreamer, at that! A gangly kid who carried a few books around the hills and talked big but had nothing. As soon as they reached the Comstock, he'd see that Glenn Donovan stepped out of her life. Then he'd have a talk with that girl. She wanted to be an actress, a singer and dancer? Fine. He'd help her and himself. But if being alone with Donovan had messed her up emotionally, he wanted to know that, too.

The straight truth of it, of which he hadn't needed to remind her in months, was that she owed him. Owed him for taking care of her and keeping men out of her bed more than once. The girl didn't understand the first thing about men. What they really wanted from a woman, as opposed to the sweet lies they could tell. He'd protected her from the ugliness because he knew it well. He wasn't a fool. There would come a day when she'd find out, but by then she'd be stronger inside.

How old was Fay? Seventeen? Dade brooded on the realization. Some women married at seventeen, others became prostitutes. Those were the options, and Fay didn't realize how she was damned lucky not to have been forced into either choice—because of him.

What, though, if something *had* happened to her with Donovan? Not physical. He was certain of that. She wasn't the kind to lie, and he doubted she could. But maybe the Irishman had caused a stirring inside.

"Damn him," he hissed. If that was the case, everything would change. He'd be right back to where he was four years ago. And that wasn't good.

He let his mind shift back to that day in San Francisco when he'd come to get her. Scrawny as a chicken and red-eyed from crying, ugly and needing him. Back then, he'd had no intention of keeping Fay. His path to success hadn't included a little girl tagging along from mining camp to mining camp. But no one would take her. No one except Anse Palling and his fat wife, who would have worked her ceaselessly in their dry-goods store. Even that might have been the way of things if he hadn't caught old Anse looking at her budding hips and breasts. He'd almost killed the man right in front of the customers before grabbing Fay and putting her on his horse.

Dade smiled, feeling the whiskey glow inside. He wasn't proud of much, but that counted. Paid off, too. First time was at Durgan Flat near the Yuba River. He'd entered a camp and managed to start a faro game with about seven hard-eyed prospectors. As usual, he'd let them take the first few hands, then discovered they were passing signals so he couldn't recoup his money without calling a showdown. Against seven men, it would have been fatal. He'd quit them cold, furious at himself for not realizing their game sooner. They'd been in high spirits, and one of them, in a drunken state of exuberance, offered Fay a pinch of gold dust just for the pleasure of hearing a female voice singing "Old Dan Tucker."

Fay hadn't wanted to, but he'd taken her roughly aside and spoken his mind. They needed the money! A pinch of gold wasn't much, but it was enough to get him into another card game.

God, she'd been scared! On the first note, he'd thought she was going to choke up and quit. But she hadn't. And after a couple of strained lines, she'd calmed down and her voice steadied. Steadied and came out clear and as pure as spring water. Rich it was, and with a haunting loveliness that gripped a man by the throat and made him listen. Those miners, who'd been ready to laugh, grew silent, and a faraway look crept into their eyes. It was a look he was to see again and again in the coming years. Some of 'em even cried. Especially when she sang "The Forty-Niners' Lament":

I lives way down in Maine, where I
heard about the diggin's,
So I shipped aboard a darned old barque
commanded by Joe Higgins,
I sold my little farm, and from wife
and children parted
And off to California sailed, and
left 'em brokenhearted.
Oh, I'm a used-up man, a perfectly
used-up man
And if I ever get home again, I'll
stay there if I can.

Dade had no liking for the song, but he let her use it because it was a campfire favorite and one miners begged for and paid well to hear. And he had to admit she knew how to deliver it, draw it out mournfully and leave it hanging in the smoke, dripping in tears. Leaving the sentimentalists somewhere back in a happier time and squinting as if they'd gotten dirt in the corners of their eyes.

Yeah, he thought, there was a magic when she forgot herself and came before an audience. Fay would change, become a different person even as he watched. Her eyes would sort of go vague, as though she was in another place, and maybe she was.

It was like . . . well, like she didn't see people or things but just . . . felt.

Magic. That's all you could say to describe the way she used her voice on people, played with their hearts and took 'em from laughing to crying as easy as she pleased. She had a talent and she had a power and he was the one who had realized it first and made it pay. Why, he'd even taken her to traveling minstrel shows just so she could watch and study their routines until she was better than they by far.

Breaking her leg was a real setback for both of them, but he knew it was only temporary. They'd pay her to sing in Virginia City even better than they had in the Sierra camps. Much better. He'd hold on to her as long as he could, and that ought to be another few years. Then she could do what she wanted.

He'd made her swear only one thing and that was never to sing for free. Men paid women for what they took from them. That was the way of it, and they never valued a thing given for nothing. Magic. You didn't give it away for free.

They'd been slogging up the Wells Fargo road for seven hours when the stage plowed around a curve and rushed toward them. It happened so quickly Glenn barely had time to lead Fay and the buckskin off the road. They yelled and waved like shipwrecked sailors. Dade leaped out into the path of the oncoming horses and grinned handsomely. The grin melted as the stage driver cracked his whip and frantically motioned them to move aside.

Dade held his ground to the very last instant, then threw himself out of the way as the stage churned mud from its big iron-rimmed wheels and barreled past.

Glenn gained a fleeting impression of a beautiful woman staring out through the window at him in wide-eyed astonishment while, across from her, a jowly man blew a long cloud of cigar smoke into the clean mountain air.

Dade jumped to his feet and his eyes were aflame with anger as he stormed, "Did you see that? He'd have plowed me under! The damned coach wasn't even full."

"He was probably afraid of losing his momentum and getting bogged down on this stretch," Glenn said. "All the same, I hope he mires to the wheel hubs."

"If he does and I get my hands on him, the man is going to know his troubles are twice what he expected."

"Dade," Fay said, "we are wasting precious time. And it's getting colder."

Glenn nodded in agreement. He was starting to worry about her. She was pale and he knew from the tight lines about her mouth that her leg was paining with the buckskin's hobble. "Maybe we ought to hunt up a camp for the night. The wind is rising."

She glanced up. "I know. I've been watching the clouds all morning build up on those peaks. Do you think it's another blizzard?"

He and Dade exchanged worried glances. Dade shook his head. "I think we'd best cover some more ground if we can. There *has* to be a stage stop pretty close. One team of horses can't pull a Butterfield stage over this whole damn mountain."

He was right, Glenn thought, but they'd better find it soon. The elevation was over six thousand feet, and this time he couldn't help but think of the Donner party.

An hour later, they saw the stage mired down where the roadway dipped through a gully.

"Would you look at that," Dade said with a malicious smile. "I think maybe we ought to just hike on by and let them freeze."

Glenn shook his head. He could see two women and a heavyset gentleman out beside the coach, while the driver was up with the team. All three passengers were mud-covered and straining against the back wheels.

"I don't know about you, Dade, but I think we've got to help them."

"Why should we? They damn near ran me over."

"Look at it this way. I haven't got enough money to buy a stage ticket. Have you?"

Dade flushed. The look on his face said plain enough that he didn't.

"If we help them out of this fix, maybe we're entitled to something in return."

"Like free passage." Dade nodded. "I had my mind set to whip that driver, but could be you're right this time. Fact is, I know you are."

"Then all we've got to do is get them out of the mud," Glenn said. "They look to be in pretty deep."

"We can do it. But first I'm going to make it clear to the

driver how we stand to gain. If he doesn't want to go along, I'll drop him and we'll leave them cold.''

Dade's reasoning was tough, but fair. If the driver was obstinate, their demands might just sway the passengers into insisting on the terms. Either way, Glenn wanted Fay out of the saddle and the cold.

"Agreed."

Dade Taylor grinned with satisfaction. "Donovan, I'm beginning to think more of you all the time. Maybe you'll do to travel with."

Glenn's lean jaw muscles tightened but he said nothing. Whether or not he could abandon those passengers was something of which he wasn't sure, but it seemed wise to keep his reservations to himself for now.

The passengers quit shoving when they saw help arrive.

"'Afternoon. My name is Glenn Donovan."

The heavy man, in his late fifties with sharp eyes that peered through gold-rimmed spectacles, detached himself from the women and waddled self-importantly out to greet them. "Good thing you came along to give us help. My name is Bevis York," he growled in a deep voice. "This is my daughter, Holly."

Holly was in her early twenties. Her cheeks were rosy and she already possessed a matronly look uncommon in one so young. The girl was soft-appearing, short like her father, with brown hair and a smattering of freckles that she probably hated. Yet, unlike her father, she had a genuine smile, wide and unguarded. It made Glenn think better of the father. He turned to the other woman, who was looking away. "Ma'am?"

"Julia Matson," she said in a clipped, small voice.

He stared because he couldn't help himself, and he felt uneasy under the look she gave him. It was as though he'd said or done something wrong. Yet he did not glance away because she had a quality that would make any man take a second look. Green eyes, auburn hair, and a beautiful face which mirrored more pain than any woman her age had a right to know. Her complexion was flawless, with skin so clear and white it reminded him of a porcelain figure, glazed and ready to crack. A voice came from behind him. "My name is Fay Taylor and you'll have to excuse Mr. Donovan's lack of good manners," it said icily. "The man who went to see the driver is my brother, Dade."

Julia nodded, some of the tightness evaporating from around her eyes. Then she noticed the splints. "Miss Taylor! Let's get you down and into the coach. You're hurt."

"Thank you."

Holly bustled forward to help just as Dade's angry voice cut between them.

"What the hell do you mean it's up to Mr. York! You're the driver, aren't you?"

The man dropped to the ground with a lightness that belied his size. When he bunched his leather-clad shoulders, he gave the appearance of a bull ready to charge. Glenn saw Dade take a backward step, not liking what he saw, and for good reason. The driver showed no fear or intention of backing down. In fact, he looked like the kind of man who'd tear you apart. He had a square jaw and looming brows which drove out over a fist-busted nose. He was draped in a full-length woolly buffalo coat and his beard was so thick and heavy Glenn couldn't tell where it ended and the coat began.

"I'm telling you, mister, this is a special run, paid for by Mr. Bevis. Now, if you help us and mind your tongue, I'll see you get to the Pine Tree Station up ahead. But if you bring me any more grief, I'll drop you where you stand."

There was a stubborn finality in what he said. The explanation hadn't a trace of apology. Just fact.

"We've a girl," Glenn interrupted, motioning toward Fay and stepping in between. "Her leg is broken and it pains her to ride."

The driver pushed around and his sunburned brow furrowed as a look of real concern touched his eyes. Glenn noticed he had a slight limp as he went to the horse and smiled up at Fay. As if in explanation, he said, "Miss, I know all about busted legs, as you might have been able to see. Mine was set crooked. Can I look at yours?"

Fay looked at him, then nodded. He inspected it very carefully, and, apparently satisfied, said, "It's a good job. The way mine should have been. It'll heal fine " He reached up and plucked her out of the saddle as though she weighed nothing, then set her carefully inside the coach. "I'll try to miss the bad holes, if we get out of here. Don't you worry about anything, young lady. Clayton James is in charge."

Fay leaned close to his ear and whispered something none

of them could hear. But when the driver straightened, he said, "I'll not hurt him if he lets me be. Now, you just rest easy."

Dade bristled, because the meaning was so clear, and he stepped aggressively forward.

"Hold on," the driver warned. "Before you make like a frog and jump into fast water, I want you to know I'm blood brother to a Paiute chief and I was weaned off a grizzly bear. Whatever you're thinking, it's wrong for your health. Chew on that. Roll it around in your mouth, but then swallow it hard, 'cause it's better for you than what I got in mind."

Dade actually did swallow, and though Glenn knew he was as brave as the next man, he saw him back away with only a warning intended to save face. "We all have got to work together or we'll never get out of here. That makes you a very lucky man."

"Mister, I'm the most unlucky man you ever met," the driver said flatly. "The only thing that could scare me would be living my life over again."

When the stage finally got under way again, Julia Matson thought about what the driver had said and *how* he'd said it. Strange and haunting, the way he'd put it. But then, she'd noticed Clayton James was a strange man himself, tough and physical and even intimidating when he needed to be, yet strangely vulnerable in some indefinable way that manifested itself only when he was trying to help someone, as he'd done with her and, today, with the injured girl. Yes, and he'd even exposed his hurting, in order to avoid the necessity of harming Mr. Taylor.

Julia distrusted handsome men now, maybe even hated them if she allowed herself to think about it. Clayton James was anything but handsome—therefore, no threat. Not like the brash young Mr. Taylor, who kept trying to catch her eye. He would, of course, open with some pleasantry and probably turn out to be quite charming. Fortunately, though, Holly York had him wrapped up in a discussion about how deep the snows became up above. Not a very promising topic, Julia thought, considering the skies. But she was nevertheless grateful to Holly, whom she had gotten to know quite well in the course of the journey together. Holly was a sweet girl and completely open about anything and everything. She was also a talker, and that had been good, for it kept Julia from thinking about yesterday, about tomorrow. The girl had a strong resemblance to her father, but it was only surface-deep. From what Julia could tell, Holly was more interested in helping people than in taking their money. She'd worked in the hospitals of San Francisco—which Julia could tell irritated her father—and she felt the Chinese were terribly oppressed...and what about the poor Indians of Nevada? She'd read alarming stories about how they'd suffered because men cut down their piñon pines and thus robbed them of their main source of winter food supply.

"Miss Matson, have we met before?" Dade asked.

The question was asked right in the middle of what Holly was saying, and it caused a strained silence Julia could not ignore.

"No."

He grinned, just as though she'd said yes. "Don't be so certain of it. Are you from San Francisco?"

Julia looked at the others. They were pretending not to listen, and she had no choice but to answer. "Yes," she said, giving him nothing.

"Lovely city! Fay and I have had the pleasure of visiting it many times, and—"

"Fay. That's a pretty name," she blurted. They glanced at her and she felt ridiculous but pushed on. "How is your leg feeling, Miss Taylor?"

"Much better."

Julia tried harder to bring her into the conversation. She could feel Dade's displeasure. "How did you injure yourself?"

The girl shot a look at her brother, then said, "Our horse fell."

"Oh."

Conversation died and Julia was about to rest her eyes when Dade asked, "Do you know Tom Bryerson? He's one of the city's leading businessmen."

Julia shifted uncomfortably. Why did they never leave her alone? "I'm afraid not, Mr. Taylor."

"How about—?"

"I know him," Bevis York interrupted. "He and I were on the Board of Supervisors together almost six years. Good man. We made a killing on the stock exchange four months ago. Where did you know him?"

Julia saw an alarm go off behind the calm self-assurance that Mr. Taylor gave. She probably knew Tom Bryerson as well as Mr. York did, and she doubted the young man across from her knew him except by name. In spite of herself, she almost smiled. Unwittingly, Mr. York had called his bluff.

Dade cleared his throat noisily. He leaned forward to reply to the gentleman addressing him. "Well, I . . . saw him a few weeks ago. Thought he was looking very fit. Fit indeed."

"Hmmm," York mused. "I met him last Sunday and he was unwell. Told me he might have to leave the city and go back east. Better doctors, you know."

"Of course." Dade turned back to her, but Mr. York was not finished.

"Trouble is, as you well know, young man, he's got that mercantile down on Montgomery Street, not to mention the warehouses."

"Quite true."

Julia bit the inside of her lip to keep from smiling. Bless you, Mr. York! There will be no more name-dropping. Up to now, the businessman hadn't spoken two words of conversation. But with the mention of a friend in commerce, he seemed to come alive.

"You know, Mr. . . ."

"Taylor."

"Yeah. Well, Mr. Taylor, I warned Tom about sinking all his money into buildings. But he didn't listen, and now, with the news to break of this new silver discovery, well, everyone is going to want to invest in the Comstock, and he'd lose heavily if he sold. Wanted me to go into partnership, but of course I wasn't interested. Not with the Comstock opportunities waiting so close!"

"Wise decision, sir."

York nodded emphatically and almost smiled. "Most people your age think that making a fortune is tough, and maybe it is, but they don't realize it's just as easy to lose."

When there was no answer, the older man leaned forward. "I forgot to ask what line of business you might be in."

Taylor blinked, hesitated, and Julia wondered.

"My brother and I are in theatrics, Mr. York."

"Theatrics?" He said the word as though it were foreign to him.

"That's right," Dade said quickly. "We are going to the Comstock to inquire about building an opera house."

Julia saw the girl's eyes widen, but she evidently decided to remain silent.

"What the hell do you want to do that for?" Bevis growled. "An honest banker wouldn't touch it."

Dade flushed with anger but his voice was controlled. "There's good money in the entertainment business, Mr. York."

"Well, maybe so," he conceded. "Always seemed like kind of an unsavory crowd. Nothing solid about those performers."

"That's ridiculous!" Fay said angrily. "Just because traveling artists don't own real estate or trade on the stock exchange doesn't mean they're unstable or immoral. And if our reward for doing a job is applause or . . . or smiles, tears, even a standing ovation, well, that's just as important as money."

Julia felt a sudden enormous admiration for the girl. Good for you! she thought.

The old man was taken aback. "Young woman, I meant no offense," he said stiffly.

"Of course he didn't," Holly York said quickly, and took her father's hand. "I'm sure if you and Mr. Taylor brought entertainment to the Comstock, it would be greatly appreciated by all of us. Including Papa."

She looked straight into Dade's eyes and said, almost wistfully, "You must lead a very, very exciting life."

"It has its ups and downs, Miss York."

She smiled, and there was nothing predatory or condescending about it. Julia Matson thought how much she would prefer to be Holly York than herself.

Right now, all she wanted to do was to get out of California. Hide behind the Sierras and try to forget about yesterday. She wasn't fool enough to think it would be easy and she wasn't a woman of means who could survive very long in a man's world unless she built her own life and somehow found a safe, respectable means of support. Quickly.

She was afraid. Afraid she might make another mistake—and this time there was no one to help. No one at all.

"Miss Matson. Do you mind my asking what takes you to the Comstock?"

Her heart was pounding; she pretended not to have heard the question, but though she was staring out of the window, she could feel him leaning in toward her.

"Miss Matson?"

"Oh, look," she whispered shakily. "God help us, it's beginning to snow."

3

Glenn could not see the road now, and he had no idea how Clayton James could either. The snow was slanting into their faces, hard and cold and driven by a wind that cut off the frigid slopes above. The horses were laboring, slipping and scrambling to keep their feet, and he could see white clouds of steam rising off their hides.

Beside him, the driver sat hunched in concentration, a mass of hair and snow, with a grim purpose in his eyes as he seemed to guide the team up a mountain he could not see but only feel. Sometimes a horse faltered and Glenn would see the driver tug sharply at its rein, and by his very will lift it from a fall. And when they rounded a curve, he pushed steady on the brake and the wheels would miraculously slide through the bend and throw off their clinging weight to churn into the straight ahead.

Glenn cupped his hands around his numb lips and shouted into the face of the storm, "How much farther?"

"Three miles. Right at the top."

"Will we make it?"

Clayton shot him a glance under his ice-layered brows. "Nope. But we'll get damned close!"

He could feel the stage resisting as the snow rose inch by inch. It was as if every turn of the wheels added a pound of weight. And finally, when the horses were almost bucking through more than a foot of rising snow, Clayton knew they'd had enough and pulled them to a stumbling, steaming halt. He set the brake and leaped down, walking from animal to animal, talking low with praise as he worked to pull away their traces.

Glenn jumped down and yanked open the door. "Put on everything you own," he said quickly. "We're going to have to walk to the next station."

"In that!" Bevis roared, pointing at the driving snow.

"Yes, but it's not far."

"How far?"

"Not far," Glenn repeated sternly. "But we have to get moving!"

Bevis scowled. Holly appeared almost excited by the prospect, and Julia Matson seemed strangely eager to escape the warmth of the coach.

Dade unloaded first and gave them a hand out. Glenn noticed that he helped Julia more than was necessary.

"All right, Fay, it's your turn now," he said, reaching for her.

"Are you going to carry me?" she asked with a mischievous grin. "If so, I hope you told Mr. York the truth. I'm no feather."

"I know how much you weigh, remember?"

Dade's hand pulled him roughly aside. "She's my sister! If anyone takes her in his arms, it'll be me."

"Suit yourself, Dade. I just thought you might be planning to help Miss Matson."

Dade colored, but a grin touched the corners of his mouth. "Blizzard or a heat wave, that woman is cold all the same. But I don't plan to give up."

He backed out of the coach. "Maybe I will help Julia. But you watch how you put your hands on my little sister."

"For God's sake, Dade!" the girl cried. "We're in a raging snowstorm."

"Just the same. Watch it."

Glenn reached back in and lifted her out, almost slipping and falling in the process.

She pushed her face into his collar. "Glenn Donovan, watch where you place your feet!"

"How can I?" he shouted. "With you in my arms I can't even see them!"

That made her laugh, and it was a good, happy sound, with her breath warm in his ear. Even so, as he trudged up the snow-filling road into the wind, he hoped it wasn't too far.

The procession moved slowly. Clayton James had roped the team and Dade's buckskin together and they helped to block the wind and trample the deepening snow. Even at that, it was tough going. Holly supported her father, listened to his bitter complaints about the stage driver, the road, Wells Fargo, and the damned penny-pinching fools who'd spread the stations so far apart. All this, Glenn heard in snatches as the wind batted the words around.

Dade was also trying to help Julia, but from what Glenn could see, she was having no part of it. Her head was bent low and she said nothing as he bellowed into the snowstorm.

Of all of them, Glenn knew he was having the hardest time. The air was thin and icy to his pumping lungs. Fay kept up a steady banter in his ears and he was glad for the diversion as his arms and legs started aching with weariness.

"There it is," Julia cried, and Glenn saw a long cabin made of logs with a big open-fronted shed off to one side. He smelled a fire burning and watched the front door open and then two men slog out through the drifts to reach them.

"God damn, it's Clayton James!" one hollered.

"Sure it is. Who else'd be crazy enough to run into the teeth of a blizzard? Well, let's get 'em inside and the horses taken care of 'fore they freeze and we all git fired!"

The last thirty yards to the station door were an agony for Glenn, and when he staggered inside, the warm air hit him like a furnace and made him weave dizzily. His legs buckled and he folded to the floor, rolling Fay on top of him so she wouldn't get hurt. The first thing he knew, the whole crowd was bunched around and Fay was calling for a glass of whiskey. It flooded into his mouth and burned all the way down, making him gag and sit up straight.

"You didn't have to shove the bottle down his throat," Fay said angrily.

Dade laughed. "Sure I did. Besides, look at him now. Face is as red as flannel underwear."

A lean, sharp-faced man with a gray-stubbled beard and no hair on his head at all, except for around the ears, stepped into the circle and spat a stream of tobacco juice into a roaring log fire.

"Ladies and gents, my name is Pete Dekins and I'm in charge of this here station. We ain't used to puttin' folks up overnight, but since you're here and can't leave, we got no choice."

"Your hospitality overwhelms us," Dade said cryptically.

Dekins chomped on his plug of tobacco and eyed the speaker with unconcealed dislike. Then he turned his attention to the others. "Couple of winters ago, somethin' like this happened and in the middle of the night we had a terrible fracas when some jasper climbed under a lady's blankets. Later, he saw it was a mistake."

Pete's eyes crinkled with the remembering. "It was a mistake, all right, the lady damn near clawed him to pieces. Won't happen again, because on this here run, Clayton is the one responsible, according to company policy, for all of you till you reach your destinations."

"Then where is he!" Bevis demanded. "I've got a few things to say to him."

"They kin wait," Pete said evenly. "Right now, he's out under the shed trying to rub down the team and dry 'em off so they don't get the chest hacking deep inside."

Dade's mouth went thin and tight. "If he's in charge of the passengers, why the hell isn't he in here and you out there?"

"Because. He favors horses over people even more'n me." Dekins spat his tobacco juice as though it had suddenly become distasteful. "Now, what I was about to say is that Clayton is probably gonna want the men to sleep in one room and you ladies in the other. That way, they'll be no mistakes like the one I told you about."

"Hell," Dade griped. "There's seven or more of us. Nothing is going to happen."

"I'm sure of it," Julia said stiffly, "and Mr. Dekins' idea is wise and prudent."

Dade was overruled and smart enough to know it. But when he looked at Julia, his eyes slid down her voluptuous shape and Glenn noticed she seemed to shrink back as though he'd privately touched her.

Darkness came quickly, and the blizzard continued to pour its fury down the mountain. They ate on rough benches and no one talked very much as they listened to the wind and felt it shake the building.

It was obvious to Julia that the burly stage driver was in command of their fates, and she was somehow glad. There was a no-nonsense way about him, and without coming right out and saying it, he seemed to exude a quiet kind of authority.

Julia listened intently as he ran through a checklist of information. How much food did they have? What about hay and grain for the animals? He'd seen there were two or three cords of firewood stacked out back, you fellas been working. Yes, and what about snowshoes in case somebody had to go for help? Long as there was food and fire, they'd get by. Sure hoped no one came down sick. Not much medicine. Closest doctor is still in Placerville.

He turned to Fay and said, "Finish eating, and then, if you don't mind, I'll have another peek at that leg, miss."

She nodded.

"Pete, I hope you've got a good stock of horse liniment and salve."

"Sure do, Clayton."

Fay's eyes widened. "You're not thinking of using them on me, are you?"

"Only the liniment, miss. It'll take down the swelling, suck out the dark coloring where blood vessels ruptured." He smiled. "I won't use the salve on you. Stinks pretty bad, and almost strong enough to burn hide."

He looked up at Dade. "Mister, you been setting in here for two hours or more doing nothing but looking good. Don't you know that buckskin of yours needs doctoring?"

The question hit its intended like a punch and Julia saw Dade flash with anger and humiliation as everyone looked away with stiff embarrassment.

"What's wrong with him?" Dade grated.

"His legs are all chopped up," Clayton snapped harshly. "Don't tell me you didn't notice."

Dade's fork clattered on the table. "Driver," he breathed, "you've got a team of animals and a bunch of passengers to worry about. But when it comes to me and that buckskin, you're out of line. Way out! You cross it again, you'd better strap on a gun, because I won't be pushed or talked down to by any man!"

Clayton shoved his chair back and it scraped loudly on the hard plank floor. Before she quite realized it, Julia was on her feet. "Mr. James didn't mean to insult you, Mr. Taylor. Really he didn't!"

She whirled back to the stage driver and saw a stubbornness in his eyes, but also a questioning. "I'm sure Mr. Taylor would have doctored his animal if he'd known there was medicine available."

"I ain't!"

Julia had a temper of her own, though it had been a long time since she'd used it. "Mr. James," she said angrily, "you've no right to insult any of us that way!"

His eyes locked with hers, clashed with them in unspoken battle.

"Miss Matson," Dade said, "I don't need anyone to stand up for me."

"Of course you don't!" she cried. "But are you going to kill each other over something this trivial? And what of the stage? Are you willing—or capable—of driving these mountains and taking us out of here?"

Dade's eyes fell.

"Of course not!" She pivoted back to Clayton. "You did something for me in San Francisco, remember?"

His face relaxed. The lines around his eyes softened and he nodded. "Sure I do, but—"

"I told you then and I'll tell you now, Mr. James. I *need* to get out of California. I'm *your* responsibility and that's why I'm asking you to drop this nonsense and apologize."

"Apologize!" he exploded. "For what? Tellin' a man he shouldn't be setting around acting special when his horse needs doctoring?"

"You didn't tell him, you challenged him."

The man took in a deep breath, then let it out slowly. "Damnation, woman. Maybe I was a little rough, but—"

"There! Mr. Taylor accepts your apology and that's the end of it."

"Damnation!" Clayton swore, starting for the door, yanking it open and barreling outside.

For a moment, they heard a howling. It could have been the wind or it could have been a wolf. Julia knew it was neither.

Sometime later, Julia was standing off by herself watching the others when Dade excused himself and came over to speak. "I appreciate what you tried to do a little while ago," he began, "but it wasn't necessary."

"I disagree, Mr. Taylor."

He brushed his hair with his fingers, a habit she'd noticed him repeat often.

"Well, you needn't worry about me like that."

"I wasn't," she said flatly.

"You're a hard woman with your words. But then, maybe there's reason."

She could see the questioning. The probing he would use to find something vulnerable. And yet, Julia almost felt she saw true concern in his eyes. An interest beyond the mere physical.

"Mr. Taylor, my troubles are personal and they'll stay that way."

He was rebuffed, but only for a moment. "A woman needs to share her troubles," he said simply. "Is there someone in Virginia City?"

"No."

He reached out and touched her shoulder and she made herself grow still and not show fear.

"You need someone to talk to. To help. Just call my name. That's all."

Julia saw Holly York watching them with a look that was troubling. When the girl realized she was being observed, she quickly turned away.

"I'll remember that, Mr. Taylor. But I'm going to do fine on my own."

He smiled. "That's what we're all hoping. Even that rich old man. By rights, he should have stayed in San Francisco and finished out his days in a rocking chair counting his money."

"If you were he, is that what you'd do?" As soon as she asked, Julia regretted the question. She didn't want to know how this man thought. What lay behind those cool blue eyes.

"Now, that's a hard one to answer. I've always gone where the money's to be found, and even if I had as much as he does, I'd probably want more."

"I don't understand that."

"Neither do I." He shrugged. "Maybe it's the way some people are. In fact, I know it is. Hundreds of times, I've seen prospectors strike it rich in these mountains. Rich as kings! But do you think that satisfied them?"

Julia waited, knowing the answer.

"Of course not! They'd go over to San Francisco and gamble it all away, trying to get even more. Some of 'em could have gone back home to their farms and cities in the east. Retired wealthy. But they couldn't. Always had to have one more spin on the roulette wheel or turn of the card."

"That's greed, Mr. Taylor. And I feel sorry for them."

"Don't," he said curtly. "It's the way of people to want what comes hardest or what someone tells them they shouldn't have."

His eyes slipped from her face, and Julia involuntarily took a backward step.

"Goin' after something easy isn't worth the bother, Miss

Matson. And that's human nature. What keeps us all driving forward."

"Have you...have you ever gotten anything that you wanted very badly, then kept on wanting it?"

He closed his eyes and thought for a minute, and when he looked at her, his expression was troubled. "Up to now, I haven't. Gold maybe. But then, I never seen anything, even in the best saloons of San Francisco, as beautiful as you are."

Julia flushed deeply and left him chuckling at her discomfort.

"Mr. Taylor," she heard Holly York call, "would you come over here for a minute, please?"

"Sure, but—"

"Thank you, Mr. Taylor."

Julia needed air, needed to go outside into the gusting wind and let it blow away the trouble she felt. For several moments she rocked under the icy blasts that swept around the station. They buffeted her against the log wall and stung her cheeks with icy pinpricks. When she glanced up, she saw the horse shed in the pale yellow light. For a moment she hesitated with indecision, then followed Clayton's already filling prints in the snow. He was squatted down under the buckskin, smoking a corncob pipe and humming softly to himself while his wide hands and spatulate fingers busily applied medicine. A powerful odor reached her nostrils and it was like camphor, only stronger, and it caused her to sneeze.

He observed her without comment, then returned his attention to the animal, still humming softly.

"Mr. James?"

"Yeah. What do you want?"

"Nothing," she replied, sensing his unfriendliness, and deciding to leave.

"Miss Matson, would you hold this animal's head still? Wants to nip at me when I put this stuff into the cuts."

"All right." She hurried forward, relieved to do anything that would occupy her thoughts.

He peered up, and his shaggy eyebrows formed a question. "You ain't crying over this here beast, are you?" he asked quickly.

"No. It's the medicine that's causing my eyes to water. How do you stand it, Mr. James?"

"Takes getting used to."

Julia nodded. "I want you to know about back in there."

"I don't want to hear it," he said abruptly. "You said what you wanted. Everybody did. I shouldn't have apologized. Riles me to think about it."

"We need you."

He removed the corncob from between his teeth and packed it with his square-tipped finger. "Maybe. Maybe not. It ain't a good thing to need anybody, ma'am. Ain't a good thing at all."

Julia couldn't imagine a man like Clayton James needing anyone. "That's easy for you to say. You're strong and sure. More than anyone else here, you fit this country."

His expression was thoughtful for a moment before he spoke, and when he did, it was without rancor. "Yeah," he conceded. "I like this country fine. But it's the people I'm torn between. When I was a kid, I was too wild for the towns—for folks. Soon as I could ride and shoot, I lit out and became a trapper. But then the forty-niners came pouring in ten years ago and that was the end of beaver. For a time, I tried to prospect, but gold doesn't mean that much to this horse. So I drifted and come to rest in a Paiute camp. Nevada Territory."

He grinned self-consciously. "Chief Numaga took an interest in me. I became a member of his council, though I never butted in. He's got a sister and we took a liking to each other. Her name is Windflower. And that's why, ma'am, I'm torn between red and white. Mixed up inside just the same as you. Probably even more. I can see what's happening to the Indians and I understand there's nothing anyone can do to change things. If this new strike is for real, the Paiutes are going to get blown away same as the Modocs and all the others who held this ground before the prospectors arrived. That's sad. It pains me deep, ma'am, and it makes me angry 'cause I can't do anything to stop it."

"Maybe," Julia said slowly, "it won't happen again. In Nevada, I mean. I've heard it's all desert. Surely not farming land."

"That's generally true, although there's some valleys you'll see as pretty as any in California. But Nevada is like a road from east to west, and more crossing it every day. And they'll flatten that road and everything on it. Numaga understands that, and so does his tribe."

"What . . . what about that girl? Will you take her for your wife?"

"I could, and I'd do it if I thought it would be right." He looked up. "You ever see a half-breed, ma'am?"

"No. At least I don't think so."

"Well," he said slowly, "I have. They're generally handsome people, but godalmighty sad and unhappy. They're usually not accepted by either the Indians or the whites. It's as if . . . as if they done something wrong. And if I married Numaga's sister, our kids would be as torn up inside as me. Does that make sense?"

"Yes," she whispered. "It makes good sense."

"That's what I figured," he said in a troubled voice. "Windflower doesn't understand that. She's innocent, you see, when it comes to the way some folks treat others who aren't the same. But I've seen it and I know. And I'd fight for my kids! Lick any man for the hurtin' of 'em. But . . . but if something happened to me, I couldn't help them. That'd make me fearful. All the time worrying."

"So what can you do?" she asked. "If you love . . ."

"Pretty soon now," he was saying, "I'm going to have to make up my mind about things. Decide whether I'd be causin' Windflower more grief than not by marrying her."

He finished the rubbing, capped the tin of foul-smelling sticky white salve. "You ever been married?" he asked, rising up before her. He looked massive and strong.

"No," she said in a tiny voice.

"But you need to be, don't you."

It wasn't a question and she wasn't prepared for the jolt that left her sagging into his powerful arms. If he'd said anything more, done anything more than stand rooted and steadying, she'd have cried. Julia couldn't look him in the face. Not yet.

"Ma'am, don't you worry none, 'cause I ain't going to say anything. And I'll help you, if I can."

"How did you know?" she asked raggedly.

"Oh, little things. Like that San Francisco dandy I threw outta the coach. And seeing you in the mornings, and how you're scared when that Dade feller looks where he oughta know better'n to. And the way your color shines when the sun strikes your cheeks. A special way, ma'am. Maybe I just see things keener than some because of my upbringing and being around animals so long. Carin' for 'em and such. Maybe I talk too much. Huh?"

Julia squeezed him and held her face down against his

chest. "Mr. James, when I left San Francisco on your stage, I swore I'd never allow another man to touch me. Now I'm hanging on to you as if I were drowning. You're different. The most different man I ever met."

"Yeah," he replied, stroking her hair gently. "That's what I was trying to tell you. But it ain't necessarily good, and it sure ain't easy."

She peered up into his broad, strong, not-so-handsome face. "I need a friend, Mr. James. And I'm going to need some of your strength in the months ahead."

He beamed. Fidgeted in his soft leather jacket, and because she knew he was aware of her own feelings toward men in general, he stuck out his thick, rough hand and they shook. Julia's own fist was dwarfed in his, but she felt a gentle power flow into her.

"You're, if you'll excuse me, a hell of a good man, Mr. James."

"And you, ma'am, are a hell of a good woman. Anytime you need help, you call. If I'm not in town—as often I won't be—leave a message at the Wells Fargo office. I'll come. Even . . . even if I marry Windflower, I'd still come. She'd know I was doing the right thing."

Julia brushed his face. Shivered at the feel of his whiskers. Thick, as he was. He pulled her hand away quickly.

"I don't want you to see what's under this beard, Miss Matson. Ain't pretty to look at. Grizzly bear. Kinda rough on a woman's eyes."

"It wouldn't bother me," she told him. "We're friends, remember? Things like that don't count."

He squinted down at her. "Nice of you to say that, but it's still ugly for one so pretty as you."

"Is that how you hurt your leg?"

"Sure is. He chomped down on it like a drumstick before I could get a blade in his throat."

Julia shivered.

"Ma'am, you shoulda told me you was getting cold. We'd better go inside."

She nodded. With Clayton James's help and friendship, she no longer feared Dade Taylor and his lusting eyes.

Holly York was talking as fast as she could, but it wasn't keeping Dade's attention. His gaze kept shifting toward the doorway, and she knew he was thinking about Julia Matson and wanting to leave. Not that she could blame him. Miss Matson was stunning, really, and few women could hope to compete with her beauty on an equal basis.

Once or twice, as she strove to continue what had become a monologue, Holly saw Bevis glance over and scowl. She knew he was thinking that Dade Taylor wasn't good enough for his daughter—not by half. Holly loved her father, but he measured the world and its individuals in dollars. She was all her father had left, and he needed her and zealously protected her from all outside temptations—especially men like Dade Taylor.

Actually, Holly thought, his job was rather easy, because anyone as handsome as Mr. Taylor wouldn't give her a second glance. She'd once tried to explain this to Bevis, and failed dismally. Oh, he'd invited a few men to their home for dinner, but they'd been more interested in finance and investments than in her—with one notable exception, a man who'd drunk too much of Bevis' liquor and tried to wrestle her down on the front porch.

Holly had to smile when she remembered Mr. Paul Haddock, middle-aged, overweight, and with bags slung under his watery eyes like hammocks. But at least he'd shown that he could distinguish a woman. And she was a woman! One who'd give anything to be beautiful and as shapely as Julia Matson. Just once, she thought, I'd love to have men look at me the way they do at Julia.

She was twenty-one, and except for clumsy old Mr. Haddock, whom she'd completely discouraged by shoving over the porch rail into the rose garden, no man had ever wanted her—except for her father's money. And because of the wealth she would someday inherit, Holly's sense of mercenary interest was as finely tuned as a Stradivarius violin. Thus, if a man paid her a compliment she felt was undeserved, she always looked deep into his eyes for the image of dollar signs. And without exception, she found it. Holly knew she wasn't ugly, but not pretty either. Men thought her plain. Plain, no matter how she fixed her hair or selected her clothes.

Her figure was another disappointment, though certainly not a total disaster. To begin with, she was too short, not much over five feet in high-heeled shoes. Then, too, even though she was careful to watch her weight, most of her curves had a disgusting tendency to slip from the upper to the lower. Oh, for a tiny waistline!

Sometimes she almost gave up hope of finding a man who wasn't tomcat-ugly or viewed her only as a sizable bank account. And though she loved Bevis and revered the memory of her departed mother, Holly yearned for a man of excitement and dash—commodities of which she'd seen precious little in her own life. It was very hard to share her father's enthusiasm at the rise of a mining stock or the price of lumber futures.

That's why Dade Taylor, even though he hadn't the least interest in her, was so appealing. There was a boldness in him that she could almost feel, and a danger in his eyes that excited her. In all her silly fantasies of someday being swept away by a handsome buccaneer or even a dashing young gold hunter or adventurer, she'd never visualized anything like Dade Taylor.

He was the best-looking specimen of a man she'd ever seen. Tall, beautifully proportioned, and, yes, mysterious. Holly suspected he was not a gentleman in the strictest sense of the word, and she'd seen the hesitation in his eyes when her father got to talking about Tom Bryerson; she'd also divined a keen, hard intelligence. And despite whatever character failings he possessed, there was something very noble about a man who'd taken it upon himself to further his sister's career. It was a sacrifice few would even attempt to make, and that, in her opinion, redeemed him completely.

"I've got to talk with Fay," he announced out of a long silence, as he came erect and moved away, leaving her in mid-sentence, talking a mile a minute.

Holly sighed. He moved *so* gracefully. She watched him interrupt a conversation between Fay and Glenn Donovan and it occurred to her that she and the young Irishman had something in common besides their ages. Glenn, though nice-looking in an underfed way, was also aiming for the stars with Miss Taylor. Brother and sister, they possessed a special kind of physical magnetism. Holly was certain poor Glenn wouldn't see that girl again after they arrived in Virginia City. Mr. Taylor would see to that. He was as protective as Bevis.

Holly detected a dispute among the trio. She saw Glenn's face grow angry and the girl talking earnestly. Then Dade turned and said, "I have an announcement. My sister, even though she cannot perform as she is accustomed, has agreed to sing for you."

Everyone looked at the girl with sudden interest.

Pete Dekins slapped his hands together. "I've got a fiddle and I'll saw along."

"Good!" Dade shouted. "Why don't you all gather around the fire and join in. Miss Taylor has lightened the hearts of thousands in the few short years we've traveled together."

And their pockets, too, I bet, Holly thought mischievously.

Several minutes later, she found herself as surprised and pleased as everyone else when the music began. The girl had a lovely voice and Mr. Dekins was surprisingly adept with his fiddle as he scratched out one song after another. It was somewhere in the middle of "Oh, Susanna" that Holly noticed Dade slip into the other room, and thought it curious. One minute, he was leading the clapping chorus, and the next, he was gone.

Then it struck her. She smiled, made herself walk casually around the small group of singers, and positioned herself just outside the door, where she pretended to sing along with the others. When she was certain no one was paying her the slightest attention, she pushed open the door and entered.

For one instant she saw him bent over her father's luggage, hugging a match and going through papers. The match went out and the room plunged into darkness. Holly took a quick breath and heard him slam the case shut. She waited, afraid even to move, yet unwilling to retreat.

"Mr. Taylor?" Her voice was quavering but she pushed on. "It's silly for both of us to be standing like cats in the dark."

"What are you going to do?" he asked guardedly.

"What are *you* going to do, now that I've seen you going through my father's belongings?"

There was a long silence. "I don't know," he said tiredly. "Honest to God, I don't."

She took a deep breath and approached the voice. "Why don't you strike another match, Mr. Taylor? Then put everything back the way it was. I think . . . I think that would be the best."

The match flared and she saw him begin to replace her father's papers. Papers she knew to be assignments of credit, a few letters of introductions, and countless sheets of stock quotations and mining-cost figures.

"Did you find them interesting?" she asked coolly.

He glanced at her. "I might have, Miss York, if I'd had more time and understood something about the stock market."

He snapped the case shut and rose, his face grim and set. "All right, I'm not one to beg, if that's what you want."

"That's not . . ." Her voice trembled. "That's not my intent."

"Then . . ." He smiled. "You want me to kiss you, that's it, isn't it?"

She nodded, because it was true. And she was grateful when the match went out in his fingers. "That's all I want. Just this once. Just so I know how it feels."

His laugh came to her as he did. And when his arms went around her, Holly felt the world turn like a beautiful ballet dancer. His lips found hers and she swayed under his power and felt something wonderful grow and grow until it stretched into exquisite pain and burst inside.

"No more, please!" she gasped, falling away and hearing her own breath, which filled the space between them. She was thankful that he couldn't see the tears in her eyes.

"Now . . . now," she breathed raggedly, "each of us has something on the other to be held in secret. Don't *ever* try that again."

"What? Stealing your father's money or kissing you?"

Holly retreated until she felt the door latch. She pulled it open a crack and studied his face. "Stealing from my father," she whispered, and then, with his soft laughter in her ears, she floated into the other room, just as Fay Taylor ended "Old Virginia Shore."

Far, far into the night, when she could hear Miss Taylor's and Miss Matson's easy breath of sleep, Holly lay staring into the blackness of their room. She *should* be ashamed—but wasn't. Someday a good man who went to bed with numbers on his mind would ask her to marry. And because she was not pretty and couldn't bear the thought of living her life alone, she'd accept. And they'd sit down right after the marriage and he'd want to discuss investments, and she'd accept that, because she was lonely and accustomed to such things. And maybe . . . maybe, if she was very fortunate, they'd have children.

Not a daughter—please, God, not a girl—because plain people begot plain children and Holly never wanted a girl to feel the way she was feeling now. Lying here, having something new and strange and wonderful slowly melt inside and knowing it would never return again. Knowing it couldn't, because someone who looked like Dade Taylor had no interest in women who were not beautiful.

But she'd had her moment. While she could still almost

taste his lips and relive her passion, she wanted to hold on tight and make the feeling last.

Holly York did not sleep at all that night. And she was glad she'd caught him stealing. And that she'd made him kiss her, as she'd always dreamed.

4

With Clayton James at the reins and the horses eager and well-rested, the stage lunged through the final avenues of pine, where the snow lay warm and melting. Up near the summit, the branches were hung with crystal and the sky was pale and cloudless. They passed through Strawberry Valley, near the timberline, where giant granite boulders cluttered the skyline, and finally they reached the top. Clayton had let the horses breathe and his passengers take one last gaze at California, the miles of verdant forest, streams and rivers which glistened in the sun and tumbled happily into the green, plush valleys of the Sacramento. Everywhere, they saw beauty, and a country pregnant with life.

"Look at it well," Clayton advised ominously, "for when you see Nevada, you'll believe that the good Lord must have grown weary when he reached the summit."

They'd thought his words strange as they'd piled back into the coach and glided down to gasp at the sheer magnificence of Lake Tahoe. Emerald and sapphire it was, changing colors as the sun and wind touched its rippling surface. It seemed like a jewel carelessly dropped among the great forests and granite escarpments which plunged down to the water's edge. Thirty miles long, fifteen wide at its girth, the lake was a mile and a half above the sea and far deeper and clearer than coastal waters. Clayton called out these statistics as they rounded the southern shore and once again pulled upward out of the basin.

"They say if it sprang a hole at the bottom, her water would have to rise up to the Carson Valley. Maybe it hasn't even got a floor to 'er. Across the lake is Emerald Bay. Over two miles long and almost landlocked. I wintered there four years ago. Never wanted to leave. That big pile of boulders, they call Cave Rock. We could all go inside her—horses, too—if we needed shelter. Washoe Indians hold their medicine dances in there. Zephyr Cove is that one with all the trees right down to the water. Good fishing!''

Everyone grew silent as they left the Tahoe basin. The grade was steep, and once again Clayton pulled in to let the horses breathe.

''Take a hard gander ahead and see where we're going. Beyond that little strip of valley down below is a land gone to hell forever.''

''Where's Virginia City?'' Bevis asked.

They traced his finger eastward. ''We go down this mountain, and it's a wild run, so hang on inside. Below us is Mormon Station. They built it, and there's good grass under timber. Mormons had to pull stakes, though, 'cause they got called back to Salt Lake City by Brigham Young. Story is, and I happen to know it's fact, when those Mormons left, nobody would give 'em half what their land and improvements was worth. So they cursed that valley and all the others up against these mountains. Why, they was so bitter they cursed the whole of Nevada Territory with droughts, floods, and the strongest winds a man ever faced. Call 'em Washoe zephyrs they do, and they've been known to blow horses and cows clear down to Death Valley. Nevada is tough. It's either chilling your bones or so hot your lips shrivel up and your eyes stick out like the horns on a snail.''

''It doesn't look *that* bad,'' Julia said hesitantly.

He smiled. ''You're seeing the very best part. Spillover from California, I reckon.''

''You still haven't pointed out Virginia City,'' Bevis said stubbornly.

Clayton looked at each of them, then turned and directed their gaze to a purple-gray mountain rising in one smooth sweep to point an angry finger at the cloudless sky. It looked treeless, devoid of life, bereft of water. ''That's Sun Mountain,'' he whispered. ''That's what you're leaving California to live on and dig into. You can't hear the picks and shovels ringing against her yet—but you will. They tell me it never stops, except when the wind gets to moaning up the canyons.''

Glenn stepped closer. "I thought we'd be some of the first."

" 'Fraid not. I don't know where they're all coming from—maybe across the desert from the east, or down south where the Sierras kind of play out around Death Valley. Some even from Oregon Territory. Wherever, they've come."

Bevis cast a worried glance at his daughter. "Maybe," he growled, "but there's thousands more behind us, and we've beaten most. Should be some good claims still going cheap. I mean to buy. Buy a ledge of silver."

"It's nothing to me," Clayton said good-naturedly. "I earn my living in the clean air where I can see things. Not down in some hole like a rabbit. Well, the team is breathing easy again. Let's roll."

And roll they did! Clayton drove his team down a spine-stiffening series of switches and cutbacks that had all the passengers grinding their teeth. Through Friday's Station they barreled, then hurtled down the street of the old Mormon settlement and on into Carson City.

They changed teams and headed east on the old immigrant road leading toward Dayton. They were in desert now and the wagon traffic began to thicken. Some five miles out, along the lusty, spring-fed Carson River, they veered north into the barren hills. Boiling sulfur hot springs gurgled a foul-smelling steam that hissed like a den of vipers. The hills leading up to Sun Mountain were tarnished, crumbling things, where piñon pine and juniper competed with runty sage for existence.

Inside the coach the passengers were quiet and seemed oppressed by the barrenness they saw everywhere. Fresh in their minds were the Sierras, green and alive, but this—this seemed like another world gone dead. Gold Canyon closed them in with its heat-seared, ice-cracked rock. At one point, the canyon walls pinched tight and tall above them and the stage creaked to a halt. "DEVIL'S GATE TOLL—50¢ EACH," the sign read, and an extra dollar for the horses.

Clayton paid the hawk-faced toll-gateman, but they heard him grumble in anger as a small cascade of pebbles bounced down onto the road from above, where two riflemen stood guard. Then they were moving again and the canyon widened to a quarter-mile. And they heard it, the sound Clayton spoke of—a sharp jangle of steel on rock, a ringing chorus of echo which assaulted the crumbling, denuded hills. The hard whack of ax into the last of the trees to be burned for firewood or used in the deepening pits they called mines. And rearing its head above, seeming to watch it all with haughty amusement, towered Sun Mountain.

They slipped under its shadow and the air grew colder and a hard wind blew grit from the molehill-like piles of tailings they witnessed popping out of the red earth about them. Tailings fresh dug by men who wrestled dirt and rock from the skirts of the mountain and lived in every kind of shelter imaginable. Tents and shacks, they were accustomed to, but not pits feebly covered with boards and sagebrush. And the miners themselves were lean and dusty. Unwashed. Hard-eyed and heavily armed. The passengers stared at this grim breed of men and were stared at in return.

The canyon grew very steep and the horses settled into a laboring, muscle-cramping walk. Their hooves dropped into cadence with the ringing steel. And suddenly they were at the divide and Virginia City burst into view.

Fay, Glenn, and Dade had all seen gold camps. Few of them were built to last more than a week or a month. Usually, however, there was a protected feeling to them, nestling close in by some bend in a gold-running river with trees crowding in to bank the wind. But not here. Not in Virginia City. This was a windswept, clinging collection of shacks and shanties which appeared to quake in fear of being blown off the mountain.

A thousand men moved, purposefully, with quick, choppy steps which belied their hardship. And as the coach rolled up C Street, the passengers witnessed an ugly, ragged line of buildings and miners in red shirts and unkempt beards swilling whiskey beside sullen, vacant-eyed Indians. Every third business was a saloon, and despite the blowing grit, their doors were wide open and heavily trafficked by men and, occasionally, painted-faced women in fancy dresses. They almost ran over two whiskey-soddened miners fighting in the dirt while a raucous crowd of onlookers shouted encouragement and passed bets on the winner. Somewhere on the street below, a gun blanked twice, sharp and hard, and it was instantly answered by others as men stampeded out of the saloons and raced down to see the newest fatalities.

The coach stopped before the office of Wells Fargo. Clayton jumped down and swung the door open. "End of the line, folks. Welcome to Virginia City."

* * *

Dade Taylor had accomplished a lot of thinking since they'd crested out of the Lake Tahoe basin and bolted over the Carson Valley. Like the others as they'd gazed into the desolate Nevada Territory, he'd been shocked and even a bit intimidated by the naked harshness. He remembered that in his years of gold-camp rambling, he'd never gone hungry. The Sierras were too rich. You could fish the streams, hunt game, pick berries, or return to San Francisco, where jobs were for the asking. There was always a way to get by until a man's luck swung in the right direction. California took care of its drifters and seekers of fortune.

But standing on the mountaintop, he had an image of what life could be in Nevada. And he didn't have to think very hard to know a man could starve or freeze in the high desert or, almost as bad in his opinion, be forced to go to work as a hardrock miner. One month of that life and Dade knew his fingers would become thick and bent to fit a wooden-handled pick or shovel. And once that happened, he was no better than the filthy hordes who drank and gambled, fought and whored their lives away. It made him shudder.

Fay was of no value until her leg healed and, in truth, a liability, because he'd have twice as many expenses. These were his thoughts until Bevis York had angrily stated he intended to buy himself a ledge of silver. Right there and then, Dade knew he'd been looking up the wrong tree because of his fascination over Julia Matson. Julia was so good-looking, she'd addled his thinking, dulled his wits. York had the money and his daughter was the key to all of Dade's problems.

And so when they'd gotten back into the coach, he'd made himself ignore Julia and focused his attention and charm toward the grumpy old man and his sweet, virginal daughter.

It was easy. In fact, by the time they'd passed through Carson City, Dade had about convinced himself that Holly York was almost cute. She had a good sense of humor, a winning smile, and acted delighted at his sudden interest—the poor girl wasn't used to flattery. By the time they crossed the divide into Virginia City, Dade's mood was very optimistic. He could read the disappointment on the girls' faces. Virginia City was uncivilized and lawless. Dirty and hard. Yes, he thought, but it's also prosperous and wide-open—a perfect gambling man's environment. To him, every saloon was its own silver mine, a den of opportunity where a quick, smart, and gutsy man such as himself could prosper mightily. And that was in addition to whatever happened with the girl. Just to be sure there would be no resistance, he'd made it very plain to old York that he had plenty of money of his own and they'd no doubt be bumping into each other in the course of property investments.

Sizing up Virginia City, Dade felt so emboldened, he turned to the old man. "Do you mind if I call on your daughter?" he asked, helping the girl down from the stage.

"Huh?" Bevis asked distractedly as his mind seemed already preoccupied with business.

Dade was slow in releasing the girl and he saw color rise in her cheeks as she remembered the last time he'd held her. Of course she did!

"I said," Dade repeated, "I'd like to call on your daughter when you get settled into a hotel."

"What for?"

Dade blinked in surprise. For a moment he thought York was going to refuse; then he realized the request was so novel the man really didn't understand.

"Well," he said quickly, "this appears to be a pretty rough town, and I thought your daughter might need an escort."

"Sure. Sure, young man. If she agrees. Fine. Over there," he muttered, pointing and trying to squint something into focus. "Doesn't that say 'Mining Property for Sale'?"

"Yes, it does, Mr. York."

York fidgeted, wanting to leave.

"Father, you go on," Holly said. "I'm sure Mr. Taylor can get us rooms at this hotel. Come back soon, and don't rush into buying."

Bevis actually heard the last part and swung around. "Don't you worry, my dear. I've never bought in haste, and before I spend one dollar in Virginia City, I'll have walked every foot of it and talked with half the miners on the Comstock. I'll know this mountain as well as if I had been born and raised on it!"

Holly smiled and the insult went out of his beefy face as he peered at Dade. "Would you mind checking my daughter and our luggage into this hotel, young man?"

Dade kept his face straight. "Of course not. I guess we'll all be staying here."

Clayton James, his arms filled with luggage and with Glenn helping right beside, called, "This here's the Silver Slipper Hotel, Mr. Bevis. Don't forget, or you'll never get back. I got over three hundred dollars coming."

Bevis was ten yards away and shuttling along fast. "You earned it, driver," he called. "I ll pay you when the banks open up in the morning."

"What are you going to do with all that money?" Glenn asked.

"Got a big family north of Reno. After this winter, they'll be hungry. Ought to buy some provisions and a couple head of cattle for 'em. First though, we'll get that pretty girl to a doctor. Though he ain't much."

Holly took Dade's arm. "I didn't think Mr. James was the kind of man who'd have a big family," she said, watching them enter the hotel.

"A man like that, Holly, well, you never know."

He started to turn but felt her hand stiffen on his arm.

"Mr. Taylor?"

"Dade," he corrected gallantly.

"All right," she conceded as the smile on her face died. "Why the sudden interest today? These past few hours?"

He tried to laugh, but it didn't come off right. "Why, Holly!" he exclaimed with a tone of injury. "Why does any man show interest in an attractive young lady"

"I'm not attractive. And you're not *any* man, Dade Taylor. So let's quit playing games!"

"Holly!" He tried to pull her closer.

"Stop it!" she cried. "I won't say I haven't enjoyed your attentions. I have. Shamefully. But I'll not be used for my father's money. Not by anyone—not even you."

He swallowed and was unable to dredge up the smooth denials. There'd been too much truth and anger in her words. Yet... yet, he needed her money and wasn't about to let someone else beat him out of it.

"Dear lady," he said quickly, "what would I have to do to prove you wrong?"

She stepped back, and her brow furrowed with concentration. At last she glanced up. "I know you must be broke. Otherwise you'd never have attempted to rob my father. I guess the only thing you can do to convince me of your intentions is to make your own hard-won prosperity in this awful town."

Her voice took on emotion, thickened with something close to pleading. "Oh, Dade! I know this sounds cold and awful. Something that a rich girl would say, but I can't help it! Make something of yourself! Prove to me you don't need my father's money."

He scrubbed his face wearily. Didn't even attempt to inject levity into his words. "Is there some specific amount I need in the bank, Miss York? How much? A thousand? Ten? Twenty? What price is your precious trust?"

Her soft eyes filled with tears and she tried to pull away, but he held her firm. "Tell me!"

"Dammit, I don't care about the money!" she swore. "It's pride!"

"How much!"

She looked down into the street and whispered, "For you, just a thousand. That's not so much for my pride, is it?"

Dade's hand tightened. "I could use a stake," he said coldly. "Give me twenty dollars, Holly. I'll pay you back and I'll earn the thousand before too long."

She fumbled in her purse and brought it out, along with a lace handkerchief which she used to dab at her eyes. "Dade, I'm sorry. You've been so nice to me. And that kiss . . ."

He felt her shudder in his hand as he took the twenty. And when she broke away and he heard her steps pounding across the hotel lobby, he smiled with grim purpose. A thousand dollars was a cheap investment, considering the stakes. Cheap even for one's pride. He liked that. If it took marrying, he wanted a girl who undervalued herself. It always had made things a lot easier.

Glenn stood beside the coach, trying desperately hard to look cheerful and failing miserably. Saying good-bye to Fay wasn't easy.

"You don't have to wait," Fay said quietly.

"Oh, I want to."

"How come you're not checking into the hotel with us?"

He thought of the small handful of change in his pocket and shrugged nonchalantly. "No sense in getting spoiled in a bed. Besides, I'm used to sleeping out-of-doors, so I'll just take my blankets and find a place to camp."

"You be careful," she warned. "I've got the feeling every inch of this mountainside is staked."

"I'll be fine. As skinny as I am right now, it won't take much room."

"Glenn?" Her worry flooded to the surface all at once.

"Glenn, I'm afraid I won't see you again. And what are you going to do if all the good claims are taken?"

He reached out and his rough fingers stroked her cheek. "I'll find work—or make my own."

"But you'll never get enough money saved to go to school, earning wages!"

She was right and it was something he had to face and which had weighed heavily on his thoughts since passing through Devil's Gate Toll. He knew as sure as the sun rose tomorrow, he'd find no claim unstaked. But there was another way to earn money—if he could regain his weight and stand busting other men's faces, given the right odds. He thought of it as a last resort. "Fay, don't worry about me," he told her. "I'll be visiting whenever I can, no matter what your brother says."

"Never mind him," she said hotly. "Besides, he's got enough on his mind."

"Holly York?"

"Yes. And her father's money."

Glenn nodded. Everyone in the coach understood Dade's motives. He felt sorry for the Yorks, but even sorrier to leave Fay.

"I'd better go," he said. "It's getting dark and I don't want to be stumbling around out there and get shot as a claim jumper."

There was so much he wanted to tell her, yet words caught in his throat and he knew he couldn't express what he felt. Someday. But not now, like this, while he was broke and full of big dreams but very little else. And he'd have kissed her, except there were too many people around, so he just left. Left, wondering when he would see her again and how he could save any money from wages.

Julia Matson stood in the small unpainted room and watched Clayton James set her trunk in the corner and go to wait awkwardly beside the door.

"Guess I'll be leaving, ma'am. The horses need tending and they'll be hounding me to take the stage back to Sacramento. Probably with ore instead of people."

"Yes," she said, "I suppose that's true. Will you have to leave tomorrow?"

"No. Leastways not on the stage. I'll borrow a horse and a

few pack mules from the company and go north to visit the people."

"Windflower?"

He nodded. "You'd like her, ma'am. Know you would. There's something besides pretty in you both."

She tried to smile, put some gaiety in this farewell. "I'm sure I would, Clayton. Will I see you again?"

"If you want. When I return for the stage, I'll come by. Maybe..."

"Maybe what? Tell me."

"Maybe if you wouldn't..." He flustered. "Maybe we could get a bite to eat together when I come back. I'd clean up some."

A lump rose in her throat and she walked over and stood toe to toe with him. "You come anytime, Clayton. We're friends, and I'll thank you not to forget that."

A big smile creased his face. "Not likely. Not likely. Say, do you need any money? Kinda to hold you over?"

"No," she said quickly. "I've plenty."

He laid a big rough hand on her shoulder and then he kissed her cheek. "Adios," he whispered, closing the door.

"Adios," she whispered silently after he'd gone. In her purse was fifteen dollars. With rooms at one dollar a night, if she ate only once a day, Julia figured she could hold out perhaps a week to ten days. But, she told herself, it won't take that long to find work. She must find it soon. Even tomorrow. Then she'd save for the baby. And she'd find a way to live in peace and forget the yesterdays. For herself. For the child. She must!

Clayton James felt good toward the world as he rode north into the desert. Roped behind him were three company mules loaded with flour, cornmeal, salt pork, and other provisions he intended to give to Chief Numaga and his tribe when he reached Pyramid Lake. And, oh yes, there were two bolts of calico cloth for Windflower's family and a Mexican silver necklace which he knew would brighten her eyes with joy.

The land stretched out before him, shimmering into the gray distance. Nothing moved in his field of vision. The whites called it a godforsaken desert, but the Paiutes made it their home. Pyramid Lake sustained them and probably had for centuries, and as long as the Truckee River splashed down to replenish the dead lake, the people would stay unless driven out by the whites.

To survive, the Indians had learned to use everything and waste nothing. Fish made up an important part of their diet. Each year, they caught the strange-looking cui-cui fish. And in the spring and the fall, there was great excitement among the people when the salmon-trout spawned in the Truckee River. The men and boys would hurl spears and nets for the spring cutthroats they named tamaagaih and, later in the year, for the long beautiful hoopagaih with the bloodred throat and firm pink meat.

Those were the best times of the year, when the fishing was good and women cleaned and filleted the salmon, then dried and smoked them for winter. If the spring rains were generous, the hunters would stalk pronghorns and bighorn sheep along with mule deer that came down from the snowy mountains to graze. But the deer were fewer each season and the Paiutes found other foods to keep them alive.

The battle for survival never ceased among the people. Through the long summer, Clayton had watched young boys stand for hours camouflaged with reed mats waiting to snare ducks and geese, while their sisters reached deep into still waters with nimble fingers for the new shoots of cattails the tribe ate to quench their hunger for green things. Sometimes, too, they found eggs in the marshes and carried them in green tub baskets. And everyone helped with the rabbit drives. The frightened animals were driven from the sagebrush by a line of walkers toward concealed nets. The meat was for food, the skins for winter robes.

But of all the sources of food, the one that sustained the Paiutes through good year and bad was the squatty blue-green piñon pine. They gathered pine nuts, and it was good to see the women carrying baskets, the men and children racing through the trees, laughing and trying to outpick each other. And when the baskets were filled, the Indians knew they would not starve through the long winter.

Clayton thought of these things and of Windflower as he crossed the desert where alkali and sand, like spilled milk, curdled whitely. He'd often wondered why the people stayed in this land instead of remaining in the Sierras, where they sometimes went in the heat of July and August. There, they'd camp and enjoy the cool days and fresh breezes that rattled the quaking aspen, cottonwood, and pine forests and lifted the human spirit to that of the eagles which soared above the peaks and canyons.

At last he crested the hill over the big meadow beside

Pyramid Lake. Clayton saw the island of the pelicans, and just beyond and near the eastern shoreline, the great pyramid rock which lifted three hundred feet out of the water and had so inspired John C. Frémont that he'd named the lake in its honor. He gazed at the sharp, wind-sculptured rocks which jutted out into the northeast waters like bleached fangs. Inland sea gulls lofted gracefully above on warm, invisible desert currents. The vast lake seemed to change color as he watched, green to gray to blue, as the sun and clouds played the painter.

Clayton smiled and then looked down at Numaga's camp in the meadow. He saw women at work beside their willow frame, grass-covered karnees, and the smell of smoking fish rose to build a hunger inside. His eyes found Numaga's hut and he threw back his head and a wild, building roar echoed from his lungs. The cry floated down the hillside, rolled through the encampment, and instantly caused a reaction as heads swiveled toward him. Children at play froze in mid-stride and warriors burst out of their karnees with bows and arrows. When they were all staring up at him, Clayton bellowed again, and this time his call ended in a high, happy sound.

Then they were motioning excitedly to each other and pointing, and a young woman, slender and lithe as a doe, broke free and began to run toward him, calling his name over and over.

Clayton dismounted and, with long strides, went to her, knowing such moments were the finest of his life.

He sat cross-legged at the council fire and waited for the pipe to travel the circle five times as he knew it must before talk. Somewhere behind him, out of the ring of firelight, he could feel Windflower's eyes, and they warmed him and made him sit straight and tall beside the grave Paiute leaders.

Directly across the fire, Numaga gazed impassively at the flames, and his eyes reflected a troubled light. He was a magnificent figure, about Clayton's own age of twenty-seven. Responsibility had given him a quiet dignity and self-possession that set him apart from the other leaders. That, and his size and strength. Numaga looked up for an instant; his keen black eyes shone with an intense and steady gaze across his features—high, prominent cheekbones, Roman nose, wide mouth, and strong chin. Everything about Numaga was big and strong and good. In the years he'd known the chief, Clayton had never seen him lose his temper or treat anyone unfairly. Maybe it had something to do with his immense physical power or even that as a young man he had been sent to learn the white man's customs and language with the mission fathers in California's Santa Clara Valley.

"It's time to speak," Numaga ordered. "I have waited until our brother has eaten and rested from his journey. His eyes have warmed to Windflower, but I have also seen them tighten with pain at the hunger of our people. His gifts will still the empty rumbling of our children's bellies and give strength to those of us who must hunt after this bitter winter of famine and sickness."

"How many died, Numaga?"

"Three children. Four old ones grown weak with cold. The snows were deep. Ice covered the waters. Many horses starved."

"I should have come sooner," Clayton whispered. "Could have made it over on snowshoes but . . . but, well, I was working two jobs, saving money for the people. And then about a month ago the company offered me a hundred dollars if I could get this rich fella over, and I took it 'cause I knew you'd need all the food I could buy."

Clayton twisted his big hands together, knowing his words had sounded lame and weak and that he'd been wrong to stay in the gentle womb of San Francisco while the Paiutes were dying of hunger. A terrible guilt rose up in his chest, until he found it difficult to breathe.

"My brother," Numaga said gently. "You did well for us. Even your long rifle could not have kept the hunger from our karnees, the cold snow from killing. We know your heart is good and you are not like the whites who swarm into our lands like locusts."

"There will be more. Many more," Clayton said quietly.

"I know. My scouts have told me they come on foot and on horses. From the east, the Shoshi say they gather in their moving houses on wheels. We have always welcomed the white man, but this is no longer so. They dig holes in the ground and cut our trees to put inside." Numaga's voice grew hard. "This winter, they have cut many, many trees for the ground and for above the ground and for their fires. They have killed the piñon which gives us harvest. They dirty our water and then, like coyotes in the night, they steal our women and send them back with an evil sickness in their wombs. This I know!"

Clayton felt the council's eyes boring into him. He was one of them, they trusted him, but *still* he was one of the whites, too.

"Some white men are good," he said. "They have helped your people."

Numaga nodded. "They have changed. At first, they were good, asking only to cross our lands, and they did not defile it with holes, or cut the trees, or look to our women and horses. But those who come now are filled with hunger for that which is ours. They would kill our warriors and use our women. They are evil."

Clayton nodded. When there had been only a few white men like himself, they'd respected the Indians' rights because they were afraid or because they knew Indians well enough to treat them with respect. But the miners, the gawddamn lusting miners, didn't give a plug about anyone or anything except gold and silver. All they wanted was to strike it rich and return to California's pleasures. Numaga was right—this silver bonanza was bringiing in a godless, selfish breed who'd exterminate the Paiutes just as they'd done the Modocs in the gold country ten years ago.

"I don't rightly know how you can stop 'em, Numaga. If you unleash killing, they'll band together and drive you from here. Hound you into the Black Rock Desert, where you'll starve."

"This is true. I feel it in my bones. But the killing has already begun. After you left, two whites were murdered. The people of Carson City said it was because of my people."

Clayton leaned forward. He hadn't heard about this. It was just the kind of thing he'd dreaded.

"Chief Natchez, son of Chief Winnemucca, and I journeyed to Carson City to say that this was wrong. I am war chief of the Paiute nation, and I did not order the kill."

His black eyes dropped to the fire and seemed to tighten as though it hurt to see back into time. "It was cold. Our horses were thin and weak from hunger. On the way to Carson City, we were shot at many times, though none were hurt. A bearded man called Major Ormsby showed me arrows. His eyes were accusing and mean, like a snapping dog's. I told him the arrows were made by Washoes."

"Washoes!" Clayton swore. "Chief Jim would never allow his people to murder anyone."

"Washoes," Numaga gritted. "Then Ormsby asked me to help him get Chief Jim to bring in the murderers if what I said was true. His eyes slapped my face with insult."

Clayton bristled. "That Ormsby is too full of himself since he built that hotel. Thinks he's the governor of the territory or something. Says Carson City is going to be the capital of a new state and that big adobe hotel of his is gonna be turned into the capitol building."

Clayton got a hold on his temper, but promised himself on the way back to Virginia City that he'd have a word or two with Major William Ormsby. He wasn't the law; in fact, he wasn't anything but an agent of the stage company. "Then what happened?"

"I sent five of my best warriors to Chief Jim's camp to bring him and the guilty men back to Ormsby. They went bravely, knowing the Washoes might kill them. One day later, they returned with Chief Jim and a dozen of his tribe. Three were accused, though I judged them innocent."

"Who accused them! Ormsby?"

"Yes. But Chief Jim said no, that all of his people were at Pinenut Valley when the murder was done. The whites became angry. Their faces grew ugly and their tongues shouted vile names I will not repeat in council. Then they began to throw rocks, and ropes were unsnaked over tree branches."

Clayton's jaw became rigid and his teeth were locked in fury. He could visualize how it must have been—he'd seen lynch mobs before, when only a boy. It was something he'd never forget.

"A young girl, younger than Windflower, threw herself into the dirt at my feet and begged me to save her husband. She cried . . ." Numaga's mouth worked silently until the choking words were bitten out. "She cried, 'Oh, Good Spirit, come! Oh, come into the hearts of these people. Oh, whisper in their hearts that they may not kill my poor husband. Oh, good Chief, talk for him!' "

Numaga shook his head with bitterness. "The woman's cries and the flying rocks drove fear into her husband and he ran. The two others followed. Before any of us could stop them, bullets filled the air. The husband fell with blood running from his back. He died. Another, too."

"Damnation!" Clayton swore vehemently. "What about the third?"

"He stopped running and Ormsby silenced the rifles and he was spared. Chief Jim is shamed. He swore I had betrayed him and that their blood was on my hands. He vowed the dead warrior's spirits will haunt me all my days. I believe this."

"Numaga, listen!" Clayton pleaded. "You did what you had to do in trying to keep peace under the promise of justice."

"What peace!" Numaga raged, leaping to his feet and towering across the fire. "The Washoes *were* innocent. White had murdered whites and were hanged. This, Ormsby himself found to be true!"

Clayton rose. "I'll talk to Ormsby, but there's nothing can be done now, and you kept the peace."

Numaga's heavy shoulders bunched. "Soon it will end," he spit. "When the snows melt, the whites will come in great numbers from the west. And to the east, my scouts watch them killing more trees for shelter. They are building a Pony Express."

"What's that?" Clayton asked disconsolately.

"We do not know. Only that it will bring others across our lands."

Clayton nodded. Maybe Ormsby could tell him more about that, too. But right now, he felt sick for the people—what was happening to them—and what was going to happen. And about the children, who might never live to be free, and the old, who'd starve because the pine nuts were gone. And about Windflower. Beautiful, good, uncomplicated Windflower, who huddled in the darkness and loved him and heard the words of her brother and cried her innocence.

"We will not be starved and cheated," Numaga warned. "We have spoken of this many times and would rather die in battle than like old, shivering men in our karnees. The women and children would also have it so. All have spoken from their hearts."

"If the people are tested, I will join them to fight!" Clayton vowed with determination. "Never again will I leave when the snows fall on this land!"

Then he left the council fire and strode across the earth to stand before the great dead lake and gaze at the white dagger rocks ripping into the quiet, star-sprinkled heavens.

And, soft as the moonlight, Windflower glided in beside him and took his hand in her own. He squeezed it, hard; but the expression on her face did not tell him this as they began to walk along, where the dark waters kissed the quiet sands.

* * *

Clayton stood with her, apart from the others, and looked deep into eyes that mirrored a trust that made him feel humble. She had, in the two days they'd been together, asked for nothing but his presence. And after that first night at the council meeting, she soothed the fear from him and returned lightness to his world. Now he was going, and he knew she was sad, but letting nothing betray her thoughts to cause him unhappiness.

"Windflower," he told her, "this time, I will not be so long. One moon, perhaps two. I will come back and you will build me a karnee."

A wondrous expression touched her face and she shivered with joy. She stood poised before him with dignity so as not to shame her family. This, he understood.

"You are my woman and I have asked your brother to prepare for the marriage ceremony."

She nodded quickly, couldn't seem to keep her small moccasined feet from dancing. "Soon, Clayton. Soon, please."

He grinned wide and strong. "Very soon. First, I want to go and earn as much as I can so the tribe will have food this next winter. You ever eat canned peaches?"

"Peechez?"

"Yeah, peaches. Big, drippin' yellow things."

She shook her head; the glistening black hair shimmered. "You will," he promised. "I'll buy a can for every family."

"I do not care about peechez," she stated quietly. "Only you, Clayton James."

He swelled up with pride. Looked at her deep and long. "It's a puzzlement," he said, "how someone so damned beautiful could want such an ugly critter as me. Specially one all clawed and crippled."

Windflower reached out and traced his lips with her fingertips, then said, "I love you with all my heart and spirit and body, Clayton James. You are not critter. *You* are beautiful."

He swallowed painfully, then took her into his arms and kissed her in front of the whole tribe, who thought it very funny and started laughing. Then, while the smile was still on his own face, he mounted his company horse and moved away, the three unburdened mules trailing behind. At the crest of the hill overlooking the big meadow, he reined up and saw her waving, a small, trusting figure. Clayton knuckled moisture from the corner of each eye and let his horse carry him south toward Virginia City.

5

Julia buoyed herself with the knowledge that she was saving almost fifty cents a day out of her earnings at the Silver Exchange Mercantile. She'd found employment that very first day, and although she was weak by evening, she hoped she'd grow stronger as her body accustomed itself to the long hours and constant activity that stocking shelves, waiting on customers, dusting, and pricing required.

In only two weeks, Mrs. Raney had persuaded her indolent, tobacco-spitting husband to raise her wages ten cents a day. Julia suspected it was because since she'd come to work, the business around the cracker and pickle barrels had increased enormously. The Raneys were good with figures and knew how to squeeze a dollar.

Everything was expensive because it was hauled by mule from Sacramento and San Francisco. Even so, Julia felt the Raneys were gouging the miners. For example, they paid three dollars a pound for flour and sold it for five-twenty-five. Coffee and beans were marked with an equal profit margin. Picks and shovels were eight-ninety each and salt pork was seven dollars a pound. There were three other general stores in Virginia City, and Julia knew Mr. Raney visited them each time a new mule train arrived and that prices were fixed. And though she didn't speak of it, Julia thought the store owners, in their greed, were just asking for more competitors.

"Julia?"

She was kneeling on the dirt floor, arranging little boxes of baking soda on a low shelf, when her name was called. Julia pushed herself erect, feeling a slight dizziness. "Yes, Mrs. Raney?"

The woman was thin, sharp-featured like her husband, with

deep-set gray eyes and silver-streaked hair pulled back tight in a bun. Mrs. Raney could hear a coin drop in the dirt from across the room and recognize its value.

"Mr. Raney and I were talking last night and thinking it might be to our advantage to stay open two more hours each evening. None of the others do."

It wasn't posed as a question, but Julia knew her opinion was expected. "I believe that would be a good idea, Mrs. Raney."

"Good." She seemed relieved. "And if that proves to be successful, we think it would just as easily apply on Sundays, don't you?"

Julia swallowed a growing apprehension. "I suppose so, but—"

The woman cut her off abruptly. "Of course, Mr. Raney and I have noticed how well you seem to take responsibility. That's why we thought it fair to give you that extra ten cents a day."

"Mrs. Raney," Julia said, feeling disappointment and anger, "I earned the raise."

The woman's lips drew down at the corners. "You must agree, young lady, we've taken a great deal of trouble in your learning. That robs us from other work and has been expensive."

Julia bit her lip and forced herself to remain silent. She couldn't help but feel trapped and resentful, especially after she'd been so grateful to the Raneys for the small raise.

"I'm glad you understand that, my dear. Mr. Raney said you would, and, you're such an intelligent girl, I agreed." She seemed to brighten with good humor. "Now, getting back to those extra hours you'll be working. We feel that since you have only just received the extra—"

The door jangled shrilly as two miners entered. "Take care of them. We'll continue this discussion in the back room when they leave."

Julia nodded stiffly and hurried down the aisle, past the glass case holding gold-cased pocket watches and silver buckles, around the tables of work clothes, and under the dangling pickled hams strung like an aerial trapline.

The two customers watched her approach with obvious enjoyment, and she recognized and catagorized them as more talkers than buyers.

"'Afternoon, ma'am. Nice day out, ain't it?"

"Yes," Julia said, not thinking it was so nice at all after her conversation with Mrs. Raney.

"You got any more newspapers in lately?"

"To rent or buy?"

"If we return 'em without tearing anything out, we get fifty cents back, right?"

Julia nodded. She knew very well they were just creating talk. "The newspapers are right over there," she offered, pointing toward a stack.

"What else you got in new?"

"Since yesterday?" She was certain they had been in the afternoon before.

One elbowed the other in the ribs, and they both grinned sheepishly. "Well, the truth of the matter is, ma'am, we aim to take you to the dance next Saturday night down in Gold Hill. It's—"

"I'm sorry." She turned to leave.

The taller man stepped around quickly and cut her off. "Take it easy. You ain't even had time to hear about it yet."

The other closed in behind. She could smell whiskey. "If you don't like dances, we could think of something else."

Julia inwardly stilled herself. Where were the Raneys? She could call for them, but didn't want to create a scene. She cleared her throat and said firmly, "Thank you for the offer, gentlemen, but no. Is there anything *here* I can do for you?"

"Yeah, plenty, if you want to lock the door and close up shop for tonight."

Harland Raney's old Navy Colt cocked ominously in the background. "Gents, either make a purchase or get the hell out!" he wheezed savagely.

The intrusion startled the pair, and their eyes banked around sharply to see Harland standing at the storeroom door, with the pistol aimed and ready. He was tall and skinny, except for a small potbelly, and the Navy Colt was wrapped in fingers like spider's legs. He spit tobacco and waited with his lean, coyote-shaped face an incalculable mask that seemed all the more frightening because it lacked any sign of caring. Harland was like that, and Julia was once more reminded the taciturn store owner frightened her. Especially when she was working alone and suddenly glanced up to find those insect eyes of his probing into her. It was as if they hunted her down in the poorly lighted store and crawled over her in the gloom.

"They . . . they just wanted a newspaper, Mr. Raney."

"I know what they want," he snarled, motioning with the pistol. "The papers are over there. Look 'em over quick."

They nodded and almost fell over each other reaching the stack and grabbing the top issue. "This will do, Mr. Raney. Yeah. We ain't seen it yet," one said, tearing a dollar out of his pocket and setting it on the counter. "Thank you kindly!"

When the door closed, Julia turned and was surprised to find Mr. Raney almost touching her. She retreated. "I . . . I don't think they meant anything."

" 'Course they did!" he graveled, shoving the gun into his baggy work pants and spitting tobacco. "Those varmints wouldn't have bought anything if I hadn't stepped in. Probably have stole something when your back was turned."

She nodded dumbly, realizing she'd been foolish to think he'd interfered on her account.

"You stir up the blood," he said after a pause.

"I'll finish stocking those boxes of dry goods, Mr. Raney."

"Hold on. I'm not finished. I just sent Mrs. Raney on home so's we could talk alone."

Her lips formed the question "Why?"

Raney scowled, knuckled his long nose. "Well, it's what she spoke to you about, keepin' the store open late and on Sundays."

Julia made herself stand up to him. "I can't take that kind of hours. And—"

"Sure you can! You're strong, and younger by twenty years than the missus. Hell, a girl like you oughta be able to work from sunrise to after dark and still have plenty left to dance all night or please a man."

"Mr. Raney!" She needed this job badly, but not so much as to be degraded by such openness.

"Aw, now. I meant nothing, girl," he said soothingly, aware he'd overstepped propriety.

She waited irresolutely, unsure of what he intended to say next.

"The thing of it is, me and the wife trust you enough to let you close up at night and handle the money on Sundays."

Julia took a deep breath. "I appreciate that, Mr. Raney. I really do. But . . . well, you saw what just happened. What if I were alone here one evening and the same thing occurred?"

He scratched his potbelly. "Hadn't thought about that. You've got a point. Tell you what. For the first month or so, I'll stay, off and on. You can wait on the customers and I'll keep mostly to the storeroom and do the ordering and heavy work. After the men get to know I'm around, they won't try anything."

"I'm tired," she protested wearily.

His voice hardened. "I know what you're a-holdin' out for, and though the missus won't like it, I'll give you another ten cents a day for the extra time and two dollars for Sunday—if the business carries it."

Julia balanced her fatigue against the money and knew she had no choice but to accept, with the baby coming. Yet she didn't want to appear overeager, and held her silence.

"Listen, girl," he said roughly, "there's others we could hire and they'd thank me right proper for the chance to make over nine dollars a week!"

She didn't like the implication he'd thrown out, and her anger flared. "You're telling me to work eighty hours a week, Mr. Raney! Even the miners don't put in that kind of hours, and they make nearly twice as much."

"Are you wantin' to up and quit? Maybe be a miner?" His wedge-shaped face split to reveal a mouth full of tobacco-stained teeth, and he chuckled meanly. "Hell, lady, you wouldn't last an hour workin' like they do. If the walls didn't drop down and cover you, the crews would!"

Her face went hot. "Mr. Raney, I won't be spoken to like that."

He laughed. "You got no choice. In case you don't understand it yet, you oughta be down on your knees thankin' me for this job. Only one other way you kin earn more in Virginia City, and I don't have to spell it out."

"I quit!" she snapped in anger.

He blinked, then seemed to realize she wasn't bluffing. "Wait a minute. I meant no insult. Yore a growed woman, not a girl. Maybe I was wrong to say it out plain like, but that don't mean it isn't the gospel truth."

"The truth," she said coldly, "is that I'm no slave that you can intimidate or bully or insult, Mr. Raney! I am not at your service."

His lips drew into a tight line. "You're right there, Julia. We don't pay slaves back where I come from—just use 'em as suits our pleasure."

She wanted to slap him but was afraid. "I *am* quitting,"

she declared staunchly. She'd found this job easily enough—she could find another.

"'Fore you do," he said quietly, "why don't you simmer down and state your wants plain out. Like I said before, you're good for our business. Never had so many men flocking around. Most just want to gawk at you, but some feel obliged to buy. Adds up."

Julia expelled a deep breath of pent-up anger. She stared down at the floor and past her waistline, which was, even now, beginning to expand. In another two months, it would be noticeable. And then how many men would flock in to buy? And if her value decreased, she knew the Raneys would fire her without notice. She *had* to swallow her pride and drive her fleeting advantage while it lasted.

"All right," she gritted. "I want twenty-five cents of every dollar I sell during the extra hours, rather than a wage."

"What!" he roared. "I won't hear of it! Neither will the missus!"

"Yes, you will, once you've reconsidered," Julia vowed. "If I don't make you money, I won't cost you any."

He scrubbed his day-old whiskers, and his face went hang-dog. "I'd like to, but we just can't. Our profits ain't that large."

He was lying through his teeth, because he'd forgotten she knew exactly what he paid and sold his goods for. She decided to remind him of the fact. "They're fifty or sixty percent, and we both know it. I tally the invoices and mark the prices, remember?"

He actually winced, and Julia watched him run the calculations through his head. "But you could earn over five dollars of our money a day!"

"And you'll make four times that and it will be over and above anything you've earned up to now. You've nothing to lose."

"That's a lot of money," he said dispiritedly.

"For both of us!" What did it take to make him understand? "All I'll do in the extra hours is wait on customers. Sell them, Mr. Raney. I'll smile and laugh and . . . and I'll even flirt if I have to in order to get them to buy."

He studied her closely. All the trumped-up indignation and opposition were gone, and he wasn't looking at her like a woman now. More like a tough bargainer, and that gave her confidence.

"You're pretty ambitious, ain't you?"

"That's right," Julia replied. "Have we got a deal, or do I

go to work for one of your competitors tomorrow under the same terms?"

His mouth flew open and his big hands clenched, but she knew she couldn't show fear or everything was lost.

"I'm sure, of the three, at least one is smart enough to want to be the biggest in Virginia City. The man who drives the others out."

"You'd do that?" he asked softly. "Go to work against me?"

Julia looked straight into his little muley eyes. "It's as I said, Mr. Raney, I'm no slave, and I'll not be used."

"You're usin' your body on me," he told her.

She opened her mouth, then clamped it shut. Maybe he was right. It didn't matter. He'd spelled out her alternatives loud and clear. If she was using her body for profit, she'd use it well and it would be far cleaner than going up on A Street and joining the other women of the night.

"I'm leaving," Julia said, twisting away. "You and Mrs. Raney talk it over. Think about it very carefully. Get out a pencil and figure it out over a month. Consider how it will be when the Silver Exchange Mercantile becomes the largest general store in Virginia City."

At the door she paused, and he was standing next to the rope-strung hams.

"Think about how you've got nothing to lose and everything to gain."

Then she closed the door and left him working up a spit. As she passed down the street, Julia felt her heart beating excitedly. He'd think about it, all right. And because he and his wife were smart, they'd accept. Then she'd finally have her chance, and Julia promised she'd do whatever it took to make it pay. There was so little time left.

Dade sneaked out the back door of the hotel because he was a week overdue on the rent. He edged around the corner of the building and smoothed his new gray suit, flicking off a spot of dust with his manicured fingernails. Then he waited for Bevis York.

In the weeks since his arrival, Dade had gotten to know Virginia City as well as any man. It was rough and ready, without law or justice. The saloons favored roulette and faro and the proprietors had instantly pegged him as a professional gambler. Reluctantly he'd had to pay a third of his profits for the bartender's help and the establishment's cooperation. It seemed an exorbitant price, but every day he saw new gamblers arriving and competition for the miner's dollar was fierce. Hell, a good part of the night, he was being forced to match his skills against other professionals. Skill against skill and, often, lady luck was the deciding factor.

Dade tipped his hat to a successful-appearing gentleman and glanced at his gold pocket watch with its new ten-dollar chain. He smiled, remembering it was Julia Matson who'd sold it to him over at the Silver Exchange Mercantile. And since he'd won eighty-five dollars the Saturday night before, he'd hung around the woman until she'd relaxed. When she'd told him about her deal with the Raneys to earn a share of the profits, well, that's when he'd decided to buy the watch and the new suit, just to see appreciation flood her eyes. Dade had figured his purchases alone must have earned Julia ten or twelve dollars. But his satisfaction had been short-lived, because there'd been a lot of other men trying to impress her. Hell, if she kept that up each Sunday, she'd soon be working for herself and put all of the rest out of business.

He'd left the Silver Exchange Mercantile feeling kind of low that she was prospering so greatly. If she ever came on hard times, he might have a better chance with her, but now that seemed unlikely. And the minute he'd spent most of the eighty-five dollars, why, damned if she hadn't turned her smile on someone else! Her businesslike attitude had only made him more determined to have her someday. But with every dollar she'd rung on her till, that seemed ever more remote.

Dade stiffened and his eyes, dark and puffy from gambling at night and trying to impress Bevis during office hours, narrowed as he saw Holly's father appear. After only a few weeks in Virginia City, Bevis already had everyone bowing and scraping to him as though he were some kind of king passing out favors. And, in a way, he was. It hadn't taken the community long to find out that old York was loaded.

"Mr. York!" he called, dodging across the street and getting the impression that Bevis didn't even notice the new suit and gold chain. Never mind, Dade had some news that the old man would perk up and listen to.

The financier squinted through glasses that enlarged his eyes, then scowled. "Oh, it's you."

Dade nodded, a frozen grin wanting to crack.

"Mr. Taylor, isn't it?"

"Yes, sir."

Bevis nodded once, checked his watch, and continued walking.

Dade followed along beside him, trying to look equally prosperous and self-important as the man who was rapidly becoming known as the Comstock's wealthiest and shrewdest investor.

"Mr. York, I have some news that could be very important to you."

"I doubt it, young man."

"It's about the main ore body. I have it on good authority that it is changing direction."

Bevis stopped in his tracks. The irritation was gone now, and Dade had every bit of his attention. "That's preposterous!"

"No, it isn't," he insisted. "And my sources are very reliable."

The man studied him like a bug. He started to walk away, but couldn't. "I'm in no humor for jokes or rumors. Tell me your sources!"

"That's impossible right now, sir." All his years of gambling came to the fore. He wanted to create doubt, but not to reveal that Virginia City's best geologist was a very poor gambler, and one with a powerful addiction to a deck of cards. After three nights of losing, he'd been more than eager to swap confidential information for his debts. Now Dade was hoping he'd bargained well. Five hundred dollars was a lot of money, but if the geologist's knowledge was accurate . . .

"I said," Bevis repeated, "what is the nature of your sources?"

"I'm afraid I can't reveal them, sir."

"Then they're worthless to me," Bevis huffed. "I don't listen to unfounded rumors."

He started to go, but Dade reached out gently and stopped him. "You've bought heavily on the upper slopes of this mountain, Mr. York?"

Bevis rudely swept his hand aside. "That's right, and I'll continue to do so, because the value is increasing every day."

The old man couldn't hide the triumph in his voice. "Some have doubled in a week."

Dade looked him in the eye and said flatly, "In another month, they'll be practically worthless."

"Young man," Bevis said after a long pause, "either you are an irritable fool whom I don't want around my daughter any longer—or you know something I would prize. Which is it?"

"The latter, sir."

"Very well, we shall see. Come along. My daughter has prepared a meal and she is a fine cook."

"Thank you."

"I don't want your thanks. You've piqued my curiosity, and after our meal, I expect you to tell me exactly why you have made this wild statement about the direction of the lode. I have no doubt you are wrong, but since I have listened to this much, my curiosity demands I hear it through."

"You won't be sorry, Mr. York," Dade promised. "We're both investors, and . . . well, I've been thinking about what you said concerning theatrics. Perhaps you're right. I may just start investing my assets in mining property."

Bevis looked at him quizzically and almost smiled. "Do you have any idea the price of a running foot of ground is commanding?"

"Ten dollars. Maybe fifteen."

"Double it," Bevis said crisply. "And next week, triple that. I tell you, we are only starting to see the real bonanza under our feet. Before it's through, we'll uncover a wealth that few can even envision."

Bevis ate quickly, but Dade enjoyed the meal and complimented Holly lavishly.

"Now, then," said the financier, placing his napkin down on the table. "Let's hear it from the beginning."

Dade leaned back in his chair, sipped his coffee. "Mr. York, what I am about to tell you will seem preposterous at first. But it's not. In fact, it's so valuable a piece of information that it could well decide your own future. The fact of the matter is that everyone thinks the lode dips to the west directly into and under Sun Mountain. They are wrong."

"On what basis do you make this rash assertion?"

"Assay reports. Mine logs. Geological principles. Which—all together—leave small doubt that the main lode of silver is beginning to straighten up and change directions. Still running north and south, it is now dipping eastward."

Bevis toyed nervously with his napkin before speaking.

"Do you realize what you're saying, young man? I've bought claims on the west side and ignored the east as virtually worthless. If I'm wrong, I'll be ruined."

"Not if you sold out now," Dade said quickly. "In fact, you'd reap profits by grabbing cheap claims on the eastern slope at a fraction of their true value."

"Proof, Mr. Taylor. I still need proof!"

Dade glanced up at Holly. She was watching him as intently as her father, and he caught a warning signal in her eyes, telling him he'd better not be trying to cheat her father.

He took a deep breath and leaned forward, knowing that if the geologist was wrong, his own hopes were lost. "To begin with, the Poker and Yellow Dog mines have started to sink vertical shafts east and west and are discovering that the silver is east. They're not certain yet, and they are under strict orders of secrecy; but they're changing directions. For another thing, I've been informed that the geological rock formations indicate that, up to now, the lode has gone west because it is faulted by an earthquake. A fissure erupted and quickly became saturated with hot water. The water carried the silver downhill, not up into the mountain."

"What else?" Bevis asked quietly, his frame tight with concentration.

"Tomorrow you'll see the Belcher Mining Company begin a new shaft. If you observe closely, Mr. York, you'll see that it is *east* of the original shaft."

Holly sat down with them, and Dade noticed the financier looked to her for comment. "Dade may be right, Father. You can't afford to ignore this information."

"Of course I can't," Bevis said wearily, "nor do I intend to. It's just that . . . well, if what he says is true, then I've almost ruined us."

"But Mr. Taylor will have prevented that," Holly said. "If he's correct, I think we owe him a real debt."

"*If* he's correct," Bevis grumbled, coming to his feet. "And to my mind, that is a *big* if. However, if what you say *is* true, Mr. Taylor, rest assured you'll be amply rewarded. How much do you want?"

Dade blinked at the suddenness of the question. Numbers—big numbers—ran through his mind like thumbed pages in a book. It was his chance to make thousands, and all he had to do was to mention a figure. Dade felt the sweat pop out under his suit. If the geologist was lying, he'd kill him. But if the man was right . . .

"Your price, Mr. Taylor! I must get back to my office and begin a quiet investigation at once."

Dade swallowed, told himself not to say what he was thinking, but he did it anyway. "I want nothing, Mr. York, but your trust and friendship."

Bevis chuckled out loud, and his entire body sagged with escaped tension. "That's not what you really want, is it?"

"What do you mean?"

"I mean you don't give a damn about this old man's trust and friendship. I understand you perfectly, Mr. Taylor. You are young and ambitious. Even more, you're a gambler with the courage and audacity to back your play."

Their eyes locked for a moment and Dade finally glanced aside. "All right, I admit to what you say."

"Good!" Bevis thundered with satisfaction. "You *can* tell the truth if you have to. There's another thing you should know. Holly informs me of your devious intentions and that, despite them, she has agreed to let you call, under a certain provision."

"Yes," Dade said gravely. He couldn't help but feel a sense of betrayal. "Your daughter told me I had to make one thousand dollars."

Bevis clucked his tongue with disapproval. "She set the price far too low, Mr. Taylor. Far too low. I say it must be ten thousand."

"What!" He was stunned and outraged. The man might as well have said a million. "Mr. York, ten thousand dollars is an impossible figure."

"Think big, young man! If you are as mercenary as I suspect, you should have much grander plans than that. Besides, I'll make you a guarantee that if my investigation proves that you are correct about the main silver body changing directions, I will give you five thousand."

"But I'd still need twice that, according to you."

"That's correct. And my advice would be to take the five and leave the Comstock a far wealthier man than when you came. Do you catch my meaning?"

Dade nodded sullenly and watched Bevis rise to kiss his daughter and then walk hurriedly out the front door. When he was gone, Dade whirled on Holly and wanted to choke her with both hands. "Why? Why did you have to tell him about the money?"

"Because it is *his* money you're after and he has a right to know."

"Has it ever occurred to you that you're wrong? That I might really want Holly York instead of her father's money?"

She looked away quickly. "There is nothing in this world I'd rather believe, Dade. But . . . it's going to take some convincing."

He roughly pulled her to his chest and his fingers dug into her hair as he turned her face up to his own and cruelly ground his lips into hers until she was writhing in his arms. Then he pushed her away and watched her try to steady her breathing.

"Holly," he graveled, "you want me so bad I can taste it on your lips. And, some way, I'll get five thousand dollars and live to see your father eat his high-and-mighty opinion of me. But I'll tell you one thing right now."

She waited, her lips bruised and parted.

"Once we marry, you'd better know who comes first in your loyalties. Me, dammit, not him!"

He strode to the door.

"Dade!"

"Yeah?" He was angry. Angry with her and at Bevis for treating him like some kind of trash that had to upgrade itself to a set of arbitrary standards. And just as angry with himself for not saying to hell with them both. "What do you want?"

"You," she told him quietly. "Please don't take the five thousand and go. That's what father wants—hopes—you'll do."

"I know. And that's why I'm not going to. That . . . that and you, Holly."

Her face brightened. "Will it take long?"

"To get five thousand?"

She nodded.

"I don't know. Depends on the luck of the cards."

"If you win, you'll have enough money to invest in property. Especially if what you've told Father is true. Dade, with ten thousand dollars, you could have the kind of stake you've always dreamed about!"

He nodded. Felt the anger leaving his body. "I'd be a fool to take the five thousand and go."

"Of course you would," Holly said tonelessly. "Anyway you add it up, you'd lose."

Dade frowned. He could see the hurt and worry in her eyes and knew that, while she wanted him, she was also afraid—until he kissed her.

"Come here," he said huskily as he kicked the door shut.

"No, I . . . I think you'd better go now."

"Holly?" He lifted his arms and held them open for her to enter.

She trembled with indecision, and then, like a moth to the flame, she flew to his embrace and the last thread of her resistance went up in smoke. Dade laughed softly and knew everything was going to go exactly as he wanted. Holly was the key, and she dangled at his bidding.

6

He stood outside the foreman's shack and watched the Ophir Mine bucket brigade trudge wearily in and out of the hillside. Six men moving in a slow, steady shuffle, carrying heavy pails of scalding, putrid water from the bowels of Sun Mountain.

The day was cool and the water steamed like a milky brew when the bucket carriers tossed it against the hillside. Glenn stood beside the others who came each morning in hope of a job. But after four days, the Ophir had replaced only one man, a fellow who'd tripped and scalded himself badly. By afternoon, Glenn counted twenty-seven hopefuls including himself and knew that tomorrow the number would be even higher.

His belly rumbled like an echo in a cave, and Glenn tried to think of the last time he'd had a decent meal. Four or five days. Anyway, too long. Like everyone else, his mistake had been in coming to Virginia City believing he could find a claim and work it alone. There were no good claims left. After leaving Fay, he'd found himself nearly driven from the Comstock by heavily armed miners jealous of their unproductive holdings. And so he'd kept moving to the west, until he'd reached the rough semicircle of latecomers and staked a piece of barren ground.

But he hadn't found any sign of ore, and neither had his neighbors. No, the discoverers had taken possession of the surface ore, and all the rest was deep underground. So deep it took machinery and big crews willing to tunnel into Sun Mountain and risk cave-ins and seething bodies of hot water that spouted from rock with the bite of a pick.

"We're wasting our time!" an angry voice swore. "We could show up every day like this and they wouldn't hire us. I shoulda stuck to cowboying."

Glenn turned and realized the young man was talking to him. He was smallish but well-built and purposeful-looking. "I was thinking the same," Glenn admitted. "In fact, it won't be too long before someone hits on the idea of getting a steam engine up here and running a pump."

"A steam engine? What the hell is that?"

"It's powered by hot water. Turns blades and creates a suction." The young cowboy looked at him as if he were crazy, and Glenn's voice trailed off on the explanation he'd been about to go into. "Anyway, it would pull the water out five times quicker than those buckets."

"And take five men's jobs, too," came the truculent reply. "They're not paying high enough wages to eat on now."

"I don't know about that. But from where I'm standing, it seems evident that the water is holding up digging. Maybe with a steam engine, they'd hire more miners."

The small man shrugged, hitched his pants over his riding boots. "Hell, I don't know anymore. Maybe you're right. Seems like a roundabout way to do things. You know, laying off the bucket carriers to hire miners. But then, what do I know about all this? Why the devil I ever left the topside of a horse is purely mystifying in itself. Name's Bob Haslam. Pony Bob they call me, and I'm the best bronc-buster and horse-racer west of the Rockies and likely the Atlantic Ocean."

Glenn shook the proffered hand. Haslam was about his own age and had a deeply tanned face with a wry smile that was disarming. Like all the other men who needed work, he was probably discouraged. And there was no disputing he looked out of place in his high-heeled boots and with a definite horseman's bow to his legs.

"Why didn't you stick with horses?" Glenn asked. "A man ought to do what he's best at."

"Well, I mean to," Haslam drawled. "Fact is, the only

reason I'm here at all is because of a rumor about something they're calling the Pony Express. There's supposed to be a big meeting down in Carson City one of these days. But nobody will say anything, and I've got to eat until they make up—"

"All right, men," called a familiar, almost apologetic voice, "you might just as well leave for today. The Ophir won't be needing more help."

Glenn turned and recognized Cy Peterson, the Ophir Mine superintendent. Every afternoon, his announcement was a familiar story, and the groans of disappointment grew louder, angrier, just as they did at the handful of other large mining operations. And once again Cy patiently explained how the bottom of the shaft was filling up with hot water so quickly that ore extraction was at a near-standstill.

Glenn and Bob Haslam lingered behind, watched the lucky men on the payroll emerge to receive their day's wages, then file away. When they glanced at the two hungry men, they looked almost sheepish and hurried past.

Glenn stopped one of them, and after a few questions, he turned to Haslam, saying, "Are you as hungry as I am?"

"Hungrier."

"Then let's see if we can talk ourselves into a job."

"What do you mean?"

Glenn smiled. "I mean, we'll starve to death waiting for that superintendent to hire us. And I've been to all the other big mines and it's the same story. If we want a job, we're going to have to talk ourselves into it. We haven't a damn thing to lose by trying."

"But—"

"Listen," Glenn said quickly, "In another few minutes, Cy Peterson will come out of that shack and go home. He's just waiting for everyone to leave so they don't buttonhole him for work. When he appears, I'm going to have to talk fast. I'm not good at that, but I'll try. Back me up, and I'll speak for us both."

Haslam nodded briskly. Hope rose in his eyes. "Fine! I still don't have any—"

"Shh! Here he comes. Say, Mr. Peterson."

The superintendent almost stepped back inside, but Glenn was on him fast. "Sir, if we could save you money, would you hire us?"

Cy Peterson dug his hands into his pockets. "Why . . . why, yeah. But it's like I told you a few minutes ago, we—"

"I'm talking about profits," Glenn said, moving around him and entering the mining shack, "and the way to increase profits is to increase production. And to do that . . ."—he hesitated until Peterson leaned forward—"is to install a steam pump. Twenty horsepower ought to be enough. One of your men tells me he's working the shaft about a hundred and fifty feet down."

"Tell me something everyone on the Comstock doesn't already know," Peterson said cryptically. "And make it damn fast, 'cause I'm hungry."

"All right. Just give me three minutes to explain, and then, if you're not convinced I understand the principles of engineering, steam mechanization, and hydraulics, I'll leave. And my partner here just happens to be a first-class surveyor. A man who single-handedly laid out the truest line of ore tracks ever seen in Mexico."

"The hell you say!" Cy glanced at Haslam with sudden interest.

"Three minutes," Glenn pleaded. "That's all I need to draw you a diagram or two on hydraulic engineering and mine extraction."

"That don't mean nothin' to me, young fella. I'm just a forty-niner who's in over my head. I take orders from the owners same as everyone else."

"Yes, but don't you also share in the profits? Isn't that the way it's done here?"

"Sure, but—"

"Good! Then I'll make your income rise, too. Steam, Mr. Peterson! It'll cut costs and increase your output, and I can prove it on paper."

"Yeah," Haslam echoed, "you have to lay off them water-bucket toters in order to hire miners and track layers. And us specialists."

The superintendent's eyes tracked back and forth between them, and finally he nodded. "Go on," he said wearily. "I've heard of steam-powered vessels, but not pumps. And I sure don't know what this talk of surveying track is all about. But . . . well . . . I am stumped on what's going to happen in the weeks to come. Every morning when I open the shaft, the water is deeper at the bottom. Takes a good three hours to empty it, and the steam is so hot a man can't breathe. We got problems—all of us on this mountain. So I'm willing to listen for three minutes."

Glenn forced himself to speak slowly and with great emphasis. "The pumps are new," he conceded, "but they work, and I saw two of them in San Francisco last fall. They were shipped from a company in Baltimore."

"Hell, we can't wait that long!"

"I could take the stage out tomorrow," Glenn countered quickly. "Bob Haslam will stay here—on the payroll, of course."

Glenn saw the protest starting to form and said, "But first we'll need to go down in the shaft, take some measurements, and figure the load and slope. How much water is seeping in a day?"

"Well . . . I don't know. Maybe a thousand gallons. Likely more."

Glenn nodded. "I'll measure it now. Base my estimate on fifteen hundred, then return in the morning and calculate the exact flow."

"How will you do that?"

Glenn didn't bat an eye. There was a formula in Arthur Kurzweil's engineering book on calculating liquid mass. And there were several others on slope and resistance based on gravitational principles. He understood them, could almost see the equations on the page he'd studied by firelight. But could he apply them? He just wasn't sure. Yet, he'd have to—tonight. By tomorrow morning he intended to arrive with everything penciled out plain and clear. And, some way, he'd make this man and his superiors believe that a steam pump could solve underwater problems and also be used to pull ore carts up an inclined track. A track he and Bob Haslam would lay.

Glenn looked up. "Mister, I'm not an engineer, but I've studied to be one. If you'll show me your mine and promise to have the Ophir owners listen in the morning, I'll present my case. Not only that, but I'll show them cost figures that will make 'em sit up and listen."

"He can do it, too!" Haslam chimed in enthusiastically.

"Very well," Cy Peterson said with slow decision, "I'll take you down there, but if this is just some kind of trick to see what the Ophir has discovered and the size of the ore body we're uncovering, I'll see you run off the Comstock. I mean that."

"Fair enough."

At the mine opening, the superintendent hesitated. "You haven't told me what you want."

"No, I haven't. And I won't until I face the owners," Glenn replied.

"Smart," Haslam drawled.

They entered the mountain, holding their carbide lamps and following the incline which dipped sharply to the west.

An hour later, they emerged and Glenn knew enough to begin his night's work. The Ophir people had attained a depth of just one hundred and ten feet, but already they'd scratched the greatest body of ore ever seen by man—thirty feet wide at least! There was a fortune buried down there, just begging to be mined. Yet, the rock was crumbly, damp and unstable. Only when they'd reached the ore body had the earth's color and composition changed to glistening quartz and solid rock.

Glenn looked back at the tunnel entrance and gratefully drank in the cool, fresh air of outside. He'd never been that far underground, and it had been almost eerie, knowing tons of rock hung overhead, supported only by a row of puny doorframelike timbering. It was something he doubted he'd ever get used to.

"What do you think?" Peterson asked.

"We can build the tracks," Glenn said, "but I'm worried about your shoring. Have you had any cave-ins?"

"Plenty," Peterson gritted. "It's like trying to tunnel through sand. We buy the finest timbering around, but it still breaks under the ground weight. No one has died—yet."

"Maybe I'll go to San Francisco with you," Haslam said quickly. "You might need some help."

Glenn suppressed a grin. Haslam hadn't said a word all the time they'd been underground. It was pretty obvious he wasn't cut out to be a miner.

"Now, wait a minute. You fellas better understand that the Ophir owners aren't the kind of men who'll put up with any extra expenses. There's no reason why Haslam couldn't be surveying it out while you go to San Francisco after what's needed."

Haslam started to protest, but Glenn interrupted. "We're getting ahead of ourselves. We can discuss the details in the morning."

They agreed. Cy Peterson gave him directions on where they were to meet and left him with a warning. "I hope you boys will be ready. My bosses count their time precious, and I'll catch hell if it's wasted. Don't make me have to apologize for you."

Glenn took a deep breath. He was going to have to prepare graphs and figures around a campfire. And furthermore, he wasn't at all certain he could work all the formulas out correctly. Philip Deidesheimer could. But then, he was a real engineer.

Glenn stood before the building on C Street and felt his insides tighten. In his fist was a roll of papers he'd pored over up until an hour ago, when he'd struggled back down into the Ophir to remeasure the night's seepage.

Haslam prodded him forward. "Go in there and show 'em, Donovan. Those gents you'll face may have the money behind them, but they aren't engineers. Make 'em listen!"

"I'll try." He smoothed his clothes down, trying to wipe the dirt and creases away. He looked awful and felt drugged and jittery from too much of Haslam's coffee. But if he could sell these people—well, maybe it was the break he'd need to earn his schooling money. With that in mind, he opened the door, took a clerk's directions, and passed into the meeting room.

The walls were polished oak, as was the long table that closed off four men in wait. They were all dressed in suits with vests and heavy gold watch chains. They examined him with something akin to irritation. Maybe it was the fact that his clothes were dirty and he'd forgotten to shave or even comb his unruly hair. And it could also be that they'd expected an older man, someone with a scholarly bearing instead of an unwashed Irish lad. Whatever, the moment he entered, Glenn felt their disapproval.

But then, from a side door Bevis York strode in and nodded to each of the four on his way to the vacant center chair. He deposited some papers on the table and took his seat. For a moment everyone waited while he arranged his pen and notations. When he was ready, he glanced up and said, "Mr. Donovan, it is good to see you again. Now, I and my fellow board members are at your disposal. We would ask that you present your opinions concisely, but in their entirety. In short, leave nothing unsaid."

The others nodded solemnly, but now there was something different in their attitude. Glenn unrolled his sheets of figures, the diagrams and charts. A corkboard was instantly brought to his side, and the clerk who'd directed him in with an air of superiority was now busily helping tack up the pages for all to see.

Glenn cleared his throat and forced himself to relax as he opened one of his soiled engineering books to the chapter entitled "Principles of Mining Hydraulics." He reminded himself once more not to become overtechnical, but to stress the application of knowledge. Taking a deep breath, he began.

It was midafternoon and his voice had ground to a whisper when Bevis York called an end to the discussion. Glenn took a seat and waited while they went into a huddle. Once Bevis strode outside and was gone for what seemed like an eternity. When he finally returned, there was an expression of determination in his jawline.

"Mr. Donovan, I have in my hand a telegram. Before I reveal its content, I wish to assure you that we believe you are a young man of learning and intellect. However, it seemed imperative that we verify your engineering background and that steam pumps are feasible in our mining enterprises."

Glenn's mouth formed a thin line. "Who did you contact?"

Bevis studied the telegram for a moment. "A Mr. Philip Deidesheimer. I remembered your mentioning his name several times during our earlier contact."

"Sir, you had no right to bother Mr. Deidesheimer!"

"On the contrary! And you should be pleased I did so. You see, I was convinced—from the very beginning of your presentation—that your ideas are sound and worthy of consideration. But my colleagues needed additional persuasion. Believe me, we are constantly being assailed by all kinds of charlatans and dreamers. I face them here, as well as in regard to my other properties."

"What did Mr. Deidesheimer say?" Glenn asked quietly. He understood the need of these gentlemen for professional confirmation, but it still wounded his pride they hadn't at least advised him of the fact.

Bevis York looked to each of his colleagues; then his gaze settled on the young man who waited. "He supports your recommendations and has personally guaranteed your integrity."

Glenn wanted to leap into the air and shout with joy. Bless you, Philip Deidesheimer, he swore to himself. Bless you!

"Mr. Donovan, my associates and I are prepared to gamble on steam. We have little choice but to become pioneers in its application. And, while we do not expect overnight miracles, we do expect results. If you agree to our terms of employment, you may proceed at once."

Agree to his terms! Didn't they realize he was practically

starving until this moment, without hope for even a water carrier's job? Glenn's chin lifted, "What are they?" he whispered.

"Simply this. No big salary. In fact, a small one at first. Then, if increased production becomes a reality, we'll give you a percentage—two, I think—of the overage. *But*, if you fail, you get nothing. Is that agreeable?"

Glenn swallowed dryly. My God! Two percent of the overage! Why, that could run into hundreds of dollars. Maybe thousands!

"Yes, sir!"

Bevis smiled for the first time. "Excellent. Then it's settled. A contract will be drawn. You'll leave tomorrow."

"What about my friend Bob Haslam?"

"I'll place him on the payroll, but he'll have to work for his wages just like the others."

"But Mr. York . . ."

He smiled tolerantly. "Don't be foolish and make an issue of this, Donovan. Your friend is no more a surveyor than I am. And I won't have bluffing, which could endanger our success and the lives of others. Tell Mr. Haslam I'll find him a good position—aboveground. Our superintendent, Mr. Peterson, told me your friend looked ill after coming out of the shaft."

Glenn nodded in agreement. Bob Haslam would have been good company and some help in San Francisco, but if this Pony Express thing came up and he missed it . . .

"Donovan, I'd like to ask your opinion of our current shoring methods."

Glenn noticed the sharp attention the question brought. "Not good, sir. Those doorframe supports are weak. Mr. Peterson told me they fracture under stress."

"Do you have a better idea?"

Glenn shook his head. "I may have later. I'm not sure. You'll probably need a whole new system."

"Talk to Mr. Deidesheimer about it," Bevis suggested. "Tell him we may be seeking his expertise in addition to your own. Like the hot water, we expect the timbering to become an even greater problem. If it's possible, I'd like to minimize the risk of losing men in cave-ins. Though, to be honest, in mining it's not feasible to eliminate all danger. Now, if that's everything, our clerk will draw your travel money and lines of credit. Also, there will be a list of people to contact." For the first time, he hesitated, seemed uncertain. "By the way, Mr. Donovan, if you don't mind the inconvenience, I'd like you to buy a decent wardrobe before conducting business."

Glenn nodded stiffly and told himself the suggestion was not meant to be insulting but helpful.

"I'll not have anyone in my employ looking as though they are ill-paid. Regarding the necessary mechanical equipment, you should buy wisely—at lowest prices—but do not tolerate any delays. I expect the steam engine, pumps, tracks, ore carts, and pipes to be in place by the end of the month."

"If they're delivered by the end of next week, I can do that. But it's a tight deadline."

Bevis allowed a smile. "I know that. Now, give my regards to your friend Mr. Deidesheimer. Tell him I look forward to meeting him. And one more thing."

"Yes?"

"In your opinion, is it possible the lode could shift directions? Like from westward to the east?"

"Quite possible, sir."

"Thank you. And good luck. Come back in an hour and your money will be waiting."

Outside, Glenn was relieved to find that Bob Haslam was elated to get a job aboveground. The fact that he didn't have to pretend to be a surveyor seemed to take an immense load off his shoulders. And though Haslam pleaded with him to celebrate their sudden change in fortune, Glenn declined. He wanted a bath, a shave, the new clothes Bevis York had promised, and then to pay a visit to Fay Taylor. It had been weeks since he'd seen her. He'd made himself stay away until receiving some kind of good news.

As he approached her hotel, Glenn felt stiff and awkward in his new suit, white shirt, and tie. But he'd let Julia Matson pick them out and fit him properly, and she'd told him the clothes hung elegantly on his tall, lean frame and that if he also got a bath, shave, and haircut, he'd appear as fine and prosperous as any man in Virginia City. It had been nice to see Julia again. She'd looked very tired, but seemed quite happy with her work. Obviously the Silver Exchange Mercantile was one of the busiest places in town, and he was pretty sure it was because of Julia's beauty.

Now, as he came to the hotel entrance, Glenn paused to study his reflection in the window. In spite of himself, he drew a deep breath of surprise. The image that looked back at him was a total stranger. The coat gave him a wide, strong look, and the white shirt and tie seemed as if they belonged to some prominent young man quite unaccustomed to the rigorous life he'd been living. Even seeing his ears, now that his long hair was shorn, was a novelty. My heavens, he thought, Fay won't even know me!

He entered the hotel, noticing how the clerk behind the desk nodded with respect. Glenn liked the effect, but still he couldn't help feeling deceitful and that at any minute someone would point an accusing finger in his direction and holler that he was a fake.

His new shoes squeaked as he strode across the lobby. "I'd like to see Miss Fay Taylor," he announced.

"Yes, sir. If you'll step right around this corner, you'll find her in the next room."

The man leaned forward confidentially. "Miss Taylor, I'm sure, will be delighted at your calling. It's refreshing to see a gentleman ask for her for a change."

Glenn's eyes hardened. "What's that supposed to mean?"

The clerk's eyebrows raised and he tried to smile up at Glenn. "Nothing, sir. I meant no discourtesy. It's just that... well, go around and see."

"I will."

He rounded the corner and entered a small, windowless room. Fay was seated at a table with a bearded man who had his eyes closed as he talked. "Now, then, Emmy, I don't want you to sell that good brindle cow of our'n unless you gotta."

"Slow down, Mr. Yost," Fay said, never looking up as she wrote quickly. "All right, go on."

Yost opened his eyes, grinned sheepishly at a man who waited close behind, and said, "Emmy, I know you can't read nor write either, so you'll have to find someone who kin to know what I'm a-sayin'. But, one thing sure, keep the young 'uns in school, and if I don't get back for a couple of years, they kin save you money by readin' this lady's hand themselves. I'll keep trying for work, Emmy, 'cause I know you and the young 'uns need money. I am still strong and in good health, but thinner. Tell Jason that brindle cow is worth eight dollars at least. I... I miss you all and am sorry I ain't struck it rich like I said I'd do. Tell Jim Henderson and old Ned Arnold to keep to their farms like I shoulda. Has our dog still got mange?"

There was a long pause before the miner nodded with finality. "I guess that's all, Miss Taylor. I'd . . . well, I'd like it if you'd pretty it up some. Write Emmy something to make her feel better. She gets low sometimes. And the kids are a torment. Four of 'em, Miss Taylor. All boys, and hellers."

"I'll say it nice," Fay promised. "I'll try to put in something cheerful. Maybe about how you're hoping for a job soon."

He slapped money on the table, but Fay gently pushed it back at him. "When you've got that job. All right?"

Glenn saw the miner's eyes tighten as he struggled with the decision. Necessity won out. "Fair enough, miss. But you keep tabs. Hear, now? Mailin' expenses, too."

"Sure."

"I can't pay either, ma'am," said the next man. "But my woman will pay the letter freight when it arrives, and . . . and, well, by God, I've never chiseled anyone on a debt and I sure wouldn't start with a pretty girl like you. In fact, my first payday, I'll buy you—"

Fay laughed, but it had a faint, scolding tone. "You be careful what you say, John, or I might write your wife and tell her all you've promised me."

"Aw, Miss Taylor! You know how we all feel about you."

Fay's eyes dropped to her tablet. "First your name and where to write. Then you use all that romantic stuff on your wife."

The two men beamed and then Glenn listened to another lonely Comstock fortune-seeker tell of his trials and disappointments while Fay wrote in a strong and flourishing hand. And as he listened and watched this girl, once again it struck him how much he loved her and how she seemed destined to become very special.

When the others had gone, Glenn stepped in behind her, saying, "You'll never get rich on credit, ma'am."

Fay looked up quickly, then a cry of happiness sprang from her throat. "Glenn Donovan!"

"In person," he laughed. "I was afraid you wouldn't recognize me."

"Well, it would serve you right if I didn't," she scolded. "Why haven't you been to see me? And look at that suit! Did you strike it rich?"

In a rush of words, Glenn told her about his sudden stroke of good fortune and how Bevis York had offered him two percent of the increased production. Fay listened intently, and he could tell she was as happy as he was at the good news.

"Oh, Glenn, I knew you'd do it. Knew it!"

"Hold on," he said easily. "Finding the machinery they want is the easy part. Making it pay off will be tougher."

"I'm not worried," she said matter-of-factly. "If you were smart enough to figure out the need, you're smart enough to make Bevis York a lot of money and finance your schooling."

"I hope so. Mr. Deidesheimer will give me some ideas on installing the pump and tracks, but . . . well, I think I've worked it out properly."

He knelt down beside her, remembering how it had been when they'd weathered the Sierra blizzard. Funny, it seemed like a distant time, something that had happened long ago. "What about you?" he asked, uncomfortable because all their talk had been about his success.

"I'm fine. Really. And I get paid for most of the letters I write."

"Is it enough? Does your brother help you?"

Her eyes darted away, then came back. "I don't see him much anymore. He's courting Holly York and gambling every night. I'm worried."

"He can take care of himself," Glenn said abruptly. "It's you I'm concerned about."

She looked pleased. "Now that you've a job and could earn a lot of money, perhaps you're thinking I need taking care of?"

"Well, maybe . . ."

"No, thank you, Mr. Donovan! The doctor says my leg will be fine to dance on in another month. And all this time has given me the chance to practice new songs. Why, I've even learned how to accompany myself on the guitar. In fact, tonight I've rented a room next to the Silver Run Saloon. I'm giving a performance. Want to come?"

"Nothing could stop me," he vowed. "But first I'll take you out to dinner."

Fay smiled with bright expectation as he lifted her up from the chair. She balanced precariously on one leg; then he slipped his arm around her waist and escorted her away. And though she seemed as bubbly and irrepressible as ever, he thought he felt an underlying tension in her body. And he'd held her enough to know she'd lost weight. Damn her brother! It was obvious the man hadn't bothered to look after her at all. One thing for certain, now that he had employment and a chance at some money, he was going to be seeing a lot more of Fay Taylor after returning from San Francisco. And no matter how she protested, he was going to help her financially as much as he could. If that meant his education would wait a few months longer—so be it!

Through the paper-thin walls of the Silver Run Saloon, they could hear the wild, slamming noise of a badly played piano and a screeching fiddle accompanied by thunderous hand-clapping and shouts.

Glenn had placed wood planks across empty whiskey barrels for the people to sit on, but so far he was the only customer in the room. Fay avoided his eyes and nervously fidgeted with a decrepit-looking guitar she'd borrowed. The door was open to C Street, and each time heavy clomping boots sounded on the walk, they both looked up quickly. Always the miners went on by, and they heard the thump-whack of the adjoining saloon doors.

He leaned forward on the first bench. "I put up your sign, Fay. And twenty cents is a piddling small amount to hear you sing."

She tried to smile. It didn't work very well. "Hard to compete with the noise next door. And, well, they've got some new saloon girls. That doesn't help either. Kind of thought Dade would have come, at least."

Glenn swore silently. Just thinking about Dade got his blood up. But there was no sense in saying that, because Fay looked upset enough already. "Why don't you go ahead and begin? I'm a paying customer."

"All right," she replied with a defiant toss of her hair, "I will."

Her voice was strong, strong enough even to compete with the boisterous crowd next door. Glenn watched her fumble with the guitar strings, work to reach the proper frets, and then grimace when she missed a chord. He'd have preferred she just put the damned guitar down and sing. Fay's voice was special enough by itself. But then, he sensed this was something she needed as a challenge, and so he kept quiet, though his own body struggled with the instrument just as if he were the one playing.

Fay was midway through "Sweet Betsy from Pike," missing all the most difficult chords, when a cutting voice from the doorway shouted, "Hey, you in there! Bill Fogerty says he can hear you through the walls! Says it's messing up his piano playing."

Glenn swung around on the bench and looked at a couple of rough-hewn miners.

"Yeah, I'm talking to you and the lady."

The second one leered. "Rich man. Hired his own room and woman to sing. Damnedest thing I ever saw! Wait'll the boys see this!"

Glenn stood up quickly. "They'll have to pay," he vowed, "and I'll do the collecting."

The two men burst out in hysterical laughter. Fay stopped playing and seemed to be trying to fight back tears.

"Say, lady, don't you quit on us. We was just starting to enjoy ourselves."

"Yeah," called the other. "Hang on while I go next door and tell 'em. Twenty cents is damned cheap for a belly laugh these days."

The man vanished, then returned a moment later with a collection of drunk friends.

"That's it!" Glenn swore. "Fay, I'll not have them laughing at you."

"No," she said quietly, "I've set my price and if they pay, then I'll sing. I'm a professional, Glenn. That means I sing for money."

"But not to this bunch! You can't!"

"Watch me," she said tightly. "And collect the money, because I need it."

He could tell by the expression on her face it was no use trying to argue with her. None at all. So he let them in and took their money as they hooted and laughed their way up to the front rows of benches. He wanted to strangle each and every one of them.

A silence descended on the revelers when they saw how young and pretty was Fay Taylor. But then someone dropped his whiskey bottle and three men left their seats in a dive for it, causing a big uproar of laughter.

Fay was ready now. Her expression was pale and almost waxen. Glenn recalled how she'd sung at the Pine Tree Station and felt his heart ache for this girl. It was the guitar that had her frozen up. Why didn't she just put the damned thing aside and sing for them the old ballads and mining songs that she did so well? Her voice was magic.

Fay tried "Old Dan Tucker," and she got off to a fine start until she missed a chord and the guitar twanged off-tune. The miners were waiting for just such a mistake, and they erupted in gales of laughter.

"Quiet!" Glenn shouted, stepping in front of them with his fists knotted. "Give her a chance."

He might as well have yelled at the moon, and his words seemed only to nettle them. Faces grew surly. They were here for sport, and sport they'd have. As Fay struggled on, a slope-shouldered man got up and began prancing around, mimicking her, as if he too were fumbling with the strings. His dirty hand clawed at the imaginary guitar's neck, and his face was screwed with fear. It caused wild peals of laughter—and it also caused the final link of Glenn's self-control to snap.

He threw himself at the mocker without thought of anything but destruction. Yet, as he barreled forward, the old lessons taught by his father made his body react with perfect control and timing, even as his mind was obliterated by fury. Glenn's fist arced to explode savagely against an unsuspecting jaw, and there was a vicious crack as the miner shouted and reeled off balance. Before anyone could react, Glenn was winging punches with deadly accuracy until strong arms pinioned him. Glenn slammed a boot down on a yielding foot and struggled free, backing to the wall.

"You want sport!" he cried. "Fine. *I'll* provide it for you. Come on, one at a time, and I swear you'll all have your turn."

His knuckles were raised and he waited with grim anticipation.

The biggest man of the lot slammed his bottle of whiskey down on the bench and spat into his palms while his friends shouted their encouragement. Glenn pushed off the wall and swallowed dryly as he noticed the oft-busted nose of a fighter and the scarred knuckles half again as wide as his own. No one had to tell him he was outweighed and facing a brawler. He'd seen that cruel look in the eyes of other fighters and knew his opponent was the kind who would take a punch to give a harder one, shrug off pain, then glory in administering it to a weaker man.

The brawler grinned, and his front teeth were missing. His voice rumbled ominously. "I'm going to mess up those fine clothes you got on, city man. I'm going to make that white shirt run red."

Fay cried something he didn't hear, and Glenn, his eyes never leaving the man who approached, said, "Don't move, Fay. Just stay out of this."

The brawler roared and charged; his fist whistled. Glenn ducked and came in underneath, delivering two wicked punches, one against the ribs, the second hard to the exposed kidneys; then he danced away before the bigger man could grab him.

A small circle had formed around them, and men crowded forward expectantly as the fighters moved toward each other. Glenn flicked a fast pair of lefts into the brawler's nose and took a numbing punch to the shoulder before he skirted away.

"Stand still and fight, God damn you!"

It was the last thing he intended to do, unless it was absolutely necessary. He ignored the rising taunts of the crowd and waited for what he knew would be another fierce charge. He didn't think about what could happen if he lost, only that if he whipped this man, the others would seem easy. He might even hope to beat three or four more before his strength and speed deserted him—before a lesser fighter knocked him senseless and the remainder laughed at his prostrate form.

He saw the quick tightening of shoulder muscles and knew, before the brawler moved his feet, the man was coming. This time, Glenn went in to meet him. He blocked a looping swing and whipped a driving uppercut to the jaw that sent arrows of pain up the length of his arm. But his opponent's eyes glazed and the man seemed to shake through his entire body.

Glenn recognized the symptom and rooted his feet to the floor with the intention of putting all his weight into one knockout blow. Yet, as his body pivoted, something struck him in the back so violently he felt broken in two as he slammed down on the floor, cracking the side of his head. It was like alarm bells going off inside. Dimly he realized he had to move. To get on his feet. He tried. For what seemed an eternity, while loud voices shouted all around, Glenn managed to raise his body into a kneeling position. His vision detected something, and he lurched sideways as a fist grazed his cheekbone and he spun around in a heap.

Fay Taylor's voice ripped through his dulled senses, cleared the descending fog away. He raised his head in time to see her lift the guitar and bring it down like an ax on the brawler's skull.

The instrument disintegrated into a thousand bits and hunks of wood, and a head popped through as the guitar came to rest on a pair of wide shoulders. As the big miner clawed wildly at the tangle of wires about his face, Glenn rolled forward and tripped him down hard, snapping the guitar's neck and bringing a roar of pain.

Glenn made himself stand, and he waited until the man was almost erect before hitting him. An uppercut brought the miner out of a crouch, and a straight left hand drove him staggering into the crowd. His friends caught and then propelled him back. They shouldn't have. With every ounce of muscle and fiber in his lean whipcord body, Glenn applied a basic principle of physics which declared that when two onrushing masses of great force come together, there's going to be a *hell* of a collision.

Glenn didn't just punch, he put his fist through the scarred face, and the man's legs jerked out from under him as if they'd been chopped away.

For long moments, nothing moved until Glenn wheeled around and faced those who watched with grim disbelief. "Who's next?"

No one stepped forward. They didn't even meet his eyes.

"Gentlemen," Fay said, an unmistakable sarcasm belying the warm, swimming pride in her eyes as she gazed at Glenn Donovan, "my next song will be 'Farewell, Old California.'"

Glenn stared at the pieces of guitar strewn across the room. "Sing it like before," he rasped. "Sing to me." The miners, totally subdued, remained motionless, as if awaiting further instructions.

And she did sing. Her eyes were for him alone, though her voice was for all to hear. It came pure and sweet, full and strong. Rich with feelings of love, and pain, and remembering, that seemed to reach out and grip those who listened and to demand that they feel and remember, too.

Almost reverently, the benches were replaced as men began to sit quietly, their bottles of whiskey forgotten now. After a time, Glenn realized someone had started to play the melody very softly and well on a harmonica. And from the streets, others filed in to take their places after paying, just to sit and listen to the finest, loveliest voice ever heard on the Comstock. Glenn finally made her halt when the weariness came to her face and the hour grew very late. And he supported her through a grateful crowd of men who leaned forward to press money into her hands.

A short time later, he eased Fay down on her bed and tiptoed away.

She pushed herself up. "Glenn?"

There was an immediacy to her call, and he stopped, then turned. "Yes?"

"Must you go? I . . . I mean, I noticed your coat is torn. Let me fix it."

"It's all right. I'll be leaving on the stage very early. You sleep now."

"I am tired," she sighed, "but stay. Just be here to wake me. And I'll mend your coat like new. I *can* do some practical things, you know."

Glenn smiled. "I never doubted it. All right. I'll sleep right here in this chair."

"Good. Know what?" Her voice was drowsy now, barely audible.

"What?"

"Don't worry about the guitar. It was in the way for me anyhow."

"It sure was," he told her. "You've got everything you need right inside."

The soft flutter of her breathing told him she was asleep now, and he moved the chair over to the side of her bed so that he could watch her through the night. She *did* have everything she needed. If he'd ever had a doubt before, seeing her transform that crowd was enough for a lifetime.

But, in a way, he knew that very gift of hers would always be the thing which separated them.

7

"Be patient?" Dade echoed with exasperation. "I have been patient! It's been over a month since I told your father about the Comstock Lode shifting directions."

"I know," Holly said, feeling his anger and believing it justified. "I'll speak to him tonight. I promise."

"Do that! I realize he's your father and that you love him very much, but what about me?"

His question hung unanswered between them and made Holly ache to reach out to this man, hold him tightly, and say everything would be all right. Didn't he know that the waiting was tearing her apart also?

"Holly, I've won almost two thousand dollars this month and I've never gambled harder in my life or taken such chances."

She nodded. Every night for weeks, she'd gone to bed praying he would not be pushed into reckless cheating. If he did, and were killed . . . Holly shuddered, because it would be her fault. "Please be careful, Dade. If anything should happen to you . . ."

"I can handle myself," he snapped. "And what else can I do but take risks? Even if your father comes through with the five thousand, I still need three more." His lips assumed a bitter cut. "Sometimes I want to say to hell with it! Forget this stupid dowry idea and walk away."

An involuntary gasp came to her lips. "No! Don't say that. You don't mean what you're saying." She couldn't stop the words that tumbled out in her fear of losing him. "Oh, Dade, if you only realized how many times I've hated myself for even suggesting you should have to come up with money. I'd do anything to take it back!"

His expression softened, and as she had noticed so often, his personality swung from one extreme to the other as he pulled her up against his chest and whispered, "You remind me of a little bird, Holly. Know that?"

She shook her head, laced her hands around him, and never wanted to let go.

"Well, you do," he whispered, "you live here in this house, all finery and fluff. But it's a cage, and I can't seem to break you free. And I'd like to."

"Would you?"

"Yes. I'd teach you to fly. Spread your wings and fly! I could open your eyes to life, Holly."

"I'd *love* that."

"Then go with me! We'll run away and elope. Get married in San Francisco, and I'll show you things in that city you've never dreamed existed. Exciting things. Come now!"

His voice was a command she passionately wanted to obey. She would have given anything to do as he said—to leave the cage and soar on the wings of his love.

"I . . . I can't."

He pushed her face back and his eyes flashed. "Why? It's because of your father, isn't it?"

"Dade," she gasped, "you're squeezing me so tightly. That's hurting!"

He pushed her away in anger. "It's always your father, and I'm beginning to think it always will be."

"That's not true!"

"Then why won't you elope with me? Tonight. We could use my two thousand for the honeymoon. Hell, we could even sail to the Sandwich Islands. You'd like them, Holly. They have beautiful . . . beautiful beaches."

He'd been going to say "women," but it didn't matter. She could change him, rein his appetites and satisfy him with her own.

"I'd like to, Dade. Honestly, I would. Right now. Just grab my bag and run away to get married. It would be the most beautiful and exciting thing of my entire life. But I can't!"

Muscles corded his jawline. "I love you, Holly, but I'm running out of patience. Tonight you'd better get a decision from Bevis or tomorrow I'm taking my information to a few others in this miserable city. At least they'll pay."

"If you do that," she declared stonily, "you'll never marry me, and my father won't—"

"I don't care about him! He thinks that I'm trash! Not good enough for you. A low-class opportunist."

Holly retreated. She'd never seen him so angry, and it frightened her. She wanted to say he was wrong, but knew she could not, and when she remained silent, his cheeks reddened as though he'd been slapped.

"Holly, understand this. I've been scraping and scrambling since I was thirteen, and I'm sick of it. Hear me?"

"Yes."

"And if I can get a toehold on this Comstock, I'll never let go. I'll bite and tear and club my way to the pinnacle of this mountain, and *then* I'll show you and your father what I'm made of."

Her lips tightened and fear was replaced by anger. "Are you threatening us? Because if you are—"

"Shut up!" he bellowed. "I'm tired of being treated like some kind of monkey who jumps to your tune. I'm a man, goddammit! And I'm sick to death of being jerked around. Either you talk to your father and get his answer on the five thousand or we're through and I'll do business where I'm welcomed."

Holly whirled away. Suddenly the afternoon seemed to have gone gray and cold. She listened as he strode angrily to the door, and though she hated herself for having no pride, she called, "Dade!"

"What?"

"Do you *really* love me?" She turned to study him and watched the anger play across his face. "Dade?"

He squeezed the doorknob until his fist was white and the knuckles stood out in a ridge of bone. "Yeah," he said finally, "I really do. That's why I've been jumping up to now. Trying to bow and smile when your father peers at me like a stray dog with an itch. And at night . . . at night, wanting you and making myself stay away from the saloon girls wanting me."

"Have you . . . ?" She couldn't bring herself to ask.

"What do you expect me to do? Castrate myself physically like you've done mentally?"

Holly avoided his eyes, tried to imagine what it must be like for such a man. Then slowly her chin came up with fierce determination. "You're right. I see that now, what we've done to you—are doing. I'll speak to Father. Make him say yes and tell him that to deny you is . . . is to deny me."

"Will you tell him I want to learn his business? That I need respect, too? Will you do that for me?"

She gazed at him a long time before answering. Holly saw need and avarice, but maybe her own father hadn't been so different in those early days when he'd been poor and hungering for recognition. And maybe—dear God—maybe that was the power that caused greatness among men. She just didn't know. Dade Taylor was proud and wild and violent. She loved him in spite of those things, and perhaps a little because of them.

"I'll speak to him," she heard herself promise. "I'll make him see you as I do."

The relief that swept across Dade's face made her heart go to him. So powerful it was that she leaned against the wall and knew he could take her and she couldn't possibly resist.

"Holly, I'll get the five thousand tonight and prove I can hold up my part of the bargain. Tell your father he won't be sorry. I'll learn fast. I'll . . . I'll show him." He started to come to her, but something in her eyes changed his mind. Then he left, and for a long, long time she cried alone, without realizing why.

Holly watched her father eat dinner, though she had no appetite for her own meal. A gruff, abrupt man to others, when they were alone he talked almost incessantly about the many things he was incapable of saying to outsiders. And now, after almost twenty minutes of monologue concerning the unquestionable value of a particular claim he was negotiating to buy, Bevis had finally argued and counterargued the deal until there was little else to say. He grew reflective, then slapped the table and peered into her eyes.

"I think I'll raise my price another thousand if I must. But that's the limit. Don't you agree?"

"Yes," she replied, staring down at her untouched dinner.

"You surely are quiet tonight." For the first time he realized she hadn't eaten. "Are you ill, my dear?"

"No."

This made him scowl. "It's that Dade fellow," he swore violently. "He's been around again, hasn't he?"

She nodded.

"Well, that settles it! From now on—"

Her eyes flashed. "I want to marry him!"

"What!" The fork with which he'd been gesticulating clattered onto his plate. "Holly, I do not approve of the man. I thought I'd made that quite clear. He'll never get ten thousand dollars unless he steals it from someone, and I'll not have you taking up with a gambler."

"He wouldn't gamble if you'd pay him!" she cried.

"Enough! I forbid his—"

Holly didn't let him finish. "Either you help Dade or I'll elope with him. I swear I will."

Bevis' face went as gray as dead ashes. His fist, which was poised to slam down on the table, seemed to spasm until the fingers shook, and then the arm dropped heavily at his side. Pain radiated in slow, soft lines from his eyes, and he slumped. "You mean it, don't you, my child?"

She took a deep breath and knew that if she took pity on him now, he might take it as a lack of determination. And she didn't want to hurt him again.

"Pour me a drink, Holly. A very big drink."

When he took the glass, she heard his diamond ring tinkle against it shakily as he swallowed the whiskey in one gulp. "All right, I guess we'd better discuss this man," he said huskily.

Holly led her father to the parlor and knelt beside him. She could barely stand the hurt she saw mirrored in his eyes, and she tried very hard to think of Dade and what this meant to him—and to her.

"I don't want to choose between you and Dade," she began. "Yet, I love him. Can you understand that?"

He remained silent. Locked in his own chamber of shock and rejection.

"Try!" she pleaded. "If it helps, think of how you felt about Mother. Remember? You told me her father thought you unworthy. But you didn't believe him, and neither did she."

A faraway look rose in his eyes. "I showed him," Bevis said, mouthing the words with satisfaction. "All he had was a rocky farm. But I didn't even have that much. And . . . and then came a day when I bought his pitiful little farm and gave him back the deed just to see the look on his face. It was worth it."

Holly nodded. She'd heard the story many times. It was, in a way, cruel, how Bevis had bought his father-in-law's pride, then given it back as though it were of no value. And she felt a quavering fear that Dade might do the same. But that seemed impossible. Bevis wasn't a poor, uneducated farmer—he was smart as the smartest, tough and experienced. Scrupulously honest, he'd been outdealing his contemporaries for as long as she remembered.

"Father, I want you to think about that. How it was. And . . . and try to understand that Dade feels the same."

Bevis looked up quickly. The dreaminess around his pupils went slate cold. "Are you telling me he's going to do what I did? To me!"

"No!" Holly grabbed him by the shoulders. "Maybe. . . . maybe, right now he could. Dade is burning with pride and anger. He said you treat him like a monkey on a string."

"He said that?" Bevis was astonished.

"Yes. And it's true."

"Holly, the man is sick. I never thought of him as a monkey. And—"

"Oh, Father, you don't understand!" she wailed.

"What's to understand? He wants you for my money."

Holly dug her fingernails into him until the lines of his face grew stiff, and then she said in a voice that was not her own, "All my life, I've believed I wasn't pretty. That I was even ugly. But it wasn't so. You . . . you even let me think that, so I'd stay with you after Mother died. I know it's true. That time is over. I love you, but I'm going with Dade, given your permission or not. Don't make this any more painful than it has to be! Don't drive me away."

Bevis' lips sank down at the corners. He seemed to shake himself like an old dog facing one more battle. "Holly," he said at last, "this man is no good for you. He's more than ambitious. He's a liar, a cardsharp, a womanizer."

"No! How can you—?"

"Because, as you reminded me, I was once young and ambitious myself. But not like him. Dade Taylor is the kind who'd take anything he could lay his hands on, whether or not he's earned the right."

"And you didn't?"

"You know I didn't, and you should be ashamed to ask."

He was right. Holly was ashamed.

"My dear," he told her, "this man you say loves you has agreed to earn five thousand dollars."

"Will you give him what you promised?"

Bevis considered it for a long time before he nodded. "Yes. I believe his information is true, although I suspect he obtained it in the most despicable way. But, yes, I'll pay him *if* he agrees to our previous terms."

Holly swallowed. "And if he can't earn the other five thousand on his own and I decide to elope with him?"

Bevis' brow furrowed, and each word he spoke was clipped and hard. "Then you'll do it anyway and there's nothing I can say to prevent your unhappiness. But at least . . . at the very least, I'll have the money and power to help you when he fails."

"Is that all? Because he wants me to tell you he's serious about learning the mining business. He wants to be an equal."

Bevis snorted with derision, and it made Holly so angry she jumped to her feet and started to leave.

"Where are you going!"

"To find him."

"Holly, stop. Don't go now. Not while you're feeling this way."

She hesitated, then decided to wait. Wait until her father was sleeping untroubled in his bed. Then she'd go, knowing she had to before Dade's own recklessness got him killed this terrible night.

Dade spent the early part of the evening drifting from saloon to saloon, ordering a whiskey at each, but hardly tasting them as he watched the various card games. Most were friendly and of low stakes, where a man of his talents might earn ten or twenty dollars for an evening's work. In some of the others, he'd have to watch only a few minutes to detect a professional at play, and he'd move on, searching for easier pickings.

The professional gamblers were thick along C and B streets, and Dade was able to spot them after only a few hands. Every one of them had his own system of cheating, and Dade's sharp eyes detected them as he moved about. This man was using "strippers," cards whose ends and sides had been trimmed with a razor blade, perhaps just a thirty-second of an inch. The trimming was generally done so that there was just the faintest curve to the side of the high cards, leaving the ends the same width. It took a delicate touch to notice those strippers, but, if caught, the accused was said to be "playing both ends against the middle."

At a nearby table, another gambler was using a "poker ring"—diamonds on the topside, a small needle point on the under. The point was used to punch in braille-like bumps so tiny they could be read only by the edges of sandpapered fingertips. It was a good system if no one happened to notice your fingertips were beet red with surface blood.

One game he found interesting enough to consider joining was opening at five dollars, and he almost sat in, except that one old gentleman with a long white goatee seemed uncommonly lucky as his stack of poker chips grew taller. It took Dade nearly ten minutes to realize he was a line-and-scroll artist. You didn't see many of them anymore and Dade lounged as close as he dared to admire the fellow's work. Line-and-scroll required the extreme amount of patience necessary to add very fine lines to the back of a card's design. In this case, the old man had chosen a deck of cards with a floral backing and had adeptly expanded on the leafwork design until the alterations were nearly impossible to detect by the untrained eye. Using special ink and the finest of quill pens, he'd managed to shade in certain leaves and add a stem or two which undoubtedly allowed him to denote both the suit and value of every card. If he'd had the time, Dade would have stayed to watch, knowing that sooner or later the other players would get suspicious and the clever old gambler would have to switch back to a fair deck. It would be interesting to see if he could spot the movement, because any professional who'd lived that long plying his skills had to be good.

Reluctantly Dade pushed away and continued searching for a lively game that wasn't rigged. To expect an *honest* high-stakes game was unrealistic, because wherever men laid big money down, there would be men such as himself to pick it up by any means possible. When he'd arrived in Virginia City, every sixth or seventh man at a faro or poker game was a professional. Now it was nearly every fourth or fifth. Many nights, it just boiled down to who had the slickest system. In the past, Dade had relied on his undercut shuffle. But not tonight. Tonight he had something special and was counting on it heavily. He *had* to make his money now. Through Holly, he'd given an ultimatum. There was no way to back down on such a threat, and he hadn't the slightest intention of doing so.

The game, when he found it, was a natural for what he hoped would be his biggest killing. Four men, all well dressed and with large stacks of one-hundred-dollar chips at their elbows. Dade watched for perhaps twenty minutes, sensing the familiar excitement build, even as he forced himself to act uninterested. One of the players, lean and hawk-faced with a gold front tooth, kept eyeing him with a definite unfriendliness. Instinctively Dade knew this man would be his chief rival, a fellow gambler, protective of his lucrative clientele. The hell with him! Dade thought. He stayed where he was, getting a feel of the caliber of the men he intended to beat. The gold-toothed man stared at him with unconcealed dislike, and Dade smiled. It was a waiting game now. The gambler didn't want to use whatever advantage he had because of Dade's inspection, yet the stakes were too good to let pass for long.

Dade ordered another drink, his eyes never leaving the cards. A half-hour went by before the gambler's patience broke and he began to cheat. A small, disdainful grin appeared at the corners of Dade's lips as he instantly recognized the pattern. Actually, it was one he should have guessed. The players were using the very common "club cards" provided by the saloon, with plain white backs specifically designed to frustrate the once-prominent line-and-scroll artists. The particular man who kept scowling at Dade had spilled a few drops of his whiskey and was now using his right index finger to water-spot them. It was a good system and one of the hardest to prove, because the marks could be seen only if the cards were tipped at a certain angle to reflect the lamplight. Fortunately, it was also one of the easiest systems to destroy. And Dade had a deck of club cards ready and waiting.

"Mind if I join in?" he asked pleasantly.

They all nodded agreeably, except the one, so Dade moved to an empty chair, bought two thousand dollars' worth of chips, and began to play as though he had money to lose. Two hands and thirty dollars later, Dade ordered a beer and managed to spill part of it on the table just as he was about to gather up the deck and shuffle. At the same moment, he pulled out a clean handkerchief and wiped a few selected cards, completely obliterating the gambler's system.

"No problem," he said, "just clumsy, that's all."

"Sure," gritted the hawk-faced man across from him as he scowled at what had been his carefully marked deck.

Dade grinned. "Shall I call for a fresh deck?"

"Just deal, gawddammit!"

"At your service," he replied evenly, and the cards began to flash from one hand to the other. He cut the deck honestly and in a competent manner designed to show a reasonable amount of skill. A gambler who feigned clumsiness was the most suspicious, though many still clung to the simple illusion.

"Let's keep it neat and easy," he said, passing the cards to the next man for the cut. "And let's keep the money flowing."

Dade felt the eyes close upon him and knew every man at the table was scrutinizing him with intensity. Let them, he thought, feeling the mechanical holdout gripping the muscles of his bicep and lying cold and still between the double sleeves of his forearm. The device wasn't yet being marketed, like so many in the newspapers, and that was his edge. He'd bought it from a San Francisco inventor for two hundred dollars because it still had some mechanical failings. But when it worked properly—and it usually did—the holdout was brilliant. It reached the length of a man's body, from his forearm, up the sleeve, around the shoulder by a neat set of harnesses and cords, all the way down the torso, under the trousers, and into the boot. To activate it, Dade had only to stretch his foot and a flat, deck-sized metal plate would slip a card or even a full hand into his palm. By twisting his arm one way or the other, the pulleys which cut into his shoulder would select one or five cards and obediently wait to retract the rejects.

Its complexity, which allowed a man to sit like a statue without the uncharacteristic motions of its cruder predecessors, was also its greatest weakness. In the hundred or more hours he'd practiced with the device, oiled and adjusted it to his exact body measurements, the holdout steadfastly had decided to spring forward at its own bidding about once every twenty times.

Dade had no intention of using it that often. Not nearly. Ten at most, and on every one of those occasions the sweat seemed to flush through his pores and drench his undershirt. A man could sometimes explain his way out of an extra card on the floor as a clumsy deal, but if he were caught with a mechanical holdout, he'd best draw his gun and start firing, because he was trapped by indisputable evidence.

When the hand was dealt to everyone's satisfaction, Dade peered down at his cards. Moments later, he dealt himself two more and watched the chips stacking up for a high bet.

"Mister," drawled the gambler, "I said I'll just raise you and the rest four hundred dollars. You going to play or fade out?"

Dade stared at the three kings in his palm. Not good enough for the bets being wagered. Slowly his foot began to straighten under the table, and the polished steel plate edged down his sleeve.

He grinned tightly and pushed his chips forward, wondering if the fourth king was still in the untouched deck and knowing he was going to have to take his chances to find out. "I'm in, and I raise you another two hundred."

The gold tooth disappeared, and as the professional glanced around at the others, Dade's foot reached full out and his arm twisted as a card silently brushed across the tender skin at the base of his wrist. Without a flickering of the eye, his covering hand removed the second card in line and shoved a deuce in its place.

"Gentlemen, I call," he breathed, feeling the contraption scramble up his forearm like a squashed metallic rat. "Four of a kind. King high."

They kept pawing at her! Pawing and laughing and trying to buy her a drink and take her upstairs. Holly was almost frantic, because she'd been searching for Dade more than two hours and still hadn't found where he spent his nights gambling. And now she was growing desperate to find him before he took a foolish gamble with his life and ended the only chance for love she might ever know. Over and over she remembered how he'd seemed before leaving. How there'd been a recklessness in his eyes and voice when he'd said he *would* earn the money tonight. Now those words and that expression haunted her, drove her to search through this awful night.

All the saloons looked alike to her by now. Just smoky rooms with laughing, leering men and bars upon which they clung for support. How could Dade frequent this kind of establishment night after night? She peered into some faces bloated with drink and devoid of expression and saw others filled with anger and sickness. Only the bartenders seemed alive—and the gamblers. Yes. Some of them glanced up at her with a trace of curiosity, then seemed compelled to go back to their cards. She wondered if they gambled as desperately as Dade this long night.

Holly stood beside the doorway of another saloon and tried to keep tears of frustration from smearing her face. She didn't want him and his friends to see her all red-eyed and puffy. It would shame Dade, because he was accustomed to pretty women, and she did so want to seem pretty to him. To that end, she'd worn her most provocative dress, though from what she'd seen on the dancing girls this night, it was dowdy in comparison. But now one sleeve was torn where a miner had tried to drag her out onto the dance floor, and her hair a tangled mass. Her skin felt dirty and she reeked of cigar smoke. But at least she still clutched her handbag with over two thousand dollars of savings, and there *couldn't* be many more saloons.

Holly glanced up the street, saw two men emerge from a lighted doorway and halt to stare owlishly.

"Why, god damn! Ain't seen that one before."

"Me neither!"

They swayed forward and she dashed into the saloon with them close behind.

"Dade!" Her cry was a desperation plea, and as everyone seemed to freeze, a hand grabbed her by the shoulder and jerked her around.

"Dade!" she screamed as foul breath and a hairy face swam closer.

He jackknifed out of his chair and bumped the table hard, collapsing more than three thousand dollars of poker chips out of their neat stacks. The mechanical device, which he'd agonizingly been forced to use almost thirty times, performed once more. It obediently sped down his forearm and dangled forgotten from his sleeve in a pathetic offering of royal faces and precious aces.

Dade was twisting from the table when the gold-toothed man raged hoarsely, "Cheat! I knew it. The man's a cheat!"

The deadly accusation split the saloon down its center and galvanized everyone into action. Experienced men dived for the floor and the bartender ducked for cover. Holly felt the grip vanish and saw hands flashing for guns even as Dade threw the poker table over and streaked for his own weapon.

The holdout flopped against his gun butt and spewed cards into the air as his pistol clattered on the floor. Holly didn't need to see anything more to know that Dade was going to be shot. She unhesitatingly threw herself at him, pleading for those behind to spare his life.

"Get away from him!" a voice ordered. "Get away, I tell you."

She could feel Dade's heart beating as wildly as her own as they huddled together against the wall. "Do as he says, Holly. Just get away from here fast."

"No. No, please!" She turned, spread-eagled to protect Dade, and faced those who would end his life. "You don't understand," she said brokenly.

"The hell we don't!" one of them spit. "Look at that damned thing hanging outta his sleeve!"

"That *doesn't* matter. Not anymore. You see... he doesn't need the money now. Take it. Every bit of it."

"Holly!"

She ignored him, willed herself to make these men who would kill him understand. "I'm begging you to give me his life! I swear he'll never cheat again."

"Uh-uh," one said, gold flashing in his mouth.

"Now, wait a minute," said another, "he came in with a couple thousand. We could split it and it'd still be a good night's work."

Two others solemnly nodded. The ugly one with a gold tooth did not. "You know the rules," he argued heatedly. "Make one exception, every cheat in Virginia City will take advantage. I say a bullet or a rope. Besides, we get the money anyway. Them's always been the way we handle cheaters."

Dade pushed Holly sideways, his hands raised. "This

woman is going to be my wife," he said. "I needed the money for a ring."

"Damned expensive ring, and at our expense, too."

"I'm sorry. Like she says, I won't do it again."

"Oh, hell, let's let him go." Clearly, now that their tempers were appeased, they wanted money, not blood.

The gambler was overruled and he knew it. And maybe the thought passed through his mind that he'd inevitably be caught at his own game. He lowered his gun and began to collect the scattered poker chips.

Holly swung around and stared at Dade. His face looked as though it were sheeted with ice. "Come on," she whispered, "let's get out of here. You wanted to take me to San Francisco? To teach me to fly? I'm ready. I'll never be as ready as I am right this moment."

"All right," he said stonily. "If you've got the money. That was all I had."

She took his arm, but as they started to leave, Dade lashed out with a boot, and the murderous gambler squealed in pain as he rolled clutching his side. "My ribs! You broke my goddamn ribs!"

"Too bad," Dade whispered, bending close and reaching inside the man's coat. A frozen grin touched the corners of his lips as he withdrew a handful of secret cards, then stood up, holding them before the astonished players.

"You three can split both our chips," he said quietly. "But not him." With the device still dangling for all to see, he dropped the prostrate man's cards one by one, to flutter to their rest on him. "Funny, isn't it?" he mused to no one in particular. "The only other cheat at this table was the one who'd have voted my death."

The gambler tried to get up, but Dade, taking Holly by the arm, stepped on his fingers and ground them until the bones mashed under his boot heel. And with his scream in their ears, he escorted Holly away.

There was a stage that left an hour before daylight, while Bevis still slept. One other passenger tried to board, but Dade said something that made him abruptly change his travel plans, and they found themselves leaving Virginia City together and alone.

As they passed over the divide, he reflected, "You saved my life."

She snuggled up against him, feeling his hard, strong body next to her own and wishing she could see his face better. "And you saved mine."

"Did you speak to your father?"

"Yes. Everything will be all right when we return."

"I'll marry you, Holly. You want it to be down in Carson City?"

"No." She didn't dare take the chance that her father might hire men to seek and find them. Holly wanted to go as far away as possible until they were husband and wife.

"Then where?"

"San Francisco. The city I've lived in but you say I've never really known."

He twisted around on the seat until he was hovering over her, bracing himself against the side of the rocking coach. His lips clashed against her own, searching, seering in their hunger.

"Holly, I can't wait that long."

She didn't try to answer. They had more than an hour before the next stop. It was still dark. The shades were drawn.

Holly reached for him, passion driving away all thoughts but to satisfy the craving inside that only he could quench. And then, as his hands moved expertly up and under her straining body, she knew the waiting was finally ending.

8

Glenn stood poised outside the Ophir Mine, uncomfortably aware that hundreds of onlookers were holding their breaths as anxiously as he was. The fifteen-horsepower steam engine they'd bought in San Francisco seemed pitifully inadequate to meet the dual expectations of suctioning hot water out of the mine and also drawing loaded ore wagons up the shiny new track.

Once more Glenn checked the gauges for pressure, while

his ears listened to the throb of the mighty little engine. Then he opened the valve. Ten seconds passed before he heard it—the gurgling suction of water. He smiled hugely and gave a thumbs-up sign as the steam engine powered the water out and spit it down into the hillside. The crowd reacted with a rousing cheer and raised toasts all around.

Glenn felt his confidence surging like the pump. Now, if only the little engine moved the ore wagon as briskly. Inside that mountain, and down one hundred feet of steep track, it crouched on its iron wheels, loaded with a good thousand pounds of ore. It didn't seem possible the little engine pumping away nearby could meet the task. There was only one way to find out.

Glenn threw the switch, heard the screeching protest of the cable as it drew tight and hummed with tension. The steam engine altered sounds, its throb deepening. It wasn't going to make it. Not pump out the water and pull the ore up at the same time, it wasn't. Glenn's hand came forward and, just then, the cable began to wind angrily around the big steel spool. For the first thirty seconds the engine grunted and worked like fury as it belched black smoke into the clear Nevada sky. Then it performed like a runner and got its second wind. The cable began to sing as it dragged the shiny new ore cart faster. Too fast! Before Glenn could slap the switch down, the cart rocketed out of the shaft, catapulted into the air, struck, and unceremoniously flipped its valuable contents all over the hillside.

He winced at the aftermath—spectators scooping up silver, and the ore cart, twisted, all wheels flattened outward like a squashed beetle. He didn't have to be reminded that the cart and the freighting of it cost over six hundred dollars.

Bevis York frowned; yet, as he watched the miners scrambling and whooping with glee over their unexpected good fortune, almost a smile came to his lips.

"Don't worry about the damage, Glenn. I'll have the blacksmiths on it all night. Bad as it looks, they'll have it fixed and on-track by tomorrow."

"Just needs a slight adjustment. I'll make it work right next time."

"My boy, you have performed admirably. Few besides the two of us realize what this experiment will mean to our futures here on Sun Mountain. It will create jobs and wealth for the entire nation."

Bevis smiled and waited for the crowd to finish cleaning up

the hill. Then he raised his sausagelike arms and proclaimed, "Gentlemen, the Ophir Mining Company is proud to have footed the bill for this historic breakthrough. It will bring us prosperity. We'll all benefit!"

"But you most of all, Mr. York!" a man crowed.

Bevis nodded enthusiastically, then motioned all eyes to Glenn. "My colleagues and I gambled on an idea—on a man—this man! He possessed the vision and the knowledge to pull off this breakthrough. Let's give him a big cheer!"

Glenn blushed, but felt ten feet tall. It *had* been his idea. And there'd be others, too. Especially when he could afford the kind of education he hungered for. And later, when the crowd was gone, Glenn thanked the financier and asked him straight out if he'd earn much for the percent of overage.

"That depends on what you can devise on the timbering, young fellow. We'll be going down fast now, but if the timbers won't take the pressure..." He shrugged fatalistically. Glenn had his answer. If the Ophir started caving in, all they'd have accomplished this day would be to hasten and compound an underground disaster.

As if reading his mind, Bevis said, "Put all your efforts into strengthening our shoring. Think about a better system. Think about how your life and those of my employees depend on a new solution. By the way, did you see Deidesheimer when you were in San Francisco?"

"Yes," Glenn replied. "I told him we may be needing his help."

"Good. Ahhh..." Bevis struggled for words, finally bit them out. "You didn't happen to see Holly and that...that chameleon she ran away with, did you?"

Glenn shook his head, noticed the way Bevis's face sagged with disappointment. "Don't worry, sir, they'll come back."

He nodded slowly. "I hope so. Guess I'd best get used to the idea that my daughter is a married woman by now. At least she'd better be!"

Glenn said comfortingly, "Holly is a fine girl. She could have done a lot worse."

"A damn sight better, too! How come you didn't show any interest? Oh, never mind. I remember now. Your eyes were full of Dade's sister. Am I right?"

"Yes."

"Well, she's the class of the pair, and there's no denying

that." He looked around. "I'd better get to the telegraph office before the whole town does. Our stock is going to go sky-high today. I want to buy up whatever I can before it's gone."

Pony Bob Haslam rushed up to him a moment later as he was adjusting the tension on the big cable reel. "Say, did you hear the news!"

"What news?"

"The Pony Express. They put notices up all over these parts advertising for help. There's a meeting tonight in Carson City. You coming?"

"Why not?" Glenn shrugged. "It sounds interesting."

Glenn had no intention of working for the Pony Express, so he stood against the back wall and studied the job seekers. What an assortment! The hall was packed with every type of colorful individual ever seen on the western frontier. Over two hundred of them, ranging from shaggy old buffalo hunters to gamblers, clerks, prospectors, and even a gunfighter or two with their holsters tied low to their thighs. Some applicants looked screwed up tight with eagerness, while others were drunk, and the rest acted bored, as though, by their seeming uninterest, they would appear important.

A tall man dressed in a black suit and starched white shirt took the podium, and the room quieted.

"Gentlemen, it is a proud day for me because, at last, I can announce what the people of this continent have been waiting for all these years—fast overland mail service."

How fast? Glenn wondered, along with everyone else in the hall.

"But first, I should introduce myself to those of you who are strangers or have ridden all the way over from California for this meeting. My name is Bolivar Roberts and I'm the superintendent in charge of the Pony Express between here and Roberts Creek, four hundred miles east."

He grinned. "No, the creek wasn't named after me, but I've swum in it."

There was polite laughter, but it ended quickly, as everyone was eager to hear the big news.

"And, just so you men know I'm no con man and the Pony Express is genuine and legitimate, I'm here to tell you it's owned and completely financed by Russell, Majors, and Waddell, names you've all heard spoken with respect and admiration."

Glenn nodded. Russell, Majors, and Waddell owned the greatest western freighting and stagecoach operations west of the Mississippi. Their business ethics and success in moving both people and goods across the west were legendary. Some men said the government might go broke, but you could bet Russell, Majors and Waddell would be there to buy 'em out and make a profit.

"You should know that I'm honored to tell you about the historic endeavor we are about to undertake. It is the boldest of gambles. An effort of heroic proportions!"

Bolivar's voice quivered with zeal, and the crowd strained forward. Pony Bob Haslam, a little more anxious than prudent, yelled, "Quit flogging the trees. Git to it, Mr. Roberts!"

"I will! I'll come right to the purpose of this gathering. We need riders who can stick to the back of a horse and withstand the punishment of racing a hundred miles through dangerous territory."

Once more Haslam shouted, "I can do it! What are you paying?"

"The real pay is glory! A chance to have your name go down on the pages of history."

"We can't eat the pages of history. What's the dollar pay?"

Bolivar laughed openly. "I understand your temporal concerns and am happy to report that Russell, Majors, and Waddell are hiring at fifty dollars a month and found. That's not quite what you can earn on the Comstock. We know that. But after buying whiskey and food in Virginia City, you don't have enough left to mail a letter on the Pony Express. Go with us, and in no time you'll have a fair savings."

"I'll take it," Haslam shouted as others immediately echoed his feelings.

"Whoa up!" Bolivar yelled. "First I've got some things to say. We need *small* men for riders. If you weigh over a hundred and thirty pounds, you're too damn big."

There was a loud groan. Some angry muttering.

"There's a good reason. Our stations will be placed every twenty-five miles. And we'll buy the finest horseflesh available. But there ain't no horse can run that far under big weight. That's why we've had a special saddle designed to weigh in at less than thirteen pounds."

A lot of the men who were obviously too big started to leave. "Hold up, gents. If any of you still want to be a part of making history, then consider becoming a hostler. Same pay and less risk. It would be your job to have fresh horses saddled and waiting for the riders. And since we're setting up twenty-five home stations where our riders can sleep and another one hundred sixty-five swing stations for trading horses, we'll need far more hostlers than riders."

"Would we have to cook, too?"

"Sure," Bolivar answered, "and a hell of a lot of other things, like toting water, being responsible for the horses, and fighting off Indians if you must."

"And you damn sure will have to!" Clayton James roared as he plowed into the meeting hall past Glenn to eye the speaker. Clayton was dust-coated, and Glenn had the impression he'd just jumped down from a coach or off a horse.

"And what kind of warning is that?" Bolivar Roberts demanded.

"A damned plain one, mister. I've just talked to the war chief of the Paiute nation. Numaga says you've no right to trespass. You neglected to ask his permission."

The crowd's reaction was instantaneously vicious. Someone yelled what Numaga could do with himself, and Glenn saw Clayton James's cheeks burn.

Bolivar Roberts raised his hands for silence. When he spoke, his voice was laced with genuine concern. "I know you, Clayton. Most people here are aware of your reputation, and we'll take your word you've seen Chief Numaga. And I'll say right here and now, before every man in this hall, that the Pony Express wants peace with the Indians whose lands we'll cross."

"You shoulda asked them before you made plans!" Clayton thundered.

The crowd erupted in a babble of shouting voices. Glenn saw a man push Clayton roughly from behind, and that sent him forward with the intention of helping the infuriated stage driver. This was no place for Indian sympathizers. Not when trouble could cost these men their scalps in the lonely Nevada desert.

"Next man who touches Clayton James gets thrown out of here!" Bolivar spit, and the crowd drew back. "Now, listen, Clayton. I agree the Pony Express should have consulted the Paiutes first. But there just wasn't time for negotiations. And now I've got orders to build a string of stations across the territory, and that's what I'm going to do, Numaga or no Numaga. But tell him this. We want to be friends. If he leaves us in peace, I'll order my employees to respect his piñon trees and feed his hungry when they ride through."

"Be damned if I'd feed a stinkin' Indian!" raged a tall buffalo hunter. "I'd as soon shoot 'em on sight!"

Clayton James shouldered two men aside as he bulled a straight path toward the speaker and then nearly beheaded him with a bone-crunching fist. Several men surged in on him and Glenn tripped one, shoved another off-stride, and belted another. A gun boomed and men hit the floor yelling.

Clayton's pistol smoked. "Next man who lays a hand on me or insults my friends gets a fast trip to the Promised Land. My guarantee!"

"You have my word no one will be hired who wishes blood with the Paiutes," Bolivar said, stepping down to face him. "Furthermore, our riders will be armed with only a light pistol and will have instructions that they are to *outrun* any and all trouble. We demand they deliver the mail, and it should be accomplished by the fastest means possible. That's why we're taking only the finest horses money can buy. Paying an average of two hundred dollars each, when top saddlehorses go for sixty. Flight, not fight. That's our plan."

"Good," Clayton said. "I'll tell Numaga that and how you're sorry you didn't ask first and that all stations will feed their hungry. I'll tell him the Pony Express does not want the land itself, but only freedom to cross it in peace."

"Thank you."

Clayton nodded and strode through the crowd, forcing men to separate in his path.

"Gentlemen," Bolivar announced, returning to the podium. "That man may have just saved the Pony Express from being stillborn. And what I said to him is my bond."

His fist clenched and he slammed it down hard. "We *are* going to carry the mail across the American continent, from St. Louis, Missouri, to San Francisco, California, which is a distance of exactly 1,965 miles."

He drew a deep breath, seemed to look into each of them. "And the time? Gentlemen, when we prospected during the forty-niner gold rush, we received our mail via Cape Horn and it took six months. Right now, the Butterfield stage boasts that its circuitous southern route through Texas and Arizona can deliver mail out from the east in only twenty-five days.

"That's fast—I guess," he added, "but the Pony Express,

using the overland route which Russell, Majors, and Waddell are gambling will prove worthy of their receiving a new government mail subsidy, intends to do it in . . . *ten days*!"

It was as if someone had punched them in the stomach, the way the crowd gasped in disbelief. *Ten days!* Why, that was impossible!

Bolivar smiled. "You look just like I did when I first heard that schedule. And it took Mr. Russell almost an hour to show me it could be done. Done with fast horses, tough men, stop-watch schedules, and peaceful Indians."

"When do we start?"

"I'll be hiring tomorrow and for the entire week. One thing you all should know before you come by is that any man who signs on *stays* on. I'll have no quitters. No deserters. And no horse thieves, because this country ain't big enough to keep us from hunting them down and stretching their necks."

There was a certain deadliness in his voice that left no doubt that special plans had been made to deliver swift justice to thieves. "One more thing. As an employee of the greatest stage line in this country's history, you'll be required to swear to an oath over one of our free Bibles."

"What's the damned oath say?" a hard-faced group near Glenn demanded.

Bolivar held up a paper and read it to everyone so they'd understand what they were getting into:

> I do hereby swear before the great and living God that during my engagement, and while I am an employee of Russell, Majors, and Waddell, I will under no circumstances use profane language; that I will drink no intoxicating liquor; that I will not quarrel or fight with other employees of the firm, and that in every respect I will conduct myself honestly, be faithful to my duties, and so direct all my acts as to win the confidence of my employers. So help me, God.

"I'll add one more thing. You'll have to swear to leave the goddamn Indians alone!"

On May 11, 1860, the Comstock took the day off to celebrate the momentous occasion when a lean rider by the name of Warren Upson conquered an unseasonably late Sierra blizzard to carry the first Pony Express mail into Nevada. Julia, along with thousands of others, watched Upson pass the especially designed mochila off to Pony Bob Haslam, who raced east. A few of the mounted onlookers tried to keep pace with Pony Bob, yet they were soon left far behind as the superb horseman quickly evaporated into a thin trail of dust on the purple-saged horizon.

To Julia, that first sight of the Pony Express was both thrilling and unforgettable. Through Glenn Donovan, she'd come to know Pony Bob, and that made the occasion even more special. As she gazed at the fading plume of dust, she couldn't help but think how small was the man against the sky and earth.

Everyone knew the express route the riders would travel, for it had been faithfully printed in the *Territorial Enterprise*, as well as every other newspaper in the country. Straight into the Nevada desert by way of the Carson River, quick relay changes at Dayton, William's Station, Fort Churchill, and then on, clear through Salt Lake City and beyond, over the vast prairies, until it reached St. Louis, Missouri.

The Comstock returned to its work, but nine days later, everyone streamed back down toward the Carson River and cheered wildly when the first westbound rider sped by on his way to San Francisco. Bob Haslam owned this stretch, and with a wave of his Stetson and a broad grin, he had just long enough to yell out the triumphant news that the Pony Express was on schedule! Tomorrow night the eastbound mail would reach the Pacific Coast! The impossible dream was about to become a ten-day reality.

"Julia?"

Her mind jolted back to the present. "Yes, Mr. Raney?"

He stepped in close to her. So close she could smell the foul whiskey and tobacco on his breath.

"You look a little pale, girl. Why don't you go lie down on that cot the missus keeps in the back room. I'll hold the rein on things out here in front until closing time."

"That's all right," she answered quickly, "I'm fine."

He didn't look relieved or happy. "I don't know," he said, scrubbing his long stubbled jawline. "Been watchin' you these past couple days real close and thinkin' something ain't right. Maybe I'll have the missus take you by and see the doctor."

"No!" She realized she'd betrayed her fear. "No," she

repeated carefully. "I do feel a little poorly, but it will pass in a few days."

"Oh. I see." His brow furrowed. "Well, you call if you need help. Guess I'll make use of that cot myself, since you won't."

"That's a good idea, Mr. Raney. Take your rest. A man your age..."

She didn't need to be told she'd spoken foolishly, and Harland Raney's face flushed with scarlet indignation. "My age!" he squealed, sucking in his ridiculous little potbelly.

"I didn't—"

"How old do you think I am?" he demanded. When she didn't answer, he said hotly, "I'm at my prime age. Strong and seasoned. Experienced, too, in ways a woman like you would appreciate!"

There. He'd finally said it. Spoke the thing she'd known was on his mind from the very beginning. Julia felt her heart thumping. She should slap him and leave. Quit. But...but tomorrow was Sunday! Sunday, when she'd be able to earn ten or twelve dollars, and, dear God, she needed the extra money! For the baby who grew stronger each day as she grew weaker.

"Miss Matson," he stammered, "I...I didn't mean to say it that way."

Julia thought of the money. The precious few Sundays she'd be able to play this charade. And so she nodded like a mute.

Her lack of indignation seemed to embolden him. "Julie, honey," he whispered, "I could make things awful easy for you. Put a chair up front for you to rest on when you feel peaky. And that cot back there..."

"Mr. Raney, please. I don't feel well. I want to leave now. I...I feel awful!"

He tried to pat her, but she whirled away, knowing his touch would make her flesh crawl. And as she stumbled to the door, he hollered, "I was sayin' that cot back there is strong enough for two. Me and the missus, we used to..."

She clamped her hands over her ears and ran outside, just as Clayton James was pulling his stage into C Street with a coach full of new and expectant arrivals.

"Clayton!"

His face, thick with a luxuriant growth of beard, opened in smile and he waved heartily. "How about dinner, Julia!"

"Yes!" she cried, knowing that dozens of men up and down

the street were watching, and she didn't care. Clayton was the one person in the world who could soothe her just by his presence.

She was still feeling that way later in the evening as they sat enjoying after-dinner coffee. Clayton had changed into a fresh shirt, and gotten a bath and haircut, along with having his beard trimmed. No woman would consider him handsome in the cast of Dade Taylor; but he was, in a rugged way, very good to look at.

"Anyway," Clayton was saying, "after that Pony Express fellow gave me his promise, I rode to Numaga and told him there'd be no trouble. For using his lands, Bolivar Roberts said he'd feed any of the tribe that was hungry and passing through."

Julia nodded. She didn't need anyone to tell her how important it was to keep peace. A lone rider would be easy quarry in Paiute territory. "Did Numaga seem angry?"

"He wasn't pleased. But he agreed to let the express riders pass as long as they behaved themselves."

Julia switched the subject. "And what about you? Is marrying Windflower in your plans?"

Clayton glanced aside uncomfortably. "She needs me," he said quietly. "And . . . and, well, I guess I even need someone. For taking care of. To think about and make me stronger when hard times come, as they always do."

He glanced up. The corners of his eyes wrinkled deeply. "Julia, don't look at me like that," he said disconsolately. "You're thinking I won't be around to help you. That's it, isn't it?"

She nodded. How could she tell this man that his gentle presence meant so much to her? That she needed him? Not physically. But spiritually. And that there was no one else who could make her feel safe and protected, even good and decent, despite the illegitimate child in her swelling womb?

"Tell you what, Julia. When it comes time for you to have that baby, why don't you let me bring you up to Pyramid Lake? You could live with us. Have the child and rest until you were ready to come back here or move on."

She was jolted by his suggestion. Go up and live with Indians? Have her baby in a . . . tepee.

"They're good people," Clayton said roughly, as if divining her repulsion at the idea. "And they'll be more understanding about your condition than some white people."

"I'm sure you're right, but—"

She was interrupted by loud shouting and angry voices. "What do you suppose is going on? Look! I see people running! They're carrying pitch torches in the street."

Clayton pushed erect. "We'd better see."

An excited crowd was swarming in front of the Delta Saloon, swelling by the moment as heavily armed men came running. Some were shouting and almost incoherent with either rage or panic. Others stared at their guns with set purpose in their eyes. The upraised torch flames danced in the breeze.

"What's going on?" Clayton yelled.

"It's the Indians! They've massacred the employees at William's Station. Burned the Pony Express station and four men inside plumb to char!"

"No!" Clayton shouted, his face ashen. "They wouldn't do that!"

Julia grabbed him, tried to pull Clayton off the street before the excited mob focused its hatred.

"Something's wrong, I tell you! Numaga gave me his word there'd be peace. He wouldn't lie."

"Hey," a man snarled, "that's the same Indian lover who was sticking up for 'em the night Bolivar Roberts spoke."

Clayton went rigid. His eyelids dropped to slits and his voice was cold as melting snow. "Get back, Julia," he growled.

She didn't want to leave him. Not when she saw the almost maniacal expressions forming a human ring about the stagecoach driver.

"Get out of here!" he repeated, batting a reaching hand away. For a moment they just circled, almost snarling and waiting for someone to close.

Julia was knocked aside, and then the ring collapsed on its prey, as terrible oaths pierced the night air and a high shout rose toward the moon. "Kill the Indian lover! Kill him!"

Julia tried to pull them away. She grabbed and yelled and tugged, but they were frenzied and striking Clayton with their fists and boots. She laced her fingers into someone's hair and he spun around and backhanded her so savagely she nearly lost consciousness.

Less than fifteen miles away, William's Station lay smoldering with the stench of death. It was close enough to taste, and it drove a bitterness and hatred deep into the people of the Comstock. The murderers weren't here to punish, but their goddamn Indian-loving friend was. *Kill him!*

Julia staggered to her feet and lurched back at the melee. This time she grabbed a holstered pistol. It was heavy and clumsy in her hands, but she managed to cock it and point the weapon just over their heads. Then she fired. Cocked. Fired again, and again as the tangle of bodies unwound and scattered, leaving only one—Clayton. Clayton, with dirt and blood covering his whiskered face. When she saw what they'd done, Julia, in a haze of fury, emptied three more bullets at them, not caring whether someone died or not.

Her second wild volley of gunfire sent the men scrambling into the cover of darkness, bent on nothing more than escaping with their lives. Julia hurled the empty gun at them and folded at his side.

"Clayton! Can you hear me?"

He showed no sign of recognition. Yet, he was breathing. She leaned closer as the sound of running boots made her jerk upright. A tall, clean-shaven man came to a sudden stop.

"Is he alive?"

"Yes." She tightened. "Who are you?"

"My name is Bob Tillman, U.S. marshal from Carson City. I help the sheriff up here on Saturday nights."

He glanced around. "We've got to get him off the street or I'll have a riot on my hands."

"The doctor's office."

"No. Someone might go there and shoot him through the window. Where do you live?"

She told him quickly; then he somehow managed to lift Clayton, and she was off running toward the doctor's office.

The doctor was a crusty veteran used to treating the losers of frontier brawls. When he was through with the examination, he said, "You give him this medicine—if he wakes."

"If!" Julia repeated in astonishment. "You mean . . . ?"

The doctor shrugged. "I don't know. Right now, it's anyone's guess. When I see hemorrhaging from both the ears and nose, I think there's been some cranial damage. Maybe it's just a concussion, where the brain has bruised itself—then again, it could be serious enough that he'll die."

Julia sagged in despair. She glanced over at Clayton, who lay very still, his breath coming fast and ragged.

"When will we know?"

The doctor shrugged, fastened his bag, and ambled to the door. "If he's still alive in the morning, I'd say he'll survive.

I've seen more of this kind of brain damage since I've been in Virginia City than I care to admit. It's a rough town, lady. Fights, mine cave-ins. We lost a couple a week. I should be a mortician instead of a doctor. The money's better."

Long after he'd gone, Julia sat by Clayton and studied his face in the lamplight. Once she submitted to a compulsion and ran her fingers through his beard until she found the rigid scars along his left cheek and jawline. They'd healed badly, probably due to infection. Julia stared at them and her lips smiled wistfully. Windflower hadn't found the marks difficult to look at, and neither did she.

What of Windflower? If Clayton died, someone would have to tell the Indian girl or she would be forever tortured with the thought that Clayton had deserted her. A cruel fate that Julia knew she would have to forestall.

"You *must* live," she whispered fervently, hugging his chest. "For Windflower and . . . for me!"

Bob Tillman stood over the still-unconscious Clayton. He was a thoughtful young man with bright red hair and clover-green eyes. There was a definite air of tension in his quick movements about the room. "He's going to live, and that means we'd best get him out of Virginia City."

"Are you certain?" Julia asked quickly.

"Yes. His life ain't worth a damn if they find him up here in this little room," the marshal said bluntly. "I saw what was left of the William's Station victims, and it wasn't pretty. Right now, Major Ormsby and over a hundred men are riding hard toward the Paiute stronghold, and they figure to more than settle the score."

"But, Marshal," Julia said, "perhaps there's a reason. I'm sure—"

His voice crackled with cynicism. "You're an Indian lover, too, aren't you, lady?"

When she didn't answer, he expelled a breath. "I'm sorry, ma'am. There was no call for me to say that. It's just that I was one of those who helped bury the dead beside the Carson River. I'm no Indian lover, but I'm no hater, either. But when I saw the way they died . . ."

"How many Indians were there?"

"Ten, at least, by the pony tracks."

Julia frowned, her thoughts returning to Clayton. "What are you going to do with him? He's done nothing to be arrested."

"No arrest, ma'am. Protective custody. I'll wait until after dark, then freight him down the mountain. When things settle and he's fit to ride, I'll tell him to strike out of this territory."

"Can I come down to visit him before he goes?"

Bob Tillman's striking green eyes crinkled at the corners with amusement and, at the same time, appreciation. "The more often, the better, lady. You can visit my jail anytime."

She nodded self-consciously, smoothed Clayton's brow, and prayed for a complete recovery. "Thank you, Mr. Tillman. I have no doubt you've his best interests in mind."

Julia sat beside Clayton on the hard jail bench and whispered so the marshal could not hear them. "You look *much* better. The doctor says you'll be fine in a couple of days."

Clayton forced a tired smile. His eyes were ringed with purple and his beard was still crusted with blood. "I wish I could remember their faces. I'd give *anything* for the chance to repay them that took me down."

"Clayton, you can't think of them now. What's important is getting the marshal to let you go. Then you must go away until this is over."

Clayton scowled. "He says I'm in here for my own protection. But I can't stand being penned like this and wondering what's going on up north. How many did Major Ormsby take with him?"

"Just over a hundred," Julia answered. "I've been told half of them were drunk and acting like they were going to have a party. Ormsby himself gave the expedition a motto—'an Indian for breakfast, and a pony to ride!' "

"The stupid sonofabitch!" Clayton breathed. "They don't have any idea what they're riding into."

"Can they lose?"

He snorted with derision. "If they're drunk, poorly armed, disorganized, or badly mounted—they'll die in their folly. Numaga is smart. He'll be expecting them and he'll pull a noose around them like he was trapping rabbits!"

Julia shuddered, and his analogy was still haunting her when she bid Clayton good night and stepped into the waiting coach she'd hired. She really couldn't afford the expense, but to use that as an excuse was unconscionable.

It was late that night when she returned to Virginia City, and though her body longed for sleep, it was not to be. For only moments earlier, the first of Ormsby's partygoers had reached home. And Julia, stunned and horrified, listened to the grisly account as he raved almost in hysteria.

"We kept seeing tracks on the ground, but no Indians. There was snow falling the last night and we almost froze, and some got sick for drinking all the whiskey. Major Ormsby, he tried to stop the drinkin', but everybody was cold and tired and just wanting to shoot an Indian and go home.

"Three days we rode until we came to the meadow leading into Pyramid Lake. Still no Indians! It just wasn't right, I tell you. I was spooked, an' so were the others. Some wanted to turn around, but Ormsby said no, and he shamed us along with some of the older ones. We shouldn't have listened to them! Shoulda run!"

There was a long pause while the man chewed his dirty knuckles and stared with a faraway look that made Julia's heart go out to him.

"Come on, mister. Get it said. We have to know how it went. How many died?"

"I don't know. Maybe all except me. I don't know!"

There were sharp intakes of breath as the crowd rocked back in one disbelieving body.

"We rode into that meadow, and it was so deadly quiet I could hear myself sweating. All of a sudden, they appeared across the meadow. The biggest goddamn Indian I ever saw, and six others. They just sat on their horses, waiting.

"Some of those still drunk spurred forward, with Ormsby telling them to hold back. 'Wait!' he kept screaming. But they paid him no never-mind. And . . . and when nothing happened to them and the big chief whirled as if to run, why, all of us got brave and followed."

His eyes dilated and a muscle began twitching in his face. "That's when they started killing us. And just kept on and on and on and—"

"Get control of yourself!" one of the interrogators bellowed. "You ain't telling us anything. How did they kill you? Do they all have rifles? Are they fixin' to overrun the territory?"

"Probably," came the dull, uncaring reply. "They're tasting of blood now. We got caught in their trap good. They were hiding. Thousands of them, and it seemed like they sprang outta the ground from little holes. They were jerking men offa their horses. Clubbing 'em out of the saddle. Shootin' guns and arrows. We couldn't get out!" the man shrieked.

Someone grabbed him, and he fought like a crazed animal. "Let me go! Let me go! They're after us. They never stopped, once we got outta the meadow. They *rode* us down. I could hear men screaming as they got yanked off their horses! Let me go!"

And they did. The crazed man dashed shouting into the night, heading for the divide and beyond. His terror spread among them like a cancer. Within the hour, everyone on Sun Mountain was either preparing for attack or racing for the safety of California. Several had themselves lowered deep into the mine shafts, where they huddled in everlasting darkness and pictured Indians with bloody scalps raised to a dark and foreboding sky.

Of the hundreds who raced down from the Comstock in those nightmarish predawn hours when fear held the whip hand, Julia Matson was the only one who disdained escape. She remembered the hours she'd spent listening to Clayton tell about Numaga and the Paiutes. In the first place, she knew the tribe numbered less than a thousand—not enough to overrun the territory. Also, Clayton had said Numaga was intelligent enough to understand he could not overcome the whites and that his only hope lay in peace. She didn't understand things about battles, but one fact kept repeating itself to her: Numaga had been attacked. He'd not yet ridden against a town.

No, she repeated over and over to herself as the rented carriage twisted its way back toward Carson City, the Indians were not going to overrun the towns and settlements. And as soon as the panic died, there would be an upswelling of vengeance the likes of which the west had never seen. And someone would remember Clayton James—the Indian lover. When they did, his life would be terminated.

Julia held on tightly to the carriage door. She *had* to get Clayton out of jail before they came for him. Would the marshal let him go? What if he was unreasonable and refused?

The muscles of her jaw clenched tightly. One way or the other, she *had* to set Clayton free—and quickly!

9

Carson City appeared to be a nest of fireflies in the desert night as half the Comstock fled to her. Julia's carriage rounded the corner of Curry Street and careened to a halt before the marshal's office. In an instant she was hammering on the door.

"What is it?" Bob Tillman's rough voice demanded.

When she told him, the marshal let her in quickly, then shut and bolted the door.

"You know, then," Julia said, going over to stand near Clayton, whose fists were clenched whitely around the bars.

"Yeah, I know," Tillman snapped. "This whole town is about ready to bust wide open."

"Someone will remember Clayton is in their jail, Marshal. When that happens, you can't stop them from killing your prisoner."

Bob Tillman's forehead was creased with deep worry lines and his expression was bleak. "My kid brother went up there with Ormsby. I begged him not to go, but . . . but he wouldn't listen. Always said I was too bossy. But I know Ormsby. He's no military leader. I tried to make all of 'em wait until the U.S. Army sent help. But do you think they'd listen? Hell, no! Drinkin' and laughin' and yellin' about an Indian for breakfast and a pony to ride. What the hell kind of talk is that?"

Julia and Clayton said nothing. Both realized the young marshal was nearly in a state of shock.

"Crazy talk!" he boomed. "I knew something awful was going to happen up there. I've felt it in my gut the last few days."

"Your brother may be riding here at this very moment. But what are you going to do with Clayton?" Julia asked point-blank.

"Protect him, of course! If I set him free, he wouldn't last ten minutes before he was drawn and quartered."

"I'll take that chance," Clayton barked sharply. "I can't stay here. I've got to reach Numaga. Try and find out what caused this whole thing. Maybe if—"

"You're a fool!" Tillman shouted. "Don't you understand what's happened? First William's Station and now God only knows how many of the best men in Carson City! All slaughtered!"

He whipped his fist down hard on a battered desk. "It don't matter now! Right or wrong ain't got nothin' to do with it anymore. We're talking about justice, revenge—*vengeance!*"

Julia glanced over at Clayton. His expression mirrored her own deep anxiety. Marshal Tillman, worrying over his young brother, was nearly out of control. If it turned out that his worst fears became a reality, Julia thought it a definite chance he might even hand Clayton over to the crowds in his grief and hatred.

"You've *got* to let him go," she persisted. "Clayton James has done nothing wrong. We all know that. And—"

"Shut up! Yeah, he hasn't done anything wrong—yet. His only crime is being an Indian lover, and that's enough to get him strung up this night. *But,* if I turn him loose, he'll go straight to those Paiutes and tell 'em everything. Hell, if they realize the state of panic this town and the whole Comstock is in right now, those goddamn tribes might just decide to join forces and overrun this territory."

"That's crazy talk, Marshal. Let me go and I'll try to prevent more killing."

Bob Tillman's face grew resolute. "No," he said tersely. "I can't take the chance on what you'd do up at Pyramid Lake. Too many lives are at stake. Reckon I'll have to keep you right here."

Clayton shrugged as if in defeat, but his eyes flicked once between Julia and the marshal's gun.

Julia snatched the gun out of Tillman's holster and darted out of reach as he whirled. At the same instant, Clayton's strong arm reached through the bars and clamped around the marshal's neck and pinioned him.

"Get the keys, Julia. They're in the top drawer."

She found them, and moments later, Bob Tillman was locked securely in his own cell. His complexion was as red as his hair and his voice shook with fury. "If I had any compassion for you, mister, it's just been wiped clean. I'm a U.S. marshal, and neither of you can get away with this!"

Clayton took a deep breath and let it out slowly. "Think what you want about me. But I'm asking you not to do anything to Julia."

"Why shouldn't I?" he demanded hotly. "Are people supposed to believe I locked myself up by mistake?"

"Tell 'em it was a stranger. Or he wore a mask. Tell them anything except what really happened." Clayton paused. "You could live with your conscience if I were hung—do you think it would be the same if a mob got to her?"

Tillman scowled as he debated inwardly with himself. "All right," he conceded as he turned away. "Why don't you both just get the hell outta town?"

Clayton nodded. At the door, he paused, then pitched the keys to Bob Tillman, who stared with open bewilderment.

"You don't hate Indians," Clayton told him quietly. "And why don't you stop tearing yourself apart and go discover what really happened to your brother?"

Hope flared in the marshal's eyes. "You think—"

"I don't know," Clayton said, cutting him off. "But if I were you, I'd be going to find out."

Tillman scooped up the keys. "I guess I will," he said. "If one made it to Virginia City, others could. That's where I'm heading."

"May I ride along?" Julia asked suddenly.

"What for?"

"I live in Virginia City," she told him simply. "And I have a job there."

"Suit yourself," Tillman growled, freeing himself. "I'll get horses. I won't wait for you."

"I'll be ready."

They watched him stalk out. A good man, but one twisted with worry.

"He'll do," Clayton said. "I'd best go now."

Julia couldn't meet his eyes. Deep inside, she'd hoped that he might change his mind about leaving her for Windflower. But now she knew that even though she might have just saved his life, he was still going north to help the Paiutes. And it wasn't fair!

"Julia? What's wrong?"

"Nothing." She'd barely gotten the words out.

"I have to go," he said. "You know that."

"Do I!" she cried, pulling back. "All I know is that I've a child and you're the best man I've ever seen. At least Windflower has her family. I have no one."

Pain seeped into the creases of his face. "Julia, I didn't know you felt that way."

"Now you do. Will it matter?"

"I . . . I don't think so."

"Why?" she demanded. "Is it because Windflower has seen your scars and still loves you? Well, so do I!"

He didn't believe her. She could tell by looking that he didn't. "Julia, you're tired. Upset. You're working too many hours and lacking sleep. If—"

"The Indian lover!" a voice boomed out of the night.

Clayton reached out and pulled her close. "Listen, girl! Pairing us up would be like planting a rose in a bed of thistles. I can see that now, and someday, you would too. Find a good man. One with education and money in the bank. A city man. Not someone like me."

She wanted to tell him she didn't care about money in the bank. Or fancy things. No! For once in her life, she just wanted a good, solid man she could love and trust and . . .

"He's over there! By the marshal's office."

"Good-bye, Julia. Maybe . . . maybe I'll come back."

"I love you," Julia told him simply. "When you decide—"

A bullet exploded in the night and Julia heard a fleshy thud and saw Clayton twist in pain as he shoved her aside and stumbled around in the corner of the building.

"Clayton!"

Three men skidded to a halt beside her. "Look! I told you I got him. Blood."

"He hurt you, lady? Don't worry. We'll track that Indian-lovin' sonofabitch down. He won't get away! Come on."

A sharp pain made her cramp up inside, and suddenly the world began to spin and she could feel herself falling.

Julia awoke in her own bed with Bob Tillman pressed up tightly against her warm skin.

"So," he chuckled, stretching lazily against her, "you finally woke up."

She screamed. Screamed and tried to rake his laughing face with her fingernails. Bob grabbed her wrist, twisted her arm down, and clamped a hand over her mouth.

"You don't want to scream and have everyone come running in here and see us like this, do you?"

She tried to bite his hand, tear herself free from his grasp. Her shouts were muffled protests and her efforts to break away were hopeless.

"Now, listen, Miss High-and-mighty," he said evenly. "I didn't tell anyone you helped Clayton James and I'm the one who got a doctor to see you. Whatever he prescribed musta been strong, 'cause I've been waiting more than a night and a day for you to come around and show me your appreciation."

She relaxed, hoping to get him to lower his guard. When Julia saw the smile reappear and felt his hand slip from her wrist and move across her hip, she scratched at his eyes.

He grunted in pain as her fingers dug into the flesh of his brow. "Goddammit, woman! It's a taming you need, and I'm just man enough to do it!"

She fought with every ounce of strength in her weary, pregnant body. But it made no difference to him. In fact, her desperate struggles seemed to heighten his passion as he took her fiercely, using her for his own rough pleasure. Julia bit her lips until they bled and she squeezed her eyes shut and tried to pretend this wasn't happening. Or, failing that, it was Clayton James who was making love to her and it meant they would be together always. He would be the father of her child, her protector and provider.

"Julia?" he whispered down into her face. "You can't keep your eyes closed forever. Besides, it wasn't that bad, was it?"

"It was terrible!"

There was a long pause, and when he spoke, his voice carried evidence he'd been wounded. "I never had any complaints before. Fact, just the opposite."

"Did you also rape them?" she hissed.

His voice roughened. "You *owed* me. Besides, don't give me that holier-than-thou routine about chastity and your virtuous reputation. Julia, you're a used woman!"

She shuddered under him. It was true. She pretended respectability, worked and slaved to make it a reality. But it *wasn't* a reality.

"Julia! Quit biting your lips and cutting them to pieces like that. I can't stand to see a woman who looks like you hurt herself. Open your eyes and look at me."

"No." She wished she could will herself to just cease to exist.

He forced her eyes open with his rough fingers. "That's better. I'm not an ugly man, Julia. In fact, I'm a lot handsomer than that Indian lover of yours."

"Get off me," she ordered dully.

"Is he the father of the child you're carrying?"

Julia felt a cold shiver sweep through her veins. He knew! And why shouldn't he? Unclothed, the roundness in her belly would plainly reveal her secret.

"Answer me," he snapped. "The Indian lover is the father of your baby, isn't he?"

To admit otherwise would have killed her, and that was surprising, because she'd thought there was no shame left inside. But there was. And so she found herself nodding.

"That sonofabitch!" he snarled. "And I heard him say he was going to marry the squaw!"

Bob Tillman's lean, hawkish face hardened, with his eyebrows slanted down in the middle, almost coming together. Tight lines cut into his cheeks.

"I shoulda let them hang him. If I'd known—"

"No. No, listen. I was lying," she pleaded.

He clamped his hand over her mouth. The anger vanished, and in its place she saw almost a gentleness. "I don't want to hear about it. He's gone and I'm taking his place."

She shook her head violently. "Get off me, Marshal. Please."

"I will," he told her. "When I'm done, and that's going to be quite a while."

"Marshal, please. What . . . what about your brother? And the Paiutes? What about—?"

"My brother's dead!" he choked. "Out of over a hundred, only twenty or thirty got out alive, and they were riding the best horses. Indians . . ."

He scraped a rough forearm across his eyes. "Indians ran them down. Chased 'em halfway to Virginia City. Billy . . . Billy almost made it. His body was one of the first ones brought in."

Julia swallowed. Ground her teeth together as he moved back into her.

"He was just a kid!" Tillman choked brokenly. "And I loved him. Now . . . oh . . . now I got no one who gives . . . oh, *good*, woman . . . a damn about me 'cept you!"

* * *

Bob Tillman peered down at the street. "The funeral procession is starting to form. I should be down there, Julia. In memory of Billy."

She said nothing. Only watched him. He had raped her, but he'd also shown her his pain and that he was capable of love. And because of that, she didn't hate him. She felt nothing. Maybe . . . maybe she was incapable of ever feeling anything again. Could that be how it was to die in spirit?

"Julia, I want you. Knowing what you've done doesn't change it. We *need* each other."

"No."

"Yes!" He strode over and yanked the covers from the bed and stared at her nakedness. "Even with child, you're the most beautiful woman I ever saw," he whispered fervently.

"Get out of here."

Pain flashed across his face. "I want to *marry* you. Think of the baby, dammit! It needs a father. I'll be one . . . do it up proud and treat it like my own."

She shook her head fiercely.

"Why the hell not?"

"Because . . . because I don't love you," she replied brokenly.

"What's that got to do with anything?" he bellowed. "You need me."

"I'll survive," Julia said dully. "I've made it this far—"

"On your looks, you have! Dammit, Julia, for you, the dance is over. I'm asking real nice to take you home and see you're taken care of. The baby, too. And who knows? Maybe you'd come to love me, too, someday."

"I don't think so, Bob Tillman."

"You'll change your mind," he vowed, "and it won't be long. About as long as it's going to take for people to notice you're *with* child and *without* husband. Then I'll have you for my wife, and anyone who says or acts like they're thinking bad about you or the child will answer to me!"

She didn't understand him. His dogged persistence was something she'd never dealt with before.

"Listen, you're my woman now. Only thing is, you don't know it yet. But you will. And soon."

Business was good at the Silver Exchange Mercantile for the next few hectic days. Julia worked feverishly to handle orders for the extra provisions, guns, ammunition, and all the supplies needed to either withstand a siege or, if that didn't materialize, then for a second expedition into Paiute country.

Many fled, and those who stayed gobbled up claims and vowed to fight to hold them against both the former chicken-hearted owners and the advancing Paiutes—whoever came first.

Though Julia declined to join them, most of the women and the handful of Comstock children were corralled each night in Peter O'Riley's half-built stone hotel. The walls were thick and tall enough to repulse the Indians, and as soon as everyone was inside, the open doors were barricaded as men gripped their rifles and waited.

Down the mountain in Silver City, the emotion was also running high as those who remained vowed to fight to the death to protect their diggings. Just above their town, where Gold Canyon pinches into Devil's Gate, a staunch band of defenders climbed to the top of the Gate and built a stone fort, and believing that a fort is nothing unless protected by cannon, they made one. It was bored out of a huge pine log, hung with iron bands, and aimed down-canyon. They crammed it full of chains and scrap metal. By God, if the Paiutes chose to come up this canyon, they'd be blown to smithereens!

Everything went fine for several days until the protectors of the fort began to wonder if their homemade cannon really would deter a large attacking force. Doubts started to spring up like weeds after rain, and finally the canyon below was cleared and the order given to "test-fire."

They rigged a slow match to the enormous weapon and scrambled for cover. When it blew, thunder shook the earth, and the tree, scrap metal, chains, and the fort itself exploded. Debris flattened the land for a hundred yards in every direction.

"Julia?"

She looked up from the cash register and into the troubled face of Bob Tillman. "Go away."

"I am," he said quietly. "Today we're going north up to Pyramid Lake."

Julia's fists clenched. "Hasn't there been enough bloodshed?"

"Not *Indian* blood," he said bitterly. "Aren't you even going to say good-bye?"

"No."

He grabbed her wrist. "You're still thinking about Clayton James, aren't you?"

"Let go of me or I'll call Mr. Raney."

"Call him, then. Never liked him anyway. Besides, I just wanted to say I'm planning to arrest your Indian lover and charge him with treason."

"Treason!"

He smiled. "That's right. Against the United States of America. I can make it stick, because he's aiding and abetting the enemy. Telling 'em about our defenses and arms."

"You're crazy!" Julia raved. "Clayton James would give anything for peace."

"Well, I hope so, because if he don't surrender peaceably, then I'll kill him myself. This time we'll beat 'em, Julia. We've got Colonel Hays in command, and he's an Indian fighter. Captain Storey and over two hundred regular soldiers are also coming, in addition to more than five hundred sober civilians. On top of all that, we've been sent Army mini-muskets and a pair of twelve-pound mountain howitzers. We'll make them remember what they did to Major Ormsby and Billy and all the others."

"It won't bring them back," Julia said. "And Clayton wasn't even—"

"Never mind him! The man is gone. He either dies or gets hung."

"Please."

Tillman's facial muscles corded. "I'll be back for you soon, Julia. A woman's place is with the man who'll stand by her. *I* will. *He* didn't. It's that plain."

Then he pulled her into his arms and kissed her. Roughly at first, then tenderly. When he stepped away, he reached into his pocket and dragged out a small bag of gold dust. "Keep it for me, woman. It's not that much, but if I don't come back, it's yours."

Julia was stunned for a moment and almost dropped the sack. "You . . . you actually do love me."

He chuckled. The corners of his green eyes crinkled. "My, oh, my! Not only beautiful, but smart! Yeah, I love you. Have since the first night I laid eyes on you, sitting beside the Indian lover up in your room when you thought he was going to die. I wish he had."

"Don't say that."

"It's the truth, Julia. I'm not so stupid as to think he's going to forget you over some squaw. Come a day when he'd show up and see you trim and sleek like a well-groomed racing filly. Then he'd want you back and I'd have to kill him. Better now. For you and for me."

"It won't change my feelings about him," Julia vowed. "And—"

He reached out and pressed both of her hands around the sack of gold. "Julia, if . . . if I don't come back—well, none of this talk matters. All that counts right now is that I've given you everything I own in that sack. Consider it a price."

"What price, Bob? I can't. Won't—?"

"Just tell me," he whispered, "tell me I'm not such a bad fellow and that you don't hate me for what I did. Would you give me that much, Julia?"

This time, he was *asking* her. And there was an urgent necessity in his asking that could not be denied. "Very well," she told him, looking deeply into his imploring eyes, "I don't hate you. And you aren't a bad man. In fact, I suspect you may even be a very good one. But—"

He laughed, pressed a forefinger over her lips. "Shhh. No more. Not until we meet again."

Julia watched him go, and a deep sadness welled up in her. He *was* a good man in spite of himself, but so was Clayton. And one of them, without question, was going to die in the next few days. How long would this senseless waste of life go on? Would there be anyone decent left when the blood had seeped into the desert sand?

"Julia?"

She turned quickly, caught off guard. "Yes, Mr. Raney."

"The marshal. I saw him give you a sack. Was it gold?"

Her eyes dropped to the small bag of gold dust. It couldn't have been worth more than a hundred dollars. But to her, and because it was all he had, it somehow was more.

"Yes. It's gold, Mr. Raney."

"For what?" he demanded. "He bought nothing."

"It's mine, Mr. Raney," she told him while slipping the precious dust into her purse and turning to face him. Julia had come to despise this man—and fear his lecherous gaze that seemed to probe her body all through the working day.

As if he read her thoughts, the eyes seemed to take her measure, and a contemptuous sneer formed on his lips. "You're with child," he pronounced. "That man's child. And he's just given you money for your favors."

"Mr. Raney!" she breathed, looking into his triumphant face.

"Deny it!" he challenged. "Go ahead. The missus saw it last week, but I said, 'No, Julia Matson is a good and decent woman.' You sure fooled me."

"Stay back," she gritted. "Don't you come any closer. I'll scream."

"Hold it, Julia," he whined. "I'll stay back. All I want to know is your price. Whatever he's paying, I'll match it and then some. You oughta be worth—"

Her palm smacked his face viciously, and he raised his own to her just as a man came into the store.

"Got any more ammunition?"

"Take care of him, Julia!"

She did. He was very agitated and spilled the box of cartridges all over the floor. By the time she was finished helping him retrieve them, both of the stern-faced Raneys waited.

"You're fired, young woman," Mrs. Raney hissed. "I'll not have a loose woman working on these premises."

Julia's cheeks flamed and her entire body shook with anger as she viewed the self-righteous woman who'd as much as branded her a harlot.

"I quit," she said in a trembling voice. "I don't know why I've stayed on here so long anyway. Every other store owner in Virginia City has practically begged me to work for him."

"You're a liar and a fool, young woman. As for the other stores wanting you to clerk for them, well, that will change in a hurry once people realize your immorality."

"Don't count on it! My baby is due in two months, and somehow, I'll be right back to work. And I swear I'll win away all your customers."

Both of them rocked back, fear and hatred twisting their faces.

"Pay her!" Raney shouted. "Go into the back room and make her leave that way. I don't want anyone ever to say she left here by the front door!"

"I'll go any way you want," Julia gritted.

Less than three minutes later, she had her wages. Mrs. Raney had cheated her by over ten dollars, but she didn't argue. All she wanted was to leave.

"Back door, like my husband said!"

"I'll get my purse," Julia said hotly. "And you can tell your lecherous husband he can go to hell!"

Mrs. Raney gasped. She threw her hand over her mouth, and Julia smiled as she left. He was holding her purse and shoved it roughly into her hands as she slammed by and out the door.

It was done! Her blood roiled with fury and indignation. She detested those people! Loathed them. Vipers! Never mind what happened tomorrow. She'd find another job. If she pulled her elastic waistband even tighter, she could get by for another week or two. Maybe even more. Then she'd have enough money to live on until the baby arrived.

She *could* make it. Tomorrow she'd accept one of those job offers. Probably the one from Mr. Tooey at the Virginia Exchange. He was nice. Old, too. Sixty or seventy, at least. Yes, she thought Mr. Tooey would understand.

"Stop her!" a familiar voice cried. "Thief! Thief! I've been robbed!"

A flood of horror knifed through Julia as the Raneys charged out of their store shouting and pointing at her.

"No," she whispered, striding away as quickly as she could. "No!"

The shouting grew in intensity, and she realized the Raneys were following her down C Street, yelling and drawing a crowd. Suddenly a man latched onto her arm. He wore a gun and a badge, yet his voice was kind, almost apologetic.

"Miss, I think we'd better hold it right here until I find out what's going on."

"Please, let me go."

"Thank heaven you caught her," Raney wheezed, puffing up to them with his wife in tow. "She robbed us!"

"That's not true!"

"Open her purse. She took half the money in our till. Still in the business envelope the bank provides. And I wouldn't be surprised to find she's taken other stuff, too."

Julia's eyes dropped to her purse. It dangled in her hand and seemed to assume a threatening quality as she realized what was about to happen.

"Ma'am, I'm afraid I'm going to have to take a peek."

She nodded. Handed it over as her heart slammed against her ribs and her breath came faster.

"There!" Raney trumpeted. "That's it! And look, she stole three of our watches!"

"Doesn't surprise me," Mrs. Raney quipped. "She's a tramp and a thief. Probably trying to steal it for that bastard she's a-carryin'."

Julia went for her. Fighting and kicking and screaming, she wanted to kill them both. Then the sheriff clamped his arms around her and lifted her from the ground.

"Where are you taking me?"

"Off the street and into my office," he graveled. "I think you've put on enough of a show for one day, young woman. Mr. and Mrs. Raney, you pressing charges?"

"Damn betcha, Sheriff. Lock her up!"

"Hellfire!" the sheriff muttered out of the corner of his mouth. "As if I ain't got enough problems. Every man in town is going to want to get arrested and jailed tonight. Dammit anyway!"

Julia strode with grim purpose down C Street, past Union Street, until she reached the Virginia Exchange. Spending the night in jail had been a humiliating experience and would have been even worse if the sheriff hadn't decided not to arrest anyone else. As a result, after midnight, when it became apparent that the town was "wide open," the miners had raised special hell. Many of them still felt that the Paiutes were certain to annihilate the white man in Nevada and that by now they'd slaughtered the second military force and were on their way to the Comstock. With that kind of outlook, they drank with an even greater zeal than usual.

The sheriff, realizing one more night like the last would suffice to destroy Virginia City before the Paiutes could get to it, had decided to set bail at twenty dollars. Julia had gladly paid, but it had taken some of Bob Tillman's gold dust.

Now, as she smoothed her hair and tried to pull in her waist, she was aware that men were watching her with unconcealed contempt.

"Good morning, Mister Tooey," she called, stepping inside and facing the old white-mustached storekeeper.

He glanced up; his smile dissolved. "Miss Matson. What do you want?"

She was taken aback by his abruptness, pushed off balance by the brusque greeting. "I've decided to accept your offer," she said, forcing cheerfulness into her voice.

"Offer?"

"Why, yes. You remember, about employment."

There were several customers browsing around, and Mr. Tooey kept glancing nervously at them. "Well, ah, you see, I'm afraid this Paiute thing has cut into my business and—"

"I understand," she said doggedly, "but your customers still need meat and beans, coffee and bottled whiskey, pork, medicine, shirts, and pickaxes."

"Miss Matson, I don't need you anymore. I'm sorry."

He started to turn away, but she pushed around in front of him. "Mr. Tooey, you're not telling me the real reason, are you?"

When he didn't answer, she pushed on. "I was framed by the Raneys. What they said was a lie. If a man like you won't believe me, no one will!"

"Miss Matson, I *am* sorry about the unfortunate things that are being said about you. I don't know if they are true or not, but it doesn't matter. You see, I can't buck all my competitors. Harland Raney made me promise not to hire you, and he's done the same with the rest."

Julia swallowed with fear. "Then I'm beaten," she whispered tonelessly.

"No, you're not. There'll be a trial. If you can prove—"

"I can't."

He wrung his hands together, kept glancing expectantly at each of the browsers, hoping one would call for his attention.

"Mr. Tooey, I'm begging you to let me work. I *need* the money."

A wintry look stole into his eyes. "Yes. For the baby. You should have thought of the consequences of your immorality, young woman. You had me fooled as much as the others."

Julia's chin snapped up. Her eyes burned with anger. "You are no better than they are, Mr. Tooey. Furthermore, *you* had *me* fooled."

"I don't have to listen to this!"

"No. No, you don't. But I'll tell you one thing and you can pass it on to the other four 'competitors' as you choose to call them. I know how you collectively set prices, and one way or the other, I'm going to come back and drive you all to your knees. It won't be hard, because I'm not greedy like the rest of you. And I *will* see each and every one of you humbled!"

His face, usually so benign, reddened furiously and his

mouth worked in silent rage before he finally swore, "Thief! Harlot! Get out of my store! Go back where you came from."

Julia twisted away and ran. She wasn't going anywhere. Even if there had been a place to return to, she couldn't afford the ticket.

"Clayton!" she sobbed. "Clayton, I need you!"

10

The bullet hole was low in his side, deep and burning. As soon as he was certain no one from Carson City had followed him in the darkness, Clayton reined in the stolen buckskin gelding and stuffed the wound with strips of leather hacked off his deerskin jacket. The wadding quickly swelled to pack the bullet wound and slow the loss of blood. But after he'd skirted Reno and continued on in the predawn hours, a deep lassitude assailed Clayton and he knew he was becoming dangerously weak.

Just after a pale salmon-colored sunrise, he toppled from the horse and crashed to rest in a dry stream. The buckskin snorted and tried to pull away. He held it by the trailing reins and talked soothing talk until its nostrils no longer dilated and the whites of its eyes lost fear. It cost a great deal of his last reserves of strength to pull himself back into the saddle. Yet he did so, because to fail was to die, and there were too many whose lives depended on his own.

He tied himself in the saddle with the morning sun blazing on the western horizon and frost steaming off the sage brush, rabbit brush, and greasewood. Clayton didn't notice the quick gray jackrabbits or the earth-matched coyote that glided across his trail. In fact, he rode for many hours, drifting in and out of a blurry pain until he became aware of the great birds hopping around on the desert floor. Vultures! He choked with revulsion and the buckskin shied, almost pitching him to the ground. Clayton's eyes blazed with outrage at the scavengers and dead men strewn carelessly along the ridge he traveled.

He laboriously drew his pistol and kicked the horse forward as the vultures watched with small and hostile eyes. At sixty feet, some of the larger males began their drunken, bobbing weave—advancing, screeching, flapping their powerful wings, then retreating with snapping beaks.

Clayton shot two before they ran into their struggling flight, scolding and clacking into cloudless sky. The bodies filled him with bitter sorrow and the signs of struggle on the desert revealed how each man had died. Around the brave, the earth was marked and torn with the battle, while about others there could be seen only a few prints and, most often, the victim had died on the run with a spear or arrow between the shoulder blades.

Clayton's eyes stung with tears—for those who'd already died, whom he could not even stop to bury, and for those who would die before the Paiute war was finished.

The miles passed slowly as he continued northward. Terrible visions came to him, and sometimes he was jerked into consciousness by his own gunfire and the heavy beating of black wings. He didn't know how long the nightmare lasted. Only that, finally, he awoke to find Windflower pressed tightly against him under the fur robes. And later, when the wings of death rose up before his eyes, he groaned and clutched for the woman as though she were life itself.

Windflower enfolded him, breathed warmth and then fire into his body, and drove the demons away. Clayton gripped her with all his ebbing strength. Julia Matson seemed far, far away, as if in another world. And so, as a cold wind pushed rain clouds east, and drops began to pelt the sides of the new karnee she had built for him, Clayton took Windflower and kissed her eyes and told her that he would always be her man. She moved passionately in his arms until their breath came quick and hard and reason was swept away.

Deep into the night, they lay together, warm and close, while the rain fell soft upon their new home. Windflower carefully explained the wedding ceremony they would go through when there was time. But no matter. For now, because she had given and he had taken, the bond between them was forever.

"And see how I have built our home? It is tight against the weather. Even in the time of deep snow, we will be warm and dry together."

"Windflower," he said gravely, "I must talk to Chief Numaga. There is an army being formed. Soon they will come to destroy your people. To punish them for killing Major Ormsby and his riders.''

''You will go and fight? Maybe become a chief someday.''

''I . . . I don't know,'' he said quietly. ''Some of those who advance are my friends. Men I've lived and worked with for years.'' He sat up, feeling the pain in his side. ''I'd like to stop this killing before the Paiutes are driven from their lands.''

''We have many warriors. The Utes, Bannocks, and Washoes will all join us. You must help them too, Clayton James. The white raiding party did not come to talk peace. Those who follow will seek only revenge. We must fight or be driven like cattle to our graves.''

He nodded, sick at heart, because she was right. Besides, he really had no choice. Back in Carson and in Virginia City, they'd almost killed him just for trying to prevent a war. He couldn't go back. The woman beside him had just given him her maidenhood. Freely. Without reservation or hesitation. And he *was* a man of honor. Windflower had become his wife. These were his people. His destiny was that of the Paiute nation. There was no return.

As if sensing his decision and understanding his loss, Windflower said, ''My husband. I have dreamed of you often.''

''What did you see?''

Her eyelids lowered and a calm resignation edged her words. ''I saw you on a hill while I was far below. Men were riding down on our village and I held to the sky a thing worth more than my own life.''

He pulled her face to his own, not wanting to hear any more. ''It was only a dream. Let's not talk of it. Dreams mean nothing.''

''But this one. So real!'' Windflower quivered as though an icy chill had passed through her slender body. ''In it, you called my name. I heard you. And I saw your face—angry and terrible in vengeance. Then—''

He clamped his hand over her lips. ''No more!'' he said harshly. ''These days are full of dark dreams and we must not think of them again or speak of them, for that is like planting poisonous roots.''

She wrapped herself onto him and stroked his beard gently. ''Yes! Yes, you are right, my husband. Let us talk no more. Let us be one!''

* * *

"You ask me why this murder at William's Station came to be," Windflower said in a troubled voice. "I tell you. Two young and pretty girls of our tribe went to gather medicine roots. The place where they are found is far south, down near the river. All day they were gone, and by nightfall they had not returned. We grew fearful."

"Didn't the girls know better than to go on such a long ride unprotected?"

Windflower shook her head. "They were well mounted and had gone before. Besides, we believed the Pony Express men were our friends. But it was not so. Only later did we hear that Walking Bull had ridden into the change-horse-place by the river. He did not see the girls or their horses. But the men who lived in this place wanted to trade many cans of powder, boxes of caps, and lead bars for Walking Bull's pony. He accepted and they took his pony to their barn. When he asked for that which was promised, the four whites laughed. Walking Bull, thinking perhaps it was a game, laughed also but reminded them he still owned the pony."

"Yeah, but it was no game," Clayton snarled. "I should have known Bolivar Roberts couldn't order men to change their nature. What happened to Walking Bull?"

"They set their dogs on him and his legs were bloodied by their fangs. He ran into the barn and grabbed his pony and mounted, with the dogs snapping their teeth. And that is when he heard the voices."

"Voices?"

"Yes," Windflower said, a bitter twist to her pretty mouth, "of the Paiute girls. They seemed to come from the very earth itself—wailing and sorrowful. But Walking Bull had no time to think of them, for the men were trying to pull him from his pony. He escaped. When he returned to this camp and told of this thing, Chief Natchez, along with the fathers of the girls and six others, made a raiding party."

"What happened when they reached William's Station?" Clayton asked tensely.

Windflower's eyes fell and then she rose and quickly dressed herself. "I will bring Chief Natchez," she told him. "It it better you hear it through his eyes."

The chief's voice was like the sound of grating rocks as he squatted beside the doorway and narrated the tale. And as he listened, all hope about convincing Numaga or the whites to talk vanished from Clayton's mind.

"We came upon them when the sun was dying and smoke rose from their chimney. We call and they step out. Four whites. They scared. Eyes lost like rabbits. I ask, where girls? They say they no know. Lies!"

Natchez stabbed the earth with a blunt forefinger. "One ran. I send warriers to bring back. The others talking very fast; like wings, their mouths flap. 'No. No. They have not seen our girls. Maybe look somewhere else' I say, 'You lie! Why he run if not lie? He run for his life. He know he is guilty and will die.'

"Another man run. He jump in river and drown. My warriors bring back like fish. Biggest one think we murder and drew his knife. I grab and pull arm up behind back. Bone snap like twig and he scream plenty, begging for his life and telling of girls under floor of barn."

Clayton took a deep breath and expelled it slowly. "Then you killed them."

Chief Natchez' eyes burned with hatred. "We find earth door. Girls under ground on floor with rags in mouth and hands tied. They were crying and bloodied between legs. I give order to kill! We run to whites and strangle like rabbits! Then we burned them in their place and prayed their spirits scream forever."

Clayton didn't know when Chief Natchez left. For hours he stared into nothingness. Four bestial men had committed a terrible outrage on two Indian children and deserved to have been tortured. But like a pebble bouncing down to trigger a rockslide, the entire mountainside was beginning to engulf all in its path. In a few days, when he was strong enough, he would ride back to Carson and Virginia City and tell them *why* the Paiutes had killed those men at William's Station. But Windflower had stated it truly: it was too late for facts to matter. Nothing could stop the days of killing which lay ahead. The hour for peace was gone forever.

"No!" Numaga spit. "You will lead our women and children north to the land of Black Rocks when the whites come. In the lonely canyons, where men become lost and the spirit withers, they will be safe. Take all the food and water that can be carried."

"Listen," Clayton protested. "Let someone else do that. I

can talk with whoever is in charge of the U.S. Army, and maybe—''

''They will not listen! And I would not have you throw away your life.'' The powerful war chief's voice softened. ''Some must stay to take the women, children, and the old to safety. You will be responsible for this. It would not be good for you to kill the whites. Some may be your friends.''

He understood. Clayton knew he'd fight if the women and children were attacked. Fight to the death, if need be, to protect them. But to wait in ambush? He just wasn't certain. Numaga, in his wisdom, had sensed this and given him an honorable way out.

Clayton nodded. ''I will do as you say.''

The chief turned to the others. ''Tell our warriors this will be like an antelope hunt. We will act like we do not know they are here. When the whites come forward, their hearts will lift at the thought of easy victory, and like before, they will charge down into our karnees. A few will run to pull them closer. Then, when I signal with my pelican feather, three hundred of our warriors will attack when they are almost at our doors.''

The chief was sketching rapidly in the dirt, cutting bold, sweeping battle lines for Chief Natchez and the other council members to see. ''The mounted warriors will come at them like a giant arrowhead, and behind them will come our bowmen on foot.''

''Would it not be wiser to send them in from the sides?'' Chief Natchez asked.

''No. That is what was done before. They would remember. This time we shall drive them back and out of the meadow to the steep ridge, where I shall wait with those who use the white man's rifles. We shall be like the rocks. Still and unmoving. When the whites are driven past, we strike like rattlesnakes! Each warrior will fire as though his belly were hungry and his children starving. None shall miss!''

Clayton examined the drawn trap and felt his insides constrict when he thought of how many on both sides would die. ''It is wrong, this which will happen,'' he stated. ''It is the time of year when fish are to be speared, cooked, and dried. When the women and girls collect eggs from the nesting birds and the red berries await picking. When children laugh for the coming of spring and—''

''Go,'' Numaga said heavily. ''Go to Windflower, for the

days that come will bring you little happiness together. Remember, my friend, you must stay in the land of the Black Rocks until we return."

"And if you don't return?" Clayton gritted.

"Then the future of the people is in your hands, Clayton James. You will lead them to life—or death—as befits your wisdom."

Julia lay in her room, staring at the ceiling and wondering what she was going to do next. She'd given up hope of finding another job. Besides, every waking hour was filled with worry and doubt. Could she support herself and the baby? What would happen to the army that had ridden north under Colonel Hays and Captain Storey? If they were defeated, then surely there was nothing to stop the Paiutes from driving the whites from Sun Mountain. They might even yet be overrun.

But more than all these things, Julia thought about Clayton James. He'd told her about Windflower, but she'd also told him of her need. Maybe . . . maybe he would change his mind after seeing Numaga and come back to her. Julia prayed for this, yet feared the Clayton might have died from the bullet wound she'd seen him take outside Marshal Tillman's office.

The days had passed with agonizing slowness and Julia scarcely left her room except for meals.

"Julia! Julia, are you in there?" a rough but familiar voice called.

She'd been sleeping fitfully. The afternoon had almost gone when he yelled and began to pound on her door. In that first moment of awakening, Julia thought he'd come back to her. A smile formed on her lips and she cried, "Clayton!"

The door splintered open and Marshal Tillman, a Winchester rifle in his fists, crashed through. He glanced around and then lowered the weapon and said, "Clayton won't be coming. I'll be taking his place."

"Get out of here!"

He kicked the shattered door closed and sauntered over to gaze down at her. "What are you doing lying here in the dark in the middle of the day?"

"I feel awful. Weak and sick. Leave me along. Please."

Tillman swept the curtains aside and opened the window before slumping down beside her on the bed. "I don't know what I'm going to do with you, Julia. Here I've been gone only two weeks, and already you're failing."

He pulled the blankets off her and Julia's fingers curled like talons. "You'll have to kill me this time," she hissed. "I swear you will!"

"I do believe you mean that," he said matter-of-factly as his hand brushed her leg in a tender, soothing motion. "You've lost weight, Julia. A lot of weight."

When he pulled the blankets back over her, Julia's fingers unbent and she relaxed. He wasn't going to try to rape her again—at least not for the moment. Something was different. His eyes. Still an arresting green, but no longer bright with mirth and challenge—now they were dull and sunken deep into their sockets. Julia smelled him, and he was gunpowder and horseflesh and sweat. Bob Tillman *had* changed—the boyishness was gone. He'd aged two decades in two weeks.

The hardness in her voice drained away. "You haven't been eating so well yourself, have you?"

He shook his head, thumbed back his dusty gray Stetson and scrubbed at his bloodshot eyes. "No, it hasn't been easy. Eight days ago, we came to Pyramid Lake and they tried to draw us all down to their settlement; but it didn't work. Colonel Hays sent in a small detachment under Captain Storey."

Tillman drew a long breath. "Them boys didn't have a chance. When they reached those cone-shaped huts, the Indians poured out of them, and just as it looked like Storey was going to whip 'em good, hundreds more came riding out of a gully. They came in like an arrow and split Captain Storey's detachment as if they were melting butter. It was awful. We saw it happen from up on the ridge and damned if me and all the others didn't want to go to the rescue. But Colonel Hays said the first man who broke ranks was going to get back-shot."

Julia bristled. "You mean he just let Storey and his men be annihilated?"

"No, they retreated. Most all of 'em reached that narrow trail leading out of the meadow. When they got back on the ridge, Hays gave the order to charge. Right then, this big Chief Numaga and his warriors started firing rifles down at us off Pinnacle Peak, but we were moving fast and those cavalry boys had their sabers out and tore through the Indians like a sickle through old winter wheat.

"Our troopers advanced up Pinnacle Peak, where Numaga

and his sharpshooters were hiding, and them mountain howitzers started tearing up the chief's riflemen. When we met Captain Storey, the whole lot of us dismounted and formed a walking line. That did it! Those Indians mostly had arrows and spears, and we mowed 'em down with rifle fire. They couldn't stop us. We walked and fought clear back down to the meadow, and we killed the last of 'em in the village. Later, we burned it to the ground like they did William's Station. Someone told me they called them wood huts karnees. I don't know. But they burned like pine-pitch torches!''

Julia shut her eyes. She could almost picture the death and carnage as he described the battle. And what of Clayton and Windflower, Numaga and all the others? What of the old and the children—were they also killed in the heat of victory?

''Hell, Julia, don't go to crying on me. It had to be done and Hays told us not to kill the women and children. He didn't need to, though, 'cause they were gone.''

Tillman raised her chin up. ''I saw Captain Storey take a bullet right square in the chest. He was leading his men up Pinnacle Peak near the end of the shooting match. That big Chief Numaga was going crazy up above. Shouting and screaming and firing a rifle that looked like a toy in his hands.''

Bob Tillman clucked his tongue, marveling. ''You know,'' he said quietly, ''me and everyone else was aiming for him, but . . . but it was as if he was there and he wasn't. Then, after Captain Storey went down, his men were crazed for the killing of Numaga. They seemed to forget the other Indians, and all of 'em charged him. A lot of them died right there, but they got that big sonofabitch!''

''Numaga,'' she whispered. ''Clayton said he wanted peace.''

''Peace!'' Tillman's eyes were bright with hatred. ''He's the one caused it all! I saw him fall, get up, take another bullet, and fold up again. His warriors carried him away. Like Storey, he was hit bad. It sorta took the fight out of those Indians. They broke and ran and we lost 'em in the rocks when it started to get dark. But the very next morning, we buried Captain Storey to bugle and drums, along with the others who died. Then Colonel Hays set up patrols to hunt down any Indians left near the lake. We drove the survivors into the Black Rock Desert and they'll die there before we let 'em come out. It's finished.''

Julia *had* to know the question that burned in her mind, even though she knew it might provoke the marshal's fury. She forced her eyes up and looked into his worn face. "What about your job?" she whispered. "You said you were either going to arrest or shoot Clayton James."

"Damn!" he raged, leaping to his feet. "That's all you really care about, ain't it? You aren't sorry about the good men who died up on Pinnacle Peak to keep you and everyone else from being overrun by bloodletting savages. No, you don't give a damn about anything but that turncoat Indian lover of yours!"

His fists knotted and his whole body shook with a terrible inner battle. "I . . . I don't know why the hell I care what happens to you and that baby you're carrying. I swear I don't!"

"*Please*. Tell me!"

Something inside of him snapped, and in one powerful wrench he tore her out of bed and hurled her to the floor. A pain shot through her body; like a hot knife, it ripped deep inside and doubled her up in convulsions of pain.

He was instantly down on his knees beside her. "I'm sorry!" he cried. "Dear God, I don't know what got into me. Julia. Julia! Are you all right?"

He gently lifted her back onto the bed. Julia felt waves of pain, like circles in a pool, spreading outward into her extremities. Tillman was sponging her face with cool water, almost beside himself with guilt.

"I have to know," she panted heavily.

For a moment the damp cloth in his hand faltered; then he continued stroking her forehead. "Are you all right now?" he asked shakily.

"Yes," she lied.

"Okay, then," he said, inhaling deeply. "Clayton Jones is dead."

She writhed on the bedcovers with a new kind of pain, and he bent low and cradled her in his arms, saying, "I didn't kill him, Julia. I swear I didn't. They . . . they just found his body out there. He didn't make it back to Pyramid Lake that night he escaped from jail. He's dead. Forget him! Julia, I'll help you forget him. Give you and the child my name. I can make you happy! You have to trust me."

Julia bit off her reply. In a hundred years, Bob Tillman couldn't make her love him. She didn't understand why. He wasn't as handsome as Dade Taylor, yet he was an attractive man nonetheless. But . . . but how could she make herself fall in love with a man who had raped her, then forgot his temper and physically punished her? And even had he not done those things, Julia knew her heart would always remember Clayton.

Salty tears rivered down her cheeks as she tried to keep from crying and failed. With the news of Clayton's death, it was as if a tiny ray of sunshine and hope had been shut away forever. And so she cried with her heart and her body, knowing she would never really stop.

"Come on," he said gently, "it's not good for you to stay cooped up in a dark room. Besides, what about your precious job?"

She told him then, told him about how the Raneys had tricked her and smuggled watches and money into her purse. And how she'd been jailed and humiliated as well as publicly branded a thief and harlot.

As he listened, Bob Tillman's complexion grew scarlet and his emerald-green eyes lost their dullness to glittering purpose. When she was finished, he stood up and marched to her wardrobe.

"What do you want to wear?" he asked brusquely.

She didn't understand. "I'm not going anywhere."

"The hell you aren't, woman! Get out of that bed or I'll come in after you!"

Julia sat up fast, then wrapped the blankets protectively about her. The pain from her fall moments earlier returned, but she ignored it.

"Here," Tillman swore, yanking out a dress, "can you still wear this?"

"Yes, but—"

"Then put it on!" he shouted as he grabbed her bags and began stuffing things into them.

"What *are* you doing?"

He pivoted. "I'm checking you out of this place."

"And if I refuse?" She was angry now. Who did he think he was? Her owner?

"If you refuse, I'll arrest you on charges of helping Clayton James escape. That's enough to get you down to Carson City."

"I won't stand for this! I'll . . . I'll go to the sheriff here."

"Fine. Do that. He's my friend, remember? So come on and get dressed—or do you need my help?" he asked, advancing menacingly.

"No. I can do it."

Julia had never seen a man move so fast once he was set on

doing a thing. Before she had her dress buttoned, Bob Tillman had her entire trunk packed and downstairs to the lobby. She heard him order the desk clerk to send someone for a buckboard. Moments later, he was back and helping her down the stairs. Across the lobby they marched; then he steered her north up C Street. She kept glancing up at him, but his eyes were riveted ahead with grim determination.

"Where are you taking me?"

"You'll see."

At the Silver Exchange Mercantile, he shouldered inside and she tried to fight free but his grip was like an iron manacle on her arm. Down the long aisle, he dragged her with little resistance. Julia saw Harland Raney step through the back door. When he noticed them, he reacted with hatred.

That's when Bob Tillman let go of her arm and lunged forward. His big sinewy hands clamped together like a vise on Raney's thin gobbler neck and fairly jerked the squawking store owner off his feet.

Tillman's lips were a bloodless line as he shook Raney until the man's face was purplish and his eyes bulged.

"You lied about her, god damn your stinking hide! You planted that stuff and lied! Admit it. Admit it or, so help me, I'll choke you to death!"

Julia grabbed him by the forearms. "You're killing him," she cried. "Let go!"

"Admit it, I say!"

Julia did the only thing she could do. From the table she grabbed a sixteen-inch cast-iron frying pan and bashed Tillman alongside the head.

He faltered. A trickle of blood appeared over his ear. And slowly he let go, whispering, "Don't do that again, Julia. Don't ever hit me like that again."

Raney slumped, made a feeble attempt to escape, and found himself once more in Tillman's grip and heard him say, "One time is all I'm going to ask. Then I break your arms. You are going with me down to the *Territorial Enterprise* and you're going to beg the editor, Dan De Quille, to print a retraction, stating that you now realize you made an awful mistake about Miss Matson."

Raney shook his head and Tillman grabbed his arm and twisted it up to his shoulder blades as the man hollered in agony.

"All right. I'll do it! Please. Stop!"

The arm came down and Tillman shoved the merchant toward the front door. "Come on, Julia. After he sets this straight, I'm taking you out of this town."

She nodded quietly. There was something too powerful about this man to deny. And she was beaten, sick and demoralized by the death of Clayton. She could no longer fight, or even put up a token resistance. Besides, as Julia hurried along after Bob Tillman and they entered the newspaper office, she felt a deep, deep sense of vindication and even gratitude. Nothing, not even being acquitted in a trial, could have cleared her name and reputation except this—now, almost miraculously, she had both, and with it some pride and decency.

Dan De Quille was a tall, spare man whose daily prose in the young *Territorial Enterprise* was the delight of the west coast. No one knew more about the people of the Comstock than this outwardly grave chronicler of human events. And none could write about their everyday trials and tribulations with such wit and humor. Dan listened intently, a chilliness in his countenance toward Raney. By and by, he asked a few questions, and when finished, the newspaperman smiled coldly. "We all make mistakes, Mr. Raney, but in this case you seem to have nearly destroyed the reputation of a beautiful woman. I'd be more careful, sir, in the future."

Raney glanced at Bob and then asked plaintively, "Is that all?"

"Yeah. Get outta here."

Julia felt Bob take her arm and steer for the door. He wrenched it open. "Say, Dan," he called back, "I forgot to tell you another piece of news for your paper."

"I'm listening."

"You can write on your social page that Robert A. Tillman, U.S. marshal in Carson City, is marrying Julia Matson—today."

"Well, congratulations!" De Quille appeared genuinely shocked. "Would you care to give me any particulars? You know, like where the lovely lady grew up. Her family. Choice of wedding gown. Those kinda things."

Julia's eyes fell to the infant she carried—the innocent baby who needed a home, food, and protection. And she thought of her shattered dream of being Mrs. Clayton James.

"Julia? Dan asked you a question."

She glanced up, scrubbed the dampness from her eyes, and raised her chin high. "Just tell your good readers . . . tell them the bride has no family. She . . . she has no one."

11

The Black Rock Desert shimmered into a distance of hot and glaringly white alkali plains, scorched volcanic rock, and sun-withered sage. Clayton James stood on a hillock and peered around until his eyes had drunk in the full circle of dear land.

"It won't support the People much longer, Windflower. That spring down in camp is starting to dry up, and it makes the babies sick. We've got to leave here soon."

"I know. Numaga is well enough to travel. But where will we go now?"

Clayton knew the answer. They all did. For generations the tribe had managed to sustain its livelihood from Pyramid Lake. It was their home, the place where they were born and where they died. It was unthinkable that they could survive anywhere else.

"We cannot go back," Windflower told him gently as she read his mind. "The soldiers have remained beside the lake."

"Goddammit!" Clayton swore. "We can't stay in this desert. The animals are starving, the People are becoming thin in front of my eyes. Soon it will be fall, and then winter. Food must be gathered if we're to make it."

Windflower took his hand and he pulled her to him, feeling the bones of her ribs and hating it, because his woman was suffering from hunger. How long before the children and the old ones started to die? Another week? No, these were hardy people, and if the poor water held out, they would last at least another month. But no matter. If they went into autumn without storing food, they would all starve. Something had to be done. And quickly.

"Clayton James. Do not be so troubled. You are a strong, brave man. Everyone knows this. It is you and the long rifle which have kept our people in food."

"It's getting more difficult," he said tightly. "Last trip, we had to ride nearly up to the Oregon Territory for antelope. Everything north is just like this for a hundred miles."

He lifted his head as if to challenge the land, willing it to provide. A strong, hot wind blew the shaggy ends of his dark hair. He shook his fist at the desolation in bitter frustration. "They're using you to kill us slowly!" he cried. "But you will *not* have the satisfaction of bleaching our bones white as alkali! No! I swear, we are leaving."

Windflower held him tightly. There was great power in her man. Yet, his heart bled, as did that of Numaga, to see the passing days stagger the people with its terrible heat. And beyond the sanctuary of these canyons, mountains, and blind arroyos, the long-knives waited. Twice they had entered, only to be caught in Numaga's traps.

The Black Rock Desert spared the Paiutes from a quick death for a much slower one.

Clayton gently pushed the girl away. "I'm going to talk to Numaga and Natchez. They *have* to know that the man who waits with soldiers at Pyramid Lake will stay until we die. Last week, when we rode down there to scout, I saw him and knew I'd seen him before. Then, just this morning, I remembered his name. It's Colonel Frederick Lander."

"What kind of soldier is he?"

"I'm not sure," Clayton said uneasily. "I can't recall hearing much good or bad. He rode in my stage from Sacramento to Carson City one time. Seemed agreeable enough."

Windflower's expression said clearly that the assessment of Lander wasn't encouraging.

Clayton mopped his sweating face with a bandana. "Look, woman, I'm going to ask Numaga if I can go down and speak with Lander."

"No! They would shoot you on sight."

"The miners and those folks in Carson City would, but not the cavalry. I'll circle around and ride up from the south, so they think I'm bringing news from town. And even if someone on guard does recognize me . . ."

"Cut your face hair."

Clayton shook his head. "I can't."

Windflower laced her hands behind his neck. "Do you think my people do not know of the bear scars? They are marks of bravery. You should wear them proudly."

Clayton started to object. Maybe to an Indian such a facial disfigurement was to be worn with pride; yet, among white people. . . He stopped. He no longer cared about offending whites. He'd married an Indian and he'd chosen their life.

"That's the way you feel?"

She nodded gravely. "I do not want you to die by their hands. Let them think you are a new man. Husband of Windflower. I give you a new name."

A faint look of amusement crept into the corners of his pale blue eyes. "Let's hear it."

"Bear Claw Man."

He dug his fingers into his beard and felt the white-ridged scar tissue, and for the first time in his life he was ashamed of his vanity.

"All right, Windflower. I'll whack 'em off now, then go see Numaga."

"Bear Claw Man," Numaga said, looking deep into his eyes, "you have been good to my people. I cannot allow you to ride to this Colonel Lander alone."

"You must. There is no choice."

"We can attack. There are not so many soldiers as before."

"And not so many warriors, either," Clayton reminded him gently. "Also, I have seen, along with your other scouts, the fort they are building. Many of the tribe would die in the attack, and it would not be successful."

"Then go," Numaga said finally. "Tell this Lander we wish peace. But if they do not go from our land, we will continue to stop the Pony Express. To burn stations and steal their horses."

"I'll tell him that," Clayton promised. "They think they've beaten you, but it would take thousands of soldiers to drive us out of this desert—if they could find us. And they won't want that kind of war."

The chief smiled sadly. "It's a good thing they cannot find our tribe to see how quickly we will perish in our desert stronghold. Because if they could . . . they'd leave us alone, until we were no more.

"Go, Bear Claw Man. Judge this Lander through the eyes of a Paiute warrior. If his heart is true, bring us together."

Clayton excused himself, leaving the chief to brood quietly. Together he and Windflower gathered up his traveling things and an Indian pony to ride. The saddle he used was the one he'd stolen the night he'd been shot escaping from Carson City. It seemed like years ago that he'd stood outside the marshal's office and held Julia Matson. And, God forgive him, he'd even halfway promised that he might come back someday.

Now, he couldn't, ever. His name was Bear Claw Man, and though his skin was white where he'd shaved, soon it would be a deep mahogany brown, except for the tendonlike scars. He would never go back to see Julia and witness the shock as she saw his disfigurement. But . . . but, dammit, why couldn't he forget that woman! The way she looked and felt. A hundred nights he'd lain with Windflower and cursed himself because, staring into the darkness, he'd seen Julia.

Clayton angrily scrubbed the ridges on his cheek. He would never cover them again with a beard. Thse scars, and the look they would evoke in the whites, was reminder that he was Bear Claw Man. Husband of Windflower. Paiute warrior until death!

"Colonel Lander," the guard called at the closed tent flap. "There is a visitor who demands to see you at once."

"Who is it, Corporal?"

"He says . . . he says his name is Bear Claw Man, sir. And that he's a Paiute!"

Colonel Lander piled out of the tent fast, then froze. "You're a white." His eyes seemed to be magnetized by the line of ragged scars.

"I was, Colonel. But now I am one of the People. I have come in hopes of a treaty."

"Come inside . . . ah . . . Bear Claw Man. Are you a spokesman for Numaga?"

"Yes."

"Good! Very good. I'm sick of this desert heat, and it's costing the U.S. government a fortune to keep us provisioned out here. Listen well, there is nothing I or my officers or men would like more than to leave Numaga this damned dead lake, just get the hell out of here and back to civilization."

Before stepping inside, Clayton looked about. "You say one thing. I see another."

"You mean this stockade we are building?" Colonel Lander asked grimly. "If we make peace, they come down. They're just for temporary protection, and something to keep my troops in condition."

"How can I believe that?"

"Easy," came the short reply. "Numaga agrees to stop all hostilities. Let the Pony Express go through, we rope and pull the walls down before leaving. How's that for a guarantee, Bear Claw Man, or whatever the hell your name is?"

Clayton James nodded with satisfaction. He appreciated this officer with his abrupt, straight way of putting things. "I like it fine, Colonel."

He thought of the People, of their washboard ribs and how he could see the knots of Windflower's spine when she bent at work. Truly, very few months remained. It was time to send scouts into the desert mountains near the lake. They would return, carrying piñon boughs upon which were the first ripe cones. All the People would gather then. He, beside Windflower, would watch the celebrating. The pine-nut dance was an age-old ritual and would last from dusk to dawn. Prayers would be thrown at the heavens, asking to protect the cones from sickness. Afterward, as sunrise washed across the lake and the earth beyond, the People would begin the harvest, and with it, the tribe's lifeblood would be replenished once more.

This was the hour. It had taken Clayton almost a week to negotiate this meeting between Colonel Lander and Numaga. The day was a scorcher, and several hours before, when Clayton had presented the two men to each other, Numaga had almost ruined hope by saying, "I will look hard at you first. When the sun is low, we will talk."

And so they'd pitched little canvas shelters over the brush and squatted in the dirt to sweat and slap at flies until the evening. Then Numaga rose and the council began with a ceremonial pipe which passed through Clayton's hands five times.

Lander spoke first. "I have come to listen to all Chief Numaga has to tell the Great Father of the whites. I shall listen well, but I am only a listener who makes no promises. When the Great Father hears your words, he will know what to do."

Numaga smiled with sardonic humor. "You can write President Buchanan and tell him we want only peace. But this is not what has been given us. Ten, twelve snows have fallen since the first white man passed over our land. Then they were few, and they were poor and hungry. We feed. More come. Take our land. Use our women. And always they make promises that they will give us flour and food, blankets, powder and lead that we might hunt the antelope they drive far away with their own guns. No promises have been kept. All lies."

Numaga's teeth were clenched. "I am glad *you* do not make white man's promises. I would not believe."

Lander flushed deeply with anger and started to rise, but Clayton's iron hand held him firm. Even so, his words were addressed not to Lander, but to Numaga.

"Brave War Chief of the Paiutes, you have spoken out of pain rather than wisdom. I understand, because the People have seen their lands taken, their food and wealth destroyed. Even so, this man who would make peace with you has proved he is not like others, with easy words meaning nothing. Listen well, Numaga. And guard your anger—for the People!"

Numaga's reaction was frozen in an impassive expression. But Clayton knew the chief would listen now. If he were not going to do so, Lander would be dead.

"Chief Numaga, I know of your anger," Lander said quietly. "I, too, was angry when I saw the graves of those who rode with Major Ormsby and died. But that is past. Promises have been broken, and I would not try to tell you they will not be again. But they must be given—and accepted—in trust. For if they are not, there can be no hope of peace, of justice. If you will give me your word to call off your warriors from attacking the Pony Express and wagon trains, I will seek a just peace and will leave your village so that you can return."

"To be trapped and slaughtered?" Numaga asked. "Over the mountains, the others agreed to such terms. They accepted the promises of the white man and found them empty, like their bellies. When they got hungry and stole some cattle for food, the whites came and murdered."

Lander scrubbed at his face. It was an effort for him to speak. "If you are talking about what happened recently over in Mendocino County, yes, that is true. But this . . . this is different. The land here is not good for raising cattle or farming and so it is not wanted by the white men. The fish in your lake are also unwanted by the whites, and while it is true that your piñon pine trees were cut on the Comstock, they will not be touched out here."

He leaned forward intently. "I do not believe I mislead you by saying such an outrage as happened in California would never occur here."

Numaga's eyes bored into Clayton's, and the questioning was evident. "You must try," Clayton said.

"Bear Claw Man. If this is a trap, if later we are slaughtered, are you strong enough to live with those words?"

"Yes."

His chin dipped. Numaga unfolded gracefully and stood. "I will send runners north to old Chief Winnemucca and east along the Humboldt to tell of a peace. If your promise is true, we will bring our women and children from the dead land of Black Rocks."

"Excellent!" Lander said, breaking into a smile. "I have, I believe, demonstrated my trust of honor by agreeing with Bear Claw Man to come alone. Now I ask you to do the same and accompany me to the soldiers' place by the Carson River. It is called Fort Churchill, and I want you to meet and tell the soldiers there that you are acting in peace."

"Only if I go, too. As an intermediary," Clayton said flatly.

Lander nodded. "I don't know who you really are, Bear Claw Man, and I don't care. As far as I'm concerned, you've just saved both money and lives—white and red. Hell, yes, you can come! I want to ask you some questions. For instance—"

Clayton silenced him with a single wave. "My name is Bear Claw Man. I am married to Numaga's sister, Windflower. And I will kill any soldier at Fort Churchill who thinks he, too, might have an Indian for breakfast and his pony to ride."

Lander blushed deeply. "Yes," he whispered, "we heard about that. I'm deeply sorry. With your permission, I'll leave now for the fort. I want to make dead certain they understand, and that no trooper decides he wants a place in the history texts."

"Colonel Lander." Numaga's voice was edged with emotion. "Tell your President we will fight no more for as long as there are stars in the sky—if the white man keeps his promise."

"I'll tell him. I'll tell all of 'em." He pivoted to go. "From the depths of my soul, I pray we have made a lasting peace. Thank you, War Chief Numaga, and you who now choose to be known as Bear Claw Man."

Julia Tillman knew her time was very near, and the dread within her loomed greater each day. To bear an illegitimate child was a sin, yet to deny it love was unforgivable and would damn one's soul to hell. For a child, she believed, is a precious, wonderous thing, pure in its innocence. The child had not asked to be conceived and it cared not for the pettiness of the world into which it was born. A baby demanded love and care because, without them, it was the most helpless creature on earth. And deep in her heart, Julia believed an infant would know if it was unwanted; once this was perceived, its spirit would wither.

And so, as the day of her baby's arrival grew ever nearer, Julia tried to will herself to love the child she carried. Because of it, she cared about eating enough food and getting enough rest, in spite of Bob Tillman's frequent nocturnal demands upon her distended body.

It was just such a night, when he rolled over to force himself upon her, that Julia finally objected. "It hurts, Bob! You must wait until after the baby."

He ignited the bedside lamp. "It's hard, woman. We only been married a while, and I can't seem to get my fill."

Julia forced the anger out of her voice. Since their marriage, she had learned very well how volatile his temper could be. Yet, he could be reasoned with, provided his feelings weren't damaged.

"Bob," she told him, "you know that I want to. It's only for a short time. I'll be as happy as you when I'm not so . . . pregnant."

"You will?"

Julia nodded.

The tightness in his body melted away, and with it, the anger. Suddenly he was tender. "I'll wait. It's just that I've got to leave for a couple of days and . . . well, you can understand."

Julia felt a stab of alarm. "Oh, Bob! You can't leave. Not when the baby is so near!"

"I don't want to go," he hedged. "Dammit, I sure don't. Even if the kid ain't my own. But I couldn't do much here anyways. Tomorrow, after I go, you see the doctor again. Tell him about those pains you been getting."

She nodded, afraid to speak because of her own disappointment. Julia didn't love this man who'd taken her by force, yet she knew he did love her in his own hard way. And he'd protect her. Fight for her welfare. No one else would do that except for Clayton—and he was dead.

"I got no choice in the going, Julia," he murmured apologetically, shifting closer to her and stroking her leg under the covers. "Like I said, I might be gone for several days."

Julia made herself lie still, although she could feel what he was working up to.

"Bob, please, you could hurt the baby!"

His hand froze on her hip and she could sense his quick anger, but she didn't care. "Why do you have to go just now? Can't it wait a little longer?"

"No," he snapped. "It's in the line of duty. I've got to ride out to Fort Churchill tomorrow. It's about that treaty they're signing. Since it's taking place in my jurisdiction, I gotta sign the thing."

"Yes, I suppose you do," she whispered. "I haven't heard much about it since that first day when it caused so much excitement." Julia tried to get his mind distracted with official business. "How did it happen?"

"Hell, woman, I don't know but what I've heard. Seems this Colonel Lander was fetched up to the Paiute territory."

"He went alone? Wasn't that rather foolish?"

"I think so," Tillman admitted. "But the way I hear it, there was this white fella all dressed in skins and beads that set the whole thing up."

Julia blinked. "Who was he?"

"Nobody knows. But they say he's big and ugly. Calls himself Bear Claw Man."

Something began to quake deep inside Julia. "What else?"

Bob Tillman seemed to find the line of questioning of no interest. His hand returned to stroke her hip.

"What else?" she repeated sternly.

"Who knows? I'll see him tomorrow. Only other thing I've heard is that everyone in Nevada thinks he's some kind of savior. Seems he got Numaga to agree to stop his raiding parties and quit burning out the Pony Express stations. That mail yesterday was the first they've let through in over a month. I hear it's damn near bankrupted Russell, Majors, and Waddell, trying to keep things going. Horses stolen, men run off and worse, stations burned to the ground. They say this Paiute war has cost them more than one hundred thousand dollars."

"Who is Bear Claw Man?"

Bob Tillman grinned. "Who cares?" He pulled her close against his chest. "Come on, woman, I might be gone for a week."

"Just tell me," she pleaded. "I'm curious to know, Bob. Tell me and . . . and then we can stop talking."

She could feel his desire, even hear it in his voice. "I don't know why you care, but they tell me this fella has these awful-looking scars running across his left cheek."

Her body went ice cold. She began to shake.

"The story is that he's married to the prettiest squaw in Nevada. Numaga's own sister, who's called Windflower."

Julia screamed inside.

"Now that I've told you everything, like you said, the talking is over."

Julia tried to push him away. He'd lied to her! Clayton wasn't dead! She wanted to cry out her happiness, but there was enough reason left somewhere deep inside to know that Clayton's life was safe only if he wasn't recognized by men such as her husband. Was that possible? She thought so, because she'd felt those terrible ragged scars and knew he'd covered them with a beard because they would dominate the eyes of anyone who saw him. And if he was clad in Paiute skins, the transformation might be complete.

Bob's hard, insistent body lifted to mount her and his animal passion stirred a deep hatred inside her. Maybe Clayton had heard of her marriage and it had driven him into taking Windflower as his squaw. Bob's lie, in that one blistering-white moment, seemed to have killed any chance she'd ever have for her own happiness.

"Get away from me!" she cried, raking at his face. "Get away!"

In the flickering lamplight, the marshal recoiled in shock. He loomed above her, then touched his face and stared at the blood she'd raised.

"God damn you! The baby ain't no cause for that!"

He slapped her—hard. Once. Twice. Three times.

Julia's fingers curved and stabbed at his eyes.

It was a mistake. She should have submitted. Her action sparked his rage as he straddled her body and punched her again and again until she could no longer resist. And as suddenly as his fury was born, it died. Bob Tillman collapsed in ashamed tears on top of her.

Julia vaguely realized he was crying, but it did not matter. Her entire body seemed to glow hot with fire. And down in the pit of her womb, where the child lay, she felt a deathly stillness that blotted out every other feeling—even that of Bob Tillman as he wiped away the tears and gently made tender, frantic love on her body.

Clayton James tightened the cinch of his saddle and felt good as he prepared to leave Fort Churchill with Numaga. The talk and ceremony of signing were done, and he was glad to depart knowing the People had gotten fair treatment. All of Pyramid Lake and the surrounding country was to be their reservation. The military were to police it and remove any white squatters who might choose to settle there in the future. Also, Clayton had been insistent that the government agree to put aside twenty thousand acres of valuable timber near Verdi for the tribe.

The government, in payment for lands taken, would build a timber mill near Verdi, and Clayton was very optimistic that this would provide his tribe with a good source of income for generations. And as a final gesture of good intentions, Colonel Lander had agreed to let the Indians choose their own white agent.

Numaga and Clayton huddled over that for some time. In the end, they'd agreed that Long Beard Warren Wasson, a staunch friend of the Paiute and fearless mountain men, would be acceptable. Everything seemed promising. Peace was a prayer.

"Hey, Mr. Bear Claw Man!"

Clayton turned to see the U.S. Marshal. And in that moment, he knew Bob Tillman had not been fooled by his new name and appearance.

"What do you want?"

"To talk. In private."

"About what?"

"About Julia. My wife."

Clayton's mouth twitched. Without another word, he pivoted and stalked away until he came to a halt some distance from the others.

"This suit you?"

Tillman's hand was very close to his gun. "I oughta kill you, Clayton James."

"This knife in my belt says you'd never have a chance," Clayton drawled. "Better stick to talk, Marshal."

"Julia almost died a couple nights ago. She was calling your name."

Clayton felt the strength wash out of his legs. "Why?"

"'Cause your son was born dead!"

Clayton's hand blurred downward and the bowie knife flashed up. Before Tillman quite realized it, cold steel furrowed the skin across his belly and a trickle of blood rivered under his belt.

"Speak plain or I'll gut you like a deer."

Tillman swallowed noisily. He was scared, but there was an angry meanness in him. "She *told* me it was yours. She loved you, but I said you were killed that night. Shot dead when you raced out of Carson City."

"Go on!"

"You *are* dead. As far as my wife knows, you no longer exist. Do you understand that?"

Clayton lowered the knife. He felt helpless and beaten, yet managed to ask, "You treatin' her right?"

"Yes."

"You'd better. Or I swear I'll hear of it and skin your hide."

Bob Tillman backed up. His eyes sizzled with hatred. "I'm warning you, Clayton. If you ever get tired of your squaw and come sneakin' around Julia, I'll see you hang."

Clayton turned to leave, and as he passed, there was a dead calm in his words. "We've each said our piece. You treat that woman right, like she deserves, I'll never come by. She can . . . she can think I'm dead. But if you beat her, I'll come to life so as to take yours."

He left then. Left with the sickness deep in his belly and a realization that Julia Matson really had loved him—and that, God forgive him, he'd loved her. But as far as Julia was concerned, he was a corpse.

12

In the months following Glenn Donovan's successful use of the steam engine, the Ophir Mine prospered. Deeper and deeper into Sun Mountain the miners went, angling now down and westward as Dade Taylor had prophesied. The small fifteen-horsepower steam engine was coupled with another of equal size so that one pumped and the other did nothing but pull up the ore carts.

Production soared. Within hours of the steam engine's initial demonstration, buyers were rushing over the Sierras to purchase similar equipment. And with the stockholders' approval, Glenn spent long hours advising other mine operators about the complexities of laying track and suction pipe. Gone were his initial self-consciousness and lack of confidence. He had become *the* expert on Comstock mine engineering and the use of steam. And when he wasn't down in the murky caverns, he was studying his engineering books, applying the laws of physics, and always struggling to improve mine safety through a better way of timbering.

In the first four months of steam production, his share of increased profits was minimal due to the capital investments required to finance the innovations he had incorporated. But now the Ophir was netting well in excess of four thousand dollars a month. Bevis handed him his first overage money—three hundred dollars—and he went crazy with excitement and rushed out and bought Fay Taylor a pretty cloak for the coming winter.

Not that Fay couldn't afford her own these days. She'd become a sensation on the Comstock and her frequent performances were always packed with avid admirers.

No, Glenn thought as he strode down the Ophir tunnel, everything was going remarkably well—better than he could ever have expected. They were now working at a depth of 170 feet and carving into a solid ore body so rich it defied belief. Tons and tons of silver and gold! The silver vein alone was forty-five feet wide, thicker than ever seen before in the history of underground mining.

The problem was bringing it to the surface. The traditional doorframe timbering just wouldn't hold up the immense underground caverns in which they needed to work for extraction. Millions of pounds of rock and the ever-dangerous oozing clay created enormous pressures. Trees were not long or thick enough to bear the suspended weight.

Glenn came to a halt at the bottom of the shaft in a cavern two hundred feet square. Ahead of him, he watched a team of miners labor at the wall of silver ore with pick and shovel; Bevis had three crews working around the clock. Glenn noted their progress. His brow furrowed as he studied the hanging ceilings.

Cy Peterson approached. "Mr. Donovan, I'm telling you we can't go much deeper or expand this cave. There's nothing holding it up."

Glenn nodded. He knew damn good and well they'd been pushing their luck. Right now he could feel sweat running down his back under his coat. The deeper they went, the hotter the air; it became steamy and putrid. Four days earlier, they'd punched into a small pocket of hot water, and one miner had been scalded badly. Accidents like that were unavoidable; having the wall bury a dozen was not.

He finished his inspection. "Something has to be done, Cy. Look at the silver! It's just hanging off the walls and roof. Yet, if we start pulling it down, the whole thing will follow."

"So what do we do?" The superintendent walked over to one of the doorframe timberings. "These things won't keep us from being buried."

"Of course not," Glenn said testily. "We need a better system, and I'm not enough of an engineer to come up with it."

Cy Peterson looked at him strangely. "Don't take it so hard, Glenn. Bevis and the others have you running day and night with the machinery and laying new tracks."

"No more," Glenn said flatly as a pair of brawny miners finished loading another cart and yanked a bell for the cart to be pulled to the surface.

"Do me a favor, Cy."

"Sure. Name it."

"Go up and find Mr. York. Tell him I'm closing things down when this shift is over. I want him and as many of the other shareholders down here as he can round up in the next hour."

"Are you certain?" Cy Peterson looked dubious. "They're going to scream like they was stuck."

"Can't be helped." Glenn shrugged. "I'll wait right here."

He fished out a pad and pencil and began to draw angles and rough diagrams. Maybe if they placed the timbering . . . He quickly wadded up the paper and threw it away in disgust. Dammit anyway! He needed Deidesheimer—a *real* engineer.

"Cy, what do you . . . ?"

The man was already gone. Disappeared up and out of the tunnel. Glenn forgot him and returned to the same old problem, knowing he was in over his head—tackling something too big for him.

He wasn't aware of exactly when it began. Just a tremor in the floor. Then silence as the picks and shovels froze. Suddenly they heard a loud yell float down the tunnel. Everyone jumped as the timbers began to squeal in protest and then snap like brittle bones.

"The tunnel!" he shouted. "Get back!"

Instantly his warning cry was drowned out in cries of terror as the miners stampeded toward the only avenue of escape. Glenn saw two dash headlong into the long tunnel, their arms and legs pumping like pistons. All at once the weak surface light was snuffed away. There was a tremendous blast of compressed air that exploded into the cavern and knocked men over like clay statues. It hurled them with indiscriminate savagery into the rock wall, breaking their bones, tearing their head-worn carbide lamps away, and then leaving them battered and scared in the total darkness.

Much later, Glenn pushed himself up onto his elbows and coughed violently in the dusty blackness.

Someone moaned.

"Don't anyone move," Glenn said raggedly.

Minutes stretched by, and when the rock ceased to tremble, Glenn lit his carbide and peered at the others. Fear was etched deeply on their grit-coated faces. Only the whites of their eyes and teeth shone in the beam of his lamp.

"Is everyone all right?"

"No!" a voice gasped. "I'm hurt bad."

The voice was shattered with anguish, and Glenn hurried over to a young man who'd been thrown against a wall with such force the top of his scalp was badly torn and bleeding profusely. Glenn motioned one of the crew over, and a compress was quickly applied.

"If he dies, he'll be the lucky one among us," a voice grated with bitterness.

"Shut up!" Glenn snapped. "We've got water, and each of you has a lunch pail of food. There's enough air in this cavern to last maybe a week. We can survive."

Someone else lit his carbide, and Glenn told him to turn it off. They'd use them one at a time until all were gone.

"Go to hell," a burly miner rasped. "We're as good as dead men, and that's a fact. There is over two hundred feet of tunnel between us and daylight. It'll take months to get here!"

The man was almost hysterical. Glenn stood up and walked

quickly to his side. Over the months since arriving with Fay, he'd grown accustomed to regular meals, and by that very fact, had undergone a striking physical transformation. He was solid now, layered with smooth muscle. Once he'd seemed ungainly because of his height and angularity; now his stride was graceful.

"Take it easy, Ernie," he soothed. "We don't know the whole tunnel fell in. Maybe it's just a few yards that have to be cleared.

"You're crazy! We're dead men and—"

Glenn's fist connected on the man's jaw, dropping him in an unconscious heap.

"Someone get a rope and tie him up. Shove a handkerchief into his mouth." Glenn moved over to where the tunnel had been, and he stood poised beside the rocks for nearly an hour before he heard a distant concussion. That would be Cy Peterson and a rescue party blasting away the infill. They were a long, long way off. One hundred feet—maybe all the way up to the surface; it was impossible to judge.

He pivoted. "I can hear them," he said, trying to sound optimistic. "They're working like hell this very minute to get us out. But no matter how hard they work, it won't be soon enough unless we move rock to meet them."

"But that'll take up oxygen faster!"

"True." Glenn snatched up a pick, drove it into the rubble, and grunted. "But that's the gamble we take. So let's get to work."

He drove them by example. Hour after hour, they slammed and tore at the rubble. Glenn's carbide lamp died, then another and another, as men lost track of time. The work was slow, made even more dangerous by the shattered timbers buried in the fallen rock. Sometimes, just when it seemed the excavation would go more easily, they'd feel the earth shudder as tons of new rock fell to replace that which they'd just hauled back into the cavern.

And at last the final carbide lamp died and they were plunged into the most absolute darkness found in this world.

"Who's got a match?" Glenn stared into nothingness. Waited for an answer.

"I do."

"Then light it, man. We'll find the candles and get back to work."

The match flared and died. Glenn felt a crawling fear as the man lit another, then said, "They're wet. I laid my shirt down, and you know how damp this place is."

"Who else?" Glenn turned blindly around in a circle.

"You know the rules, Mr. Donovan. No smoking underground. We all light our carbides topside. Ain't no reason for matches down here. They can touch off explosions."

Glenn shook his head and fought away despair. He took a deep breath and said, "Then, boys, we're just going to have to sit tight until help comes. We sure can't be pulling rock in the dark; someone would get buried in a hurry."

They had plenty of water, though it was hot and tasted like rotten eggs. And one by one they crawled and dragged themselves to the upper end of the cavern and listened to the dull vibrations that were coming to them from above. Hours slipped into days, days uninterrupted by light or air or change of any kind. It was as though they were suspended in a frozen black crystal of ice.

"Whose watch is that ticking?" a man yelled, startling them all. "It's driving me crazy!"

"Take it easy," Glenn breathed.

"Then tell whoever it is to stop that gawddamn watch from ticking or I'll come and do it myself!"

The watch stopped. Silence, like the darkness, became absolute, and Glenn would have preferred the watch sound to the total absence of noise between outside vibrations.

The food ran out. No one protested. No one talked at all anymore. Only listened. At first they'd kept telling each other that the sounds from the tunnel were getting much louder each day. But now . . . now they'd grown weary of the promise that never became a reality.

In the absence of food came the dreams of food. Meat and beans and flapjacks with maple syrup. They tortured themselves in the way of starving men. And once, out of the deep hopeless silence, a bloodcurdling shriek pierced their hearts. It ended in dead silence, and as the hair on their necks stood on end, it repeated itself. Suddenly it died in wild laughter.

"Who is that?" Glenn called. "Answer me!"

More shrieking. Higher, louder, almost inhuman. Then another sound that all identified as running feet. A sickening thud of flesh on rock.

Glenn cursed and lunged into the blackness. He *had* to stop the man!

But it was like clutching at a ghost, and the running feet scrambled frantically away. Again the heavy breathing, then the sound of lungs collapsing and a cry of pain.

"Get him!" Glenn bellowed. "He's down!"

Men cursed, grappled with each other in blindness. More running, and that eerie, tortured shriek which culminated in a dull crack like a melon splattering on the street. And afterward there was no sound at all.

Glenn Donovan clenched his fists until his entire body was rigid. Then, when he was certain he was under control, he whispered, "No more silence in here. From now on, we are going to talk to keep from going crazy. I'll begin with the story of my life. I'll tell you everything I ever did or remember. When my voice goes, someone else will take over, and so on, until we're released."

"What about whoever . . . ?"

His answer was flat and decisive. "Whoever it was—leave him be. If he's still alive, he's beaten himself into merciful unconsciousness. None of us need a wild man's lunacy."

Glenn thought back to the early days of his childhood. "My earliest friends," he began, "were the drunks at my father's saloon, who used to talk to me because only a small kid would listen to them anymore. My father . . ."

Seven men told their life stories before the rescue team broke through the topside plug of rocks and cautiously moved thirty yards to the final barrier. It wasn't thick, and they labored furiously because time was running out and they feared another cave-in.

Like swarming ants they worked until at last the final rock was cast aside.

Glenn saw a beam of light pierce into the cavern and felt an incredibly cool and fresh current of air brush his face. He roughly scrubbed away tears, but he needn't have, for they were on each of the survivors' cheeks. Two employees had died running through for the tunnel mouth. But the one that made Glenn and his companions shudder was the man who'd gone insane among them and had finally received mercy in the form of a broken neck.

Fay Taylor and Bevis York were standing at the Wells Fargo office when Glenn arrived with his small trunk.

"I don't like this," Bevis said. "You've been out of that mine only three days. That's not long enough to recover from that kind of ordeal."

"I'll be all right. There will be plenty of time to rest on the trip over to San Francisco."

Bevis frowned. "Are you certain it's necessary for you to go personally? I could simply telegraph him a very generous offer and—"

"No." Glenn was firm but willing to explain. "Philip Deidesheimer has his own successful practice and he doesn't like to travel. It's going to take some persuasion."

"Can you do it?"

"I think so. What I've got to do is present him with a few of my own ideas on a new timbering system. Then he'll point out their weaknesses, of which I'm already well aware—and I'll challenge him to come up with something better." Glenn smiled broadly. "It should work. Philip can't resist a challenge. He'll seize it like a bulldog, and I'll drag him back with the bone in his teeth."

"Good!" Bevis York looked toward Fay apologetically. "I know you want to say good-bye to her last, so I'll come right to the point."

"Let me guess first, Mr. York. You very much want me to find Holly and Dade and persuade them to come back."

Bevis smiled sheepishly. "I miss Holly constantly," he confided. "Tell her I mean to bury past feelings and accept Mr. Taylor as my son-in-law. I just hope they haven't sailed to the east coast or to Europe."

Fay laughed. "If I know my brother, they're staying at the Barbary Hotel in Portsmouth Square and living it up in grand style."

Bevis frowned. "They can't keep that nonsense up forever. Find them, Glenn. Bring them back with Mr. Deidesheimer. I need my daughter, and the whole Comstock needs an improved system of timbering."

Bevis didn't have to tell him how important the German mining engineer was to the future of Virginia City. Since the cave-in, the Ophir Mine had been sealed for being too dangerously unstable. Men were thrown out of work and soon there would be other mine accidents and layoffs. Next time, perhaps many lives would be forfeited instead of the three Ophir employees.

When Bevis York shook his hand and walked away, Fay

said, "He's very fond of you, Glenn. It shows in the way he speaks and acts. I can tell he deeply regrets that you didn't fall in love with Holly."

Glenn watched the stagecoach driver do a final check on the harnesses. It was about time to roll. "Fay, Bevis has been mighty good to me, but no matter how good, I could never feel about Holly the way I do about you."

She beamed. Stepped in close. "I liked you the first time we met," she declared firmly. "You set my leg and you didn't take advantage."

"Maybe," he teased, "my brain was a little froze up."

Her eyebrows lifted in mock surprise. "Be honest with yourself, Glenn Donovan! You were skinny then, but plenty strong enough to have your way. No, you were too fine a man then—as now. And I knew you'd soon amount to something. This overage thing you have with the Ophir and some of the other mines you've put steam into is going to make you a wealthy man, isn't it?"

"I don't know." That was the honest truth. If they could come up with a safe way to timber the vast caverns below . . . if the immense bonanza they'd touched held up . . . if . . . "There's a lot of things have to go right first, my girl."

"But they will!" Fay placed her hands on his broad shoulders. "Glenn, you're going to have money, as you've already gotten respect, from everyone of importance on the Comstock. You don't *need* to become an engineer anymore."

He stiffened. Looked deep into her eyes and knew she wasn't kidding. "Fay! The money has *nothing* to do with my dream. You must know that?"

"Oh, I do. I do," she said quickly. "But I mean . . . well, now that you are respected and no longer poor, becoming an engineer isn't so important. Glenn, you could *hire* them."

He removed her fingers from his coat, not liking what she'd said. "You still don't understand. Money, prestige—they're not what I'm after. I want to *do* things."

She was wounded. Her eyes could not watch his own, and when she tried to pull away, he gripped her tightly. "Fay. Tell me about your own dream—is it all just money and applause? They're nothing but trappings."

"And what if it were!" she stormed. "There's nothing wrong with either fame or fortune. I need them. They're important to me!"

He was shaken. "But surely they aren't enough!"

"What else is there?" she cried. "For me, I mean. Oh, sure. You can become the great engineer. And so you build monuments—lasting monuments out of wood or iron and mortar. And for a hundred years your work will stand for all to see and praise. They'll cry, 'Look at that magnificent trestle! An engineering marvel. Glenn Donovan built that.' "

He shook her hard. "Stop it, Fay!"

"I will not! Don't you see? When *I* perform there is *nothing* left for tomorrow. Nothing. When the applause dies, it's over until next time. And a performer does not have so many 'next times'!"

She stepped back, her eyes glinting with fire and fury. "Know this, Glenn. I'm in it exactly for those 'trappings,' as you so arrogantly put it."

Glenn took a deep, ragged breath. "I'm sorry to hear that. I thought we were both aiming for something higher."

She slapped him. Hard. And there were tears running down her cheeks when she sobbed a good-bye and ran.

He might have caught her and said something. Anything. It was terribly wrong. They'd just misunderstood each other. Yet, before he could react, the Wells Fargo driver yelled to load up. Glenn's heart told him to hell with the coach, go find her and settle this now. Reason spoke otherwise. Let some time pass, then mend their differences.

Glenn boarded with a troubled feeling. It occurred to him that less than a year ago he'd arrived on the Comstock flat broke and dressed in rags; now he was leaving wearing a fine suit and with a wallet and traveling money. So what! Back then, on that cold spring day when they'd first viewed Nevada, Fay Taylor was his girl and they'd shared a dream. Now it appeared they really hadn't shared anything at all.

As the stage lurched away, Glenn felt much poorer than when he'd arrived.

Glenn turned and pretended to look at Philip Deidesheimer's view of San Francisco Bay. It would not do to have the man notice his amusement as he baited the engineer's hook. "I understand, Philip, why a man such as yourself wouldn't go out of his way to needlessly jeopardize a well-established reputation. Why accept the risk?"

"What!" the powerful German roared. "Donovan, are you

forgetting that I am the finest mining engineer in America? And what is this you say about 'jeopardizing my reputation'?"

Glenn feigned confusion. "Well, Philip, I hoped only to spare you embarrassment. After all, the Comstock mining is totally unlike anything you've ever faced or will again. Quite frankly, I consider the problem insoluble."

"Nonsense! Didn't I teach you a good engineer never accepts defeat? He may design something imperfect—that is forgivable because we are so, *but*, whatever he does accomplish should be an improvement of the science, learning from the mistakes of his peers!"

Deidesheimer twisted the tips of his mustache. He was a short man, a trifle overweight, but every inch alive with dynamic energy that was a marvel to behold. He raised his index finger professorially. "Now, what do we know so far about the science of underground engineering?"

Glenn told him as much as he'd been able to learn, while Deidesheimer nodded, then said, "So, this standard rectangular structure is no good."

"Correct."

"Because of the oozing clay?"

"Yes."

"And the great depths to which you must go?"

"Again, yes."

Deidesheimer's eyes glinted mischievously. "Then there is only one solution."

Glenn leaned forward. This man's reputation wasn't built on half-baked answers. "You mean you have the solution?"

"Yes. Cover up the shaft and forget it!"

Deidesheimer erupted into wild gales of laughter. It was several minutes before he regained enough control to speak. "My young friend, I could not resist the joke. You forgive?"

"Of course. But . . ."

"I know. I know. Something must be done, and quickly. If you will instruct this Bevis York to pay my normal consulting fees, I will complete several smaller tasks and come at once."

"By the end of the week." Glenn extracted a large envelope from his inside coat pocket and handed it to the engineer. "It's your ticket and usual fees, paid in advance. Also, you will notice that Mr. York has enclosed an extra thousand dollars in consideration of 'prompt attention,' as he put it."

The German carefully counted the money, and Glenn saw

the smile in his eyes. Though Deidesheimer would never admit it, he did enjoy spending money.

"I think, Glenn, I will get along very nicely with your employer. Tell him I'll be on the Wells Fargo stage this Friday."

"Good! Are there any instruments, machines, or tools I should have ready?"

"No," Deidesheimer said confidently. "I will bring what is necessary and vital to solve this type of 'insoluble' problem."

"And that is?"

"This brain," Deidesheimer said with a wink.

Glenn had one more stop, and that was the Barbary Hotel. Situated a block up from the bay, past Montgomery Street, it was the hub of San Francisco. Ranged about the already famous gathering square formed by Dupont, Clay, Kearny, and Washington streets, were some of the plushest hotels, restaurants, saloons and gambling halls to be found in the world. Money and excitement gravitated to Portsmouth Square, and no expense was spared to create an atmosphere of lavish opulence.

The gambling halls were enormous, with tapestries and crystal chandeliers fit to grace the finest castles of Europe. Often they employed floor shows featuring exotic imported acts from Africa and Asia Minor. Champagne was on the house, and so were the scantily clad girls who served it, as long as a man did nothing more than give an occasional pat or squeeze.

Yes sir, they said, you could spend a year's earnings in one crazy night of celebration on Portsmouth Square and the very next morning, drunk or sober, you'd want to start saving up for next year's twenty-four-hour spree. Day or night, the glitter, gaiety, and sheer pace of living left one dizzy.

Into this carnival atmosphere, Glenn Donovan strode to find Dade and Holly Taylor and hopefully to bring them back to the Comstock and Bevis York.

At the Barbary Hotel he was directed to the Palace Club, where, it was said, a wild-animal act was a twenty-four-hour-a-day smash attraction. The first thing Glenn heard upon entering was a lion's roar. He looked up to see Dade Taylor riding the beast around the stage with a half-empty glass of champagne held aloft. Holly was unsuccessfully trying to refill it. The champagne fizzed all over Dade, who finally toppled from the animal, whose trainer helped him to stand. Then he and Holly unsteadily bowed as the audience cheered.

They were drunk, of course. Dade seemed right in his element, but Holly's condition was a total shock. She even looked different. Her low-cut dress seemed out of character and her face was heavily made up. Glenn didn't remember her hair being stacked so regally on top. She looked good, but less wholesome.

"Quite an act," he said, easing up to join their table. "Mind if I sit in on your party?"

Dade's eyes widened, then squeezed down into slits, but Holly laughed with genuine pleasure. "Glenn Donovan! Dade, honey. It's Glenn. You remember him. He was—"

"Yeah, I remember, all right. I hear you are the talk of Virginia City with all your new ideas. Got Holly's father thinking you're the greatest engineer in the world." Dade laughed obscenely. "Boy, if he only knew you weren't nothing but talk."

"He knows I'm not a licensed engineer," Glenn said tautly.

For a moment they locked eyes. Then Dade slurred, "What do you want?"

"Darling! That's no way to speak to our friend."

Dade pushed uncertainly to his feet. "*Your* friend, maybe. I never did like the way you was hanging around my little sister. Did you and her ever—?"

Glenn punched him in the mouth so hard the man crashed over two tables before he lit on his backside in an unconscious heap.

Holly went ashen, then rushed to his side.

"He'll be all right," Glenn drawled, rubbing his knuckles. That was the hardest he'd ever stuck a man. Probably because he was thirty pounds heavier.

"Are . . . are you certain?" Holly was sobering up fast.

"Dead certain. What he needs is a long ride in the fresh air." He picked up the inert gambler and slung him over his shoulder. "Don't you think, Missus Taylor, it's about time you and your new husband came back to Virginia City and set things right with your father?"

She nodded. "Both of us were afraid to. Maybe . . . maybe that's why we've been carrying on so. I mean . . . if my father has disowned me, I'm afraid of what Dade might do."

She looked straight into his eyes. "I know you probably think, after seeing us up there, we are despicable. But I don't care. You can even tell Daddy what you saw. But tell him this, too—say that I was having the best time of my life with the man I love."

"You tell him, Holly. Right now, all I want is to get you and your husband on the stage before it pulls out. There isn't much time."

She grabbed his arm. "I'm not sure I can. I'm . . . a little ashamed of myself."

"For the lion act?"

"No. For hurting my father."

"Holly, I can't help you on that one, except to let you know that Bevis loves you very much. Enough even to accept Dade as his son-in-law."

Her face transformed into a mirror of radiant joy. "He said that?"

"Yes."

"Oh, Glenn! Glenn, I love you!"

It was hard enough skirting through the boisterous crowd with Dade hanging over his shoulder, but when she tried to hug him, Glenn lost his balance and nearly toppled over a crap table.

"Come on, Holly!" he shouted as the jostled gamblers yelled in complaint. "Let's get out of here!"

By the time the Wells Fargo stage had completed the long journey across California and over the rugged Sierras, Dade Taylor had recovered. At first awakening, there'd been a moment of tense indecision, but Holly, knowing her man, forestalled an attack with the good news of Bevis' forgiveness. And when Glenn said that the old financier was ready to accept Dade as his son-in-law, the atmosphere brightened markedly.

Dade was a transformed man. No more gambling, he vowed, hugging his wife—or excessive drinking. He was going to become a businessman, a person of wealth and respect. He'd show Bevis what a wise decision he'd made to forgive and bring him into things.

In Carson City, Dade insisted they hold over long enough for him to bathe, change into his best clothes, and get a shave and haircut. That meant taking a late-evening coach, but he was adamant, so the decision was final.

Later that day, while waiting for Holly to join them for dinner at the Ormsby House, Dade was clearly in a high state of excitement.

"I've got a talent for business, Glenn. Damned if I don't!"

"That's fine," Glenn said dryly, wishing he were somewhere else.

"Bevis doesn't have any idea what I'm capable of."

"Oh," Glenn drawled, "I think maybe he does."

Fortunately the veiled innuendo went right over the gambler's head. "No chance. He thinks I'm just a card shark. No better than a common gambler. He's in for a big surprise."

"What have you got in mind?"

He chuckled. "Don't worry. I'm not going to fleece the man. But he's getting on in years. Could be he oughta retire. I mean to pick his brain clean and then take over."

Glenn's lips drew into a thin line. "You'd better go easy," he warned. "Son-in-law or not, he'll cut you off without pocket change if you try anything clever."

"Hell! I'm no fool. What I got in mind will take time, and I'll do it honestly. But one day I'm going to take over. There's opportunity for me on the Comstock. Why, I might even get into politics."

"What politics?"

Dade leaned close. "Statehood, Glenn. Before too long, we're going to be a part of the Union."

"You're probably right, but not soon. Anyway, I don't think you've got a chance at being elected to Congress."

"That's where you've got it all wrong. I'll get elected, all right. Just watch me."

"I will. Every step of the way. And I'll be watching how you treat Holly, too. Don't use her, Dade."

"Is that a threat?"

"No," Glenn said coolly. "It's a promise."

"I'm not worried," he replied. "Holly is a damn fine woman and I'll never take advantage of her for money."

"That's good to hear. But then, you know that better than anyone."

"Yeah. I . . ."

Dade's words trailed into silence and Glenn saw his mouth fall open and heard the gambler swallow noisily. "My," he breathed, "would you *look* at who's coming across the room!"

Glenn twisted around to see Julia Matson. She was as strikingly beautiful as always, yet something about her caused him alarm. Julia looked different, and as she approached, Glenn tried to isolate just what it was that had changed her appearance ever so subtly. Around her eyes, he noticed what was almost a deep, wounded expression, as though she'd seen something terrible, and still did at times when alone. It was a haunting quality. And she'd lost weight. The bones in her face seemed to press out a little tighter under very pale skin. As she came toward them, Glenn knew with certainty that she'd been gravely ill in the very recent past.

"Julia!" Dade whispered, striding across the room. "My dear woman, how good it is to see you!"

She faltered, seemed a little overwhelmed at his enthusiasm. "Thank you. What brings you to Carson City?"

"Oh," Dade said quickly, "Glenn and I are just passing through."

"We are waiting for Holly," Glenn explained. "She and Dade were married in San Francisco. They're going home."

Dade's eyes were murderous, yet his voice did not betray his feelings as he took Julia's hand. "How are you?"

Julia pulled away. "I'm fine. And I do offer you and Holly my very best congratulations. She is a wonderful girl."

"Why did you leave Virginia City?" Dade asked bluntly.

"I, too, was married," she replied carefully.

Dade actually rocked back on his heels and blinked in astonishment. "Who?" he breathed.

"Marshal Tillman. We're living here at the Ormsby House at present. Soon we hope to have enough saved to build our own place."

"That's . . . that's fine," Dade said weakly.

"Perhaps you and Holly would like to come down for supper one evening. You, too, Glenn, provided you bring Fay."

He smiled. There was no sense in spoiling things by telling them he and Fay weren't on speaking terms. Besides, it was something he meant to remedy as soon as they returned to the Comstock.

"I'll do that, Julia. Say, here comes the bride now."

Dade looked straight into Julia's eyes. "I'll be seeing you again," he urgently promised. "And if you and that marshal . . ."

But either Julia chose not to listen or just didn't hear, because even as he made his promise, the most lovely woman in Nevada slipped away and walked over to greet Holly. The two embraced like old friends, though Glenn couldn't recall them being that close.

It didn't matter. Not when Glenn pivoted to see naked desire in the gambler's eyes. Right there and then, Glenn wanted to batter the man's handsome face. And he knew that it didn't matter a tinker's damn who was married to whom, because Dade's intentions were right out in the open. Nothing was going to prevent him from eventually taking what he hungered for—not all of Bevis York's power and money and not even a U.S. marshal.

13

When they arrived back on the Comstock, Bevis York was standing in the Wells Fargo office waiting for his daughter. Holly, after a moment's hesitation, rushed into her father's arms, and when Bevis looked over her shoulder at him, Glenn could see the glistening tears.

But then Dade stepped into view. "We came back only because Donovan told us you needed help."

"That's not what I said," Glenn intoned.

Bevis waved him into silence. "I'll have no angry words to spoil this reunion. This is my daughter, and you . . . you, Mr. Taylor, are my son-in-law. And I'm prepared to treat you as a member of the family."

Dade's broad shoulders relaxed just a trifle. "Does that mean you'll teach me about mining investments and stocks?"

Bevis nodded. Both men stood rigidly, the tension almost visible between them. Glenn could feel the antagonism that was coursing just below the surface of their conversation.

"Good! That's all I've ever wanted, Mr. York. Just a break to prove my worth. I've earned the right, haven't I? It was me who told you the lode was shifting to the west."

Bevis winced, glanced around and saw that no one was paying attention. "If you and I must be partners, young man, one of the first lessons to learn is how to hold your tongue in public."

Dade flushed redly and choked down his anger.

"Father," Holly said, pushing between them, "my husband

is a very intelligent and proud man and I'll not allow you to publicly criticize him. That will be *your* first lesson."

This time it was the older man who fought to contain his angry words. But there was something about Holly that was unmistakably resolute. Glenn knew that she was prepared to leave Virginia City forever if her father launched one of his tirades.

Bevis' complexion was white with fury, but he nodded once. "Very well."

As though eager to change the subject and rid himself of Dade's presence, Bevis continued, "Glenn, what about Mr. Deidesheimer? I'd expected him to join you."

"He'll be along in a few days."

"Good. As soon as he arrives, bring him to my office. You'll be responsible for working with him to solve our timbering problems."

Glenn nodded. He wasn't a real engineer, but he knew the Ophir Mine almost as well as a real engineer would, and his own thoughts on timbering might help the German. At the very least, he'd save him from wasting valuable time on systems that had already been tried and found to be inadequate.

"Can the man really help us?" Dade asked.

"I think he can," Glenn answered. "In fact, if he can't, we are about finished here. It's just too dangerous."

"*Life* is dangerous, my friend. Raise the wages. I'll venture there will be plenty of men willing to risk their lives if the price is right."

Bevis spun away in disgust and a deep shadow of worry crossed Holly's eyes. They were all thinking the same thing. Dade was probably correct, but it was a hell of a mercenary attitude for anyone to take. And it said a lot about the man himself.

"I don't think that's going to be necessary," Glenn replied tightly. "Philip Deidesheimer has never failed yet."

"I hope you're right," Dade said with a wink. "But then, he's never seen anything like our Comstock."

Three days later, the German admitted the same as he and Glenn toured the depths of the mine. "It's big. Bigger than I've ever been in, and the rock is very weak."

"Can you help?"

Deidesheimer chose not to answer the question directly. "I've gone over your measurements and calculations and I am convinced we need an entirely new approach to timbering. None of the existing methods apply here because of the depth and size of the Comstock. Also, the amount of clay and porphyry rock. All those factors create enormous underground pressures.''

He studied a wall of pure silver. ''But I'll figure out something, Glenn. It would break the spirit to leave this wealth untouched.''

Glenn agreed. His dream and that of hundreds of idled miners depended on the engineer's resourcefulness.

That evening Glenn found Deidesheimer at work with a notepad covered with figures. Around him on the floor were scattered dozens of six-inch-long square-sided pieces of wood.

''What are these?''

''Toys.'' He smiled. ''Actually, I'm using them to represent timbers. Would you mind notching their ends?''

''How?''

''I'm not certain. Experiment with them. Use your mind. That's what you must do to become an engineer after you master the principles.''

''That's my problem, Philip. I can't seem to get enough knowledge just from books.''

''Of course not. You need an education. Remind me to write the Freiberg School of Mines and recommend you as a student.''

Glenn laughed. ''Thanks, but I'd rather build railroad trestles and bridges.''

''Oh?''

''Yes. Besides, there are several good engineering schools back east. One is called the New York Engineering Academy.''

''I know it well.''

''You do?''

''Certainly,'' the German replied. ''It's a fine school, though not as good as Freiberg.''

''No school is that good. But all the same, would you help me get in?''

''Of course! Just as soon as we finish solving our current riddle.''

''It's a deal.'' Glenn began to notch the stick ends in a way he'd already tried and found workable underground. He noticed Deidesheimer penciling in a set of flat lines. ''What's that?''

''Configuration Number One, my friend. Before this night is through, I will draw and test every imaginable one which could exist. And sometime early tomorrow we shall know if this Comstock will flower or die of neglect.''

After that, they both went to work, and it wasn't until nearly dawn that Philip Deidesheimer reassembled the miniature timbers one last time and rechecked his calculations for accuracy.

''That's it!'' he sighed, gazing intently at Configuration Number Seventeen. ''None of the others will do what this one can. In fact, it alone stands a chance of supporting the massive weights and gravitational pressures.''

Glenn stared at the drawing, then down at the replica he'd assembled from the miniature beams. It was so basic he had real doubts that it could work.

''Are you sure?''

''No. But it works on paper, and the simplicity of design bodes well for its application.''

''What you've designed, Philip, is simply an interlocking set of cubes. Each mortised and tenoned together for strength.''

''Exactly so,'' the engineer replied. ''This design would allow the mine owners to interlock cubes both vertically and horizontally. They'd be able to follow the veins of ore. What we have is nothing more or less than empty blocks which need only to be floored and ceilinged off to create identical working compartments.''

He began to extend the model, working as he talked. ''As the mine goes deeper, Glenn, these honeycomb wooden frames can be placed in such a manner that they will support each other. I knew the old doorframe method was totally impractical. The only shortcoming here is that my square-set timbering will require immense quantities of timber.''

''That's no problem. You came over the Sierras, around Lake Tahoe. We've still got plenty of access to the forests.'' He glanced up. ''Philip, can this model be empirically tested before I ask Bevis York to send men underground?''

Deidesheimer nodded solemnly. ''Let's disassemble it now and place it in . . .'' He glanced quickly around the room, then rushed over and yanked his pillowcase loose. ''We can pile those sticks in here. I'll bring the drawings.''

''You mean we're testing it now?''

''Why delay?''

''But Mr. York will want to see it.''

''He shall''—Deidesheimer winked—''*if* it proves successful. Take my advice, Glenn. Never demonstrate your theory until you've already secretly tested."

"But the formulas?"

"And never believe everything you read. Come on, young man. Let's find an abandoned hole and test at once."

The test, as Glenn found out, was unscientific yet convincing. Halfway up Sun Mountain, they found an empty man-sized hole in the rock. Then, while the engineer gave directions, which weren't really necessary, Glenn reconstructed the model. When Deidesheimer was satisfied, he placed it inside the hole, draped the pillowcase over it, and ordered it refilled to ground level.

Glenn was sure it would collapse, and he was damn glad they hadn't invited Bevis to watch this fiasco. The little model was at least six feet under.

"It's carrying four hundred pounds if an ounce," he said.

Without bothering to comment, Deidesheimer jumped onto the pile and stomped down hard with both feet.

"Six hundred," he corrected.

"Then it's flattened for certain."

"You think so, my young friend? Have you so little faith in the laws of physics?"

"No, but . . ."

"Then it's my calculations."

"Of course not, Philip, but they were only little sticks."

"And your timbers will be only twigs in respect to the earth mass they must support."

"All right," Glenn said, "let's find out."

Unearthing the square-set model proved a lot harder than burying it. Yet both men were so intent upon their mission they were completely oblivious of the gathering crowd of bewildered onlookers who'd assembled to watch the strange proceedings.

"It held!" Glenn roared, snatching the pillowcase away and raising the notched cube in triumph.

And while the crowd began to babble in confusion, Glenn heard the Freiberg mining engineer chuckle and say, "Sometimes, Deidesheimer, you amaze even yourself!"

Philip Deidesheimer's square-set timbering method was an overnight sensation as the experiment was repeated a dozen times. Bevis York started his crews to work immediately, dispatching them to the Sierras for thousands of six-foot timbers. He sent Dade Taylor first, though, sent him with orders to buy up the logging rights to every tree he could get on the mountain. Dade also had orders to acquire as many logging mills as possible for cash as fast as he could sign papers. They'd made every effort to corner the market in a single day, realizing that Deidesheimer's new square-set would ignite a run on timber.

They might have succeeded, except that other mine employees were smart enough to alert their respective owners. Dade was able to gobble up huge tracts of forest, but not all of it. And the small band of logging operators weren't stupid—not when they saw horsemen riding in with saddlebags of cash. A few were even clever enough to hang on to their timber.

News of the breakthrough sped over the Sierra Nevadas and stockholders in California celebrated as they watched the value of their shares triple overnight. Newspaper reporters from around the world flocked to Virginia City to interview Philip Deidesheimer, even as the square-sets were multiplying and pyramiding deeper and deeper into the Comstock lode.

Through it all, the German engineer remained his own man, gracious and yet possessing a special brand of confidence. During every interview, he acknowledged Glenn's assistance, and even more important, he wrote the New York Engineering Academy and sent them news clippings with Glenn's name underscored beside his own. And on a cool November evening, Wells Fargo brought the engineer a thick envelope that made him rush to the privacy of his hotel room. When he emerged a short time later, his eyes were bright with anticipation. He headed straight for the mine office and approached the man on duty.

"Where's Glenn Donovan?"

"He's out walking with Fay Taylor. I swear, he's head-over-heels for that girl. She's all he thinks of these days."

Philip Deidesheimer ignored the remark. In his hand he held the letter of admittance that would lead to Glenn's becoming an engineer. It was the younger man's dream, his ticket to greatness, because Deidesheimer knew the Irishman was destined to be a leader in his field.

"He'll forget her as soon as I show him this letter, and he'll want to leave the Comstock tomorrow."

"What for?"

Deidesheimer looked the stranger right in the eye, and didn't blink when he said, "To become like me—an engineer!"

* * *

Fay Taylor stood overlooking the valleys of rock and sage which reached far, far to the east. "You know something, Glenn, I can't believe we've been here almost two years."

"Why?"

She pulled her shawl closer about herself. "Oh, I was just remembering how we arrived—each of us with our dream and knowing we'd be leaving as soon as possible. I was going to return to San Francisco to become a famous dancer and singer."

An uneasiness stirred in Glenn as he watched her. "Are you unhappy, Fay?"

"No," she said quietly, "but though I'm well appreciated on the Comstock, I'd hoped to achieve more recognition."

She smiled. "I guess that sounds terrible. You know, self-serving and all, but . . . but I'm still only nineteen and I've gone about as far as I can in Virginia City."

He took a deep breath. "Then why haven't you left? Certainly you can afford to. Is it Dade?"

"Heavens, no!" She reached out her hand and he took it. "Glenn Donovan, everyone tells me how smart you are. And I listen—but I don't believe them."

"You don't?" He didn't understand this girl at all. Never would.

"Of course not. Because I know that if you were *really* smart, you'd know the reason I haven't left Virginia City is you."

"Fay!" Glenn didn't know what to say. He was stunned. Ever since he'd known Fay, she'd been telling him about her plans for the future. Her dream. And now she was telling him something entirely different.

Fay moved into his arms and lifted on her toes. "Well," she said with the old familiar touch of mischief, "you do remember my name. Is that all?"

He gathered her close and she folded against his chest. "I'm . . . I'm just trying to make sure I'm not dreaming," he whispered. "That what you're saying is real."

"I'm saying that I think I love you, Glenn, and that I'll stay as long as you do. I would be content as both your wife and an actress right here on the Comstock."

He squeezed her with joy, but then, remembering something he'd been avoiding telling her, he drew back slightly. "Fay, I haven't said anything to you yet, but I'm expecting a letter any day. There's a possibility that Mr. Deidesheimer can get me admitted to the New York Academy of Engineering.''

She stiffened and firmly pushed herself away. ''Glenn, we don't need to go back east. Everything we want is right here. You're already an authority on mining and we're both earning lots of money.'' She seemed to be groping. ''Besides, President Abraham Lincoln's election is sure to push the North into war with the South. No one knows what's going to happen back east. *This* is where our futures lie. Here on the Comstock.''

''No,'' he said gently, ''I don't care what people are saying, someday we'll carve all the ore out of Sun Mountain and Virginia City will wither and die.''

''Let it!'' she said angrily. ''You're one of the best mining men in Nevada. If you weren't, every operator on the Comstock wouldn't be clamboring for you to install their rail and pumping systems.''

Fay took his hands. ''Glenn, there is nothing to worry about. Why . . . why, we'll each make so much money these next few years we can retire young and wealthy.''

He realized she still didn't understand. And looking into her eyes and knowing he loved her, Glenn didn't know himself why he felt he must become a licensed engineer. Maybe she was right, that they were assured of enough money to meet their needs—but what of their dreams?

''Fay,'' he said gently, ''I love you and—''

''And I love you, too!'' she cried, returning gratefully to his arms. ''Oh, Glenn, let's be married!''

He closed his eyes, smelled the fragrance of her hair, and knew he would always remember this moment. She was right, dammit! Would becoming an engineer make him any happier than he felt right now? Of course not! And what good would he be without Fay?

Glenn raised her head and brought his lips down to hers. Yes, yes, he thought. We *will* be married!

Philip Deidesheimer cleared his throat loudly. ''Ummm, excuse me, please, but I have been hunting you for nearly two hours, Glenn.''

Fay glanced at the engineer, then disengaged herself. ''What could be so important that a famous engineer would go to so much trouble?'' she asked coolly.

Glenn suppressed a smile. Fay was seething at the interruption. ''What is it? Has something gone wrong with the pumps?''

"No, no, my friend! I bring you *good* news." He reached into his jacket's inside pocket and offered the thick letter.

Glenn's heart leaped. His mouth went dry. "You mean...you mean they've accepted me, even though I had only six years of formal schooling?"

Deidesheimer nodded, his eyes shining with pride. "It's all there, Glenn. My personal recommendation and the newspaper account of your assistance to me in designing the square-set timbering were enough to overcome the lack of classroom education. You're scheduled to begin classes in two months."

"Two months! But I thought you were going to apply for next fall."

"You did?" Deidesheimer glanced at Fay. "Hmmm," he mused, "I guess I misunderstood. Sorry."

"You didn't misunderstand anything," Fay cried, her eyes blazing at Deidesheimer. "You've been against me from the first. Always talking about how wonderful it is to be a 'real' engineer. Telling Glenn he has to go to college in order to amount to anything."

"Fay, please!"

"No!" she stormed. "I know how much you revere this man. Value his opinion. But what you don't seem to realize is that you are already successful. We both are!"

She lifted up her hands, then let them drop hopelessly. He could see the glistening of her tears. "Glenn, if you go away now to New York City, I'm leaving here too."

"Thank God!" he breathed. "Fay, we can—"

"No!" she exclaimed. "I won't be going east. It's soon to be a war-torn land and the cities will empty as the men go off to fight. The theaters will close. I couldn't stand to be there for that."

"But you said..."

"I'd go away too. And I will." Her chin lifted. "A few minutes ago I was willing to settle for the Comstock and being your wife. I was being foolish. Undervaluing both of us."

"Don't say that!"

"Why not? It's true. Maybe...maybe I should thank Mr. Deidesheimer."

"No need," the engineer said quietly. "You are both too young and talented for marriage. Later you will see I was right."

He handed the thick envelope to Glenn. "It's your decision, my friend. The New York School of Engineering asks four years of hard study so that you can live the remainder of your days accomplishing what we both know you were destined for—building this country. If you are meant to wed this girl, it will come to pass in its own good time."

"Wrong!" Fay said in a cracking voice. "Because I'm not waiting four years. Maybe that sounds entirely selfish, but I don't care. You see, I also have plans."

She laughed, but it was a cold, hard sound. "And I guess it's time I got busy pursuing them. Glenn, we'll both be too occupied to write, so just watch for me in the papers."

"Fay!"

They stood apart in hurt silence.

"Good night," Deidesheimer said, excusing himself in a rush and hurrying away in the darkness.

Glenn took her arm, and she struggled to pull away. "Let me go."

"Not until we talk this out."

"What is there left to say? I practically begged you to marry me and you almost said yes, until God himself butted in and handed you that envelope. And you grabbed it like a drowning man would a rope. I was a fool, Glenn Donovan. A fool to lose sight of what we are—ambitious, driven people. Like Dade, and like the great Philip Deidesheimer himself. And you know what?"

Glenn waited. He realized he'd made his decision, and in doing so, he had deeply wounded this girl. If her angry words could purge some of the hurt, he'd take them.

"What?"

She took a ragged breath. "I feel sorry for us, the driven ones. Better by far to be content with ordinary things, like marrying and raising a family, working an ordinary job like Clayton James or one of those miners. They'll never be remembered. Not like you and Deidesheimer, Bevis and, perhaps, even myself. Yet, I'll guess some of them will be much happier."

"I don't want fame."

She brushed her hair back, glanced down at her feet. "Well, maybe I do."

"Fay, you don't mean that."

She shivered, drew her shawl closer. "I just felt a chill. Do you mind if we start back?"

He shook his head, took her arm, and they walked slowly

toward Virginia City. When they reached the hotel, Fay said, "It won't be necessary to escort me inside. In fact, I don't think we should see each other again."

Glenn made himself speak slowly. "I won't let us part this way."

"You've had your choice, Mr. Donovan, and caused me to make mine. I'll be leaving for San Francisco on the early-morning stage."

Glenn's hands formed clenching knots. He could see that Fay Taylor wasn't bluffing and that he was losing her. And he swore at himself, because he alone had the power to change the separate directions their lives were taking. But he gripped the acceptance envelope and knew he had to remain silent. And he hated himself for it.

Perhaps she sensed this, because a low sob escaped her lips, and before he could stop her, Fay was racing up the steps and into the hotel.

"Good-bye," he whispered softly as he faced back toward the street. He wasn't a drinking man, but he headed for the Delta Saloon. There'd be dozens who owed him a drink for one favor or another, and he figured he'd collect all of them tonight. He'd drink enough whiskey to blot out the image of Fay Taylor and convince himself he'd done the best thing for them both. It was going to take a lot of convincing.

Besides, he never had been any good at lying.

He was gray-faced and red-eyed when the Wells Fargo stage sailed out of Virginia City going west to San Francisco. Glenn Donovan, a nearly empty bottle in one hand and an unloaded pistol in the other, swayed onto the dirt road and began to wave his arms for the coach to stop.

The stage driver who'd taken Clayton James's run didn't know him and wouldn't have believed that the tall, weaving young man was anything more than just another down-on-his-luck drunken Comstock miner. Even the upraised pistol didn't bother him, because the derelict was obviously incapacitated with alcohol.

"Hol' up!" Glenn yelled, peering at the onrushing stage. "Hol' up, I say! I gotta see my girl. Prettiest girl in worl'. Gonna get married. Tore up letter. Hol' up, dammit, or—"

The lead horse, a powerful bay weighing nearly fifteen hundred pounds, struck Glenn with its massive, driving shoulder and knocked him spinning into the roadside sage as the coach bowled on past.

Fay Taylor heard the driver hoot with derision but didn't see the body which lay sprawled like a broken doll. Her mind was wrapped in grief and disappointment. She hadn't been bluffing about her plans. She'd gathered her ready money, left Dade a note to withdraw her bank funds and send them to her, then packed her belongings and cried through the night until the stage was ready to go.

She didn't know how she'd get her start. Being well known in Virginia City wasn't going to open any San Francisco doors like Maguire's Jenny Lind Theater. But she'd find a way. Besides, she told herself over and over, marrying Glenn would have been a mistake. Their plans were incompatible. She didn't understand engineering and he'd never fit into the world of theatrics. Even if he didn't want her, she would prove that other men did.

But, dammit! Why did she hurt so badly? And why did she feel like crying again? Why? Should she have gone with him?

No matter, it was too late now. Already she'd made a fool of herself over the man while he'd spurned her for a college diploma—a lousy piece of parchment. And twisting deep inside her like a sharp, cutting knife was the realization that he hadn't even bothered to come to the stage depot this morning—not even to say good-bye.

She couldn't help it: when the driver laughed as they sailed over the divide, Fay Taylor wept openly.

14

Julia Tillman was beginning to feel alive again after the long months following her miscarriage. Though she dared not ask her husband about Bear Claw Man, she was certain the mysterious peacemaker was none other than her beloved Clayton James.

Clayton, who'd married the beautiful Indian girl Windflower and saved the Paiutes from extinction."

Clayton had done what he had to do. Julia realized this, even as she tried to forget the man and get along with her own life. In a way, the death of her baby symbolized the death of Clayton. Julia had grown to love them both, and now they were lost forever. She'd chosen life and willed her own recovery. She would survive and rebuild her own life with Marshal Bob Tillman.

He wasn't a bad man. Not really. And Julia noticed that he was particularly attractive to other women, who openly admired his quicksilver smile and the lean, easy way he had of moving. Graceful, he was, and striking, with his red hair and laughing green eyes.

Marriage and the recent death of Bob's younger brother seemed to have matured him. He now drank only moderately, and when he upheld the law of Carson City, he used his gun skills only when pressed to the wall. Even then, he always tried to get the drop on his opponent and convince him to hand over his weapon peacefully.

The time came when his contract was up for renewal by the city fathers. Bob was nervous, but he needn't have been. The mayor and City Council voted overwhelmingly to retain their marshal, and because Bob was now a married man, they raised his salary enough so that he could rent a small cottage and save for a house. The cottage was down near the Carson Livery and the Wells Fargo depot—not the best neighborhood really, but Julia had scrubbed it clean and together they'd painted the walls and made it cozy and bright.

Julia was even thinking about writing her family to tell them she was on the way to recovery and blessed respectability.

"Hello, Julia."

She turned, one of Bob's dripping shirts upraised to hang on the wash line.

"Dade." Julia relaxed and finished pinning up the shirt. "Weren't you in town just a few days ago? Maybe you and Holly ought to move to Carson City. Seems I see more of you around here than I do of my own husband."

He chuckled, for they'd grown easy with each other since both had married. "Well, you know how it is, Julia, when a man has too many business deals for his own good."

Julia reached for another shirt and kept on working. If past visits were any indication, Dade Taylor would stand around talking until she finally broke off the conversation by going inside. He wouldn't follow—everyone knew of her husband's violent temper and jealousy.

"You know," Dade continued, "I'm the overseer in charge of our logging operations. My employees are swarming all over that mountain up there, cutting timber for the mines."

He pointed at the slopes, moved very close to her. "Look, see that notched peak?"

She squinted up at the towering mountains which overshadowed the town. "Yes, I . . . I think so."

"Well, that's just one of the areas we're clearing out next month. I'm here trying to contract someone to build a mining road into that section so we can move timber out faster."

"Doesn't that create problems?"

"You mean the road?"

"No," she said, "I mean cutting down all those beautiful trees."

"Why should it?"

Julia suddenly felt uncomfortably close to the man. She could feel his eyes boring into her and smell his cologne. She tried to back up, but the clothesline blocked the way.

She reached down for another shirt, but he was quicker and picked up the wash basket for her.

Julia laughed uneasily. "Really, Dade, you're too important a man to be seen helping me hang laundry."

"I like to help you."

Julia looked away quickly. "How is Holly these days?"

"Oh, fine," he answered lamely. "She keeps herself busy with her charities up in Virginia City. I swear she's on every do-gooder committee between here and Reno. If she isn't helping the injured miners, she's trying to raise money for the damned Indians. Why, she's even talked her father into hiring some of them to haul wood and ice. Foolish as hell!"

Julia brushed by him and made herself work faster. She wanted to get these clothes up quickly so she could break away. Her husband might return at any time for the noon meal.

"Are you going to open a business down here?"

"Why should I, Dade?"

"Oh, I don't know. I couldn't help but think it must be kind of tough making a decent living on your husband's small salary."

Julia slapped a shirt down over the line with anger. "He does just fine," she said tightly. "We are never going to be rich, like you and Holly, but we're not starving, either."

"I'm sorry. I didn't mean to sound like I was talking him down, it's just that . . . that you deserve better than this rented shack."

"*Mister* Taylor. I've had about all of this I can stand. Bob Tillman is a fine man and well respected by the law-abiding people of Carson City. Or haven't you heard that he recently got a two-dollar-a-week raise?"

"Hell, Julia. That's nothing. I offered him a job as head of the Ophir Mine security a few weeks ago. Was going to double his salary."

"You did?" She frowned. Strange that her husband hadn't even mentioned the offer. It wasn't because he didn't enjoy money, either. Bob was always broke and poring through the Wanted posters, hunting for some outlaw he might capture for a bounty.

"Sure I did. And I can see he didn't bother to ask you your opinion on the decision."

She went on hanging clothes. "It's his job to decide how he earns the money, not mine."

"Maybe, but I don't understand why he'd turn down my offer. Especially knowing you deserve better than you're getting."

"Don't you fret about it, Mr. Taylor. If worse comes to worst, perhaps I could start a general store here in Carson City."

"You'd be good at it. But you ought to think about opening up in Virginia City and teaching old Raney, Tooey, and the rest of those jackals how to operate an honest business."

"I've thought about it," she conceded, "after what they did to me, and knowing how they set their prices. But my husband is here and my place is beside him."

"Sure," Dade said without conviction. "It's just that this town will always be little more than a stopover for the Comstock."

"You could be wrong," Julia told him. "The day may come when the ore runs dry. Then Virginia City, Gold Hill, and Silver City will dry up and blow away."

"Never happen," he pronounced confidently. "Every day, the vein grows bigger. We've got shifts working over three hundred feet below the surface now. I heard Bevis York say that if all the tunnels on the Comstock were joined into a straight line, a miner could walk underground clear to Reno!"

Julia thought the man was surely exaggerating, for that would be a distance of over twenty miles! "Think of all the trees you've put in your tunnels. Why, there must be a forest buried underneath Virginia City."

"If there isn't now, there will be." He leaned forward and placed his clean manicured fingers on her shoulder. Julia stiffened ever so slightly but relaxed when she saw him pointing back up at the mountain. "Right over that peak—you see the one with the rock slide on it?"

"Yes."

"Well, it's called Marlette Peak, and just this side of it is the finest stand of timber you ever laid eyes on. There's a little lake almost no one knows about. It's got beaver and everything."

"Really! I've never seen them."

"Oh, you should. I'll take you sometime."

Before she could say anything, he was rushing on. "Anyway, between Marlette Peak and Lake Tahoe is about three miles of the finest logging timber I've ever seen. I've been trying to buy it up, but there's an old backwoods type who's just stubborn enough to say no. One of these days he's got to give in."

"How many beaver, and how big are they?"

He laughed, squeezed her shoulder, and leaned very close in an easy confidential way. "Let's see, Julia, last time I was there, I counted seven. But I think just maybe the momma was having kittens."

"Kittens?"

"Sure," he said with a grin, "that's what their babies are called. Little things, and so cute it would make your eyes dance."

"Oh, I'd love to see them!"

"Then you shall. You'll—"

"You'll get your damn hands off my wife!" Bob Tillman shouted as he jumped the white picket fence and skidded to a halt. Then he shoved Dade hard, nearly knocking him down.

"What's going on here!" he roared. "I come home to eat and you and my wife are playing it cozy right here in the front yard. The entire town will be gossiping!"

"Maybe," Dade spit, "you'd rather I'd taken Julia inside."

The marshal went purple with rage. "Julia," he breathed, "get into the house."

She knew what was coming and how he'd use his fists. "No, please! Bob, we were—"

He slapped her hard across the face and the basket of clothes spilled into the dirt as she faltered backward.

"Into the house, I said!" His eyes never left the man before him. The marshal's hand crept up on the handle of his Colt.

"If you're armed, I suggest you pull back your coat and draw before I do."

Dade's eyes went to Julia. He saw the blood pulse from her split lip. "Damn you!" he replied. "I wish to God I *was* carrying a gun. You didn't have to slap her like that."

Bob Tillman took one step forward and viciously backhanded the man he faced. Dade rocked on his heels, knowing he was going to see this man buried by week's end. There was a derringer in his vest pocket, but cold reason kept him from going for it now when the marshal held the advantage.

Tillman's eyes were dilated with hatred. "I don't like you, Mr. Taylor, and the next time you are in my town, you'd better stay away from my wife, or so help me I'll feed you a bullet. Some people may be conned by all your fancy talk and those fine clothes, but I'm not."

"Is that so?" he whispered.

"Yeah. Julia told me how you married the rich man's daughter. It figures. You're still just a two-bit cardsharp."

He was being deliberately baited and knew it. "You've committed a grievous mistake," Dade breathed.

Tillman shoved a finger into his chest and poked him hard. "No, you've made the mistake. Don't make another, or that rich daughter is going to become a rich widow."

"Marshal," he replied evenly, "I happen to think you got very lucky and married the most beautiful woman west of St. Louis. Too bad, though," he said, pivoting away.

"Too bad what?"

"You keep slapping folks around, it's likely to affect your chances of living long enough to enjoy your good fortune."

He was three strides away when Bob Tillman yelled for him to halt and turn around. An icy river of fear channeled through Dade's veins, but he kept walking. He expected a bullet to slice his spine, rip through his lung or heart. But he kept walking. And each step took him that much farther from death and brought the marshal just that much closer to it.

"Stay away from my wife!" Tillman cried hoarsely. "It's your last warning!"

Dade rounded the first corner and passed out of sight of the marshal. He sagged against a fence, feeling his knees shake and a ball of ice begin to melt in his constricted gut. That was as close to dying as he'd been since the night Holly rescued him after he'd been caught using the mechanical card holdout. He'd need to be more discreet in the future if he intended to see Julia.

No, he thought, being discreet wouldn't solve the problem. It was going to take something much more permanent. But trying to outdraw the lawman would have been a very fatal mistake. Better, he told himself, to wait until the time was right.

It wouldn't be long. Maybe just a couple of days, until anyone who might have witnessed the scene would fail to attach any importance to it.

Or to the death of Marshal Bob Tillman.

It was almost a week before Holly stated that she had to travel to Reno for a hospital-fund benefit. Would he care to join her for an overnight stay? He'd declined, but appeased his wife by writing a particularly generous check. By ten o'clock that night he was riding over the last row of hills into Carson City.

The air was crisp; a strong wind blew off the Sierras, and there was a promise of first snow. Along the nearby Carson River, ice would form on the banks and frost would leave a glistening, diamondlike sheen to the sagebrush come morning, when the sun would steam it away.

Dade Taylor dismounted beside the Carson Brewery. A dog yapped in the night as he tethered his horse in shadow and strode toward the center of town.

He passed Julia's shack, saw the light move within, and then caught a glimpse of her form through the curtains. The silhouette was just sharp enough to tell him she was combing her hair and preparing for sleep—and that she was alone.

Dade hesitated. He would have liked to go inside and tell the woman he loved that she would never again be forced to endure the back of her husband's rough hand. That for her, this very night the physical abuse was over.

Instead, he walked stiffly by the shack, the livery, and the Wells Fargo depot. He couldn't predict Julia's reaction. She might rejoice and give herself to him freely and with love—but she also might recoil at her husband's death and expose him as the killer.

No, Dade thought, it was better she never realize it was he who'd freed her.

He stopped beside the first horse he found, then looked up

and down the street for its owner. There was no one in sight. Dade discovered the animal's cinch had been loosened, which meant the rider intended to make it a long evening. He retightened the cinch and checked the stirrups. They were short, so he unlaced the leathers and reset them.

Then he untied the animal and led it down the street, back past Julia's house and into the shadow of the Wells Fargo depot. Cupping his hand, he lit a cigar and squatted down to begin his vigil.

The stars sprayed the sky, and the steady wind pushed clouds until they rolled off the mountains and raced eastward. There was a moon, orange and shaped like the mouth of a jack-o-lantern. Dade finished his cigar and lit another. He checked his gun once more, shoved it back into his coat pocket, then tugged his Stetson low over his eyes. Despite the long black overcoat he wore, the cold seeped in to run goose bumps across his flesh. Out in the sage, a coyote took up its howl and the city dogs set up an answering racket that drowned out the originator.

The horse stamped. Its breath made warm vapor clouds, and when it tried to nuzzle him into action, Dade said, "Not much longer. He'll be along any minute now. It's the midnight hour."

Dade rechecked the cinch. Tightened it again, even though it was fine. When he looked over the saddle toward the center of town, he removed the cigar from his smiling mouth. He dropped the butt and ground it savagely under his boot heel. Then he mounted the horse and reined it into the street toward the approaching figure.

It was Bob Tillman. There was no mistaking the tall arrogance of him or the shiny steel badge pinned on the chest of his big windbreaker. Tillman slapped his gloved hands together for circulation. He was walking fast, trying to keep the blood flowing, maybe thinking about the woman who lay warm and accessible just beyond the door of his mean, drafty shack.

Dade rode forward, a dark, hunched figure with his Stetson pulled low.

Ten yards away, Tillman glanced up and grunted, "Howdy." It came up in two little puff clouds.

Dade waited another couple of heartbeats; then he straightened, reined the horse in, and replied, "'Evening, Marshal, going home to Julia?"

The man afoot halted. Blinked. "Yeah, but..."

Dade pulled the gun out of his overcoat pocket. "I guess I'll be taking your place," he drawled.

Bob Tillman sucked in a quick breath. His hand streaked for the gun he wore tied down on his right thigh. The gun he dared cover with his leather coat only when off duty.

Dade laughed quietly as the man clawed his jacket aside and dragged his pistol from his holster with a clumsy gloved hand. Then he shot Bob Tillman right below his badge. The marshal wheezed, half-spun around in a wobbly arc. He tried to lift his weapon. "You!"

"Yep. Good night, Marshal. I just *had* to have your woman."

A second bullet tore the oath from Bob Tillman's distended lips. Then the lawman fell like a Sierra pine tree. Dade nudged his skittery horse and the animal hopped forward, its brain terrorized by the scent of blood. He let the animal run until they came to the brewery, where Dade reined it to a standstill and hopped onto a concrete walkway. He slapped the horse soundly across the rump, and the riderless animal bolted into the night.

Behind him, he heard shouts and, one by one, lanterns blinked into existence as the dogs took to howling. It was a different sound this time.

Dade casually untied his own horse and remounted. Then, with the howling echoing across Eagle Valley toward the hills, he reined back to Virginia City. It had, he decided, been a very, very good evening. Worth far more than the check he'd given Holly for the hospital fund.

Far more.

Julia wore black on the day of the first season's snowfall. The Carson City cemetery was in the northeast part of town and was a barren, cheerless place even in the nicest weather. And as she, Dade, Holly, and a few others looked on, Bob Tillman was lowered into the earth. The preacher's black frock coat was dusted by snow. A gust of wind caught his derby and tossed it spinning across the graveyard. They had to wait until someone finally was able to stomp it down.

"Only God knows who killed this brave marshal and left his young widow to mourn her life away. But I tell you this, my friends, whoever shot Bob Tillman will roast for eternity in the fires of hell!"

Dade's eye caught Julia's, and he smiled with encouragement.

"God gives life and man violates this gift by taking it away. This makes the Lord angry, my friends. Since we don't know the murderer, we should rest in the comfort of divine knowledge that whoever did this is even now wrestling with the very devil himself. He's gonna fry! Yes, my dear friends, he will burn with Satan!"

Julia shuddered. Dade swallowed noisily. The preacher nodded to a dirty old man who stood poised with a shovel. He jumped forward and began pitching dirt into the hole. Too eagerly.

The preacher scowled at him as the dirt flew, but the old man in his threadbare coat did not turn his whiskey-shot eyes upward.

"Let us bow our heads and recite the Lord's Prayer, my friends."

And they did; as the muffled grunts of the drunk punctuated sacred words, they prayed. When it was done, the preacher nodded to Julia and it was the signal for her to go forward to the grave and wait alone until it was filled. Then she was to kneel and lay a pine branch beside the mound as a memorial to her loved one. Flowers would have been nicer, but they were out of season.

Julia stepped forward, her eyes fixed on the hole, and with each new shovelful of dirt, she blinked dry-eyed. Maybe it was expected that she should weep. If so, she was going to disappoint the preacher and the curious spectators, because she couldn't cry for someone she hadn't loved. Perhaps a week ago she might have dredged up a few tears because Bob had loved her. But he'd also hurt her—once too often.

And so, as the others faded back and the gravedigger wheezed his way into sweaty exhaustion, Julia stood with dry eyes and wondered what would become of her now. She'd been used by two men for their own selfish pleasure, and the one person who'd given her more than he'd taken was now married to an Indian princess and lost forever.

She was only twenty-two and already felt as though she'd lived to be an old woman. What now? Julia realized dimly that the shoveling had ended, so she knelt on the cold muddy ground and noticed that it was soiling her dress, even though it barely showed. Perhaps, she thought whimsically, this is why funeral clothes are black instead of white.

"Oh, Bob," she whispered, suddenly ashamed of the trivial

way her mind was running. "I am sorry you are dead. You deserved someone who loved you, but it was you who lied, deceived me about Clayton. If I'd known the truth, I'd never have married you."

She placed the pine bough over the mound of fresh-smelling earth.

Dade touched her shoulder. "Julia, it's snowing harder and harder. It won't help if you freeze out here."

She nodded. "I never loved him. Do you believe that?"

"Yes," he answered. "Come. Holly is waiting in the carriage. She and I want to talk to you."

Julia nodded. Now that the funeral was over, everyone was clearing out fast on their way back to town. Julia opened the carriage door and stepped up inside out of the wind, the slumped down beside Holly Taylor.

"You poor, poor girl," Holly said tenderly. "I wanted you to know how very sorry Dade and I are over this tragedy."

"Thank you."

Holly took her hands and leaned close. Dade climbed into the front seat and applied the whip, so that they jerked forward. "Dear Julia, I'm ashamed to tell you this, but it was Dade's idea that you come stay with us in Virginia City. I should have thought of it myself."

"Oh, I couldn't."

"Nonsense," Holly continued. "You'll freeze to death in that little house. Besides, Dade is gone so often on business that I get lonely. You'd be doing *me* a favor, Julia."

She wanted to accept. Oh, how she wanted to accept! In Holly she saw a generous, loving person who needed a friend. But in Dade . . . She pushed the thought away.

"I just couldn't."

"I'm sorry. Really I am," Holly said heavily. "Ever since my husband suggested you could take the spare bedroom—at least through the winter—well, I've been all excited. I'd even . . ." Her voice trailed off.

"You what?"

Holly wiped a tear away in embarrassment.

"Nothing, really. Don't mind me. I'm a fool."

"No, you're not," Julia said, realizing she was comforting the other woman now and feeling needed. "You're one of the nicest people I've ever known, Holly. And you're here at a time in my life when I desperately need that kind of person."

Holly smiled radiantly, then sniffled. "You have been through so much, Julia. First that terrible lie that Mr. Raney told, then losing your baby, and now . . . now, even your husband. I'm so weak in comparison. I've never lost anything and . . . yet here we are and you are the one supporting me."

Julia changed the subject. "Tell me, what did you do to that spare bedroom?"

Holly brightened. "I painted it."

"Really? What color?"

"A lovely green, Julia. Dade says it's the color of your eyes. You must see how much it would mean to us if you came to stay awhile. Please say yes."

"All right. I will," she breathed.

"Oh, Julia! Thank you!" Holly squealed happily. "Dade. Dade! Did you hear that? Julia has agreed to come live with us!"

"That's wonderful!" he called back. "Just wonderful!"

Julia squeezed Holly Taylor; then they both smiled happily into each other's eyes. "We'll be good friends."

"The *best* of friends, Julia. I know things have been awful for you. But Dade and I will change all that. I'm on all sorts of committees and things, and no one has forgotten you up in Virginia City. Why, do you remember that young Dr. Megan who kept coming by?"

"Yes."

Holly laughed, a touch of embarrassment in her expression. "I'm being shameless even to mention him, but he's never stopped asking about you. When we heard about your husband, he told me to pass on his deepest sympathies."

"Thank you."

"But Dade says that Dr. Megan is a quack. Too bad," Holly mused. "He is quite handsome."

"Yes, I suppose he is," Julia said, gazing out at the sleeting snow as Holly's words faded in her ears. This young woman was exactly the kind of person she needed to carry her through the harsh, lonely days to come. If only, she prayed, I can stay clear of her husband.

15

The months that followed were the best Julia could ever recall. Yet, she often felt a pang of loneliness when she noticed Holly and Dade touching or, through the wall, heard their soft love-making in the night. But even that did not bother her greatly, and she could accept the fact that she might never know love again.

Dade was a pleasant surprise—a gratifying one, actually. She'd been terribly fearful that he would soon be making advances, catch her alone when Holly was shopping or at one of her social meetings. But he didn't. Not once. And he'd had many opportunities. Often, though, she had caught him watching her, and then his eyes would shift away quickly. Julia was glad, because he was an extremely handsome man, the kind who she imagined was bold in the pursuit of pleasure.

But one night she was awakened by voices out in the parlor, and when they grew loud enough to keep her awake, Julia went to investigate. Perhaps something was wrong. Maybe she could help.

She opened her bedroom door and entered the hallway.

"I don't understand why your friends ostracize Julia," Dade ranted. "My God, they're supposed to be sisters of charity. Helpers of humanity. Why can't they forget about her past!"

Holly was crying little muffled sobs. "I don't know. I've . . . I've done everything, said everything I can to get them to accept Julia into our group. But they won't listen!"

"Damn them! Woman, your friends are nothing but a bunch of hypocrites! Julia has been through hell. We both know that. It would do her a world of good if she got out of this house and active in some of your women's things. So she became pregnant before she married Tillman. She isn't the first person who ever made that mistake."

"I know!" Holly choked. "Please don't be angry with me. It's not my fault! I've tried to make them give her a chance."

"Petty, gossipy snakes! From now on, I forbid you to associate with them. Drop all this charity business."

"Dade! That won't help," Holly cried. "We are doing so much good and—"

"Drop them, I say!"

Julia stumbled into the room feeling dead inside. "That won't be necessary, Holly."

The woman rose to her feet, ran across the room, and hugged her. "Oh, Julia, I'm sorry."

"No matter," she said, trying to smile. "Actually, I wouldn't be any good in that kind of setting anyway, but Dade is right, I do need to become active again. Besides, the money I had after the funeral is almost gone. It's time for me to go to work."

"Doing what?"

She shrugged. "I guess I'll try to get a job in one of the dry-goods stores. At least I know the business. Perhaps everyone has forgotten about the incident with Mr. Raney."

"Why don't you open your own place?" Dade asked.

"That's out of the question."

"Why? You'd do well," Holly said.

"Of course she would," Dade added in support. "Are you afraid of the competition?"

"Heavens, no!" Julia blurted. "If given the chance, I could run them out of business."

Holly turned to her husband. "Dade. We could help Julia get started."

"Oh, no!" she protested. "You've both done enough for me already."

"Nonsense," Dade said with a laugh. "Holly and I have been investing money all over Virginia City. Mostly, I'll admit, in mining properties, but it's always wise to diversify. How much would it cost?"

Julia looked from one to the other. They were serious. She felt a river of excitement wash away her fear. "Well"—she swallowed—"I'm not sure, because I never dared dream of opening my own place for many years, but two or three thousand ought to be enough to lease a building and stock it properly."

"Lease? Hell, no, we won't lease! I believe in owning property," Dade crowed. "No, sir, I'll but a lot on B Street and have a suitable building erected at once."

Holly squealed with happiness. "Oh, darling, thank you! I'll tell all of my friends—"

"Now, wait a minute," Dade cautioned. "If your friends, as you call them, were too good to help Julia before, what makes you think they'll patronize her now?"

Holly nodded solemnly. "I'm afraid you may be right. Well, I'll *make* them come to Julia's store. And if they don't... dammit, I'll resign from their committees and their biggest financial contributor will go elsewhere!"

Dade smiled. "That's the spirit, honey. I love it when you get your backbone up and your feathers ruffled. You should do it more often."

Holly blushed. "There you go, teasing me again."

"No, I'm not," he said quietly. "I like women with fight and spirit. Sometimes... sometimes I almost forget that you have both qualities, hidden deep inside."

Julia saw Holly's troubled expression and wanted to change the subject. "Listen," she offered, "why don't you two think this over for a couple of days? It's a lot of money, and something could happen so that you'd lose it all."

"It's a risk," Dade said. "So is everything in life. There are no guarantees."

"Perhaps not, but if you were lending that much to anyone else, you'd want some kind of collateral, in the event of failure. You can't deny that."

"No," Dade conceded. "But what have you got?"

"Absolutely nothing," Julia said flatly.

"That's not true," he told her, his eyes sliding downward. "You have a great deal."

Julia couldn't match his gaze. She felt a weakness inside.

"He's right," Holly added innocently. "We know that you're a good investment. Besides, why are we even talking about failure? You once told the merchants of this town what you intended to do to them. It's time you started showing them that the people of Virginia City are tired of being overcharged. How much profit did you say they were taking?"

"Forty, sometimes fifty percent."

"So there!" Holly said, pouncing on it like a cat on a mouse. "That's absolutely outrageous. Why, with a man earning just two dollars a day in the mines, those with families on the Comstock are facing starvation. It's appalling how hard they work for such little money. We should pay them more."

Dade flushed angrily. "Holly, we've gone over this again and again. Two dollars is a good wage."

"Not here, it isn't," she declared staunchly. "If you'd come to the Miners Assistance League meetings once in a while and hear those poor people tell about how—"

"Holly, that's enough," he snapped. Then, realizing he'd spoken in anger, Dade forced a laugh. "Besides, we've just gotten through helping Julia. Tomorrow I'll scout up a lot and hire a builder. So let's not try to solve everyone's problems in one night. All right?"

She nodded and bit her lip as Julia pulled her close and whispered thank you.

"You too, Dade. I promise you won't regret this loan. I'll pay you back with interest."

"I know, Julia," he replied calmly. "You are worth investing in—anytime."

The way he said it made Julia swallow dryly and stare into those penetrating eyes of his. Maybe she was just imagining the way he seemed to be mentally disrobing her. Maybe.

Julia looked away and squeezed Holly even tighter.

Dade found a lot on the corner of A Street and Sutton Avenue, next to one of his few competitors, the offices of Tahoe Logging Enterprises, Incorporated. The store he had constructed was big, and nicer by far than Julia had dared to expect. Dade had even insisted that floors be put in, along with a big glass window so that passersby could see Julia at work.

But he needn't have worried, for on opening day her old customers from the Silver Exchange Mercantile showed up in force and they had a regular party. Julia had made cakes and gallons of punch. They ate most of the cake and washed it down with whiskey. By the end of her first day of business, she was exhausted but pleased at how well things had gone. She would make a success of this. And why not? Her prices were lower than the other merchants' in town, but still gave her a fair profit. She had no qualms about charming the men just as she'd done so successfully before.

The last of the revelers and well-wishers had departed long after dusk. Even though it was now well past business hours and her curtains were drawn, someone knocked at the door. Julia ignored the sound and continued her cleaning. It was late and the place was a mess. She was weary from the excitement and strain of preparing for opening day. Long hours of hard work had paid off, but now she just wanted to finish up and go home to rest.

The knocking grew more insistent.

"Please come back tomorrow," she called. "I'm closed for the night."

"I want to talk to you now," a woman's voice demanded.

Julia set her broom aside and wearily opened the door to come face to face with a beautiful woman, heavily perfumed and draped in rich sable furs. Her manicured fingers were covered with rubies and diamonds. "Have we met?"

"My name is Nicole Barrie," she declared, throwing her head back and tossing her long black hair. "Everyone knows of me."

"Of course," Julia said, "please come in." As the woman passed, Julia remembered all the stories she'd heard about Virginia City's successful and legendary madam. Nicole was one of the most controversial figures on the Comstock. She was loved by the men who showered her with gifts of gold and champagne and despised by the respectable women. It was said that Nicole's French Palace was the most cultured establishment in town, and so elegantly furnished that even the toughest miner became a gentleman in her place. Nicole served only champagne and the best imported wines. Exquisite French cooking was reserved for her most favored guests, and for those less favored, her girls were the prettiest to be found and were never allowed to use rough language. To be employed by Nicole was to reach the epitome of their profession.

Julia hadn't the slightest idea why this famous woman had called. But, for whatever reason, she meant to treat her kindly.

"I . . . I wonder if you'd like some cake? There's some left."

"No, thank you, Mrs. Tillman, but it is kind of you to offer." She removed her furs like an actress and pirouetted in a full circle as her luminous eyes enfolded the room. "You must paint it soon. Not white, like everyone else, something vibrant and gay. But enough—no one likes to be told how to do what they do. True?"

"Yes." She couldn't help but stare at the Frenchwoman, because they could have been sisters, their features were so well matched. Nicole's body was full and the dress she wore accentuated every line of it. Her complexion was darker, true, and she wore makeup, though Julia could not imagine why. Nicole's complexion was flawless. Her high cheekbones gave her the same eye-catching contours that Julia possessed. Beauty and strength radiated from the madam and were mixed with airs of intelligence and dark passion. Julia could admire these same physical qualities in another woman, but never herself.

So absorbed was she in her assessment of this renowned visitor, Julia didn't realize that she was also being studied. "Well, well," the lady said, "you are every bit as lovely as I've heard, and for the first time in my life, I am almost jealous."

Julia blushed deeply and heard Nicole Barrie's laughter. "Do not let me embarrass you. Please. I came in the hope we might be friends rather than rivals. That we might even become business associates."

Julia's mouth fell open. "Did—?"

"Of course not," the madam said, reading her thoughts. "I wouldn't insult you by offering work, but if you ever . . ."

Julia suppressed a smile. "What *do* you want, Miss Barrie?"

"I want to know how your party was attended."

"Quite well."

"Good! By the way, did ladies come?"

Julia frowned. She'd been so busy she hadn't really noticed their absence. "No," she admitted with a troubled expression. "Just Holly."

"Mrs. Taylor?"

"That's right. Do you know her?"

"I do. A couple of months ago, when one of my girls was knifed, Mrs. Taylor heard of it and came to visit. Good women aren't supposed to be seen near my street, much less inside my house. But she did not care, and I now admire her deeply."

"So do I," Julia replied. "She and her husband helped me—"

"Dade helped you?"

Julia nodded, troubled by the abruptness of the question. "Do you know him too?"

"No, of course not," came the quick denial. "Anyway, I'm pleased that you had such a good turnout. Too bad Virginia City's ladies didn't support you."

"Perhaps they will," Julia said.

"Like hell, as they say. When you were with child and unmarried, they labeled you forever. Nothing you can do here will ever gain you respectability. This you must understand."

Julia took a deep breath. "I didn't realize I was the subject of so much gossip."

"All Comstock women are. Even ugly ones, but especially a couple such as you and I." She sighed deeply. "You may not believe this, but even still I am hurt by their tongues and . . . even my own conscience. But we must live, and I do it the best way I can. Let God judge me, not tongue-waggers. Only He knows how many I have saved and helped in need."

"Your generosity to charity is common knowledge, Miss Barrie."

"Thank you. But you cannot buy your way to heaven, and the townswomen will always despise me for my possessions and my freedom."

"Why are you telling me this?" Julia asked, thinking out loud.

She chuckled. "I'm not sure. You see, you are in between, my dear. You fit in no category and are thus approachable."

"I don't understand."

"All right. You're not respectable. You've been shunned by those who are. Yet clearly you also do not fit into my category. This makes you . . . different. Somehow possible to confide in."

Julia shook her head. "I'm not at all sure I follow your reasoning, but I'm happy to listen, and except for Holly, I'm without friends. May I ask why you came here tonight?"

"Out of curiosity. I've heard men speak of you quite often. Also, I did want to know if your business was well received by our ladies."

"Obviously not. No matter. I hadn't even noticed," she said defensively.

"You would later, I think. After those bolts of yard goods began to get dusty and all your ladies' things sat on the shelves untouched. They don't have to, though."

"Why not?"

"Because I will buy them. So will the others."

Julia blinked. "There are a lot of you?"

"No, only one, thank heaven. But other dozens of impostors, who can only mimic my success."

"I see."

"Good. Furthermore, you would find us excellent customers. We pay cash and do not haggle when treated fairly."

"I would never cheat you, Miss Barrie." Julia looked at all the beautiful women's things she'd ordered on credit. Stockings, lace blouses, jewelry, pretty colored yardage, and nice toiletries. None of which had even been looked at this day. "I need and welcome your patronage," she said honestly.

"Do you know what you are saying? The impact of your words? If we shop here, you are going to be attacked by every social club on the Comstock. You'll be shunned by married women, denounced by preachers, and looked down upon by some of my own more respectable customers."

"I don't care," Julia said defiantly. "I've heard the stories and already been shunned, as you pointed out."

"What about Mrs. Taylor? Will you allow her to be besoiled also? If she befriends you, she will be."

"Never! I'll move away. Try to explain things."

Nicole Barrie nodded. "I hope she listens."

"I'll make her, for her own good."

"Good. Now," she said, "we will do business if your price is right. To what penalty must we submit?"

"Penalty? I don't know what you mean. Please be specific. My prices are marked and fair. Lower than you will find elsewhere."

Madame Barrie laughed outright. "You don't know much about what goes on in Virginia City, do you?"

"Enough."

"Not nearly, my dear. But I'll say it plain, because you'd hear it anyway. Women like us aren't allowed to mingle with respectable people. I guess they think something might rub off in the daytime—though the men don't seem concerned at night."

"Miss Barrie," Julia interrupted, "I really don't see what—"

"Let me finish, please."

"All right."

"What I was about to say was that until now we've had a little arrangement with a few of the owners of other stores. We write a list of necessities and our orders are delivered in the night. For this 'privilege,' we've been paying twenty-five percent extra."

"That's scandalous!" Julia stormed. "I'll charge nothing extra."

The madam laughed again. She reached out and gripped Julia's arm. "My dear Mrs. Tillman, I believe, should you dare, we will become very good friends."

"I dare," Julia said fiercely. Her eyes dropped. "And I welcome your friendship—need it badly."

"It is yours, then!" Nicole's full and sensual lips trembled into a wide smile. Her voice was rich with feeling. "We shall celebrate. Have some of your cake and the drink."

"Fine. If you'll cut the cake, I'll pour. Tea or punch?"

Nicole dropped the knife clattering on the dish. Her delicately shaped nose wrinkled with distaste, but she was more than tactful. "You know," she said casually, "it's a slow night. I think I'll escort a couple of my nicest girls over and we'll help you clean this mess up."

"Thank you, but—"

"Ah, ahh, I insist. And I'll bring some champagne back to go with this beautiful cake." At the door she hesitated. "You...you will drink spirits, won't you, Julia?"

"Only in the company of friends."

"Good! I'll bring a bottle for each of us."

Much later, Julia was definitely tipsy when the madam and three quite pretty ladies of the night departed. She'd lost track of the hour and swayed over to peer unsteadily at the only clock in the store. She had to squint to make all the numbers stop whirling around as though playing chase with the hands. But after a long, serious deliberation, she concluded it was nearly one in the morning. She also noticed that Nicole had forgotten her beautiful furs. They could be returned in the morning.

Outside, she heard the girls laugh as they trundled unsteadily down A Street toward Nicole's French Palace. Julia smothered her own laugh and hiccuped happily. Nicole had probably chosen her very nicest girls for the impromptu party, and they'd all gotten along splendidly.

She swayed over to a mirror, cocked one perfectly shaped eyebrow, and said to herself, "Julia, you ought to be ashamed. Enjoying the company of prostitutes. Now, say you repent and swear never to do this again."

Julia waited for herself to answer contritely. When she did not, she giggled. "If it is true that we are judged by the company we keep, then I have just been ruined. Lost any chance I may have had for the respectability I've always wanted. Doesn't that make you sad?"

She puckered her lips sternly but shook her head and tried to keep from giggling again as she made faces. "Well, I guess that means I'm not ashamed."

"You should be," Dade Taylor said, entering through the unlocked doorway.

Julia whirled, caught her heel in the hem of her dress, and fell as his heavy footsteps approached up the aisle. The boots stopped just in front of her face. Julia didn't feel like giggling anymore. In fact, she didn't feel very well. Not well at all.

"Get up!"

"Go away," she moaned, pushing her hair away from her eyes. "My store is closed, Mr. Taylor. Closed for business."

"*Your* store?" he asked quietly. "Did I hear you correctly, my dear? Is it possible you've already forgotten that Holly and I own *everything*, right down to the dirt?"

She tilted her head back. He looked huge towering over her. Frightening. "I'll pay you back. Pay you and Holly with interest."

"Get up," he repeated. "When you didn't come home tonight, I came looking for you. Saw Madame Barrie and her girls. Julia, you've probably just killed this business."

She grabbed the corner of a box and pushed herself up until she was swaying under his hard, critical gaze. "Leave me alone, Dade. I'm going to be all right."

"Are you? Tonight, while you were consorting with whores, Holly was berating her ladies' group about the meaning of forgiveness. Hell, she probably even made them repent."

Julia groaned. She felt awful.

"But you can bet this little party will be the main topic of interest tomorrow. You've branded yourself as one of them, Julia."

"Go away!" she cried, trying to push by him and finding her path blocked.

He grabbed her around the waist and pulled her tight. "I understand why you've chosen to openly befriend Madame Barrie," he said roughly. "Deep inside, you're no better than they are. You're a whore, Julia. A beautiful—"

She leaned back and tried to slap him, but her strength was gone and she felt so dizzy she missed as his lips ground into her own.

He was enormously powerful, and two years of hunger for her boiled up in his passion as his hands searched for the buttons on her dress.

She bit him on the lip and he yelped in pain and surprise as she shoved away and ran crashing into the serving table. The punch bowl and rented crystal glasses spilled across the floor, and so did the knife she used to cut her cake. Julia lay sprawled in the mess.

She snatched up the knife and held it outstretched before her. "Don't come any closer," she warned. "I don't want to hurt you, but I swear I won't be used ever again. Not by you or any man!"

She held the knife, realizing she couldn't fend him off. Not dizzy and lying in spilled punch.

He realized it too, because he knelt a safe distance away and shook his head regretfully. "You realize I'd expected a little more gratitude on your part."

Julia said nothing. She could feel the wetness of the punch seeping through her undergarments. Her only decent dress was being ruined.

"I took you in, Julia, and you don't know how I've tried to stay away from you. It drove me crazy, knowing you were sleeping in another man's bed down there in Carson City."

"My *husband's* bed, Dade! Just like you and Holly—"

"Don't tell me about Holly, dammit! Ever since you've been at our house, I've almost gone wild, always pretending she was you and—"

"No!" Julia screamed, dropping the knife and clamping her hands over her ears. "No! No! No! Don't tell me that."

He ripped her hands away, drew her to him struggling and crying and violently shaking her head back and forth.

"I can't help it, Julia!" he choked.

"Dade, no. Please, Dade. Don't!" she whispered as he began to press her down under his weight.

"Say, Julia," a voice sang in the doorway, "I forgot my—"

"Nicole! Help me!"

Dade Taylor went rigid as stone. He expelled a deep breath and whispered, "Soon, Julia. You owe me. Soon."

Then he stood up, his breathing heavy in the quietness which stretched among them all. He brushed his suit free of dirt and pushed by Madame Barrie. "You ought to hire her, Nicole, she's qualified."

Julia rolled over in shame, and great racking sobs tore up and down her length.

The madam slammed the door behind him, but when she knelt beside the crying girl, her voice and hands were gentle. "Honey," she whispered. "It's going to be all right. I'm taking you to my place for the night. We'll have coffee and talk. Tomorrow you're moving."

"Where?" she asked. "I have no money, and—"

"Shhh," the madam replied. "Perhaps I can help. One thing sure, I'd be a better business partner."

Julia squeezed her eyes shut. "I'm afraid," she confessed. "I don't know how, but I have the feeling he'll have his way and I'll be helpless again."

"It could be worse. Much worse. At least he's rich and handsome."

"I don't care!"

"Julia, listen to me. The Comstock is a man's world. Totally. Women are here only for their pleasure. Wives or our kind, it doesn't matter. They keep us for the same reason."

"I don't believe that," she gritted. "What about Holly?"

"She's the only exception. And we've just seen that Dade keeps her for the money. He wants you."

"Can you help me?"

"I can try. But you must be aware that I survive only because I create pleasure and no problems for powerful businessmen like Mr. Taylor."

"You mean . . ." Julia clamped her mouth shut and actually recoiled.

"Yes," Nicole whispered, avoiding her eyes. "But we shall never again speak of this thing. It is now over."

Julia relaxed. She suddenly felt a little ashamed of her knowledge. "What can I do to stop him?"

"Pay the swine off as soon as you can," Nicole said passionately. "Never again fall into such a man's debt."

"He doesn't want the money," Julia whispered.

"I know that. If he would take it, I would lend it to you myself. But this he would not allow."

"Will I . . . will I ever be free of him, Nicole? Please, answer me."

"I can't," she admitted. "I saw his face only moments ago. The lust. The passion. I have seen much of it—but never so alive."

Julia folded. "Dear God," she breathed, "I am so afraid."

And the infamous Madame Nicole Barrie turned away in silence, for she could do nothing.

16

Dade was right; the entire city heard about Julia's late-night party. And if the respectable ladies of Virginia City had politely ignored her before, they were now openly belligerent.

Julia didn't care anymore. There was only one real lady on the Comstock who mattered to her, and that was Holly Taylor. Holly, who was both hurt and confused because her friend had fled from her home in the middle of the night.

Whenever Julia recalled that awful meeting with Holly, she suffered the pangs of despair. Knowing she could not face either Dade or his wife, she'd hired a boy to obtain her belongings and transport them to the small place on Howard Street that Nicole Barrie had located.

But Holly wouldn't give the boy Julia's things until she'd come to the store and received an explanation. Julia was so ashamed, she'd barely been able to look into the woman's eyes.

"I just don't understand it," Holly had cried in exasperation. "I thought we were such good friends, Julia, and now you've gone without even saying good-bye, or thank you, or anything."

"Holly, we *are* friends. I can never repay you for helping me after Bob was killed."

"Then why? What's wrong? Is it something Dade said when he came looking for you?"

Julia's throat constricted and she could barely ask, "You know?"

"Of course. I waited up for him, and when he came home, he was very upset. He tossed all night long. Neither of us slept, and when you didn't come in, he wouldn't speak of it. He told me to stay away from you."

"I see. Then why did you come?"

Holly's fists were clenched. "Because I prayed that whatever kind of an argument you two had could be talked out. Julia, can't you even tell me?"

She steeled herself and forced the words out like poison pellets. "No, I can't. It's . . . it's a matter of business, and we said some things that will never be forgiven."

Holly dabbed a handkerchief at her eyes. "Was it about your doing business with Miss Barrie and her friends?"

Julia seized on this. "Yes, we were in violent disagreement. I intend to sell to them, and your husband objected. He told me you almost had your friends convinced they made a mistake by refusing to deal with me."

"Yes," Holly whispered.

"Thank you. I'm sorry it all was for nothing. I've crossed over onto the wrong side of the tracks now, Holly. Your friends will never forget my choice."

"Then maybe they're not worth having as friends, Julia. No one, not even my husband, has the right to tell me with whom I can associate."

Julia wanted to reach out and hug her friend, to tell her how grateful she was for that simple declaration of faith. But she couldn't. Dade's words and the threat were now like a driven wedge between herself and Holly.

In her own guilt-ridden way, Julia tried to explain. "Holly, your friends aren't bad. Not any more than Miss Barrie. They are wrong, but you can't change that, and there's no reason to put an end to the charities you do together. We can still be friends—we must be! But please, for a while at least, don't be caught associating with me. You'll only cause yourself pain, and it won't help. Go on with your work and let me do the same, as I see fit."

Holly nodded slowly. "This is wrong. I know it is, and yet . . . it seems out of control somehow. But the day will come—I swear it will, Julia—when you and I can be friends openly again."

"I know that." She swallowed. "Good-bye."

"Good-bye, Julia." Holly stood and bit her lip. She tried to speak and failed. Then she ran away, never knowing the truth about Julia and the passion that gnawed at the heart of Dade Taylor.

Late that same day, just at closing time, Nicole Barrie entered the Emporium and placed on the counter an order list gathered from every brothel in Virginia City. The total bill came to almost three thousand dollars, and Nicole happily prophesied that it was just the beginning. Once the girls saw that the correct orders were delivered at fair prices, the houses in Gold Hill and Silver City would also be ordering from Julia Tillman's Emporium.

"Thank you," she whispered, realizing that this meant that, no matter what else, she was going to prosper on the Comstock.

"Just do us a good job, my friend. And know this: among us there are no secrets. All the girls realize what you're going to be facing. They understand and they won't fail you, Julia."

"And I won't disappoint them. That's a promise."

The madam nodded. "We're betting on you. We've cut our ties with the other businesses in town and they're furious. But who cares? Burned bridges."

Julia understood she couldn't fail now. One way or another, she'd save enough money to pay back the Taylors within a few years. Then she'd be free of Dade's bond.

Yet even this thought gave her no special joy, because she'd forfeited her dream of respectability. No matter, she, Madame Barrie, and the others were a sorority of outcasts. And the loss of respectability now seemed a pale, pale issue next to her more immediate problem—survival.

Fay tasted deeply of the Pacific breeze and marveled at the sea gulls wheeling effortlessly high above San Francisco Bay. Her trip from the Comstock had been uneventful and she'd hardly spoken to anyone, because her mind had been burdened by the knowledge that she'd probably never see Glenn Donovan again. Even now, he was being borne across this continent to its opposite shore.

When she'd descended from the Wells Fargo stage, the world of San Francisco has risen up in all its old familiarity. Before, Dade had been her constant guardian, and she had been allowed out only during the daytime. Now the city was hers to explore and experience without restriction. She was on her own—and it frightened her a little.

Respectable hotel rooms were a dollar a night, and she paid a week in advance, which left her just thirty-one dollars. Fay wasn't worried. She was certain she'd be able to land acting work within the week.

And Fay knew exactly where she'd begin. Since the Metropolitan Opera House had burned to the ground, there was really only one legitimate theater in San Francisco. That was Tom Maguire's Opera House. Though she'd never met the famous theater owner, Fay had heard her brother grudgingly describe him as handsome, articulate, rich, and as daring as any man alive. It was this last attribute that had lifted him from his New York City cabbie's background and sent him west during the forty-niner gold rush. In California he'd quickly tired of prospecting the Stanislaus and American rivers and had opened a string of enormously successful saloons and gambling halls. He did it all by hard work and fast thinking. In those wild earlier days, when he was getting his start, it was said that Tom Maguire could fold his card tables, drop and pack his saloon tents, and be at the next new gold discovery before a running prospector.

Eventually he'd landed in San Francisco, where he'd built his first theater, the magnificent Jenny Lind. After making a quick fortune, he'd ignored all his advisers and boldly introduced Shakespearean plays and English comedy. From the opening night, they had performed before a packed house. His only bad luck came with fire, and his theaters burned down quite regularly. He always rebuilt them larger and finer than before. In addition to his San Francisco Opera House, he had one in Sacramento and was rumored to be thinking of building another on the Comstock.

Yes, Fay thought, Maguire was the one to impress. If only she could, it would be no time at all before she joined the actors and actresses Mr. Maguire booked from the finest stages of New York, London, and even Paris.

Fay dressed in her nicest clothes and brushed her yellow hair until it gleamed and crackled with static. Then she arrived nervously at the famous theater and asked to see Mr. Maguire.

"I'm afraid that's impossible." The youthful doorman sighed, his gaze undressing her. "Mr. Maguire is busy auditioning singers for his new production of *Trust in the Family.*"

Fay's pulse quickened. "I'm an actress. Perhaps I could play a part. Won't you let me see him, if only for a moment?"

"Perhaps we could talk about it tonight?" came the smooth and obviously well-tried line. "That is, if you're *really* interested in an interview."

Fay made herself smile. "What is the play about?" she inquired sweetly.

He was flabby and already going bald. Really, she decided, a very unattractive young man.

"Oh"—he shrugged in a worldly fashion—"the usual drivel. Pure sentiment. The entire play centers around an Irish family in New York City. The father's a drunk and it's only through the love of his wife and children that he's able to rescue himself. A real tearjerker."

"Is there a lot of dancing and singing?"

"Of course. That's why they're auditioning."

"Then I should go inside. You see, I really do need a job, and my qualifications—"

"What about tonight?" he interrupted.

Fay ground her teeth in silent fury. But she was in no position to tell him what she thought of his manners. Her eyes strayed to a nearby hotel sign and she said, "Hotel Fremont. About eight?" she asked, winking up at him suggestively.

He slipped from his role and grinned almost lewdly. "Yeah, that'd be great, honey!"

"I'm sure it will," Fay said icily as she swept by and into the theater, knowing he wouldn't try to stop her and ruin his pleasurable expectations.

But she wasn't staying at the Hotel Fremont and she'd never fool him again—her audition was now or never.

There was a group of people coming up the aisle, and Fay's heart skipped as she recognized the tallest man approaching as none other than Tom Maguire himself. He was flanked by half a dozen theatrical performers, each no doubt angling for a favored role.

Fay backed out of the cavernous theater into the lobby, smoothed her dress, and smiled her biggest. As the lobby doors pushed open, she bowed formally and called, "Mr. Maguire, I wonder if I might have the honor of auditioning for your play."

He stopped. The chattering hangers-on bumped into each other and the room grew silent. Maguire was in his early forties, an elegant man with a long, elegant mustache, waxed and tipped. In one hand was a gold-capped cane, and in the other, his derby. He wore a beautifully tailored brown jacket and soft beige trousers. He looked smashing.

"My dear," he said in a regretful tone of voice, "I would gladly have given you a few minutes of my time, but I'm afraid I've settled on the cast—most of whom you see here."

She could tell he honestly was sorry, but also that the others were openly hostile. "Mr. Maguire," she pleaded, "I know you've probably chosen an excellent cast and that your time is very valuable. Yet, I've just arrived from a successful engagement in Virginia City and—"

"I'm sure you have," he said patiently as someone nudged him, "Miss . . ."

"Taylor."

"Well, Miss Taylor, I'm sorry I couldn't hear you perform. Some other time. This play will run only a few months. Then—"

Fay saw the gloating expressions of those surrounding him and it made her both angry and desperate. Desperate enough to outstretch her arms and burst into a touching rendition of "Farewell, Old California." She knew she did it in a manner that had never failed to bring tears to the eyes of an audience.

" 'Farewell, Old California, I'm going far away,' " she began, her voice carrying more of a shiver than she'd have preferred, but still good and solid, " 'Where gold is found more plenty, in larger lumps they say. And—' "

"If you're going, young lady, then for God's sake, go!" one of the actors squeaked in a falsetto voice that caused everyone to break into uproarious laughter, even, after a moment, Tom Maguire.

Fay stumbled over the final line, then quit and wanted to hide in shame. But something in Maguire's eyes made her go on. She shouldn't have, because her voice broke; then she forgot the words, although she'd sung it a hundred times. And as the laughter swelled, hot tears rolled from her deep blue eyes to river down her cheeks.

"My dear, please don't weep. Forgive this sport," he growled, silencing the others. "Now, I am running late and we have completed auditions. Besides, your voice, though hauntingly beautiful, lacks the projection necessary to fill my theater. You would never be heard in the gallery, which, by itself, holds over three hundred. I'm very sorry."

She trusted her voice enough to say thank you and then she bowed again as he and the others passed. As they swept outside to hail carriages, she could hear their happy chatter.

Fay buried her face in her hands and shook her head in desolation. She'd had only one chance, and now it was gone. The lobby, rich with tapestries and heavily carpeted, had sponged her voice away, and nervousness had taken the rest, until she must have sounded pathetically weak. What in the world could she do now?

"Don't take it so hard, my young lovely," the doorman whispered comfortingly as he draped his arm over her shoulders. "I'll see you have a real good time tonight with old Billy Barstow. We—"

Fay slung his arm away and her self-pity flashed with anger. "Get away from me, you pudgy buffoon!"

"Why . . ."

His mouth dropped open and Fay slapped his flabby jowls and then ran outside to see Tom Maguire and his new cast making a noisy departure. Fay moved toward them as if drawn by the company she so desperately wanted. But as she approached the last carriage, a girl not much older than herself leaned out the window and called, "Maybe you ought to try singing to Bill Barstow tonight instead!"

Hilarious laughter filled the coach. At least it did until Fay bent over in the street, picked up a muddy stone, and heaved it through the curtain. The guffaws turned to oaths, but Fay didn't hear them because she was striding away and feeling much better.

If a dancer or singer could not find work at Maguire's, it was a big step down to the next jobs. They were on the waterfront, tough places called "two-bit houses."

That's where Fay headed.

"That's enough, sweetie," the lady yelled.

Fay nodded, descended from the tiny stage, and picked her way through the funny chairs whose backs were equipped with holders for rum mugs and beer bottles. She tried not to notice the stench of cigar smoke that permeated everything.

"Was I all right?" she asked, approaching the cigar-smoking lady who ran the Dancing Tiger.

Miss Rosie Raye was a handsome woman of indeterminable age, who wore makeup so thick it cracked when she laughed and whose dyed hair was rose-colored. She was tough and talented, capable of handling anything or anyone—when sober.

"Yeah," she offered, shrugging and smoking rapidly. "Too good, really. Your voice is the finest thing I've ever had in this dump. The customers won't appreciate it, though. They're always raisin' hell and drinkin as fast as we can refill their bottles."

Fay nodded. She couldn't hide the bitterness she felt for being forced to work under such circumstances. If it hadn't been for pride and the hope that she could win her next audition at Maguire's Opera by strengthening her voice here, well, she'd have returned to the Comstock.

"Are you thinking you're too good for the Dancing Tiger?"

"Oh, no!"

"Yes, you were. And I'll tell you something, young lady, you're right." Rosie fumbled into her dress pocket and revealed a small silver flask. "Believe in drinking my own firewater, same as my customers."

Fay nodded and was shocked at the way this woman drank with such desperate need.

"Oh, that's good," Rose sighed, closing her eyes and smacking her lips with enjoyment.

"Miss Raye, how much money can I earn here?"

"Plenty, with your talent and looks." She placed one of her high-heeled shoes on an empty chair and leaned on her knee. "Here's how the deal works. You're just one of many acts I have going each night. I pay 'em all the same—two bits a performance."

"Two bits! Why, I'd starve!"

"No, you won't. If the boys like you as much as I think, they'll want you onstage over and over—maybe four or five times an evening."

Fay swallowed. "I don't know if I can sing and dance that often."

"Oh, sure you can! Thing of it is, you have to learn to pace yourself and use your voice properly. Don't strain."

"Then I wouldn't be heard." She didn't dare tell Rosie Mr. Maguire's assessment.

Rosie shook her head, blew smoke through her nostrils. "Uh-uh. Just now you were trying too hard. Not relaxing your throat muscles or using your chest."

Fay's eyes widened. "You sound as though you've had experience."

"I have. Why, up until a few years ago, I was one of the biggest names on the east coast."

"You were! Did you perform on Broadway?" Fay asked reverently.

Rosie's eyes clouded for an instant. She took another drink. "No," she admitted, "but everywhere else. I just never got the breaks or had the kind of manager you need to make it big in

New York. Hell, I should have managed myself. Coulda done a sight better. I've proven that by turning this stinking hole into the most popular two-bit house on the waterfront."

"Yes, I can see that. But . . . about my voice. Making it stronger. Would you teach me how?"

Rosie's expression changed and her eyes could still spark. "I might. Depends on how you work out for me. Whether or not we get along. I seen lots of girls come and go. If they've got the talent, like you, they generally won't work very hard, because they're taking singing easy."

"I'd work. Miss Raye, I promise I'd work hard."

"Maybe. But then you'd get to thinking you deserved better and move on. So where would I be?"

Fay could see the logic. Rosie had probably been used by more than just her stage managers.

"Listen, honey. I might just help you anyway. Besides, there's plenty of other things you need to learn."

"What?"

Rosie shrugged. "If you really want to become famous, you'll have to improve your dances, learn breakdowns and—"

"Breakdowns? What are those?"

"Black people do 'em and white people put blackum on their faces and try to imitate. It brings the house down."

"I'm not really interested in that, Miss Raye. I'll be honest with you. I've sung and danced in most all the gold camps since I was just a little girl. And I made my own way then, as I will now at your place. What I want is to get into plays."

One heavily caked auburn eyebrow flew up. "My, you *are* ambitious. But so was I at your age, so I forgive you. Still it's pretty obvious you're going to leave me for Tom Maguire at the first chance. So, again, why should I bother?"

Fay looked into her blood-vesseled eyes. "Because someone with your talent appreciates someone with my talent. Furthermore, I'll work very hard as long as you help me. I'll never cheat you or say bad things. I'll even be glad to pay for the lessons."

It was Rosie Raye's turn to register shock, and for a moment she was at a loss for words. "Well," she said finally, "I think you've just convinced me. I'll put you in tonight's lineup. Don't let the men upset you if they laugh. They're paying for their fun. Besides, they still got to obey my rules."

"Rules?"

"Yes. My customers are rough, but they leave their weapons and profanity at the downstairs bar. After you perform, you'll be expected to dance. I'll be watching you girls close, so don't worry. After each dance, your partner will lead you to the bar, where you can have your choice of a drink or its value in money—two bits. Take the money more often than not or you'll be drunk before closing time."

Fay nodded. She'd take the money every time and she could see now why these places were called two-bit houses and why a girl could do pretty well for herself.

"One more thing," Rosie cautioned. "A lot of the places up and down this waterfront keep little rooms for their girls to work on the side. I don't. My girls never leave this place until it's closed. Then we all exit together with my deskman along for protection. He takes us to the hotel across the street. Can you move?"

"Yes. I'll do it as soon as my rent is up."

"Better not wait," Rosie said. "If these men want you, they'll hang around out in the fog and jump you on your way home."

Fay shivered. "I'll change this afternoon," she whispered.

"Good!" Rosie Raye brightened now that business was over. She waltzed back to her bar and lifted a bottle of rum. "Want a drink to your successful employment at the Dancing Tiger?"

"I . . . I don't drink," she confessed, "but . . . but I will, if you—"

"No!" Rosie cried sharply; then, realizing she'd overreacted, she tried to smile. "I . . . I didn't mean to startle you, Fay. But if you want to become a great singer and dancer, never drink."

She poured herself at least three fingers of rum. "You see, like yourself, I was fortunate enough to be born with looks and talent. I even had some pretty good voice and dance teachers back in Boston."

The woman closed her eyes and seemed to drift into her youth, where the world she remembered was probably always a beautiful, magnificent command performance. Then her face changed and became etched with pain. "I fell madly in love with my first stage manager, a man named Johnny Logan," she said, snapping back to the present. "Yes, I married him when I was no older than you, my sweetness. And he taught me all about the business. How to perform onstage—and off, at the receptions I was given. But Johnny taught me one thing he never should have, and that was how to drink."

"I'm . . . I'm sorry." Fay meant it. To be that close to fame and have it all washed away by liquor seemed inconceivable. Glenn didn't drink much at all.

Rosie Raye lifted her glass. "That's my sad story and your history lesson. Now I'll drink to the future. Not mine. But yours, Fay Taylor. Because—this sounds awful—because after watching you, I can see myself about twenty years ago. And I like that."

"Miss Raye—"

"Rosie. Call me Miss Rosie, then get the hell out of here and I'll see you tonight."

Fay nodded, then left the woman because she wanted to change hotels before dark and rest a few hours. It was going to be a long, strenuous night.

As she left the Dancing Tiger, Fay could feel a lump in her throat for Rosie. Maybe they could help each other. Perhaps it was meant to be that she work here awhile before again auditioning at Maguire's Opera House.

It was just a feeling. A feeling that she and this woman were destined to benefit each other in a very special way. One thing seemed evident: they were both terribly lonely.

The past and the future—they always came together.

17

Rosie's prediction came true on Fay's opening night. By the time she made her first appearance on the tiny stage, the crowd of sailors and hard-drinking miners were intoxicated and as intent on shouting jests among themselves as they were on being entertained. But Fay wore a snug dress, and even those who had to keep an eye closed to focus hooted and whistled with more than usual enthusiasm.

She tried to project her voice over the revelry, all the way to Rosie's bar. It seemed impossible, yet as the long evening progressed and she danced with customers between her performances, Fay noticed that some of the other singers had learned the technique.

The activity onstage was fast-paced and continuous. There were dancers like herself, a pair of lady acrobats, an inept young juggler who made the crowd roar with laughter, and a host of broken-down old professionals who performed as though they were alone in the room. Maybe it helped to pretend you weren't onstage before a mob of drunks, listening to their insults and catcalls.

Fay learned very quickly that evening. When someone became abusive or disorderly, she ignored him and would concentrate on Rosie, or a tired but kindly expression, or, sometimes, she was even able to picture Glenn.

She was exhausted by midnight, but realized she'd done three performances so far, each better received than the last. And she thought no one else on the stage had come so close to emptying the bar. But the room had gotten warmer and warmer, and the cigar smoke was so thick her voice was hoarse and her eyes stung and watered. Then, too, her dancing onstage, while obviously a big attraction, was sapping her strength and the two-bit dances were becoming an ordeal.

Almost every man who paid for a dance was woman-starved. Fay had to slap more than one before Rosie's doorman, a huge Negro, began to throw them out. But even so, Fay was almost in tears long before closing time, and during her fourth performance she was so exhausted she tripped while dancing and fell hard.

A stampede of onlookers stumbled onstage and tried to help her. They promptly started pushing each other and things quickly got out of hand as fists began winging. Fay crawled offstage as a chair whistled overhead.

The doorman and bouncer sprang onstage to help, but a rum bottle across his shaved skull dropped him like a walnut tree and then Rosie herself was there, emptying a gun into the ceiling as the combatants hit the boards.

"All right, gents," she yelled, overseeing her work, "the party is over for tonight! Everyone get the hell out of here. But be sure and come back. Bring your friends, too!"

There was a lot of good-natured grumbling but it was obvious the men respected Rosie, and even with her bouncer temporarily out of action, they obeyed. Why risk a bullet? The waterfront was packed with two-bit houses.

Late that night Rosie had to almost carry Fay to her room, she was so weary.

"How much money did you earn dancing?" the woman asked, dropping into a broken chair.

Fay rolled over on the bed and slowly counted the money while Rosie uncorked her flask. "Four dollars and ninety cents."

"Hell, someone cheated you out of a dime. Even so, with the dollar you earned from me, you did very well your first night."

She poured rum down her throat, then smacked her lips as always. "Thing of it is, I can't have you falling down on the stage every night and causing a riot."

Fay put her money away. It *was* a lot for one night. But right now she was so exhausted she didn't care. "I'm sorry I tripped that way. Is the doorman all right?"

Rosie chuckled. "Yeah, Mr. Jones will be fine, but meaner than hell on 'em for the next couple of nights. I feel sorry for the ones he'll throw down those stairs. Anyway, I can see you're going to have to either give up dancing onstage or with my customers. You can't do both."

"I agree." She'd reached the same conclusion hours ago. And though it wouldn't be to her advantage financially, she much preferred the stage.

Rosie lit a cigar. "Tell you what, young lady, I'm betting you're going to draw customers. I'll pay you a dollar an appearance and you just entertain."

Fay heaved a great sigh of relief. "My feet are flattened and I've got pinch marks nearly everywhere. Thank you."

"Don't thank me, girl. It's only good business. Want a drink? Oh, sorry, forgot. You know, a funny thing someone told me . . ."

Fay tried to listen but fell asleep. When she woke up, her body was so bruised and battered from dancing with Rosie's overexuberant customers she could hardly get out of bed. At least, she thought, remembering last night's conversation, I won't have to be a two-bit dancer anymore.

Rosie Raye, tipsy or sober, never failed to give Fay voice lessons three afternoons a week. Years of theater had given her an extraordinary vocal range which even the powerful little black cigars hadn't completely destroyed.

She had Fay practiced the scales too, and worked hard to improve the quality as well as the strength of her singing. For the first month or two, Fay hadn't noticed any difference in her ability, but the customers and other performers had and were enthusiastic in their support.

She grew to enjoy the evening performances. Her dancing became a continual challenge and several of the other acts let her improvise on their own routines. Rosie even agreed that it was a good idea for her to take a few hours off once in a while to study their competition. They went together, and heavily chaperoned by Rosie's customers. The idea was to develop new dance routines.

As the weeks passed, more and more young men flocked to Rosie's to fall in love with the most popular girl on the Barbary Coast. She was the hit of the waterfront, besieged by marriage proposals and those of a less lofty variety, some from a growing number of high-society patrons. But she ignored them all.

The memory of Glenn Donovan still burned brightly, although she knew it would not last forever. Sometimes, while onstage, a young man with a more than passing resemblance to the aspiring young Irish engineer would enter the Dancing Tiger. Invariably Fay Taylor would drop a line in mid-song or ruin a dance step. But few noticed, and after that first heart-gripping moment of recognition, she would steady herself and angrily continue, knowing that Glenn was three thousand miles away.

It helped to keep busy when she wasn't working or practicing her stage skills.

"My God, Fay, sometimes I almost wish you were a drinking girl," Rosie complained. "You never let up. It's always business."

"I'm not getting any younger," she told the woman she'd come to love. In truth, if it hadn't been for Rosie's drinking and those rare but awful nights when the woman surpassed her substantial limit and became piteously maudlin, Fay might have thought of the woman as her own mother.

"Well, my sweetness, no one is. Least of all those who work so hard."

Fay glanced up. "Or drink away their health," she whispered tightly.

Rosie grew very still. She opened her mouth, then closed it soundlessly.

Fay reached over and took her blue-veined hand. "I'm sorry. I had no call. It's just that I've grown fond enough to worry."

Rosie smiled, a wide, wonderful smile that made her appear ten years younger. "I forgive, my child. And thanks for the worry. I'll . . . I'll try to cut down to one flask of rum a day."

"Will you!"

"On one condition," the woman said quickly.

Fay's spirits dropped. She should have known. Rosie Raye couldn't help but drive a bargain for everything. "I'm listening."

"The condition is that you let Mr. Jones teach you some Negro songs and a couple of breakdown steps, along with how to play the banjo."

"Oh, Rosie. No!" She remembered her terrible Virginia City experience.

"Very well," Rosie sighed, "then it's no deal."

She was beaten. "Can he really play the banjo?"

"Of course. All Negroes can play music. Even if it's only on the harmonica. Mr. Jones is an absolute master on the banjo. And he sings beautifully. He can show you a couple of easy steps. Fay, you'd be sensational!"

"If he's so good, why don't you put *him* onstage?" she challenged, irritated that she'd been used.

"I would, only they'd tease him to anger, and you know how he can be when he's prodded."

It made sense. "All right, I'll learn the banjo and Negro songs and dances."

"Shake!" Rosie ordered. And they did.

Four months later, Fay went onstage with black on her face and a banjo in her hands. While her fans eyed her skeptically, she began to play—far better than she'd ever done with that Virginia City guitar. Any musician would have noticed that she only fingered chords and a few easy notes. But what Fay did, she did very very well, especially the song that began:

Clare de kitchen, old folks, young folks
Clare de kitchen, old folks, young folks
Old Virginny never tire!

That really got them wound up and clapping to the music. She forgot about the blackum that was already beginning to streak and run down her cheeks in the hot, heavy air. She finished her song and began to play the ever-popular "The Boatman's Dance" with its "hi-de-ho" refrain.

They went wild when she tossed the banjo to its grinning owner, Mr. Jones.

"Go on and play!" she cried happily.

And while he did, she jumped into the air and began to show them her new breakdown steps. She whirled and twirled like a spinning pinwheel at a Fourth of July celebration, faster and faster, keeping time to the banjo and clapping hands. Laughing as she spun, Fay dazzled them with a grace all her own and loved every minute of it, until at last she could whirl no more.

Then she bowed to them and, one by one, blew out the little candles on the stage until she was out of breath and sight.

The house went crazy! Silver and gold showered the stage. And Fay Taylor, trying desperately hard to get her breath, came out for a bow and threw an arm out to Mr. Jones. There must have been sixty dollars at her feet—the huge black man would get it all this night. He deserved every penny. Besides, Fay thought as she stood flushed with the thunderous ovation, tonight was only the beginning. She had passed the test for stardom. Tom Maguire didn't know that yet—but he would. Right now, though, she'd settle for the pride she saw in Rosie. Yes, that and the fact that the woman's eyes were clearer these days were reward enough.

From that night on, she never thought again of money. It came to her every performance. Rosie profited too and raised everyone's wages. She expanded the room to accommodate bigger crowds and charged a small admission price. No one objected. More and more, her customers were a better class of men, used to seeing shows up on fashionable Portsmouth Square and even at Tom Maguire's Opera House.

Then the inevitable happened. Maguire himself visited the Dancing Tiger late one evening to see what all the fuss was about in a lowly two-bit house that was stealing his own patrons. Upon his entrance, the tall, dignified entrepreneur was received coldly; he even overheard the suggestion from several of Fay's most ardent admirers that he would be more at home in places other than the waterfront.

At this he laughed, and his curiosity was whetted to the point that when Fay Taylor finally did appear, he was as much a part of the excitement as the lowliest man in the room. From the moment the girl danced onstage, singing and playing and making everyone clap his hands, Tom Maguire was captivated by her grace and unflagging vitality.

The room was stifling and the clapping hands so infernally loud, it seemed impossible that her maidenly voice could reach across the melee through the smoke-filled air. Yet it did, and so clearly that every word was like cut crystal and sweet as church chimes.

He began to edge forward through the rows of chairs and the stench of sweating, unwashed bodies. Someone objected to his movement and elbowed him sharply. Tom Maguire returned the favor, doubling the ruffian up as he shoved into the front.

Fay recognized him instantly. Her voice broke in mid-note and her long supple fingers tangled in the banjo's strings. He didn't seem to notice.

"I've seen you before," he said, looking up at her.

"Yes. In the lobby of your theater, where I did an impromptu rendition of 'Farewell, Old California.' "

"Ah yes, but—"

Fay heard a complaining voice. "Excuse me, Mr. Maguire, but I'm going to finish my act."

"Of course! By all means. Can we talk afterward?"

Through clouds of putrid blue cigar smoke, Fay saw Rosie at the back of the room. The lady was ordering a drink. "Yes," Fay said woodenly. "I'll meet you backstage."

And then she sang a ballad for Rosie called "If It Were Only Yesterday." She sang it mournfully and low, until her audience swam before her tears and Rosie Raye finished her drink and snatched up a bottle.

It was much later that night when Fay knocked on the woman's door. Rosie had recognized the talent in Fay that had been her own once, and had risen above herself to protect the younger woman. Rosie, who'd taught her to sing correctly and increased her performance by adapting new dances with the banjo.

"Are you awake?" Fay whispered.

"No. Go away."

Fay bit her lip and went inside. "I've decided to leave," she admitted. "Mr. Maguire has given me a good role in his theater and wants me to begin rehearsals tomorrow."

"I guessed as much." Rosie lit her bedside lamp and sat up.

Her eyes were bloodshot—as red as her hair. She looked sick and weak.

"Oh, Rosie, why did you go and drink so much again? You're going to kill yourself."

"Probably, but it wasn't much of a good-bye party without rum *or* you."

Fay's eyes became downcast. "I feel like hell, leaving you. Just say the word and I'll stay."

Rosie shook her head. "No, I knew this was coming. I'd hoped it wouldn't be so soon, but anyone who saw you couldn't miss feeling and believing in your talent. Besides, I had my chance and I ruined it. Now it's your turn, and I'll be cheering you on every step of the way. You'll go even beyond Tom Maguire to New York City, and someday . . . someday to Europe!"

Fay tried to smile. It was all happening so fast, and she was not thinking past her first real theatrical part at Maguire's Opera House.

"Will you please not drink so much, Rosie?" she begged.

"I'll try, my sweetness, though I make no promises. Will you invite this old has-been to your opening-night celebration?"

The request was so small and humble, Fay burst into tears. Tears that never seemed to stop and left her filled with sorrow until Rosie gently pushed her away and told her good-bye.

When Fay turned at the doorway to wish Rosie well, the words curdled in her throat. She'd caught Rosie reaching for her rum bottle.

Fay closed the door and felt sick at heart.

She made her debut on stage as Pauline, the young daughter of a wealthy man. In the five-act play, Claude Melnotte, the gardener's ignorant son, falls in love with her—blindly, hopelessly so, because he can never marry so far above his class. Yet, according to the story, this dashing young man learns to paint and to write lovely poetry because, as he insists, "art became the shadow of the starlight in my haunted eyes."

Even though the gardener's son is handsome, he is so pathetically worshiping that Pauline spurns his love, as she does the advances of several other suitors, two of whom become enraged enough to plot her downfall. This is accomplished by providing the impoverished Claude with enough money to impersonate a prince. When Pauline's duped father consents and the marriage is performed, young Claude takes the girl to a wretched hovel on their wedding night. But now, seeing her tears of betrayal, he is full of remorse and agrees to an annulment. He is shocked, then overwhelmed, to discover that Pauline truly loves him and wishes to remain his wife.

For a short time, they are poor but as happy as children. Then the war comes and Claude goes away, eventually to become a great general. Upon his return, he discovers his poor wife has been sold to an old rejected suitor for her bankrupt father's debts. "Claude planked up thrice the sum" and clasped Pauline in his arms as the curtain fell, leaving the audience misty-eyed, awash in a sea of sentiment.

"Encore! Encore!" The great crowd shouted as Fay and the cast returned again and again for bows. And then, as the highlight of the evening, Fay took center stage and softly played her banjo and sang to the magnificent accompaniment of a full-pit orchestra. She did all the gold-rush favorites and ended with a rousing rendition of "Camptown Ladies."

They loved her. Overnight, she was San Francisco's darling.

Rosie Raye saw her win their affection, and her own heart soared for the girl she once might have been. After the performance, Rosie tried desperately to gain admittance to the reception, where an elite group of well-wishers thronged. But a chubby, balding young doorkeeper who recognized her as the manager of a lowly two-bit house called in others to escort her roughly outside.

"You don't belong here, lady," he snapped. "Go back to the waterfront where you belong."

And though Rosie swore and ranted, the milling mass of celebrants ignored her. The steel door to the alley clanged shut, hiding her from the offended eyes of the crowd and leaving her alone, cut off from Fay Taylor forever.

Rosie leaned against a barrel of trash and hung her head. Then she lifted her sagging chin and slowly walked away. The snotty doorman was right. She didn't belong in Maguire's. She never had.

In the ensuing months, Fay visited Rosie several times, but it was like seeing a total stranger. The spark seemed to have gone out of her. Many of the acts at the Dancing Tiger, sensing the despair and unable to change the boss's suicidal drinking, grew despondent themselves, until their performances were lifeless and they were either fired or drifted away to more popular two-bit houses.

Rosie hired replacements, but they were never as good, and finally, even Mr. Jones apologetically quit to seek other employment. At least, that was what Rosie thought he had said. But no matter. An excuse was an excuse. You gave people a job or a break and they deserted you for the first better offer that came along.

The hell with them all, Rosie thought as her tired mind wallowed in hazy self-pity. The only friend who never disappointed her now, who made it possible to face each new day, was her rum. And they were becoming very good friends indeed.

Fay Taylor learned that her third leading man in six months had just been fired. It was getting to be a joke backstage that to be picked to star opposite Fay was the theatrical kiss of death. Each succeeding actor was a shade less qualified than his predecessor, and the last one had only just learned his lines after weeks of struggle.

Fay stormed into Tom Maguire's office. She knew it well, and the man who inhabited it, because they spent long hours together talking about anything and everything. Everything, that is, except why Tom kept firing her leading man.

"I don't understand!" she cried. "Tom, do you know how difficult it is for me to play my own part and whisper the lines for yet another Claude Melnotte?"

He colored at the upbraiding, yet did not anger. "My dear, not many performers can remain onstage with you and appear adequate."

"Well, they *were* adequate. More than adequate, at first. But lately . . ." Her words trailed off in exasperation.

"Listen," he said placatingly, "I'm sorry. I guess I hadn't realized the burden you were taking."

She melted under his wide, handsome smile. And though he was old enough to be her father, she knew he thought of her romantically.

"Tom, find someone and let him stay."

"Yes, yes, of course. I promise you this new understudy will be the last."

"Do you mean it?" Relief flooded through her. "Oh, Tom, it would make my job so much easier!"

He hugged her with deep affection. "I promise."

But three weeks later, after he came upon Fay and her new

lead sitting close together, laughing as they rehearsed their lines, Tom Maguire broke his promise without an explanation.

That's when Fay realized the true course of his disfavor—jealousy.

"Admit it," she said quietly. "Tom, you've never lied—please don't start now. Are you . . . are you in love with me?"

His smile vanished, to be replaced by a wintry bleakness. "I'm more than twenty years your senior," he said. "But that doesn't seem to matter. I can't order myself to quit thinking of you night and day."

He came to face her. Then he bent and took her into his arms and kissed her mouth. Not passionately, but deeply, as though he was probing her heart.

She pulled back. "Tom, no. I don't love you."

"But you might," he argued. "Give me time. I'm in marvelous shape. Far stronger than those pink-cheeked young fools who prattled to you on the stage."

"Tom, please," she begged, "it just isn't going to happen."

"Don't say that!" he demanded. "Fay, I can give you the world. Make you more famous than you've ever dreamed. I have the money and the connections that will take you farther than Lola Montez or any of them. Think about it."

"I already have," she sighed. "I don't mean to be cruel, but I've learned I can make my own way, given the chance. My brother used me for so long, I guess I'm almost cynical whenever a man starts talking like that."

"But I'm not your brother!" he cried. "And I can do as I promise."

Fay avoided his eyes. "I believe you. But no thanks. Maybe . . . maybe I need a rest. Perhaps to visit the Comstock. I have friends there."

"A man?" he asked quickly. Much too quickly.

"I did have—once. He's gone now. Back to New York City."

Tom Maguire didn't even attempt to hide the flood of relief which washed his face. "Maybe you do need a rest. And I'll tell you something. I've been keeping abreast of things in the Comstock. It's booming and people are flooding in from all over the world."

"What are you leading up to, Tom?"

"Just this. I've decided to construct a great new opera

house in Virginia City. Bigger and finer even than this one. How would you like to make your homecoming appearance onstage?"

Something leaped in her bosom, an excitement she hadn't felt in a long, long time. They'd remember her well. She was certain of that much. And while the absence of Glenn Donovan would be painful, she suddenly felt an overwhelming desire to visit Holly, Julia, and, yes, even her brother. Maybe he'd changed.

She glanced up and laughed happily.

"Tom, build your grand theater and I'll play for you there on opening night. Play and sing and dance, even if I have no leading man."

"You will have, my dear. As always, I shall be center seat, front row."

Fay nodded. Then she had to turn away, for his love burned ever so painfully. But, she thought, I *am* going back!

18

Seasons had passed since Dade had touched her, and still her beautiful face burned his dreams, tormented his days, and left him racked with naked hunger for the heart and body of Julia Tillman.

His need was stupid and dangerous. He realized that. But the knowing did not quench the need he felt or keep him from observing her secretly each day as she arrived and departed from her business. Sometimes, when he was buying mining equipment in San Francisco, he slept with other women, the most beautiful money could buy. He even selected them using Julia as a standard, then cried her name out loud as he used their bodies. But each time, the man from Virginia City was left with only disgust and a mind-consuming passion that only one woman alive could quench.

A woman who hated him—no, despised him—for robbing her of a friend who was being cheated. Dade knew this and even felt guilt, which drove him to return from San Francisco with lavish gifts for his unsuspecting wife. He believed that Holly might even grow old in innocence and sweet naiveté. He hoped this would be the case, because she was becoming a beloved figure in Nevada. As he decayed inside, she blossomed.

It made Dade sick, made him compare his own carnal desire to her loving compassion and abhor the comparison.

As month after month passed, he drove himself to learn from Bevis York all that might carry him to riches and even fame. And why not? Already he was on his way to becoming prominent; his name was spoken as a leader in the quest for Nevada statehood.

But first, there was a war. On February 8, word had reached the Comstock by Pony Express that seven Southern states, under Jefferson Davis as President, had created the Confederate States of America. The tension had exploded into a division of loyalties among the Comstock population that nearly erupted into open warfare a few months later with the electrifying news of the attack on Fort Sumter. Within the week, a total of eleven southern states had seceded from the Union and President Lincoln was calling for seventy-five thousand Union volunteers.

One morning Dade was drawn from his office by a call to arms. Jubilant secessionists had hoisted the Confederate Stars and Bars over one of the saloons and barricaded themselves inside with enough guns and whiskey to last a month.

Not to be outdone, Union sympathizers raised Old Glory over a place directly across the street and began to open fire on their adversaries. Both groups were too drunk to do much except blow out storefront windows. But it was Dade Taylor who dispatched a rider to Fort Churchill, and shortly a company of United States dragoons stormed into Virginia City, Genoa, and Carson City to confiscate arms and proclaim martial law.

Several days later, Dade himself led a cheering crowd of over five thousand Unionists up the slopes of Sun Mountain. There, twelve hundred feet above the city, they opened cases of champagne, planted a flagpole, listened to a band play, and cheered themselves hoarse while the Stars and Stripes snapped in the crystal-clear air.

Hundreds of them volunteered on the spot to race east and join President Lincoln's army. And they asked Dade to be their leader, even though he had no military experience. It was the proudest day of his life and the only thing that he could imagine to make it finer was to have Julia there as he stood beside the flagpole.

When he addressed that sea of uplifted faces, his voice was throaty with real emotion. "By God, you honor me!" he choked. "And I would give more than life to lead you into the great struggle which will decide the fate of this country.

"But I cannot. No, much as I'd like to, I must stay here to do my part by unearthing riches which will help finance the Union cause. And to remain with my wife, who gives her own health so that less fortunate men, such as yourselves, can join the great battle."

They cheered until he held his hands aloft. "But as you leave here in the days to come, I go with you in heart... in spirit."

They fired their guns in salute, drank and cried and proclaimed the great deeds they'd accomplish for Lincoln. But in the sobering days which followed, when each Pony Express rider brought more news of Southern victories, the vanguards of patriots became a trickle, and after the Battle of Bull Run, no more left.

Julia prospered, because she never revealed her own loyalties. Her emporium became one of the few businesses on the Comstock which was patronized by the unholy trinity of Unionists, prostitutes, and secessionists.

Dade knew this and hated it, because each time the first of the month came around, an envelope was delivered to his office with a bank-deposit slip. The slip was a record of money paid on a debt he did not wish to see end.

"Twenty-seven hundred dollars paid," he whispered as he read the bank statement, then crumpled it up and hurled it into his wastebasket. "More than half in less than one year. Dammit!"

Through the glass window he saw one of their accounting clerks twist about at his outburst. Dade glared at the young man, intimidating him into an instantaneous flurry of activity.

"Dammit!" he repeated, rising from his desk and staring out the window of their land-company offices, which occupied a huge new building.

Yes, they were doing well. Very well, he and Bevis. Not that they liked each other, because they didn't, though to an outsider or competitor they seemed ideally matched, with the combination of youthful energy and mature wisdom. What it boiled down to was a wary respect and a very powerful urge on both their parts to become empire builders on the Comstock.

Dade retrieved the wadded deposit slip and dropped it absently into his coat pocket. His hands were trembling and his pulse raced. He needed a drink, but his stomach had suddenly become queasy. Julia did that to him. It was her fault and he was finally going to do something about it. While she owed him. While he dared.

"Tell Mr. York I'm on my way to Carson City. Business. I may not be able to return tonight."

He halted at the door. "In fact, I'm quite sure I won't. Suggest to Mr. York that he join my wife for dinner in my absence."

"Yes, sir. Anything else?"

Dade's fingers toyed with the ball of paper in his pocket. "Yes," he said quietly. "Tell me—didn't we pick up the mortgage on Harland Raney's Silver Mercantile Exchange a few months ago?"

"Yes, sir. Seems he isn't doing very well these days. If you recall, the loan was personally authorized out of your business account."

"That's right"—Dade snapped his fingers—"I'd forgotten. Has he been timely with his payments?"

"No. I have a note here that—"

"That I intended to give him a quarter's leeway before taking action. Correct?"

"Quite."

"I thought so." Dade nodded, knowing perfectly the exact details of the mortgage paper. Raney wasn't going to pay. He couldn't. Since Julia's departure, his business had nose-dived. When Julia Tillman's Emporium opened, Raney's place became a tomb.

"I think . . ." he mused, extracting his gold watch and eyeing it critically, "I think I'll just have time to stop by and give him a reminder. After all, we need our money to pay expenses."

"Very true, sir," the clerk said as he energetically began to leaf through ledger pages.

Dade smiled, then left. He ran his fingers through his long black hair and angled south toward the failing business. As he strode along, Dade passed across from Julia's Emporium. He noted that two well-known prostitutes, Sugar and Princess, were brazenly loitering in the doorway, chatting with Julia.

Dade said nothing, but his stride quickened and he bulled his way down the center of the walk, forcing men to step aside. Julia, he thought, no longer gave a damn about his opinion or anyone's.

It was time she had a lesson in humility. Time she was shown the realities of life on the Comstock. He was ready to collect his due. And this time—this time he would not be denied.

He crashed into the Silver Mercantile Exchange and glared into the gloominess, seeing no one.

"Raney! Raney, are you back there?"

No answer.

Dade marched down the aisle to the rear door and threw it open to see Raney propped up in a chair reading a tattered newspaper and trying to hide a pint of whiskey.

"What do you want?"

Dade walked up to the man. He lifted his polished boot, placed it on the armrest, and shoved hard. Raney went crashing over sideways, cursing and yelling and grabbing for the uncorked bottle. "Get up," Dade spit, "before I collect my money out of your stinking hide!"

Harland Raney forgot whatever he'd been about to yell. He swallowed noisily, clambered erect, and eyed Dade with unconcealed fear.

"Mr. Taylor, I was fixing to come see you today. Tomorrow at the latest. You see, me and the wife have been doing poorly. Business is—"

"Dead. That's what it is. You and Tooey and the others have all been choking to death since Julia Tillman opened her Emporium. Isn't that right?"

At the mention of Julia's name, Raney seemed to transform. His thin lips curved into a snarl and hatred blazed across his eyes. "She's a wicked woman. A harlot and the devil's siren!" he swore, spittle spraying outward.

"Maybe, but she's also a better businesswoman than you gave her credit for."

Raney's voice rattled up an octave. "She will burn in the fires of hell!"

"Yeah, but that doesn't help you and your fellow merchants now, does it? If I were you . . ." He let his words die unspoken.

"What? What would you do, Mr. Taylor? We already tried

to cut off her supplies, but she just hired another freighter. We even took a loss on some goods to beat her, but those whores don't care." His eyes pleaded. "You're a smart man. What else can we do?"

"Well, I dunno," he said, keeping his voice matter-of-fact. "You mentioned something about burning in the fires of hell."

"I did."

"Seems to me they won't come quick enough to save your business. Maybe . . . maybe you and a couple of the others should start the fires a little sooner."

Raney's eyes bugged.

"I'm not suggesting a thing," Dade said quickly. "Least of all that you should hurt Julia Tillman. Oh, no, if word got out that someone had deliberately burned down her store and she was killed inside, there'd be a hanging."

Raney's Adam's apple bobbed.

"But arson up here is a very serious crime. Of course, it wouldn't be too disastrous. I mean, there's only one other building attached to Julia's place, so the fire wouldn't spread. No danger of that."

Raney's expression suddenly brightened, as though someone had turned the wick up in lanterns behind his eyes. His pale, parchmentlike skin glowed ever brighter. "Yes, the only other building is the logging company. One of your competitors."

"Say," Dade exclaimed with a snap of his fingers, "you're right. Huh. How about that?" Dade smiled. He withdrew a good, rich Cuban cigar from his coat pocket, bit off the tip and spit it on the floor before lighting up. Then he held the flame out and watched Raney's eyes be drawn to the match. In the gloomy, fetid confines of the back room, the flickering orange flame seemed alive.

Dade dropped the match to the floor. Its fire caught dust and glowed up before Raney's boot stomped it out.

"This place could go . . ." Raney quavered.

"Yes, but those things can happen. Well, I'm off for Carson City. Be back tomorrow. I expect you'll find plenty to do in my absence. Perhaps, if your business outlook improves, I may even be able to extend your loan. But I trust there will be no need for this town to conduct a hanging in the near future."

"No, sir, I sure read your meaning."

"Then you are far more intelligent than you look, Harland,

because I really haven't said or suggested anything. Isn't that true?''

Raney's eyes dropped and he nodded. He was on his own and knew it. Even more important, Dade was certain he would be careful not to harm Julia.

''Good day. I'll see you tomorrow.''

''Tomorrow it is.'' Raney looked up and suddenly blurted, ''Only thing is, I thought you owned her gawddamned emporium, Mr. Taylor.''

''I do,'' he replied coolly. ''That's why no one would even for a minute believe anything you might say about our little talk.''

Then, leaving the man staring in bewilderment, Dade sauntered out of the building and into the brightness of day. Let Raney wonder. Because of the man's personal hatred and financial troubles, he'd do what he had to do, so no fire company in Virginia City could prevent Julia Tillman's Emporium from going up in smoke. Going up just like the fires of hell.

Gunfire shattered the early-morning silence. Julia Tillman sat bolt upright in her bed and heard a woman scream. This was followed by running footsteps and then someone pounding on her door. ''Fire! Julia, open up, your emporium is on fire!''

She was out of the bed and running across the floor, grabbing a wrap and yanking open the door to see Nicole Barrie. ''It's on fire, Julia. One of my girls tried to stop him; she was shot at!''

She didn't wait to hear any more. Julia raced out into the night. ''Not my store!'' she begged. ''Please, no!'' But as she rounded the corner of Howard Street, Julia saw flames erupting from the alley and knew her emporium was lost. Somewhere in the night she heard a fire bell. No matter which of the courageous volunteer fire departments arrived first, it wouldn't matter. Their little hand pumps could never quench that blaze.

Julia sprinted to the front door, realizing she'd forgotten the keys! Through the windows she saw yellow flames biting through the rear wall. The long room, hung with merchandise so carefully bought and priced, now glowed a soft orange. Julia could see her own reflection glancing off the jewelry display case. She had to get inside! To at least save something! She doubled up her fist and smashed in the windowpane nearest the door. Julia almost fainted as the jagged glass sliced her hand, but she gripped the doorframe and somehow managed to reach around inside and unbolt the lock.

She yanked har arm back out and saw that it was covered with blood. Someone behind her yelled to stay back, but she ignored the warning as she threw herself at the door and pitched inside. Her entrance created a draft and caused a terrible roar as flames exploded off the back wall as they drank the fresh air. They danced along the side walls, madly consuming everything. The flames were hungry, eager for more, and growing stronger each blistering second.

Julia scrambled to her feet. She tried to shield her face. Something split with the sound of a cracking tree, and all at once the rear wall collapsed inward. Julia had a fiery vision as parasols, bolts of satin and lace, and a little stuffed doll were immolated on one wall, while across, on the other, a row of new Stetsons sizzled, then burned like roasted marshmallows.

The heat was unbearable, so intense it singed her hair and bled the strength from her limbs even as she staggered to the jewelry case and tried to push it open.

"Julia!"

Nicole Barrie cringed in the doorway. Her large black eyes mirrored the tongues of flames. "The ceiling. It's going to fall!"

Julia didn't understand why her slippery, unresponsive fingers could not open the case. Why did it choose to resist now?

"Open!" she panted. "Open, damn you!"

But it would not. The heavy wood and glass stoutly awaited the flames in rigid vigil, even as its shiny varnish cover began to blister.

Julia swore at it, then shattered the glass to pieces with a heavy clothing iron.

She scooped up handfuls of jewelry. None of it was terribly valuable, but it was costly enough that she'd never allowed herself to wear the gold and silver bracelets, earrings, and necklaces which Nicole's girls so treasured as measures of their success. The jewelry didn't even belong to her. No, it was, like so many of the things she sold, purchased on credit.

"Julia!" Nicole Barrie, her face red as wine in the heat, threw herself into the room and grabbed Julia. "Leave them! They're not worth dying for!"

At that very moment, the section of roof nearest the alley collapsed and embers shot outward, burning their flesh and sparking their clothing.

Julia smelled her hair on fire. She screamed as Nicole grabbed a blanket and smothered the flames, then supported her as she began to lose consciousness. In her last flickering moments, Julia saw and felt herself dropping down, down, into the very fires of hell.

"Julia . . . Julia . . ." the voice kept repeating over and over in her ear. She wanted it to go away.

"Julia, please," Nicole Barrie whispered brokenly, "the doctor said—if you want—you will live."

She did *not* want to. And why should she listen to this voice that begged her to return to the torment she'd known before and which would now be infinitely worse? Once, there'd been a man . . . strong, brave, and yet surprisingly very gentle. A man to make her feel . . .

"Julia, honey. You *must* awaken! It's been three days. Open your eyes."

"Clayton," she whispered through her blistered lips. "Oh, please help me."

"I will help you, *mon amie*."

Julia forced her puffy eyes open until she could see. "I wish you had left me, Nicole. I didn't want to live."

"You are wrong. Very wrong." Nicole smiled. Her face was heavily coated with a clear salve. "After all," she said grimly, "in a few weeks, the doctor says we will once again become the two most beautiful women in Nevada. This is worth the living for, is it not?"

When Julia managed to nod, Nicole looked away quickly. "I have something to tell you now that must be said. It concerns your hands. They are badly cut and require a long while to heal. In the meantime, you need rest. The doctor says you are not to get out of bed for at least two weeks. The insensitive fool laughed when he told me the same."

Julia's eyes dropped to the mounds of bandages at her sides. She remembered now—the front window. Then she looked up and reached out to comfort Nicole.

"Ohhhh!" she gasped in pain, dropping her hand and feeling wave after wave of agony.

Nicole grabbed her shoulders and squeezed hard. "Listen," she pleaded, "the doctor says you have cut some of the nerves which move the fingers. The scars will be bad—very bad."

"I understand," Julia said, fighting back tears. "But . . . but will I be able to use my fingers. My God, Nicole. If I've lost their use, then you should have let me die!"

"Stop it!"

Julia beat down her rising hysteria, gritted her teeth until her face was a blistered mask of control. "I'm sorry." She swallowed. "I'm not being very grateful, am I? Or brave."

"You are being normal. Better than normal, considering this news. But you must know the doctor said you will probably never regain the complete use of your hands."

Julia couldn't help it. Tears sprang up in her eyes and a great wrenching sob escaped from her lips. She cried. Deeply. Above her, Nicole Barrie also let her tears fall silently.

"I know, Julia, you wish to die now. I understand. But you are wrong. Things will get better. I have seen much suffering and know this is true. Hang on."

Julia tried to wipe her tears away. She couldn't. "I don't believe you. Not a word you've said, Nicole. But I will try. Even when *he* comes to collect his due, I'll try."

Dread flooded across pain when she thought of Dade Taylor. But then . . . then a wonderful hope filled her bosom. Maybe . . . maybe the fire had burned away her beauty. And her hands! Couldn't the scars be her blessing? Surely he would come and see her like this and go away in disgust.

Julia smiled then, laid her head back on the pillow, and smiled as the tears dried on her inflamed skin.

Dade Taylor arrived the next evening while Nicole was perched beside her bed spooning some very good French soup.

"Well, well," he said, "look at that. What a heartrending scene we have."

Julia sat up. She stared at him, challenging him with her eyes, watching for the disgust to appear as he looked at her now.

It didn't materialize. There was no change in his expression, nothing to give her hope. Still, she knew a poker player was not one to reveal his thoughts.

"Get out of my house."

Dade chuckled derisively. "Your *house?* Come now, Julia. This is a shack, just like your last one down in Carson City."

He grabbed a chair, swung it around, and straddled it backward. "And, as for wanting nothing to do with me, you should have thought of that earlier, before we became business partners. Or do you think the fire absolved you of your indebtedness?"

Nicole Barrie was shaking with anger. "My God, Dade! Can't you see what this poor woman has been through?"

"Shut up or leave," he drawled. "I'm interested in her—not you. Interrupt once more and I'll toss you out into the street."

"You touch me and I'll cut your hands off," she breathed.

Dade ran his fingers through his hair. "Yeah, I know full well that you'd not hesitate to use a knife. Seems like I've heard a thing or two about how you stabbed a man to death in Denver a few years ago. Your husband, wasn't it?"

Julia glanced up in shock at Nicole Barrie. It couldn't be.

"It is true," she said, looking deep into Julia's eyes. "He made me earn money for his drinking. Forced me with other men. When I—"

Julia shook her head back and forth. "You don't have to explain your past to anyone. Certainly not to me."

"Maybe she doesn't," Dade interrupted, "but there are some law officers in Colorado who'd be very interested in the story."

"You wouldn't do that."

"Try me, Nicole."

"I'd be acquitted. Everyone knew—"

"All right, let's assume for the moment you would be set free. But you'd still have to go back and stand trial. That would take months. Your girls couldn't handle things. Someone else would move in and take over your business."

"I don't—"

"And what about the Virginia City Fire Company?"

"What about it?" Nicole whispered, looking away quickly.

Dade grinned smugly. "Well, I know how they're planning to make you an honorary member of their company this next Fourth of July. Yeah, give you a fire hat and belt, pull you through town on their fire engine. They think you are real special. It'd be a shame to spoil the image."

"You bastard!"

"Maybe." Nothing was going to bother him now. He was in command. "But people should know both sides of the famous Madame Nicole Barrie. Not just about how she converted her own house into a hospital a couple of years back during the cholera epidemic."

He inspected his fingernails, then said, "I imagine Dan De Quille on the *Territorial Enterprise,* or that new reporter, Mark Twain, would be real interested in the story."

"You're despicable!" Julia hissed, rising in her bed. "You can't intimidate my friend."

"I can and I already have. Nicole is too smart to try to bluff a professional gambler. She knows I'd ruin her."

Nicole's complexion wasn't red anymore. It was bone white and her lips resembled a purple slash wound.

Julia couldn't bear the pain and fear she saw in this woman who'd saved her life. "Dade," she whispered, "you can't still want me. Not like this. Not anymore."

He blinked and seemed to lose his composure as his eyes fell to his clenched hands. "Oh yes, I do!" he swore. "In two weeks you'll be as beautiful as ever, and I'll have you. As long as I want. When I want. How I want."

"And if I refuse?" she asked, not recognizing her own voice.

"You can't. You owe me nearly two thousand dollars, and probably at least that much to your suppliers. I'm going to pay your debts, Julia, and you're going to leave this shack and live in a decent house. A house I'll choose, furnish, and use at my pleasure—as I'll use you."

"No!"

"Yes!"

"Tell him to go to hell," Nicole graveled. "It's a free country. He can't make you stay."

"Watch me," Dade swore. "She tries to leave Virginia City, and I'll swear out an arrest warrant. She'll be brought back and jailed as a common debtor. And if you think that the good people, the ones who have real clout in this town, won't back me out of a sense of duty, you are badly mistaken."

"I'll hire her an attorney," Nicole vowed.

"Who? Tell me! What man is fool enough to destroy his career by backing a whore and husband killer?"

Nicole shivered with silent rage. "Then let *me* pay Julia's debt."

"My, my," Dade clucked. "Aren't we the Florence Nightingale of the Comstock tonight? My wife would be proud of you."

"Leave her out of this!" Julia cried.

"All right, I will. Madame Barrie knows I could destroy her

in less than a week. No business, no honorary fire company, just a Colorado bench warrant."

"I don't care," the woman said quietly.

"But *I* do," Julia told her. "I got myself into this and I'll get out."

"You don't know what you're saying. He'll never release you. Never."

Julia suddenly felt very dead inside. She forced her eyes to his. "Is that true? How long am I to serve?"

Something changed in his face. Guilt? Pity? Whatever it was vanished in an instant. "That depends," he said huskily, "on how you work to please me."

Julia fell back on the pillow. She stifled a cry that welled up in her throat. She heard his boots thump across the floor and squeezed her eyes shut.

"Madame, take good care of her. I'll have a doctor from San Francisco come over to work on her hands. I'm no animal. I can wait until the wounds heal."

The bootsteps receded, and as the door creaked on its hinges, Julia called after him, "I'll do it. But if you *ever* tell Holly, so help me I'll kill you, Dade Taylor."

They both heard his sharp intake of breath.

"Take good care of her," he rasped, closing the door and leaving the two women who now shared a common livelihood.

He could afford to be generous now—he'd soon begin to collect in full.

19

"Tom, look!" she cried as the Wells Fargo stage crossed the divide and rumbled into Virginia City. "They've made a banner for me!"

"Your first, but we'll see hundreds more before you've reached the top." He squeezed her hand. "My dear, it's a triumphant homecoming. We should bask in the glow of our accomplishments."

Fay smiled tolerantly. She was used to Tom Maguire sharing the billing. He'd paraded her about San Francisco as if she were his special creation and protected her from any contact with men her own age. Sometimes Tom's possessiveness was irritating, but more often she was blessedly thankful that the suitors who flocked outside her door were denied entry. Fay wasn't ready for another man—Glenn still owned her heart.

"My dear, they've even assembled a greeting party! And a band!"

Fay had written Dade and Holly to tell them of her arrival, but she hadn't dreamed they'd go to all this trouble.

As the stage rolled down C Street, men kept hollering her name and cheering as she leaned out and waved.

Yes, it was good to be back!

Dade opened the door and she jumped into his arms. "Thank you, Dade. I never expected such a welcome as this!"

"You're worth it," he beamed. "We've got a big evening planned for you and Mr. Maguire. Dinner, champagne, a speech."

"A speech?" Surely he didn't expect her to make a speech!

He read her face. "I didn't mean you, Fay. I'll do all the talking. You see, there's an election next week for the first mayor of Virginia City. I'm running for the office, and you, being my sister and all...well, it's perfect. Don't you understand?"

Fay stared at her gloved hands. When would she ever learn? Dade would never change. "Of course, Dade. I should have guessed."

Tom Maguire, always at her side, recognized the tone of disappointment and took her arm. "If you'll excuse us, your sister is very weary."

"Sure," Dade said. "Good to see you again, Mr. Maguire. We can talk business later, you and I."

A tightening around Maguire's eyes was the only sign of his anger. "Of course," he said stiffly, leading her away.

Once out of her brother's presence, Fay became determined to give a warm hello to these old friends who'd gone to the trouble of welcoming her. She smiled and shook hands with them all. It took almost an hour to reach their rooms, and when she did, Fay sagged on the bed with exhaustion.

"He's still trying to use me, Tom."

"So I gathered. Are you going to make a pitch for him?"

"No."

Maguire sat quietly for a few moments. "He'll never forgive you if he loses the election. I can tell by looking at him that it would be unpardonable."

"I don't care," she said harshly. "He used me too long and I'll not be anyone's tool ever again."

"Is that . . . is that what you think I'm trying to do?"

Fay leaned back on her pillow. "I don't know yet," she admitted.

"I see." He threw her a copy of the latest Virginia City newspaper. "We're tied together now. We can help each other—or hurt—depending on what you do. Maybe this will convince you how much our roles are linked. I'll return this evening, my dear."

Fay nodded, then stared at the headlines and front-page article.

A NEW THEATER GOING UP

> Thomas Maguire, Esq., the indefatigable builder of several great opera houses in California, has erected a magnificent Temple of the Muse for the recreation of our free-hearted mining population. It will henceforth be named the Washoe Opera House.
>
> This elegant edifice is actually eighteen inches wider than the great San Francisco Opera House and will seat sixteen hundred persons comfortably. It is indeed a tribute to the great artists who are to come to play on its boards. Moreover, it is fitting that the honor should first be bestowed on our own Miss Fay Taylor, sister of Mr. Dade Taylor, currently running for mayor. There are those of us who fondly remember Miss Taylor's previous stage performances and, perhaps, some even fortunate enough to have seen her at Maguire's San Francisco theater.
>
> To say that this new addition on D Street is a first-class establishment would be grossly understating the case—just as certainly as dubbing the lovely Miss Fay Taylor merely a first-class stage presence.

There was more, columns of praise and no little amount of speculation as to the yet undisclosed fare to be presented on opening night. The editor closed by saying that Virginia City now had a full range of entertainment for all tastes and pocketbooks. There was the Howard Theater and Topliffe's on C Street—capable of full stage productions but not as elegant as Maguire's, and at the other end of the spectrum, a number of melodeons, hurdy-gurdies, and two-bit houses. But by far the highlight at the time was clearly Fay Taylor in Tom Maguire's sparkling new Washoe Opera House.

Fay cast the paper aside and closed her eyes to rest. While she was deeply grateful for her success, there were times when she felt as though she were falling deeper and deeper into a world which had no reality, no substance. Everyone seemed to have a deeper, hidden motive. At such times, the distinction between the theater and the outside world became very blurred.

Maybe, she reasoned, that was why she'd loved Glenn so much. He was uncomplicated and direct in his hopes and dreams. When she compared him with Dade and Tom Maguire, there was a foundation laid on rock that the other two lacked. And in their lacking, it seemed as though both men were forced to constantly maneuver to maintain their hard-won but tenuous positions.

Rosie Raye was like Glenn. She was completely without guile. Thinking of her, Fay swallowed almost painfully. When this Virginia City run was over, she was going back to San Francisco and take Rosie in hand. She might get clawed in the process, but Fay knew she had to try.

The evening celebration turned out to be a political forum for Dade, who monopolized the occasion to press his candidacy. He spoke on the need for a better water system and how, if elected, he would authorize engineering studies for the development of a year-round reservoir. Furthermore, Virginia City was becoming a real city and needed a real hospital and school. He'd study those issues, too.

"What about a miners' union!" someone demanded.

Fay almost laughed at the expression on her brother's face. Being a shareholder in so much mining stock and outright owner of numerous little mines, he was naturally against any such attempt.

"My feeling," he said carefully, "is that the miners on the Comstock have to realize their livelihood depends on their employers making a reasonable profit."

"Profit! You people are bleeding us to death!"

Dade reddened. He glanced toward a group of men who

closed in on the dissenter and roughly ushered him out as the band struck up a lively tune to override his cries of pain.

Holly's fists were clenched and her voice shook with anger when she turned to Fay. "He shouldn't do that! That man had a perfect right to question him on a union. Why, every week, some miner is killed under our very feet."

"Is it *that* dangerous?"

"Yes," Holly stated flatly. "The square-set timbering solved most of the problems with cave-ins, but cables break and men fall into pits and are killed in explosions. Safety is expensive, but more could be done, starting with cutting the shifts down to eight instead of twelve hours. The heat keeps increasing as they go deeper. It's already over a hundred degrees in the lower levels. I'm going to have a talk with Dade and somehow show him how wrong he is in refusing the miners their own voice in things."

Fay was surprised at Holly. She'd always thought the woman extremely submissive. "Have you mentioned this before?"

"Of course. We've repeatedly fought over the issue of a union. He knows how I feel and that I won't keep quiet. But at least he does support a hospital and a school."

Holly's shoulders sagged. "In many ways, Dade is very good, but in others, well . . ." Her voice trailed off. Suddenly she turned toward Fay. "Let's talk about you, from when you arrived in San Francisco till now. I'm especially curious about the rumors I've heard of the Dancing Tiger. It sounds *very* exciting."

Fay nodded and told her about Rosie and how guilty she felt about leaving the woman to drink herself into an early grave.

"Offer your friend a job," Holly urged.

"I'm going to try," Fay promised, "but it isn't that easy. Rosie has too much pride to accept anything she suspects is just my charity, like helping with sets or costumes. It would have to be work she truly believed she was the only person who could handle. Besides, she's got a place of her own."

"Yes, you told me. A failing two-bit house."

"Sure, but it's her own and . . . well, you won't believe this, Holly, but sometimes I was happier at the Dancing Tiger than at Maguire's Opera House."

"Oh, I believe you. Since Dade has become so prominent and decided to get into politics, I never seem to have any time alone with him. He's gone almost every evening, making speeches and gathering votes. He says it's going to be a close race. His main opponent is a man who is trying to organize that union we talked about."

"I see. Are you . . . are you happy?"

Holly nodded. "I think so—not like at first. Our honeymoon in San Francisco was heavenly and it's never been quite the same. Your brother . . . well, you know how he is. Even Father admits he's never seen anyone work so hard to get ahead. I just wish he'd slow down, relax, and have dinner with me a few nights a week."

"You mean he's gone that often?"

"Yes. But he keeps promising he'll ease up after the election."

Fay nodded. Dade would never ease up and she was going to have to have a talk with him about neglecting his wife.

"Holly, I was reminded of our first meeting on the way over the mountains. And I thought of Julia Matson."

At the mention of the woman's name, Holly's expression grew troubled. She told Fay about Julia, the murder of her husband, and the latest tragedy of her emporium and how it had burned to the ground.

"It seems to have changed her," Holly fretted, almost thinking aloud. "After the funeral, she came up to stay with us."

"Sleep in your house?"

"Why, of course. Dade thought it was a good idea, and so did I."

Fay nodded woodenly. She tried to keep her mind from leaping to the almost-inevitability that . . .

"But she left one night—without even so much as a good-bye," Holly said in wonder and obvious hurt. "I tried to see her, but . . . but it was as if I'd become diseased or something. She couldn't even seem to look me in the eye. Do you understand it?"

"No," Fay whispered, a growing dread building inside of her.

"Neither can I. Julia said she left because she and Dade had a disagreement over her friendship with Mrs. Barrie, yet I don't really believe that. No, it has something to do with me, not our infamous madam. You don't know how many hours I've tried to think out what came between us and why she left in the night. Afterward, when her place burned down, I went to see her."

"What did she say?"

"Nothing. The poor woman is in shock. She lives in a nice

little house up on A Street but hardly ever goes outdoors. The only visitors she has are Nicole Barrie and a few of her girls. Naturally, that means none of the respectable women will visit her. I've tried often enough, but she doesn't answer the door."

"That's strange. And really sad," Fay mused. "Julia has too much beauty and life to become a recluse. Maybe I can help."

"You can try," Holly said excitedly. "And if she lets you inside, tell her I'm sorry—terribly sorry—for whatever I did to hurt her so badly. And say that I hope she's getting better."

"Getting better? I don't understand."

"It's Julia's hands. She cut and burned them severely during the fire while trying to save her emporium. I'm told that she always wears black velvet gloves."

Fay couldn't help but look at her own hands and imagine how awful she'd feel if they were disfigured. "Before I leave, I'll pay Julia a visit," she promised.

"Thank you. Try to find a way to let her know that I'm sorry about whatever came between us. I need her friendship."

"I'm quite certain she needs yours, Holly. And don't worry, I won't get too angry with my brother for leaving you so frequently."

Fay caught the eye of an acquaintance and excused herself. She didn't want Holly to notice the disquieting suspicion she felt building inside. Dade had always been a womanizer and he'd gone for Julia the first time he'd ever laid eyes on her. Fay decided to keep her suspicions hidden for a while, but she knew with certainty that wherever her brother went at night, it was not to make speeches. Julia might be physically scarred, but if she was romantically involved with Dade, the scars went much deeper. And one day, even Holly's own naiveté couldn't shield her from discovering the betrayal.

Weeks passed and Fay could not break away to see Julia. Her debut and subsequent performances at the Washoe Opera House were so popular she was hounded day and night by worshiping Comstock miners.

She probably should have expected this reaction. The illusion of grief she evoked from the play called *East Lynne* was so convincing it unleashed a nightly floodtide of emotion never before experienced on the Comstock. Even the new hard-bitten marshal wept openly.

The drama had England as its setting and Fay starred in the role of a woman who is tricked by a scoundrel into abandoning her husband and child. She believes his lies and pays the price by living a tyrannical existence for six years. In the end, deserted and realizing she's committed a terrible wrong, she returns incognito to her lawful husband, only to discover her son is fatally ill.

She tries everything to save the child she should never have left—but it is too late and the boy dies in her arms at the very instant the father recognizes and forgives her. For a while, love almost restores the poor woman but, alas, grief for the lost child destroys her health and she dies begging forgiveness. Her husband is left to face the world alone.

It was not the play that Fay would have chosen for her homecoming. Not at all. Yet, it was Tom Maguire's theater and stage company and, therefore, his to choose. And, as always, he chose well; the crowds flocked in, night after night, and men and women sobbed and blew their noses in the packed house.

Julia Tillman and Nicole Barrie wept too one evening in the darkened section of balcony seats where the town's prostitutes were allowed. It was only by chance that, during the end of the play when the famous line "Never darken my door again!" was cried, Fay saw the two beautiful women as a match flared and was held to a cigar.

Julia's eyes, filled with tears of sentiment and admiration for the young actress, met those of Fay. Then the match died and the play groaned on to its aching, heartrending, and inevitable conclusion.

The two women hurried out before the crowd, Nicole to be at her French Palace before the after-theater rush of business which would come trooping down D Street, and Julia just to be safe from inquisitive eyes and in case Dade might be waiting for her services.

He was. They had a signal, the branch of a climbing rose that threaded itself around the post. If the top was up, it meant come in. If down, try later.

Tonight he'd moved the thorny branch to point up. Julia hesitated at her front gate. A light was on in the bedroom and not the parlor, which meant he would be in bed and quickly growing angry with impatience rather than drinking alone and needing her to listen.

She swallowed, feeling a creeping numbness move across

her skin. More and more frequently she was having this split psychological reaction to Dade. It effectively detached her mind from her body until the two became separate things. Her mind would float away while her body responded to Dade's exactly as he pleased. It always happened, and later, when he departed, she would lie in bed with the smell and taste of him and know that if the blessed detachment ever failed, she would kill herself.

Julia entered the front door, passed into the bedroom, and stood framed in the doorway.

"So," he drawled, sitting up in bed smoking a cigar, "so you and Nicole Barrie made an evening of it down at the opera. Did you enjoy the performance?"

"Yes. Your sister was very good."

"Very good? Hell, Julia, she was magnificent! The election is only a couple of days off and she's going to get me voted in for sure."

"And then what?"

"The territory gets statehood and I become a U.S. senator. I'll be off for Washington."

Something stirred in her, jarred her mind back to her body. "Then will this be over, Dade? Will it?"

The cigar stopped halfway to his mouth. Forgotten. His voice hardened. "Damn you, Julia! You need me."

She shook her head violently. "No! No, I hate you. I want you gone from here!"

"Pour me a drink," he ordered harshly, his voice thick with passion and anger. "You don't hate me, Julia. And before I go away, you're going to admit you crave what I do to you in this bed."

"Never!" she groaned, turning and stumbling back into the parlor. She found the bottle and poured him a half glass, then she poured herself the same, although she rarely drank. But tonight, she had to. Maybe it was the play, *East Lynne*, and the witnessing of a sadness greater than her own. Whatever it was, as she moved back into the room and stood beside the bed, Julia knew that she must have this drink to endure what would happen next.

He took one glass, clinked it with her own, and as she stared straight ahead, he toasted, "To us, Julia. Strangers in the night."

She didn't say anything, just lifted the whiskey glass and drank.

"Julia, hurry up and get that dress off. I promised Holly I'd be home early tonight. She'll be expecting something too."

Her eyes dropped to him, and Julia wished she could kill. Perhaps he saw her expression because his laughter died and the mocking smile on his lips turned bitter. He reached up, grabbed the front of her dress, and ripped it to her waist.

An animal sound of hatred broke from Julia's mouth and she clawed at his face before remembering the black velvet gloves.

He roughly pulled her down and let her fight. "Yes," he panted, "fire at last. If this is the only way I can get passion, so be it. I'm going to strip you of everything, Julia, your pride and your clothes. When I'm done, it will be as usual, just your beautiful body and those black velvet gloves!"

She fought him as she always did, knowing it only heightened his passion, made his conquest seem a fresh victory. She fought him even though she was gloved and several of the fingers of her hands did not grasp to hurt, for they were numb and still crippled with the scars.

But she tried and she failed, and then, when she could not bear to feel him anymore, the survival instinct came upon her like a drug and, once again, she became separate, drifting and high above the passion that rutted below.

"Julia? Julia, open up. It's me, Fay Taylor. I know you're in there. I saw you at the theater tonight."

The pounding grew louder. "I won't leave, Julia. Dade, are you in there?"

"Damn!" he hissed, rolling off her and grabbing his clothes in a rush. He buttoned his pants, tore his shirt off a chair. "Get up and get rid of her!"

Julia shook her head, and he froze in disbelief. "Do you want her to find out about us? For God's sake, Julia! I swear I'll make you pay for this. Get up!"

Again she shook her head. Besides, Fay would already know about them. That's why she was here now.

Dade slapped her—hard. Hard enough to cut her mouth before he scooped up the rest of his clothes and ran for the back door.

When it closed, Julia arose and dressed. The hammering on her door seemed to bring everything back into focus—that and the blow she'd received.

"Julia, if I have to break down this door, I'm coming in.

Dade! Dade, I'm going to tell everyone about you, you bastard! You'll pay for what you're doing to Holly. I swear I'll ruin your chances at the election. Open up!"

Julia unlocked the door and waited as Fay marched inside to spin around and glare at her. "He's here; tell him to come out."

"Your brother's gone. He left by the back door," Julia replied.

Fay's voice was cold, shaking with fury. "You whore," she whispered. "You kept whore! Did you really have to take him from your own friend?"

"I would kill him if I could," Julia said quietly. "But I can't."

"Liar! You saw a chance to live it easy and Dade was plenty willing to pay your price. I *hate* you, Julia!"

She steeled herself. "Then that makes two of us, Miss Taylor. So what would you advise?"

The actress blinked. She looked away. "Do you have any idea what Holly told me?"

Julia shook her head, feeling the pain riding up behind her eyes, making them sting and burn.

"She told me to say that *she* was terribly sorry. Get that?" Fay repeated, "She, Holly Taylor, is terribly sorry for whatever she did to hurt you. Remembering that, I want to hurt you any way I can."

Julia's lips trembled. "Keep talking," she whispered. "You're doing quite well."

Fay pivoted. "Julia, you could have had any one of dozens, but you chose my brother. Well, you can tell him your little secret is safe, because I won't be the one who breaks Holly's heart."

At the door, Fay stopped. Her head was down and she was breathing as though she'd been running a long, long way. "Just one question and I'll go. Why?"

"Why?" Julia repeated, trying to think.

"Yes, dammit! And don't say it was love! Or that he's so handsome. On our way over from California, you had no trouble resisting his advances—but you knew we were poor then."

Julia wanted to tell this girl the truth if only to erase the disgust and pain so clearly etched on her face. But she couldn't. To reveal that she had no choice but to submit to Dade would result in Fay hating her brother even more, and perhaps in her shock and outrage, even in telling Holly. Julia, looking into these hot, accusing eyes, knew she had to remain silent.

Fay's mouth twisted down at the corners. "You really are something," she whispered. "It just occurred to me that you and Dade are a matched pair—both two-timing cheats!"

"Fay, I'm sorry."

"Sorry!" she cried, her voice taking on a mocking quality. "Don't make me laugh. And I've got a message you can give to my brother. Tell him to be sure and attend tomorrow night's performance."

"Fay . . ."

She was gone, running into the night full of hatred. Julia closed the door. She walked into her bedroom again and undressed, except for the black velvet gloves. Then she blew out the light and began to clench and unclench her gloved hands the way the doctor told her might someday make them strong again. And she wondered, until blessed sleep finally came, just what Fay was going to do next and how much longer she herself could endure her own life.

The huge crowd was on its feet as wave after wave of applause washed down upon her and the other members of the cast.

Fay bowed, took her encore, and then, instead of going offstage with the others, she raised her hands for silence.

The audience, teary-eyed and emotionally charged, began to clap even louder. Miss Fay Taylor was their idol, and the moment was glorious.

"Ladies and gentlemen," she cried, "quiet please."

Finally the cheers and clapping fell away into silence, and they waited, straining forward eagerly, knowing they were witnessing some important departure from the usual sequence of things.

"I want to thank you, each and every one, from the bottom of my heart for the love and affection you have shown me during my stay here in beautiful Virginia City."

A few people clapped, but it was scattered, for most of the audience knew that Fay Taylor was scheduled to remain playing at the Washoe Opera House for at least another month.

"Tonight, I'm afraid, was my final performance."

"No! No!" they shouted over and over.

"It must be," she pleaded. "But I do want you to know that I'll never really leave Virginia City. I carry her fate in my heart. And . . . and it is for this reason that I must speak out on the coming election."

The theater grew very still, though everyone was certain the actress would ask them to vote for her brother.

"Today I've visited each of my brother's opponents in Friday's election. I've listened to their views, heard their opinions as to what needs to be accomplished in order to make Virginia City the finest town in Nevada and, eventually, its capital when statehood comes, as it surely must."

This brought a thunderous ovation, and she waited until it died.

"After listening to all of my brother's opponents, it seems clear to me that the best man for office of mayor is the owner of the Comstock Miner's Supply, Mr. Aesop Beason."

If she'd blasted them with buckshot, they wouldn't have been more stunned. Fay saw Dade leap up in his private theater box and shake his fist as his words were drowned out by a chorus of loud voices.

She smiled. After all the years and his selfish, lying tricks, she was evening the score in a single stroke.

Again she motioned for silence. "Mr. Beason has a business interest in this town, but he also depends upon the support of the miners themselves. He believes, as I've come to, that you men need a union."

The building rocked with their applause. It was an outpouring from the souls of weary, hopeless men.

"And furthermore, he is willing to start a fund-raising effort to build the school and hospital to which my brother and the other candidates only pay lip service in order to garner your precious votes."

She saw Dade fighting his way up the aisle toward the side exit.

"Some of you—perhaps all of you—are wondering why I'm endorsing Mr. Beason rather than Dade Taylor. The answer is simple—my brother is a businessman, a man who could not be asked to divorce his own special interests from those benefiting this town."

Fay clenched her hands together. "I do love you all and I feel that this is my home. But I'm leaving now and I'd like to think its future is as bright and happy as you've made me and our entire cast up on this stage. So vote for a man you can depend on to represent the best interests of you *and* business. Vote for Aesop Beason!"

A bright eruption of hats sailed up toward Tom Maguire's magnificent chandelier. The roar of approval fairly threatened to blast the stage curtains away as it swept over her.

She bowed and went to gather her things. Dade would seek vengeance, but that didn't matter, because Tom could protect her. Besides, she was leaving tonight. Back to San Francisco. There was nothing more she could do about Dade, and she couldn't face Holly without telling her the truth.

She was finished on the Comstock, as washed out and sick at heart as Rosie Raye. Fay dabbed her tears, and the thought of Rosie made her realize she did have a purpose in life besides entertaining. Yes, and though Tom Maguire would be angered, Fay realized that she needed support, too—and that Rosie, the woman who never had the right manager, was going to provide it.

They'd help each other. Together. The past and the future—it stretched even beyond San Francisco. And perhaps even beyond this war-torn American continent.

20

Fay Taylor had kept her promise. Upon her arrival in San Francisco, she'd gone against the wishes of Tom Maguire and hired Rosie Raye as her manager. During the following three years Tom had never accepted Rosie, but the veteran actress had proven her worth as a friend, teacher, and astute theatrical manager. Tom would never have cheated Fay, but Rosie always saw to it that Fay's roles were tailored to her stage growth.

For its staunch support of the Union and Comstock gold, Nevada was granted statehood in 1864. Its citizens elected delegates to their new legislature. Dade Taylor was not one of them, and Fay knew it was because of her public humiliation of him. Looking back on that night, she sometimes felt a mild regret for her action, but realized she'd done the people a favor. He'd never forgive her for destroying what might have been a successful political future.

So be it. Had he not cheated on Holly, Fay could have remained silent.

On a cool evening in April, Fay and Rosie were enjoying their balcony view of San Francisco Bay when they heard the glorious news that Robert E. Lee had surrendered to Grant.

The war was over!

The cry rang through the streets and people poured out-of-doors to celebrate. Steeple bells tolled the great tidings and echoed from the hillsides out across the bay until anchored ships began to fire their cannon in response. Steam whistles, guns, barking dogs, and Chinese fireworks competed raucously until the din was almost unbearable and the streets were packed with dancing men, women, and children.

San Francisco went wild. Everywhere the people celebrated as champagne was hoisted in jubilation and exuberant throngs bulled their way into the saloons, eager to toast Mr. Lincoln and the Union. All businesses closed and the city editors didn't even bother with the day's newspaper, their reporters being too drunk to write anyway. Even the theater district locked its doors as prudent men like Maguire realized that the night's fare would be staged in the bonfire-lit streets.

The war *was* over!

Rosie lifted her cup of tea in salute. "To Mr. Lincoln and a preserved Union!"

"Yes, and an end to the destruction," Fay whispered to her friend. Rosie nodded emphatically. She hadn't touched a drop of rum since taking over as manager. And it showed in the freshness of her skin, the animation of expression, and the loss of cynicism once carried as a protective shield for her alcoholic vulnerability.

Rosie set her cup down. "Well, now that it's finally happened, do you still want to go to New York City? Broadway can be pretty tough on a westerner."

"What do you think?" Fay asked with a half-smile. "I have everything now—friends, applause, and all the money I need. Why should I take the chance?"

"You know the answer to that as well as I," Rosie said, refusing to be baited.

"Do I?" Fay wondered aloud, her expression becoming more serious as she realized that she'd been using the Civil War as an excuse to remain in this lovely city. But now her excuse was gone. The east would welcome new entertainers to lift its war-racked spirits.

"Of course you do, Fay. Besides you can't deny a man like Tom Maguire forever. One of these days he'll demand you either marry him or leave his theater."

"I've never misled him. Tom knows I'm not going to change my mind."

"Because of Glenn Donovan?"

"No," Fay said quickly. "Glenn made his decision and I'm sure it was the wisest thing he could have done. Certainly, if we'd married, I would never have come to San Francisco."

"Then I'm thankful he left," Rosie said firmly. "I was going to an early grave until you showed up that afternoon at the Dancing Tiger." She frowned. "Are you going to see your young engineering friend in New York?"

"I'd love to, but I won't, out of fear. He's special, Rosie. Always will be. And I'd never forgive myself if I let it show and perhaps disrupted his studies. Maybe that's foolish, even arrogant, to think that he still loves me. He's probably found someone else. Why, it's been over three years now and his letters stopped a long time ago."

"That's because you never wrote back and gave him any hope."

Fay's mouth crimped at the corners. "Rosie, it's history. A love story between a pair of innocent children. It all seems unreal now, the way he saved my life in that American River, and our blizzard survival—all of it. Just like a children's storybook, except in the last chapter we both grew up."

"I understand. Are you sure you want to leave all this?"

"Yes. You told me I was good enough." She smiled. "Having second thoughts, Rosie?"

"Of course not, silly girl! I'll write to my old New York theatrical agent and have him arrange your schedule for the usual booking fee. He's honest and will do a good job."

"What about publicity?"

"The theater will take care of that," Rosie said, her voice and manner becoming professional. "What I'll do is send them a box full of newspaper clippings on your triumphant performances both here and in Virginia City. They'll also want a picture."

Rosie glanced toward the street below. "Look at them," she said. "I never thought I'd see this city go as wild as it is now. I feel like celebrating myself. You don't know how much I've been hoping to see the war end and for us to go to New York City."

"How soon can we leave?" Now that it was decided, Fay wanted to go soon.

"I'll write the letter today."

But less than a week later, they were devastated by the tragic news that while attending an English comedy, *Our American Cousin,* at the Ford Theater, President Lincoln had been assassinated by the tortured actor John Wilkes Booth.

It seemed unbelievable that someone as critically acclaimed as Booth could do such a thing, and both women felt he'd damned their profession forever. And so, where only a few days earlier there had been a riot of wild celebration, now San Francisco seemed to convulse like a wounded animal, draw around itself, and suffer in silent agony. Once again, almost the entire population gathered in the streets, and this time the bells tolled slowly and mournfully. People spoke in whispers. Sometimes a loud, bitter voice was heard, sometimes just soft weeping. There was no drunkenness, and on that first night, people seemed to be afraid to go to their homes, their hotels. So they gathered like a great family and spoke in hushed tones filled with grief, and when the numbness began to wear off, their voices grew angry.

The following morning, those who'd slept found their city draped in black—with coats, shawls, blankets, and even petticoats. All stores and banks remained closed, and no one objected when the saloons and whiskey shops declined to open.

People became apprehensive; they wondered aloud if the nation could survive such a loss.

Abe Lincoln. The Union. It almost seemed that the two were a whole. That they were as the mind and the heart—each essential, working together, doomed upon separation.

There were Southern sympathizers who covertly rejoiced. Those who were stupid enough to openly proclaim their joy at the death of the Great Emancipator were beaten. Quietly. Savagely.

A grievous pall hung over the city for weeks, lasting until Fay and Rosie departed eastward. The sadness was fitting, in a way, because the night before, Thomas Maguire and Fay had argued violently. In the prosperous theater owner's opinion, she was committing a terrible mistake in abandoning the San Francisco Opera House and theatrical company. But when he had finally accepted her decision, Tom's innate gallantry came to the fore and he wished her every success and vowed there would always be a central place on his stage for her, should Fay ever decide to return.

"And you will return," he'd prophesied. "Oh, I'm aware that Broadway has its own magic and weaves a power over those who attend her courts. And I believe the day will come when you play the greatest European stages. But, just as surely, you'll grow tired of the pomp and adoration, weary of the courtiers and nobility. Perhaps then you will remember me and return to California, where your star was nurtured and grew to brilliance."

"Please find someone and marry her," she told him gently, then left because she could not bear the sadness in his face.

When they reached their overnight stop in Virginia City, Fay made no attempt to notify anyone of her arrival. The stage rolled into the Comstock after dark and was scheduled to leave early the next morning. With luck, she thought she might be able to make the restover without attracting Dade's attention.

It was not to be. Even though she wore a veil, she was recognized by the ticket man, and then the desk clerk at the elegant International Hotel as she rushed from the coach to the elevator on the C Street entrance.

The word spread like wildfire, and within an hour a delegation of the most prominent citizens of Virginia City was sent up to her room with an armful of flowers and their own pleas that she accompany them to the Washoe Opera House, perhaps to make a brief surprise appearance for a benefit which was being given this very evening for the new hospital.

Fay couldn't say no. She and Rosie were immediately swept away by their jubilant entourage and conducted directly to the theater. When it was announced that Fay Taylor was coming, a great cheer rose up from the half-filled auditorium, and by the time she'd arrived and stepped out from the wings, the place buzzed with expectancy.

Though weary from the long day's stage ride, Fay loved her Comstock audience. She responded to the greeting by giving her old friends every bit of talent she possessed. She sang and danced until she was so weary even the miners yelled for her to rest—then she made them empty their pockets before she consented to do it.

Fay saw Dade, but never looked at him. Instead, she watched Holly and was reassured by her sister-in-law's radiance. She was overjoyed to see that Holly was expecting a baby.

Maybe, she prayed, maybe a new child would change Dade, make him see that his grasping, conniving pattern of life could result only in his downfall.

But this hope was shattered early the next morning as she and Rosie waited for the stage. Dade marched into the tiny Wells Fargo office and hissed, "It's time we had a talk, little sister. Alone!"

Fay knew the look in her brother's eye, and his tone of voice betrayed only the surface of his fury.

Fay glanced at Rosie, forced a smile of what she hoped was reassurance, then followed Dade outside. All during the years she'd traveled with him through the California gold-mining towns, danced and sung while he cheated miners, she'd always been in awe of Dade. Part of it was fear, because she'd known how violent he could become if crossed, even for an instant. But it was also because she'd needed him, clung to the only person in the world who really cared if she lived or died—even if it was for his own selfish reasons.

That was yesterday. Now, facing him outside the stage depot and gazing into his hard, accusing eyes, Fay saw violence and hatred, and strangely, he did not frighten or awe her, nor would he ever again.

"I'm listening."

His eyes slitted. "I want you to know that if you were my brother, I'd have killed you the night you made your fine little speech about my not being fit to become mayor."

He laughed outright, a cold and wild sound from deep inside. "I didn't know then what a favor you did for me that night. But I do now. You see, I thought I had to be in office to gain real power. I was wrong. I underestimated the influence of wealth. Hell," he sneered, "I'd only have wasted time in office—any office. Now I realize public officials are just paid puppets. They dance to the tune of money. Whoever pays the most handles the strings."

He winked conspiratorially and Fay realized he was now talking as much for his own amusement as for her instruction. "Well, I just wanted you to know that Aesop Beason did become mayor. But then I bought his freighting company's debts and foreclosed on him the first time he had some trouble. Now I own the man *and* his office. Hell, I'm even his major political patron, though he seems in danger of losing the next election over his unexpected opposition to a miners' union."

Fay blinked. She felt herself trembling with loathing for this man. "You can't keep on using people!" she cried passionately. "Aesop Beason was a good man—"

"And even good men have their price," he interrupted.

"What was Julia's price?"

Dade's smug look faded. "She came higher than most," he admitted quietly.

"You're going to lose, Dade. Sometime. Some way, you are going to be pulled down and held accountable for your evil. And all those people you've bought, they're going to rise up and drag you screaming through hell on earth!"

He reached out, and his big hand wrapped itself around her throat. Then he began to squeeze, his face as impassive and unfeeling as a granite statue.

"I could squeeze just a little harder and you'd never be able to sing again," he told her in a calm, matter-of-fact voice. "I'd not go to jail or anything. But you'd be ruined."

Her eyes seemed to be pushed forward as a terrible pressure battered at them from behind; then he released her and stepped back as she staggered and gasped for air.

"You see, my dear, I've shown pity. Pity because you're really a child to me and always will be. And, like a child, I don't consider you completely accountable for your errors, though you deserve punishment."

She took a deep breath. "Maybe *I'm* no match for you or ever will be," she panted, "but someday the man will come who can beat you, and when he does, I'll write a song for him. This I swear!"

Dade's lip curled. He glanced up and saw the Wells Fargo stage emerge from the livery. "Holly wanted to say good-bye, but I told her I had to see you off alone. Have a good trip, my dear. I wish you great success on Broadway and the Continent. I wish it all to you wherever you go. Just don't *ever* come back to Virginia City."

"And . . . and if I do?"

He toed a groove in the dirt; then, his entire attention on it, he covered it up and adeptly worked the loose dirt into a grave-shaped mound. "No one remains a child forever," he said tonelessly before strolling toward his offices.

Fay Taylor took New York City by storm with her performances as Laura Leeson in *Time Tries All,* the comedy *The Seal of Love,* and the intense play of high drama *The Ticket of Leave Man.*

Each evening she was escorted to the theater in a carriage fitted with Comstock silver and wreathed with flowers. She met the most influential people of the city. Also the most eligible bachelors, who constantly vied for her attentions. Night after night, throngs of fans waited at the stage door, hoping for a glimpse of the lovely Comstock Canary, as she had been dubbed by all the papers.

Rosie Raye protected her even more zealously than had Thomas Maguire. And for her own part, Fay enjoyed her Broadway run immensely as, month after month, her popularity showed no sign of lessening.

Fay even performed Shakespeare on some nights and then varied the bill with an occasional evening of pure revelry. She and her fast-growing company of actors and actresses gave lighthearted performances built around her own ability to play the banjo and dance.

Scarcely a week passed without some eastern newspaper reviewing her performance with lavish praise. Offers to play in Baltimore, Washington, D.C., and Boston came, yet Rosie felt it best to remain on Broadway—at least until she'd taken the requisite European theater tour expected of all acclaimed actresses.

And so, as the months passed, Fay realized she still faced the critical test. If she could win Paris, Lisbon, and London, she would certainly be able to claim a worldwide following and enter the ranks of theatrical greats such as Adah Menken, Julia Dean Hayne, and James Stark.

It wasn't until the last week of her enormously successful New York run that, suddenly, without warning, she burst into tears during the final act and had to be escorted from the stage. An understudy was shoved out before the lights and managed to stumble through her lines, but Rosie and the entire backstage entourage were shocked.

"Out!" Rosie ordered. "I want everyone out of this dressing room except a doctor."

Fay couldn't seem to stop crying. The hurt had been building and building for months, until something just burst inside like a flood.

"No doctor," she sobbed. "I won't see a doctor!"

"All right." Rosie opened the door a crack and spoke to a waiting attendant. "Tell the reporters there'll be no interviews until we sail for London this Friday. I mean it. Miss Taylor is exhausted."

Rosie shut the door. "Now, if you're not sick, tell me what's really wrong."

"It's nothing. Really, it's not. I feel ashamed at what happened out there tonight. I mustn't allow it to happen ever again."

Rosie smiled. "Come, now. Be honest with yourself, as you've always been with me. This is Rosie, your manager *and* friend."

"You'll think I'm stupid," Fay said, her breath catching in her throat.

"No, I won't. I swear it. And if there's anything that can be done to make you feel better, then ask."

Fay stared at her interlocked fingers. "I . . . I feel awful about what I did out there in front of the audience tonight. And I had no idea it was coming. But sometimes, mostly in the night, I've been waking up and my face is bathed in tears."

"Why?" Rosie leaned forward, her expression one of intense concern.

"I'm not sure. Really. But . . ." She couldn't get it out. Now it seemed so childish.

The concern vanished from Rosie's face and there was a definite hint of anger and hurt in her deep voice. "Apparently you don't trust me. Perhaps, then, you should find someone you do."

"Rosie!"

"I mean it," the woman said. "You saved my life, and now, at the first opportunity I have to help, I'm shut away."

Fay grabbed her hand. "I'm sorry. I should have thought about your feelings. It's just that I've been so wrapped up in my own disappointment that—"

"Disappointment! What in heaven's name have you got to be disappointed in?"

Fay's eyes misted. "He didn't even come to see me," she breathed. "I thought he'd at least come for *one* night before we sailed for Europe."

"Who?" Rosie demanded impatiently.

"Glenn. Glenn Donovan! I still care about him. I can't help it!"

Rosie heaved an exasperated sigh. "Oh," she said quietly. "After all the rich, handsome young bachelors who've been pounding on your door, is it possible that you can still care so much for that hardheaded Irishman who left you for a diploma?"

Fay nodded slowly. Tried to sort out her feelings and put them into words. "It's . . . it's not that I love him. I don't think so. I mean, it's been so long that I couldn't say exactly how I feel about Glenn anymore. I've changed, and he must have also."

"Listen, Fay. I wish you'd told me about this sooner. What's happened isn't so unusual."

"It's not?"

"Uh-uh. You see, in your mind, over these past few years, this Glenn of yours has become more and more wonderful and even far handsomer. That's the way a girl's imagination works. She remembers a boy too long, until after a while he becomes her knight in shining armor. And then, no one can compete with the memory. Is that why you've ignored all of your suitors?"

Fay nodded very hesitantly. "I believe it might be, at that. I've never considered him as the reason."

"Of course you didn't. The same thing happened to me, although I was a few years younger than you."

"It did?"

"Yes. And I was just as confused, until I happened to chance across this monument to dreams I'd created."

She hesitated and Fay saw her eyes grow distant, as though she was going far back in time. "What happened, Rosie?"

The eyes snapped back to focus. "Nothing, really. We met and went to dinner. I remember it well, and how I seemed almost to float into the room. Yet, by the time the meal was over, I'd fallen back to earth. My knight was no better—or worse—than other men. He had the same little irritating habit I'd conveniently forgotten, and his chin seemed ever so much weaker than I'd remembered." Rosie giggled. "And you know what?"

"What?"

"Well, damned if he didn't even shrink about four inches, though he'd sure gained enough at the waistline. Seeing Bill again was the best medicine any physician could have prescribed. By the time I'd watched him consume nearly an entire chicken, I knew real peace. I was free. Free of illusion."

Rosie winked. "Maybe this Glenn Donovan of yours hasn't gotten so fat or even shrunk in stature, but it would be something else you'd forgotten. I really am sorry you didn't tell me this earlier. I'd have found him for you to see again. But with tomorrow night being your farewell, it's just too late."

"No, it isn't," Fay said. "He's attending the New York School of Engineering. Glenn is supposed to finish this summer, and then I'd lose track of him."

"We can't let that happen," Rosie said pensively. "I've no idea how long an illusion can survive, but it could be years."

"Then I'll visit Glenn Donovan," Fay decided out loud. "I'll hire a coach and driver and tell them to find him if we have to go all over this state."

Suddenly her spirits crashed. "But I can't!" she wailed. "Tomorrow afternoon I've promised to give the French ambassador and his staff a small performance. And tomorrow night—"

"Hang tomorrow night," Rosie growled. "If you can't get back by tomorrow night, I'll just say something about your health, which is partly true. You can leave right after your afternoon performance. Find that fool Irishman and take a good look at your illusion. Compare him to a man like Thomas Maguire in his youth, because that's the kind of fellow you can have merely by snapping your fingers."

"I will," Fay said with a new, calm resolution. "Sometimes I don't know how I'd survive without you, Rosie."

The woman blushed. "You could, my dear. I'm the weaker of the two of us. Just find the lad. I'll guarantee you'll not cry onstage again."

Fay's head bobbed. What Rosie said made more sense than anything she'd heard in a long while. Yes, she'd locate Glenn Donovan. Then she'd have her own freedom.

21

"Please wait here, driver. I'll be back within an hour."

"Yes, Miss Taylor," the impeccably dressed coachman said, wrapping his lines about the brake and then studying the heavy brass sign attached to the massive iron gateway. "Are you certain you wouldn't like me to accompany you onto these grounds?"

"No, thank you. What time is it?"

"Five o'clock, miss."

"Good. I'll return by six and still have plenty of time to get back to the theater."

"Very good, miss. You should not miss your farewell appearance."

Fay dismounted from the carriage, a vision of pink and white, her dress lace-edged and billowy. A brilliant opal hung about her neck, and her gloves were white satin, imported from Paris. She looked stunning as she marched through the heavy iron gate. Its warning stated that no access was allowed after six. Fay prayed she was doing the right thing.

The cobblestone walk was lined with flowers, but she scarcely noticed them as she approached the huge rock edifice bearing the title: "NEW YORK SCHOOL OF ENGINEERING. Founded 1808." To the right and left of the main building she could see outbuildings—probably classrooms or student quarters. Everything was surrounded by a forest so thick and heavy as to be almost brooding. And the eight-foot stone walls all about gave the place an air of militarism, almost like some of the cavalry forts she'd seen in Nevada. What kind of place was this, so sequestered from the outside world, as though it was trying to horde some great knowledge?

Fay continued forward, trespassing under the great canopy of forest shot by flickering sunlit shadows. When she reached the door of the main building, her eyes immediately rested on the notice: "Visitors—Sundays Only, 1–3."

She frowned. Her lace glove poised above the polished door handle. "Surely they'll make an exception," Fay said aloud. "I'll be on my way to Europe on Sunday!"

She opened the door and entered a gloomy foyer, her eyes trying to adjust to the sudden darkness.

"Young lady, what are you doing here?"

The question wasn't asked politely, and Fay twisted sharply toward the inquirer. She saw him only a few feet way. A tall, ascetic-looking man with sharp features and a stern, bookish expression.

"I . . . I've come from New York City to visit a friend. His name is Glenn Donovan."

"Impossible."

"You mean he's not here?"

"I mean you cannot possibly see Mr. Donovan until visiting hours on Sunday," he proclaimed with an air of dismissal. "Now, if you'll be so good as to return at that time, I'm sure—"

"But I'll be gone! My name is Fay Taylor. Perhaps you've heard—"

"I'm afraid not. At any rate, it doesn't matter who you are, the rules stand."

"Blast your rules!" Fay exploded angrily as she came face to face with him. "I *have* to see Glenn. It's very important. I can't return on Sunday, and we are very dear friends."

"That is *not* important, Miss Taylor. What is important is that Mr. Donovan not be disturbed. He is studying for a very rigorous examination tomorrow afternoon on the physical laws of stress in relation to material density."

"All I want to do is see him for a few minutes. Just a few minutes. Then he can go back to his study."

The stern-faced man grew impatient and agitated. "You don't understand. We live by rules here at the New York School of Engineering, rules that are just as immutable as the laws of physics. You and I cannot break the rules merely for convenience. Besides, tomorrow's examinations will determine whether or not he is granted his credentials."

"You mean . . . Why, I thought he'd at least six months to go." For the first time she felt uncertainty about her request.

"No. Mr. Donovan was granted special consideration based on his self-taught knowledge and its practical and very clever application to the Comstock. If he passes this final series of examinations, he will be awarded his degree. With honors, I might add."

Fay glanced around the room and spotted a board with names and numbers. She walked over to it and her eyes skipped down until they located Glenn's name and #27.

"Really, miss, I've tried to be patient but I must insist you leave at once. The gates will be locked very soon and I have duties to attend to."

"You won't let me see him?"

"Absolutely not."

"Can I leave a message?"

"You may write, but it would not be delivered until Sunday. There are eighty-nine students here, and it would be bad precedent to start delivering messages."

"Bad precedent! Why can't you seem to get it through your head that this is an exception to your silly rules?" Fay cried, heading for the door.

"There are no exceptions," he shouted back. "You would understand that if your mind were properly trained."

Fay was seething when she entered the coach.

"Please return to the city," she gritted.

"As you wish."

The carriage jolted forward with the crack of the driver's whip.

Fay clenched her hands together and felt hot tears of disappointment burn her eyes, slide wetly down her cheeks. She was a fool to let herself get so upset over this matter. Probably even lucky she hadn't gotten to see him. No telling how she would have acted.

"Glenn Donovan in Number 27, I hope . . . Oh, hell! Driver!" she yelled, scrubbing the tears away and pushing her face through the curtains. "Take me back. And hurry!"

The coach rolled up to the gate.

"What time is it?"

"A quarter to six, Miss Taylor, but—"

She jumped out. "Drive into those trees down the way and keep out of sight until I return."

"Miss Taylor, what are you going to do!"

"Find Glenn. Now, please, do as I say."

He nodded. She could tell by his expression he objected, but knew better than to say so. Maybe he could see by her face that she'd had enough of people telling her what she couldn't or shouldn't do.

Fay gathered her skirts and hurried to the wrought-iron gate. She took a quick peek inside, then dashed in and ran to hide in the trees. She'd scarcely caught her breath before the man she'd argued with emerged from the stone building and walked briskly toward the gate. He locked it almost ceremoniously and peered up and down the now-empty roadway. Then he smugly made his way back to disappear into the great stone building.

Now what? Fay wondered, as the impact of being trapped inside struck her. Unless she could get help, she might be confined inside this . . . this prison all night!

Fay pushed down a rising tide of apprehension and waited for the darkness to close in around her. It was a warm night, crickets whirred a lively tune, and now and then soft laughter floated across the grass-covered enclosure she would have to traverse.

She began to get impatient as time passed. She kept telling

herself she'd done the right thing, even if it did seem crazy. Could she locate him? Were the little stone huts numbered? All kinds of doubts assailed her as the hour grew later.

The moon was a soft golden aura floating through clouds. Somewhere nearby, an owl hooted defiantly and a night creature rustled in the leaves as Fay raced over the grass toward the little rows of huts she prayed were openly numbered.

She was scared, but excited. Glad she'd decided to break the stupid rules, yet very uneasy about being trapped until morning. She *had* to find Glenn. He would help her go free.

Fay reached the first tiny cabin and peered up at the little weathered number. It was indistinguishable, so she touched it as her heart pounded with fear that the occupants inside might sense her presence.

But they didn't. And the hut was most certainly number five. She ran down the row of huts on silent feet, trusting in faith that she would not be seen or intercepted. Luck was with her, and at number twenty-seven she made her stand and knocked. At that moment she was so afraid that, had she not been locked in the compound, she'd have turned and run.

"Who's there?"

She nearly fell off the step. The voice wasn't Glenn's! Wildly she groped once again for the number—just as the door opened to reveal a rather harmless-looking young man with thick glasses. He took an almost frightened step back and Fay was instantly struck by the realization that, if anything, he was even more intimidated than she.

"Miss . . . Miss Fay Taylor!"

Only her years of acting allowed her to answer with some measure of composure. "Good evening! I'm flattered you recognize me and I hope you can assist me in locating a very dear friend. I must find him. His name is Glenn Donovan."

The young man just stared at her in gaping astonishment.

Fay tried again. "I really am sorry to disturb you, but I thought Mr. Donovan might be inside."

The young man finally reacted by closing the door behind him and whispering, "You shouldn't have come, Miss Taylor. Not tonight, of all nights! You'll destroy his chances of passing tomorrow's exam."

"Why?" Fay demanded. "I've never been to a school like this, but all I want to do is say hello."

"Hello . . ." the boy echoed. "He still loves you, Miss

Taylor! That's how I knew who you were. Your newspaper pictures are all over the room. Why, when you came to New York, he almost broke rules to visit you. But he'd have been expelled. It took all of his friends to talk him into staying until the last exam tomorrow."

"But . . ." Fay threw out her arms in a hopeless gesture. "I'm leaving for Europe in the morning."

"Boy," the young man wheezed. "He doesn't know that or we'd never have been able to keep him. You see, Glenn stayed only because he wanted to come to see you as an engineer. It's all he's dreamed about, Miss Taylor. Why, he's even demanded they let him take his examinations early."

"They allowed him to do that?" Fay couldn't believe it. If nothing else, she'd learned that no one here broke the rules.

"Yes. Mainly because no one had ever made such a request and there wasn't a rule when he petitioned. So they got mad, but he stood up and said they had to grant his request. And they did. He's been studying night and day for weeks. Right now he's asleep at his desk. I promised to wake him when I go to sleep. Do you want me to do it now, Miss Taylor?"

Fay glanced away in bitterness, shook her head to say no. Why had she ever tried to do this anyway? She was a fool.

She tried to smile, failed miserably, and hoped it was too dark for the boy to see how badly she felt.

"May I . . . may I go inside for a moment?"

"Why, sure! My name is Bertrand Hunter. I'm Glenn's roommate, have been for two years now. He helps me a lot. Once he even whipped a guy who kept calling me Owl-Eyes because of these darned glasses. Glenn almost got expelled from the college for fighting, and I've been owing him favors ever since."

Hunter toed the dirt around. "That's why I'm saying all this. Trying to tell you what's best for him."

"I understand."

Fay's eyes were on the door. He seemed to read her troubled thoughts. "If you're going away, you could write him a note. I'll give it to him."

"After the tests?"

"Sure. After he's passed and before he goes to see you. I mean, before he'd planned to. You can use my desk to write on, since Glenn's asleep at his."

"Thank you."

"You're welcome, Miss Taylor." He gestured toward the door. "You go in alone. I'll wait here and try to figure out how to get you outside the walls."

She smiled her appreciation and entered.

The room was small, with a squatty black cast-iron stove in one corner. There were two beds, dressers, and washbasins, all of which Fay saw, yet didn't see, as she approached the sleeping figure.

The first thing she noticed was the breadth of his shoulders and the tight muscular way he filled out his heavy woolen shirt. Then, when she came around to look directly into his face, she saw a man instead of the half-boy she'd remembered so clearly. Glenn's sand-colored hair was longer now, brushed away from his forehead. He was still clean-shaven, though his jawline was stubbled, and even in sleep, she noticed deep lines of fatigue. A scar she didn't remember angled just below his left eye, but it wasn't prominent enough to detract. Fay wondered if he'd gotten it fighting for his roommate.

He looked much handsomer than she'd remembered. Rosie wouldn't like that—but it was true. And so tired! Deep black circles ringed his eyes, reminding Fay just how difficult these awful tests must be. She reached out, gently touched his hair, then backed away to sit down heavily at Bertrand Hunter's desk, her eyes never leaving Glenn Donovan.

Wave after wave of emotion for something that might have been—should have been—passed over her. If she'd hoped to destroy an illusion as Rosie had, she'd failed.

I've made a mistake, she thought dismally. I feel an ache inside that grows, not dies. She glanced away, biting her lip sharply. On the walls about the tiny room, she saw diagrams and drawings of bridges, tunnels, walls, and buildings.

One in particular attracted her, and she rose to study it closely. Virginia City was laid out perfectly, with the names of streets, businesses, and the mines he'd worked for. Glenn obviously hadn't been to the Comstock for a number of years, and Fay had the impulse to pencil in several new and important structures such as the International Hotel. She resisted.

Then Fay saw the newspaper article which had announced her arrival in New York City. Already the picture of her was fading, but he'd tacked it on the cabinet before his desk. He *did* still love her.

Fay stumbled back to the empty desk and found writing

materials. The words which followed were the hardest she'd ever written.

Dear Glenn:

I am deeply sorry I cannot be here when you awake, even more so that I depart for Europe in the early morning. But I'm glad I saw you now. Your desk is covered with pages of numbers, equations that I could never understand, just as we could never make a life together. I pray for your successful examinations and return to the Comstock to do as you've always dreamed and to take your place as a true engineer.

Please remember me and wish me well in Europe. Like you, I feel compelled to press forward on the path of my own destiny, even though, at times like this, it hurts so very deeply. I wish you success and happiness.

Yours always,
Fay Taylor

She carefully folded the letter, along with a recent picture, and whispered, "Good-bye, Glenn. I'll never, ever forget those days in our snowy Sierra cave when, like children, we dreamed our beautiful dreams. Now we've made them come true but lost each other."

Her lips brushed his forehead; then, as a tear squeezed down her cheeks, Fay pivoted to leave.

Bertrand Hunter took her arm. In the shaft of doorway light he could not have helped but notice the bleakness of her expression. "I'm sorry, Miss Taylor," he said, adjusting his glasses and leading her out into the darkness.

"Over here," he whispered, motioning in the moonlight to where vines covered the wall. "I'm afraid you'll ruin your dress."

"Hang the dress. Give me a lift up."

He did, and she hoisted herself up into the vines. Her new dress became entangled and ripped when she tore it free. No matter. He hadn't seen it anyway.

Bertrand called a soft good-bye as Fay stumbled down the road toward the trees where she knew the carriage would be waiting.

"Good heavens, Miss Taylor! Your clothes."

"I'm all right. Help me inside."

"We'll never make it in time for your farewell performance. Shall I—?"

"Take me to my hotel," she ordered, easing back against the velvet cushions and closing her eyes. "I've already completed my farewell. I could never do another this night."

It was true, and as the carriage bore her speedily toward New York City, Fay Taylor cried alone.

The door was open; he felt the draft of air and it woke him, though he was not rested. Glenn blinked awake. The draft blew papers from his desk, and he heaved himself out of his chair.

"Bert?" He decided his young roommate must have stepped outside for a breath of air and forgotten to close the door. Glenn knuckled his sleep-starved eyes, walked back over to his desk, and shuffled papers aside seeking his pocket watch. It was only eight o'clock. Not late at all—unless you were an engineering student. Then you were always tired, studying every hour you could squeeze out of every day. During examinations it was not uncommon for students to go for weeks without more than four hours of sleep each day.

But it was almost finished. Tomorrow. One way or another. Either way, he was leaving for New York City as soon as possible. It never occurred to him that he might fail the exam, because he'd worked harder than anyone else and his record to date was superior. Yes, he'd paid with long hours of study, but he found the nature of the subject to his liking. Had he chosen to, he could have quit anytime since the war and accepted any one of dozens of offers to help rebuild the North and South. Lincoln would have wanted him and others like himself to use their knowledge to mend the country. But he couldn't bear to stay in the east. Besides, the west was building too. And there was the great transcontinental railroad which would span and unite the continent. No, as much as the east needed him, so did the west, and he was a westerner first and last.

Glenn wearily pushed a sheaf of notes aside, then froze as his eyes rested on the letter—and her picture. He slumped into his beaten desk chair, unable to believe what he held in his hands. They shook as he unfolded and began to read the note. As its contents sank in, Glenn's face hardened, grew tight with unmasked resolution. She'd been here just to see him. And he'd slept! Slept while she'd written her note and watched him, knowing she was sailing out of his live forever.

He was going after her. Damn the examination and the consequences! Everyone had talked him into staying, and now look where their advice had gotten him.

He charged the door, was striding across the compound when Bert grabbed his arm.

"Let go of me," he warned sharply.

"Glenn, she wants you to finish up by passing tomorrow's test. She asked me to hold the note and picture until then."

"It would be too late!" he shouted. "You're my friend. You should have awakened me."

"No, I did what was best. And I'd do it over again. I knew what this would do to you. Miss Taylor agreed."

"Where did she go?"

"Glenn, don't ruin everything you've worked for all these years!"

But he wasn't listening as he yanked his roommate off his feet and dragged him across the grounds toward the wall.

"Give me a lift up, Bert. I'm sick of you and everyone else deciding what's best."

Bert knew better than to argue.

"What shall I tell them?" he grunted, hoisting his roommate upward.

At the top of the wall, silhouetted against the moon, Glenn Donovan hesitated. "Tell them . . . tell them I'll be ready at one o'clock as scheduled."

"But . . ."

Glenn didn't hear the rest. His shirt ripped and a vine cut an angry scratch across his chest. He completely ignored it. When his boots hit the dirt, he was running.

Unfortunately, he had a long way to go. The New York School of Engineering had been founded on the bequest of a wealthy upstate New York landowner. As such, it was over twenty miles from the city. This was felt to be an advantage by its administration, because the distance itself was an effective obstacle, rendering unreachable the unsavory temptations to which even the most disciplined student would probably succumb at some time during his long, arduous education.

Glenn was bone-weary and out of shape from the countless nights of too much study and too little sleep. Yet, his long muscular legs were suited for the road which lay ahead. At first he hoped to overtake the carriage, but as the miles passed and his lungs burned and his legs began to knot and cramp, he was forced to stop and rest for short intervals. Then he'd push himself erect and begin to run again.

To counter the pain and fatigue, he allowed himself to visualize the well-rehearsed image he'd closeted inside all those long months, the image that had kept him from rushing to her the moment she'd arrived in New York. The scenario never changed. He'd go to Broadway and buy a suit of clothing as respectable as any of Fay's admirers'. Then he'd order the best seat at the theater. Front row, center stage. And she'd come out. Everyone would stand and applaud, but when they sat, he alone would remain on his feet. Tall. Straight. Maybe not handsome, but worthy, because he would be an engineer instead of just an uneducated, hardworking Comstock miner.

She'd see him there. And then she'd smile radiantly. They'd look at each other and it would be as if they were alone. Then the performance would begin. It mattered not what play it would be, for his imagination always jumped to afterward, when he would meet her backstage. As the scene ended, Glenn pictured himself leading her away. Fay's arm on his own.

Over and over he believed this dream. It carried him steadily south to the city. At the ferry to Manhattan Island, he reached into his pocket and discovered he carried enough loose change to pay the toll. The boatman eyed him with grave mistrust as they traveled across, but Glenn didn't notice or care. His eyes were directed toward the big city just ahead. He didn't feel the cold dampness which swept off the rough, dark water and chilled the cuts on his chest. Fay was just ahead, playing at the Starlight Theater on Broadway. He'd find her and see the happiness flood into her eyes—just like in the dream.

He charged off the street and bounded up the steps into the theater, looking like a wild man—sweat-drenched and clothes hanging in bloody tatters.

"Hey!" a guard bellowed. "Stop!"

Glenn was halfway across the lobby when a big man tackled him to the floor while another tried to pinion his wrists. He wrenched free and rolled, kicking out with both feet and staggering one of them.

"I just wanted to see Miss Taylor!" he yelled, jumping up and edging away.

The one he'd kicked swore in a choked voice, and his partner sprang forward. One took him high and the other low. Glenn had the feeling they'd done it all before, and as his fist slammed into the bigger man's rocklike skull, he felt himself leaving the ground.

A fist exploded against his jaw—and Glenn's head banged hard on the floor and his vision swam. Somewhere a woman screamed, and he felt himself being pulled to his feet.

"Get him out of here!" one of the doormen yelled. "The play's over!"

There was a loud rumble of applause in the theater and they hustled him outside and threw him down the stairs to land in the gutter.

Glenn pushed himself up to his knees to see the crowd flowing out. The two guards were posted at each side of the doors watching him, making sure he didn't try again.

He managed to stand, then unsteadily walked around the corner and out of sight. Glenn clung to a lamppost, tried to keep from collapsing until the brisk night air revived his senses. When it finally did, he moved around the building to the rear exit, where waiting carriages were packed into a narrow alley.

He weaved through them and entered the building. It was a maze of stage props, dressing rooms, and equipment of all types. Glenn chose an empty corridor and hurried forward.

A door opened just ahead and a handsome young man exited into the hallway, blocking it. "Who are you?" he challenged. "You don't belong back here."

"Where's Miss Taylor?"

"You are trespassing and—"

Glenn threw himself on the man so ferociously the actor forgot his next line. "Tell me!" he demanded, balling the man's shirtfront and drawing back his fist.

"Not in my face! Don't hit my face!"

Glenn shoved him away. "Just tell me where I can find Miss Taylor."

"She's not here tonight," a deep, almost smoky woman's voice told him.

Glenn wheeled. "Who are you?"

"Her manager. Now, who the hell are you to ask?"

"Glenn Donovan."

The woman's manner underwent a sudden change from disdain to sharp interest. "Well," she said finally, "I might have guessed."

She gestured to the actor. "Leave us, please."

The young man recovered his posture quickly. "Are you sure it's all right?"

"Yes. Thank you."

He straightened his rumpled shirtfront, glanced belligerently at Glenn, and stabbed a finger in his direction. "Any more trouble and I'll be back."

Glenn laughed outright at the phony bravado, and the actor blushed deeply before leaving. If he was Fay's leading man, sparks would fly.

"Did you see Fay?"

"No, I was asleep at my desk. Where is she now?"

"Do you love her, Mr. Donovan?"

"Yes, but I don't—"

"Then go away," the woman said.

Glenn shook his head doggedly. "If you won't tell me where to find her tonight, I'll be waiting at the pier when she sails in the morning."

"If you *really* love her, you'll stay out of her life."

"I'm sorry, but that just isn't possible."

"Then I'll do everything I can to stop you."

Glenn pivoted to go. "You can't," he whispered. "I've already waited too long."

Morning found him waiting at the pier, stiff and chilled in the fog and tortured by self-doubt. Maybe he should go away. Certainly he had no wish to hurt Fay's career, ruin her send-off. With another day, he could return to the New York School of Engineering and get enough money to buy a good suit, shave, and haircut. *But there just wasn't time!*

So he was sticking. Sticking because he'd allowed others to talk him into waiting to see her and they'd brought him to this; he wasn't going to listen to anyone anymore.

The morning sun finally burned through the fog. Glenn washed his face of blood, combed his hair with swollen fingers. By nine o'clock there was a gathering crowd and at least a dozen mounted policemen who'd arrived to form an escort line.

Fay's carriage rolled up to the pierfront at eleven, and the crowd of friends, admirers, and just the curious surged forward as the mounted police tried to keep them back.

Glenn made his move, angling around the crowd toward the ship's gangplank, even as Fay emerged and marched up its steep incline.

"There he is!" an officer yelled, reining his horse in on Glenn and letting the animal's shoulder knock him down.

Glenn rolled, saw all of them coming. He did the only thing he could, and that was to throw himself off the pier.

"Fay!" he shouted. "Fay!"

The cold ocean water took his breath away, but only for a moment, as he called her name again and again.

Suddenly her face appeared along the rail.

"Glenn!" she cried, disappearing for a moment, then reappearing at the gateway. They tried to stop her, tried even as cameras clicked and onlookers stared with disbelief.

Fay had a bouquet of flowers, and she tossed them down at Glenn as he swam forward.

Then, like an actress on center stage, she waved to everyone and posed for the photographers for just an instant before gathering her skirts and jumping into the ocean. It wasn't far. Not nearly as high as she'd jumped from the rocks into the Stanislaus and Merced rivers.

They swam toward each other and embraced. She was laughing, and he felt as though he'd been given a new life.

"I love you, Fay Taylor."

"You're crazy, Glenn Donovan!" she cried, paddling to keep afloat. "You're supposed to be studying. I wrote—"

"Never mind all that. I don't care about the examination anymore!"

Fay's laughter died. They paddled over to grab a buoy someone had thrown. "You have to care, Glenn. And I *have* to go. There isn't time to talk it over . . . and I know it wouldn't do any good. I'm leaving and you're going to pass that damned test this afternoon."

"Is that the way you want it?"

People were shouting at them, holding outstretched hands down to her.

"Yes."

Glenn nodded. He glanced up as another photographer leaned out over the water for a close shot. For an instant they were blinded by the flash.

Then he gently pushed Fay back toward the pier, saying, "I hope I didn't spoil your farewell."

"Glenn? Glenn, wait!"

He didn't. Glenn ducked from view under the pier, and amid the flotsam and debris, slowly swam away.

22

Bear Claw Man sat quietly beside the desert campfire, only half-listening to the talk around him. Like the chiefs, Numaga and Winnemucca, who were seated nearby, his eyes were troubled as he brooded about the People and their future.

The time, four and a half years ago, when he and Chief Numaga had met with Colonel Lander at Fort Churchill to declare peace now seemed like another age. At first the future had seemed good for the People, and though he'd never been able to forget Julia completely, his life had been a happy one as Windflower's husband.

The battles of 1860 and the death songs for both red and white men were distant things, as distant as the war that had raged in the east to its final bloody conclusion at the siege of Petersburg and the fall of the Confederacy only a week later.

Clayton understood little of that war, only what their Indian agent had said in passing. No matter. He'd abandoned all contact with the white man and was satisfied to live in a karnee and care for his wife and three-year-old son for as long as his eyes could see game and his limbs were strong enough to bring it home. That, he figured, would be for some time yet, since he was still just thirty-two. His boy was going to be strong enough to take his place someday. This gave Clayton great comfort.

But there were deep worries, too. In the early years after the treaty, Long Beard Wasson had been their good friend as well as the Indian agent. Then, in the spring of 1862, he'd left the position to become a U.S. marshal and Wasson's successors had all been either incompetent or outright corrupt. White squatters had shoved onto the reservation and taken the best ranching land. When Clayton and Numaga protested to the Indian agent, the very official who was supposed to protect their interests turned out to be dishonest.

Colonel Lander had also been replaced, and the military leaders who followed were unsympathetic, even hostile to the People. Twenty thousand acres of timber and the promised lumber mill near Verdi, for which Clayton had argued so hard as the Paiutes' best hope for self-sufficiency, had become an empty, forgotten dream. That timber was now earmarked for the great Central Pacific Railroad, which was already beginning to crawl out of Sacramento, less than a hundred and fifty miles to the west. Clayton had argued vehemently with everyone from the new governor on down for the lumber mill as promised. An attempt doomed to failure because the value of the timber had risen faster than anyone had expected, while the Indians' welfare in peacetime was a forgotten issue.

To make the situation even worse for the Pyramid Lake tribe, hostilities between the whites and the Nevada Shoshone had broken out along the Overland Trail. Once again the whites had reacted in fear and convinced the federal government to establish a line of new forts clear across Nevada. Clayton had tried to visit each of these military outposts on behalf of the Paiutes, but had been received with contempt and distrust. An Indian was an Indian. Paiute? Shoshone? No difference. They were all dangerous and murderous scalpers. Eliminate them—the sooner the better.

Less than a month ago, Clayton and Numaga had finally taken a stand against the cancerlike encroachment of whites by attacking a large group of cattlemen down near the south tip of Pyramid Lake. Three of the cowboys hadn't run, even when the others knew better. They'd taken positions in a gully and shot Strong Elk off his pony in the first volley of gunfire. Clayton had killed two with his buffalo rifle before the third had been dispatched by a war ax.

Bad times were coming, Clayton thought darkly as he stared at the flames. Wasson and Colonel Lander gone, the peace treaty a forgotten promise, an Indian war spilling over to drag them in, and finally, the Central Pacific Railroad, which would bring hordes of new settlers westward. Could the Indian survive? And, if he did, would his future be worth anything? Perhaps not. Clayton wanted to live as much as the next man, but he'd had his day in the sun and it was gone. Just blown away by the gold-crazed forty-niners, who'd changed the face of the west forever. Ruined it, they had. He'd been sixteen at the start of the rush and hadn't realized the sweeping change that would so quickly wipe away the life he'd known as a hunter and trapper. Now the best times were past for his kind and for the Indian.

When he thought of Windflower, still young and beautiful, and his son and the Paiute children, he ached inside with a sadness he could not express and that few of the young warriors could understand. Would there be retaliation for the killing of the three cattlemen who had stolen the Paiute lands which had been earned with blood and bargained for with the President of these United States?

Time would tell.

Maybe he should have ridden at once to meet the new commander at Fort Churchill, but winter had left the tribe dangerously short of food. They'd needed his eyes and his long rifle these past two days, and he'd acquiesced to that need so that the women and children might not go hungry if the spring came late this year.

The hunting trip was successful. That was why the young bucks laughed this final night and openly bragged about their hunting prowess. Six antelope were already cut into strips and ready to carry back to the main village.

"You seem troubled, Bear Claw Man. Are you not pleased with the hunt?"

The question interrupted his reverie. "Very pleased, Chief Numaga. This meat will last our people until the sun warms the land and brings the fish and birds to our nets."

"Yes." Numaga sat down beside him, his great size blocking even the firelight. In the years since he'd been one of the People, Clayton and the warrior chief had become like brothers. So alike did they think that oftentimes one guessed the other's thoughts without words.

"It will be good to return. You miss my sister and your child."

"Yes. And my soft warm bed, with her beside me."

"Do my eyes play tricks or is my sister growing fat like a tired old squaw?"

Clayton's mouth twisted in amusement. "What do you mean?" he asked innocently. It would be like Numaga to notice first.

"You plant the seed and it bears fruit when the days grow hot. Is this true?"

"Yeah." He shrugged, feeling a touch of embarrassment mingled with pride. "The baby should come right about July."

"This is good!" Numaga stood up and called for silence. "Listen, my people. It is for us to know that Bear Claw Man is to be a new father before the salmon spawn."

The news was greeted, as it always was when any warrior's squaw revealed pregnancy, with wild laughter and gamy but good-natured comments. Bear Claw Man huddled deeper into his robes and was grateful for his beard, which hid the redness of his face. But he smiled. Smiled because there'd be some of them who'd have like news soon enough, and then he'd give 'em hell right back and enjoy every minute of the rawhiding.

"Blasted heathens!" He laughed. "Don't know why I put up with the likes of you crazy redskins!"

As usual, this caused even greater howling. Clayton bore it all with equanimity, although he scowled at the grinning Numaga. Thank God it was two hours past sundown and time for sleep! Maybe tomorrow they'd jump on some other poor soul to bedevil. Clayton sure hoped so, because Windflower wasn't due for six months. That was a long while to take a joshing—but worth it when the baby was born.

He heard the hard-scrabble clatter of a running horse, then noted its tearing gasps for air as it labored across the meadow. Clayton knew by the sound that the animal was about to collapse.

He threw his robes aside, anger flooding him at the cruel stupidity of anyone who'd run a horse to death.

It was the girl named Winona who came racing out of the night and who fell sobbing beside the fire to scream over and over that their camp had been attacked by whites when the sun was the color of blood.

"How many men?"

"Many. Many!"

"Soldiers?"

"No."

"Did any survive?"

"Some. We ran for the trees. Many guns. Few places to hide."

Clayton's anguish split the night with a terrible animallike scream as he raced for his pony. He was the first out of camp and the first to kill his own running horse six hours later—his mind eaten by fear, wondering if his wife, son, and unborn child had made it to the trees, or been slaughtered in camp.

When his horse collapsed into a running somersault, Clayton jumped free and lit on his moccasined feet, running hard; he didn't stop until he crested a hill above the Indian village.

Smoke, lazy and blue, wafted up from the charred remains of the Paiute encampment, where nothing, not even dogs, moved. Clayton's heart seized up in his great chest and he weaved down the hill, the long rifle falling unnoticed.

The bodies were strewn about like cheap dolls hurled by a petulant child-god; they lay twisted and crumpled and still.

He stumbled past them, unseeing. Tears flooded the hair on his cheeks and he found Windflower and his boy close to his karnee, huddled where they'd died.

Clayton threw back his head and roared. His hands clawed and ripped at his face and chest and he staggered around shouting at the spinning sun, wanting to go blind and crazy. To destroy himself. To end the agony which had been his life every time any happiness appeared.

He crashed to the earth and rolled and roared until finally he lay beating the dirt and cursing every mortal thing that had ever walked or flown or swam or crawled over its surface. And he cursed the God who'd made them all.

Had not Numaga himself gathered the destroyed man up and ordered him kept under guard, Bear Claw Man might have killed himself in his madness.

It was only upon hearing that the murderers had left signs that Clayton returned to some kind of normalcy—if murderous intent could be so termed.

He knew the killers were the same group of cattlemen they had fought before, and he memorized the seven horses' tracks for each peculiarity that was as distinct as a fingerprint. While the village went into mourning, Clayton prepared for the track-down, knowing his quarry would sell their stolen cattle and horses, then run with the bounty. But no matter how far—to the sea or beyond—he would find them and kill them one by one. Then he did not care what became of his own life. Death was a blessing he could yearn for—life a torture which gave, then ripped back anything a man cherished.

Bear Claw Man swore to Numaga that he would find them and avenge the tribe's loss.

"I will go with you."

"No," he'd said. "I must go among the whites, where you cannot."

Numaga, his face old and his once sharp eyes dulled with grief, had nodded. "Will you come back?"

He thought a moment. "Only to bring word of their deaths. I could not live among these people again."

"I understand." Numaga turned away, and when he spoke, his voice echoed the depth of his passion. "Take my best pony and find them, Bear Claw Man! Kill them slowly. Maybe then your pain will let you breathe and live to walk free again."

"Maybe. But I doubt it," Clayton hissed, shouldering his rifle and walking away. He left the People, knowing he'd never return, because even vengeance could not mend his wounded soul.

Clayton rode out of the desert, following the murderer's tracks all the way to Reno. The tracks were easy to follow, because the seven plunderers had had little to fear as they'd driven the Indian ponies down to the burgeoning settlement on the Truckee River.

The lone pursuer did not hurry, and scarcely glanced at the hoofprints as he steadily rode south. He would find the men, because they would sell the ponies for gold. Of this he was certain.

He was right. He had no difficulty locating the Indian ponies being held in a rickety corral belonging to a very nervous horse trader.

"The men who sold you those Indian horses—which way did they go?"

"Didn't say."

"When'd they leave?"

"I don't—"

Clayton's buffalo rifle dropped from his shoulder to the crook of his arm, and it was no coincidence that the big black barrel pointed straight into the dealer's suddenly bugged and terror-frozen eyes.

"Once more," the rider asked conversationally, "where were they headed and when did they leave?"

"Didn't say. Honest, mister! Just rode for the mountains early on this mornin'."

Clayton nodded. His shaggy head rotated toward the Sierras. Yes, he thought, they'd have cattle- *and* horse-sale money and maybe be thinking their slaughter of women and children at

Pyramid Lake might cause enough trouble that it would be healthier in San Francisco.

"Much obliged."

The Sierras layer down above Reno on easy grass hills until high up, where the trail pinches into the canyons and the cottonwoods along the river give way to juniper and pine. That is where men can be ambushed by robbers and thieves, and more than one bullet-riddled body had floated down the quick white water to float through Reno.

Clayton reached the mountain canyons after dark and kept riding. He saw over a dozen campfires, but he skirted them all and kept riding higher up toward Donner Pass, where the snows fell deep enough to bury standing trees. People still whispered about the infamous party who'd been trapped in the pass one terrible winter and had resorted to cannibalism to stay alive.

He found the band of killers around three in the morning. There were seven horses picketed back under the trees, and seven men asleep. One of them wasn't supposed to be, but he was.

Clayton dismounted, feeling every day of his thirty-two years and the aching from where he'd run those last miles yesterday to find his wife and son.

He tied and muzzled his horse downriver, because the wind blew off the higher peaks. Then he took his rifle, reversing his grip so that his thick hands were wrapped around the barrel, not the stock.

They were sleeping on a grassy patch near the spring-swollen river, and the water was so noisy he could have marched in beating a drum and they'd not have heard. The sentry died first as the rifle butt crushed his skull.

One of their horses scented the death and whinnied in fear, then began to dance on the picket line. A sleeping figure shifted uneasily, and Clayton froze until it grew quiet. Then he stepped into the grassy, dew-kissed clearing, and in the gray half-light before the dawn, raised his thick arms and screamed to the dying moon as he slashed downward to kill again. And again.

He was a mountain lion among sheep, a dervish of death that swirled and screamed and drove terror into their hearts even as they were executed.

Two fired shots; one scored flesh, the other did not. Both gunmen died as the buffalo rifle rose and fell into their horror-stricken faces.

The last murderer ran shouting toward the Truckee River, and when he saw what he might have thought was half grizzly, half man, he jumped into the roiling waters, only then remembering he could not swim.

His pathetic cries as he bobbed and thrashed downriver were answered by a lead ball through his forehead.

The seven horses were terrified by the gunfire, the smoke, and the death smell. Clayton kicked the bodies into the river and the gunpowder smoke drifted over the water, to be carried down by the pine-scented winds of Donner Pass.

Daybreak found him leading seven saddled horses tied neck to tail. His direction was north and he followed game trails which only the Paiutes knew, through the heavy forests near Verdi, where the lumber mill was to have been constructed. He rode all day, stopping only to water the horses before nearing Pyramid Lake. But he could not draw strength enough to return to the place where his family had died. So he waited. Waited until Numaga came forward to meet him in the desert.

"It is done." Clayton hurled into the dirt four pairs of gold-laden saddlebags which he guessed contained some ten or twelve thousand dollars.

Numaga dismounted. "This will feed our people for two, maybe three years."

"Trade these murderers' saddles and horses. Burn all signs of my coming and my leaving."

"It will be done." He held up a pair of the heavy saddlebags. "Take one."

"No. Your horse and my rifle. It is enough. It was always enough."

But Numaga would not yield ground on his demand. "Take this," he ordered, "for the good of yourself and the People."

"I don't understand, my brother."

Numaga stared at the dead lake beside which they talked. "Listen well," he began. "There was a day not long ago when I would have thrown this white man's money back into our waters. But now I know we need gold to buy food. We must swallow our pride. Can you not make gold from gold?"

"No," Clayton replied. "Gold is just found."

Numaga lifted the saddlebags. "Many hours around the campfire, you told me the government money was needed to build the woodcutting place. You said it was needed by our people to make money for us."

"Yeah, but—"

"Now we do not need government money. Use this!"

"Chief . . ." He searched for words as the pair of saddle-bags hung from his arm. "You don't understand. This isn't near enough to buy a sawmill!"

"Then use all of it to buy the wood cutting place," Numaga said angrily.

Clayton started to argue that his heart was dead and he wasn't any good anymore. He'd drink or gamble the money away and court death as recklessly as he could to end this tragedy he'd called a life.

"Bear Claw Man! Look at what is left of the People now."

"I can't."

"Look!" the chief ordered vehemently.

He did. He forced himself to study the sorry collection of tribesmen mourning the loss of so many of their wives and children. Clayton saw warriors bent with sorrow. "I'll do as you ask," he whispered hoarsely. "But one bag is enough."

The great chief nodded. And since there was nothing more to say, Clayton reined his mount away and rode into the barren, empty hills beyond.

He circled Reno because the Truckee River would have delivered the evidence of his revenge. But they wouldn't be able to prove he'd killed the seven. Besides, if the full story came out, the horse trader might even be forced to return the stolen Indian ponies, and that guaranteed his silence.

As Clayton journeyed south along the eastern base of the mountains, he passed Washoe Valley and then crested a hill overlooking Carson City. He was astonished to see that it had doubled in size during the years he'd been with the Paiutes. Maybe they'd have a doctor to patch up the wound under his left arm.

But even as he rode into Carson City, he knew it wasn't to visit a doctor. That was just an excuse. The real reason he was going down among the whites was that he needed to see Julia Matson before he attempted to build a sawmill.

Suddenly he remembered she was now called Julia Tillman. And what little hope he'd felt stir inside crawled out of him. To hell with it! he thought. He'd just stay back and peek at her from somewhere hidden. She was one of the few good things he had left in this world. It wouldn't be wrong. And it wouldn't do any harm.

The doctor eyed him suspiciously. "Haven't I seen you before?"

"Not likely. How much I owe?"

"A dollar for the call and two bits extra for the bandages and medicine."

Clayton produced the money. "Sure clumsy of me to have an accident like that after all these years."

"Yeah," the physician said cryptically. He didn't seem fooled in the least, but years of caring for gunshot victims had no doubt taught him the wisdom of not asking a second time about a wound.

"Doctor, I'd like to know where Mrs. Julia Tillman lives now."

"Up in Virginia City, last I heard."

Clayton tried to mask his disappointment. "Huh. Guess her husband got a better sheriffin' job."

"Nope. Got himself shot. You can find him planted in the Carson City cemetery."

"You mean Julia's a widow?"

"That's the way it usually works. Now, if I can have your money, you'll get the bandages."

"Sure," Clayton said haltingly, his mind in a whirl. Julia was alone, and that was the one thing he'd never expected. "She remarry?"

"Who?" the doctor asked, pocketing the money.

"Missus Tillman."

The man scowled and his baggy eye pouches tightened with impatience. "How should I know? Last I heard she was living alone after her store burned down. I've heard that she has become a harlot. A kept woman for Mr. Dade Taylor."

Clayton grabbed him by the shirtfront and jerked him up to his toes. "That's a lie!"

The doctor's glasses fogged and he struggled to extract himself. "I didn't say it! Now, let go of me, dammit! I got other patients waiting outside!"

Clayton dropped him, mumbled an apology, and left by the back door.

It wasn't possible. Couldn't be true. But he had to find out.

Clayton had no trouble getting directions to Julia's house. Everyone knew her because of her store, which he learned had gone up in flames a few years ago.

"I don't know what the hell she does to support herself," a

miner said, leaning on the long mahogany bar. "Any of you fellas?"

No one did, though a few made remarks about what they'd like to suggest. Normally these comments might have caused some rough barroom laughter. But Clayton stepped in and the warning in his eyes chilled the grins right off their faces as they moved quickly down the bar.

He drank alone at the Crystal Bar, a huge brooding presence in buckskins who smelled of campfire and grease, gunpowder and sweat. He was as apart from these tough, deep-rock miners as he might have been among politicians or the wealthy. Clayton half-listened to their talk about steam and heard terms like stopes, square-sets, giraffes, drifts, sumps, crosscuts, and winzes that were totally alien.

A large percentage of the miners were foreigners. Men from Wales, Ireland, the Balkans, and England. These nationalities seemed to hang together in little fraternal knots and clusters, as though clinging to their homeland was possible when far away. They worried about death by poisonous gases, and spoke of how so-and-so fell out of the cage and left pieces of himself down a thousand feet of boarded shaft, of fires, and cave-ins and accidents of every kind and description. Virginia City boasted three funeral parlors, and all of them prospered.

He continued to drink until he could think about Windflower and his boy and how good life had been for them and how he hoped that they were in heaven and happy now, even though he'd lost his own faith. Not that it had ever been so much a thing as to brag on. Now he had to see Julia once more before he struck out for the mountains to lay claim to some timber and build a sawmill. Maybe, if he was lucky, he could work himself into exhaustion so that he was too weary to recall his shattered past and hopeless future.

Clayton pushed himself away from the bar and kept the bottle he'd paid for as he moved, a trifle unsteadily, outside to find her.

It didn't take long, but then he felt a strange unwillingness to walk past the small front gate and knock on her door. He drank deeply. What if Julia *was* Dade Taylor's mistress? He shuddered at the possibility and remembered how he'd once promised to help her if need be.

It was late evening, and still he waited, pulling steadily on the bottle, waiting until it was finished before he'd go see her.

There was a light in one of the windows at the rear of the house, where he guessed the bedroom would be, and even as he watched, Clayton saw a shadow moving toward it.

He dropped the near-empty bottle and glided silently across the street to intercept the prowler. He was still sober enough to realize his reactions would be impaired.

Suddenly the intruder halted and knocked. The rear door opened and a rectangular burst of light illuminated Dade Taylor. Clayton heard the two voices, then saw the door close as he stood frozen, telling himself that none of this was any of his business. As much as he hated the idea of a woman like that sleeping with a man like Dade Taylor, there was no call in barging in and shaming her. So he'd go. Just collect his gear and . . .

She cried out, and he was halfway across the street and almost didn't hear her words.

"Dade, no!"

But there wasn't any mistaking the sharp crack of flesh on flesh, like a popping bullwhip.

Clayton spun around, and when he reached the door, he didn't even grab for the handle but instead threw his shoulder against the wood. It splintered off the hinges and he crashed into Julia's bedroom.

The flat of Dade's hand was poised above the woman in bed. Dade shouted an oath and his upraised hand dropped to the gun on his hip.

Clayton knew the whiskey had done him in. He was half-turned, trying to rise to his feet and untangle himself when he saw Dade flick the revolver out of his holster.

Recognition flashed into the man's eyes. "Well, if it isn't our stagecoach driver! Clayton James, I do believe. Yessir, weaned off a grizzly bear and blood brother to savages, if my memory serves correctly."

"Dade! Please, don't shoot him!"

Clayton stared up at the gun and felt absolutely no fear at all, only anger at his own clumsiness and a vague sense of disgust that he'd not killed this man a long time ago. Maybe it wasn't too late; he'd always figured no forty-five-caliber gun in the world could put him down to stay with the first shot.

Julia must have read his mind, because she threw herself out of the bed, dressed only in the scantiest of night clothes and a pair of black elbow-length gloves. She knelt in front of Clayton.

"Tell him you'll go," she begged. "Tell Dade now or he'll kill you!"

His head drooped and he felt a rising sickness that had nothing to do with drinking a whole bottle of red-eye whiskey. "What do *you* want, Julia? He can't keep you if you want to leave."

She inhaled deeply and her voice sounded like an old woman's. "I love him, Clayton."

"No!"

"It's true."

"He hit you, dammit!"

"I'm his woman. It's his right."

Clayton stared at her. "But you're a *kept* woman."

"I *choose* to be! It's my decision and you've no right to interfere. Now, go. Please."

He couldn't believe it at all until Julia stood up and walked over to Dade. She took his hand and placed it on the mound of her breast. Then she ran her hands through his hair and began to unbutton Dade's shirt, saying, "We fight, but it makes the loving sweeter. So, if you'll excuse us . . ."

Clayton staggered to his feet. His vision was blurred and he could feel the gorge starting to rise into his throat.

Then he left them. Left them hearing Dade laughing, and remembering Julia and those dirty black gloves. Like a whore would put on for a man's pleasure.

Clayton threw up beside her front porch and staggered away sick in mind and body. The last—the very last decent thing he'd been able to recall—was now gone.

23

Holly shifted uncomfortably at her desk chair and breathed deeply as the familiar queasiness returned. She needed fresh air. That was it. Perhaps she'd go mail this letter she'd just finished writing to Fay. But first she wanted to reread it to make certain she hadn't forgotten to say anything of importance.

My dearest Fay:

I have two exciting pieces of news which I think will delight you. The first is that your brother and I are soon to be parents! That is right, my dear friend, and even as I write this letter our baby is overdue.

You are my sister-in-law, and since Julia Tillman left this house, I feel you are my only remaining confidante and person I can trust. Oh, there are Dade and my father, but you know there are a few things which only women can understand. I am asking you, Fay, to be the godmother of this child even though I know you could not be present for its baptism. We are all very proud of your great success and do occasionally receive news of your European stage triumphs.

Until this morning, I had a great problem choosing a godfather for our baby (Dade does not seem to care and has left the choices to me, so I feel very fortunate). But guess who returned to Virginia City on last night's stage?

Glenn Donovan. Yes, Fay, he arrived from New York City. I only got to see him for a moment and did not have time to ask this special favor, but I'm sure he will accept the role of godfather; especially if you will.

Perhaps you think that last statement is a strange one, but I assure you it is not. Last night I lay thinking (expectant ladies sometimes have great trouble sleeping) about my conversation with Glenn, and the thing which I most vividly remember him asking was if I'd heard from you. When I replied yes, his face changed so that I felt a deep pang of sorrow for him. He loves you deeply, Fay, and I am sorry your careers took you from each other.

Glenn is an extremely handsome young man and should have no trouble making friends or finding employment here in Virginia City. Maybe someday you could come back and visit us and see my baby?

The last thing I wish to say is that I beg you to forgive your brother for whatever caused the trouble between you. I know Dade has some serious faults, yet he is a good man and I am hopeful this baby will change him and, at last, give him peace and satisfaction. One of my deepest regrets is that I have failed to provide these things for my husband.

I suddenly feel an uneasy stirring inside and think perhaps I will walk over to post this letter while I am still feeling up to the walk.

Please let me know if you will be our baby's godmother so I can enter the name on the birth certificate.

My prayers for your continued success and happiness.

Your friend,
Holly Taylor

She sealed the letter and found a shawl, for the morning chill was noticeable. Then Holly started toward the post office, taking deep breaths and trying to clear her head of a peculiar buzzing sound.

Because it was midmorning, she passed no one as she waddled heavily down the street. And when her first contraction came, it was so strong it nearly doubled her up with pain. She grabbed a fence and hung on until the contraction eased. When Holly straightened, her face was wet with fear. Some women had their babies very quickly. What if . . . ?

"Hi, Missus Taylor, cold out this morning, ain't it?"

She straightened, then saw the boy sauntering along, hands buried deep in pockets, not a care in the world.

"Thomas," she cried, feeling a wash of relief. "Please come here."

A whistled tune died on the kid's lips and he hurried over saying, "You don't look so good, ma'am. Something wrong?"

"Yes," she panted, bracing against the fence for another spasm. "Please run down to my father and husband's office. Tell them to call Dr. Pixton immediately!"

"You mean . . ." His eyes dropped to her bulging waistline as understanding spread across his young face. "Oh, no!" he breathed, whirling about and taking off down the street like a shot. Holly watched him run until another contraction folded her up and brought her sobbing to her knees. "Please, God! Let this baby wait until help comes. I'm sorry for anything I've done to offend you. Don't take my sins out on this baby!"

She lay still and waited until she heard the familiar voices of her father and Glenn Donovan.

"Holly," her father gasped, "what in blazes are you doing out here!"

"I . . . I felt so uncomfortable. Thought maybe a walk to the post office. Fresh air . . ."

"Damn the post office!" Bevis swore, grabbing Fay's letter and shoving it at Tom. "Mail this after you've found the doctor!"

"Yes, sir!"

Glenn scooped Holly up into his arms. "We'll have you in bed in just a minute, Holly," he promised, trying to run without jarring her.

"Aren't I the fool, though?" she gritted. "But I wanted Fay to know you're back and—"

"Never mind that. You've got enough to do delivering your baby."

"I know." She saw Bevis, his face flushed with unaccustomed exertion. "Take it easy, Father. Where is Dade?"

"He's out of the office," her father panted. "I sent a man to look for him while Thomas fetches the doctor."

Another contraction made her gasp and bite her lips as perspiration burst out across her brow. "Oh," she breathed raggedly. "Dade is going to be proud of this one. He's a fighter!"

"So are you, Holly," Glenn said. "Just save your strength because—" He didn't finish because she suddenly cried out and he felt a flood of warmth drench them wetly.

"Glenn," she cried. "Glenn, I'm sorry, but I'm going to have my baby!"

"Hang on," he gritted. "Try to hang on!" Glenn barged through her front door and stumbled up the stairs to lay her gently down on the bed.

Her eyes were closed, her color so white he could see the bluish veins under her skin. The contractions were coming fast now and when they did she clenched his hands powerfully and stifled her cries.

"Hot water!" she gasped.

"Where's the damned doctor!" Bevis roared, taking Glenn's place as he flew out of the room to get some water boiling.

Fortunately there were still live coals in her stove and he tossed wood inside, then pumped water and set it to boil.

"Where is she?"

Glenn swung about to see the doctor standing in the doorway, looking wildly in all directions. "Upstairs. First one on your right."

He took the stairs two at a bound, yelling, "If Dade isn't here, he's going to miss the birth of his first child."

Bevis came down a few minutes later and he looked a hundred years old. "The doctor told me to get out of the way," he confided, slumping down in a chair. "Said he didn't need two emergencies right now."

"Did he tell you anything?"

"Only that Holly is big and that there may be complications."

"Damn!" Glenn swore. "Maybe I ought to go help find Dade."

At the mention of the name, Bevis went purple in the face. "I oughta kill that bastard," he snarled. "If he wasn't my daughter's husband, I would have, even if it bought me the gallows!"

"You hate him that much?"

"More! I hate him more. Since I had to take him in as a partner, he's gobbled up dozens of properties and cheated me out of a fortune. But what could I do? Have my own son-in-law sent to prison? Have my daughter shamed and her child fathered by a convict?"

"No." Glenn patted the old man's shoulder. He hadn't realized the hatred Bevis carried inside. That explained his rapid aging. "Even so, I'd better help the kid find him. Any ideas where to begin?"

"Hell, yes!" Bevis choked. "But I didn't dare say so with Holly so near. You can find Dade at that woman's place! Same as he is every afternoon between four and six and half the evenings later on!"

"What woman?"

"The Tillman woman! That whore's been his mistress for years."

"Julia Tillman?"

"Yeah! I'd have run her out years ago if I could have kept it quiet. Run her out just like they did in San Francisco."

Glenn headed for the door, leaving Bevis to brood in his bitter hatreds. The man had obviously lost control of his business and was being torn apart between his love and concern for Holly and the need for vengeance against Dade. But he was probably wrong about Julia and failed to realize she was being used just as they all were. Glenn remembered the woman clearly. How she looked and how, even back then, Dade had been after her.

"Where does she live, Bevis?"

He described the place and its location. "Tell Dade if Holly dies I'll destroy him for this."

"She won't die. Just calm down. Have a drink and sit tight while I find him. By the way, does Holly realize—?"

"No. Hell no!" He buried his face in his big gray hands. "My God, she still thinks the Tillman woman is her friend."

He looked up, and Glenn realized he was crying. "Can you believe that?"

"Yes," he answered thickly. "I sure can."

Glenn took off at a dead run. It was a sad affair. Holly was the nearest thing to a saint he'd ever seen. And Julia Tillman had once been her closest friend. Hadn't Fay once told him that Julia Tillman and Clayton . . . He rejected the thought as impossible. Julia was so beautiful she'd have her pick of anyone. Even so, it was tough to think she'd chosen the husband of her best friend. He guessed he'd misjudged her rather badly.

Glenn found the house and ran to the front door and pounded loudly. "Missus Tillman, it's Glenn Donovan," he called. "I have to find Dade."

He heard a muffled conversation inside.

"Go away," Julia cried.

"Open up or I'll break this door in!" he swore. "Holly is having her baby!"

The door flew open and Dade stood shirtless with a gun in one hand and a glass of whiskey in the other. Julia was against the far wall, her face a reflection of shock.

Dade's expression changed full circle and he actually grinned. "Well, I'll be damned!" he chuckled, holstering his weapon. "Guess I'd best get on home."

Right there, Glenn wanted to smash that complacent look of nonconcern off the man's face.

Dade walked over to a chair and put on his shirt and coat. "By the way, Donovan, did you visit my sister in New York City?"

"Yes. What the deuce has that got to do with anything at a time like this?" he shouted. "Your wife needs you!"

"Take it easy, I'm no doctor." He fastened his tie, saying, "Holly got a letter from Fay. Came all the way from Paris, France! That girl sure has the Taylor touch. Always knew she'd make it big. Only time I ever worried was when she told me she loved you.''

Glenn's fists clenched.

''Hell, I knew for a fact she'd have been throwing her future away. But don't get mad. Marriage would have ruined your plans too.'' He looked Glenn straight in the eye. ''Did you really graduate?''

All he could do was nod.

''Well, I'll be! Look, I'd better go now, but you and I ought to meet later. I could use an engineer. Pay top dollar for results. Ask anyone. You see, there's a lot of projects I've—''

''Not interested,'' Glenn said, cutting him off shortly.

''No one pays better, and it's tough to do on your own.''

''Still not interested.''

Dade's eyes glinted steel and his mouth took a mean cut. ''If you don't work for me, you won't work for anyone. It's better that way, because I never liked you anyhow. You're a hardhead and I don't need hardheads.''

He started to walk away. ''Incidently, who told you I'd be here?''

His patience snapped. ''Does it matter? We found Holly lying in the street. Dr. Pixton is up there now. There could be complications!''

''Then I'm not staying here,'' Julia vowed. ''I'm packing up and moving in to help her with the baby. She'll be needing another woman.''

''Then I'll hire one!'' Dade swore. ''But she'll be a maid, not my mistress.''

Julia blinked; then her hand flashed up to slap him across the mouth hard enough to draw blood.

As he rocked back in pain and rage, Glenn stepped in between as Julia went to pack her belongings.

''She'll pay for that,'' Dade hissed, taking out a handkerchief and dabbing blood from his lip.

''You leave her be.''

Dade's hand stopped beside his face and split lip, and he grinned. ''Donovan, let me acquaint you with the facts of life in Virginia City. First off, you'll stay healthy if you realize I'm the man who calls the shots on the Comstock. Not the sheriff or the mayor—me. I own them. And not Bevis either, because he's nothing more than a sick old man who should have retired to tend a garden.''

''Are you through giving speeches?''

He sneered and started to pass until Glenn's hand clamped down on his shoulder. "Just remember what I said about Julia. You beat her up, I'll come calling."

Dade tore the hand away from his coat. "I'm easy as hell to find and plenty ready, willing, and able to accommodate whatever comes to my door. Now, get out of my way."

Glenn let him go because Holly wanted her man even if he wasn't worth a damn.

"Glenn. Before you go, I want to say thank you."

"Why do you do this?" he asked flatly. "You're not the kind, Julia."

"I have to."

"I don't believe that," he said stiffly. "You're the most beautiful woman I ever saw and could have had your choice of men."

"I did have." She swallowed and acted like it hurt. "But my choice didn't work out. It never has."

"Who?" He regretted asking. "I'm sorry. It's none of my business, but Fay once told me about Clayton James. Was he—?"

"Yes."

"How does he feel about you?"

"He despises me!" Julia cried, turning her back on him. "You see, he came here one night and found us together. It . . . it was like I'd killed him."

He wanted to go to her. Say something that would lessen her own pain.

"Glenn?"

"Yes?"

"I don't want to talk about what I've done anymore. God knows I think about it night and day already. That's why I'm leaving here. Going to help Holly recover. How is she?"

"The truth?"

"Of course," Julia whispered.

"She looks terrible. I could tell by the doctor's face he's worried."

"Holly will live, Glenn. I just know she has that kind of strength."

"What about you?"

"We'll see. The only thing that's kept me here is that Dade promised he'd not kill Clayton James."

"Clayton acts like the kind of man who can take care of himself."

"You have no idea of Dade's power," Julia said. "I don't think anyone knows what that man is capable of except me. He'd not hesitate to send a dozen gunmen after Clayton."

"I find that hard to believe."

"Believe it!" she swore.

"All right. Can I help?"

She smiled. "You're the only man in this world who can."

"How?"

"By finding Clayton and making him leave Nevada. Go far enough that Dade could never hurt him."

Glenn nodded. "Then you can leave here. Is that right?"

"After I go to the only place he can't touch me."

"To Holly?"

"Yes. She'll need me, and by the time she doesn't, maybe you'll have convinced Clayton to go."

"Can I tell him why you've stayed with Dade?"

She shook her head no. "I've hurt him enough already. Why any more?"

Glenn couldn't think of an answer. "Do you want me to wait?"

"If you don't mind. I'm a little afraid to enter the lion's den, so to speak."

If she'd attempted a joke, it hadn't come easy. "What if Dade tries something?"

Julia shrugged. "If I stay here he'll be back tomorrow. There's nothing to lose now. I've made up my mind he's not ever going to touch me again. If he tries, I'll fight and scream. Holly is right next door. He wouldn't dare."

Glenn wanted to believe her, but he couldn't. Not knowing what he did about Dade, he couldn't. How, he wondered, could things have gone to wrong so quickly in Virginia City?

The Comstock now seemed entangled in a web of power, lust, and greed. And right in the center, spinning busily away, was Dade Taylor. A poisonous spider who'd trapped Holly, Bevis, Julia, and Clayton. In one way or the other, they were all his victims.

And what could he do? Kill Dade and make Holly a widow? Tell her the truth? He couldn't. Even if she believed him, he couldn't.

Meanwhile, the web was reaching out, and he had a feeling it was moving in his own direction.

Holly gave birth to twins. A boy and a girl they named Jason and Jessica. Julia moved in without incident and Dade seemed actually excited by the twins.

"He may change," Julia told Glenn.

"You don't believe that."

"No," she admitted. "The doctor said Holly is weak. I'll be very busy helping for a while. Will you try to warn Clayton?"

"Sure. I'll leave right away."

"Thank you."

He patted her hand. A few days to hunt Clayton down was all he'd be given. It wasn't very much of a sacrifice. "Can you . . . will you be fine?"

"Yes. What about you? I heard what Dade said about a job."

"Can he really bar me from employment on the Comstock? I mean, there must be people who remember my work and need an engineer."

"Glenn, listen to me. Don't try to work here. Maybe some small mine owner would ignore Dade's warning and hire you. Then maybe he'd be found at the bottom of his mine shaft wearing a broken neck."

"Dammit, I've got to work."

"It's a big country, Glenn. This bonanza won't last forever. Besides, I'm sure you know that the transcontinental railroad will soon begin over in California. Why don't you visit the Central Pacific Railroad and apply? Or better yet, go to Nebraska and try your hand with the Union Pacific. They're bound to need engineers. Maybe that's where your old friend Mr. Deidesheimer intended to go."

Despite the way he felt, Glenn had to laugh. "I haven't even been in town a full day and already two people are trying to get rid of me."

"For your own good." Julia looked up suddenly, her eyes excited. "Just had an idea. You and Clayton could go together. They're bound to need freight-wagon drivers!"

"Julia, I'm not the kind to run. Too damned stubborn, even though I admit I'm tempted by the railroad. And if what I remember about Clayton still holds true, he won't either."

The sudden hope he'd seen reflected in Julia Tillman's eyes

went out like a candle. "Then sooner or later he'll go against you with a band of gunfighters. You'll both be killed."

He put his arms around her comfortingly. "Don't bet any chips on it, Julia, because it won't happen. Just concentrate on those babies in the next room and how much Holly will be needing you."

"I will." Julia's head lifted. "You want to know my deepest, darkest secret?"

He was a little taken aback by the directness of this woman, but managed to say, "Yes, if you want to tell me."

"I do. And it's just that until those babies came, I don't think I've ever been needed by anyone. Not for any reason to be proud of."

Glenn managed to nod his head in understanding. "Being needed or loved is something only the lucky ever feel," he told her, thinking of Fay Taylor.

Julia took his hand. "After all this time, you still love Fay and I still love Clayton. Funny isn't it, how some things don't ever change?"

"Yeah. But sometimes, for our sakes, I wish it wasn't so."

Then he left Julia and walked out into the evening wondering if he'd ever see Fay again.

Thousands of miles away, a now-famous woman had her secretary mail a letter from Paris, France, which read:

> My dear Holly:
>
> It seems years since I have received a letter from you, though I may have missed them because I travel so much. In the past sixteen months Rosie Raye and I led an entourage which has performed in nearly twenty major European cities.
>
> They are all beginning to look the same to me now, which means I have been abroad too long. I speak and sing in four languages, though none perfectly. I *miss* the Comstock, Holly! Can you believe that? Here I am in one of the most gracious and lovely cities in the world and yet I long to see that barren Nevada land reaching into the vast purple mountains and gray deserts. When I try to describe this longing to André, he grows impatient and says I am merely acting foolish as any actress will sometimes do.

André is my new stage manager now that Rosie is gone. Did I tell you what happened to her? I can't remember, but in case I did not, I'll briefly tell you again.

We were playing the theater in Vienna when Rosie caught pneumonia last winter. Her lungs filled with fluid and I was terrified she would die. Austria is so cold in winter and Rosie lay in a state of near-death for almost two weeks before I made the desperate decision to discharge our attending physician and try a new one whose name was Dr. Herbert Schober; he seemed both competent and compassionate. There was that indefinable quality about his eyes that I saw at once and trusted. It is the same look I saw in Glenn Donovan's eyes and, I think, one which André shares.

Anyway, Dr. Schober stayed with Rosie night and day and miraculously brought her back from certain death. They are about the same age, those two, and, as the fairy-tale ending goes, they fell in love.

Two months ago I gave Rosie away in marriage and lost the dearest, most faithful friend I shall ever know. I am lonely, Holly. If I thought Glenn Donovan and I could live in harmony, I would beg him to marry me. Yet, I believe, for his sake and mine this would be wrong. André understands me and my life—he has even proposed marriage. Because no woman should make such a decision at once, I will wait a little longer. But I believe, when next you hear from me, I will be Madame André Fallieres.

If Glenn Donovan returns to the Comstock, perhaps you can explain why I am doing this. Maybe too you can help him find a girl who does not speak four languages and feel driven toward fame and in need of constant stage adulation. If so, I will envy her, no matter what station she has in life.

Please write soon, Holly. My melancholy deepens. Soon we are to begin a new tour starting in Berlin in mid-April, then London in June. Rosie is, of course, happy in Vienna and I will give you her address in case you should ever lose track of me again. Perhaps, before I go to Berlin, I will visit her. André would be furious, but I do not care. He must learn that I am never going to be a typical European wife, even when I've grown old and the applause is only a nearly forgotten memory.

I miss you, Rosie, Glenn Donovan, and Virginia City. I pray for your happiness with Dade and hope you will pray for mine too.

Yours sincerely,
Fay Taylor

24

Bevis York sat in the chair and scrubbed his jowls with a weariness that went bone-deep. "I don't know what to say, Glenn, except that Dade is capable of denying you work on the Comstock."

"I find that difficult to believe, sir. Not with all the mines and projects which need an engineer's guidance."

"Listen, young man, I've never lied or cheated anyone. You know that. But now I'm ashamed to admit that I've failed in controlling my own interests these past four years. Dade is in command now. I underestimated his cleverness, and for sheer ruthlessness he is in a class by himself. I don't know if I could have stopped him even had I been in my prime."

Glenn paced back and forth. "I'm an engineer, not a businessman, but he has to be stopped."

"The only way anyone will stop Dade is with a gun," Bevis muttered sullenly. "And I don't have the heart to kill my daughter's husband."

"There's got to be a better way." Glenn stared out the window and reviewed what Bevis had told him about the extent of Dade's power. The man was now a major stockholder in dozens of properties. His sphere of influence included politicians, bankers, and stock manipulators. He ruled by intimidation and fear; each day his power grew as he gave out favors like playing cards to be collected at a later date.

"Bevis, I'll try to stop Dade, but I need your help. You know the mining industry from a businessman's point of view. Where is Dade's weakness? He has to be vulnerable some way."

Bevis lit a cigar. His hands were palsied and covered with liver spots. He blew out the match and inhaled deeply before he spoke with a great deal of reservation in his voice. "There is one small weakness which, I'm certain, he will soon recognize and eliminate."

Glenn leaned forward. "I'm listening."

"Let me begin by telling you that the Comstock mines are totally dependent on lumber for their square-set timbering. Each year we consume upwards of eighty million feet—the Con Virginia Mine alone eats timber at the rate of over six million feet per year."

Glenn whistled in genuine amazement. "I had no idea."

"Not many do. Fewer still take the time to get off Sun Mountain and ride over to the Sierras, where our timber is being logged. But I have. In the years since you and I arrived by stagecoach, they've stripped the entire lower eastern slope of timber from below Mormon Station clear north to Reno. Picked it clean as a chicken bone."

"Where are they going next?"

"Higher up the mountain," Bevis grunted.

"That would be expensive."

"Yes. But as long as our mines keep producing, it's worth going after timber at any price." Bevis leaned forward, puffing rapidly. "Keeping the Comstock in timber is going to be a hell of a rough job. I've seen those mountains. Rugged country. Nothing but trees, rocks, and a few game trails. Glenn, it's going to take a man like yourself—an engineer—to design roads to extract that timber. You've a chance to keep this whole mining area alive and booming."

Glenn frowned. All this talk of timber was instructive, and maybe he could prove useful in building roads and bridges. But what good would that do in stopping Dade Taylor?

Bevis read his thoughts like a mind reader and motioned him still for yet a few more words.

"Listen, my boy, there's a tough old bird named Cornelius Grubb who owns the logging rights to nearly five thousand acres of timber—at the southern end of Lake Tahoe. Dade attempted to buy him out but failed. He tried again and only managed to insult Grubb, who got madder than hell and ran him off with a rifle.''

''You don't say!''

''Fact is fact. Dade went back with his boys, swearing to kill Grubb, but couldn't find him. He's still up there, though, and his claim is legal and binding. I never met Grubb, but I'm told he's meaner than a scalded wolverine. He's got some big, strapping sons that can shoot the eye out of a squirrel at fifty yards.''

''Is that why Dade hasn't just moved in?''

''Yes. But it won't last much longer. He needs their lumber, and sooner or later I expect we'll hear something about Cornelius and sons disappearing from the mountain. That's the way Dade acquires hard-to-get properties these days.''

Glenn replaced his Stetson and got up to leave.

''You also going to find Grubb?'' Bevis asked, his face lighting up with unconcealed excitement.

''Right after I locate Clayton James. Sounds like I'll need some help.''

''Good idea,'' Bevis said emphatically. ''Clayton might be able to talk their language. But whatever happens, I think it's safe to say that Grubb's property is Dade's Achilles' heel. Get it, and you might be able to slow him down.''

''I'll do my best,'' Glenn said. ''What are the rights worth?''

''Whatever it takes. And I'll foot the bill. It isn't the only source of lumber remaining on the mountain, but it's damn sure the most accessible and economical. If we can gain control, it will be the most satisfying acquisition of my career.''

''I bet. Anything else to do after Clayton and I find the Grubbs and keep from getting shot long enough to somehow talk them into the sale?''

''Just one thing,'' Bevis said quietly. ''Figure a way to log and hold it when Dade and his men come storming up the mountain to bury your hides in sawdust.''

Glenn shook his head. ''After the Grubbs, maybe Clayton and I can put some thought to it.''

Clayton James knew the bird calls were imitations. Good ones, but manmade all the same. He was on Grubb land now and he'd been warned that the old heller and his boys were in the habit of shooting first and talking later. ''Mountain men'' they were called. Hell, Clayton thought, they don't know the meaning of the word.

Another bird call brought him up short and he dismounted on the old game trail which ran parallel to the mountain and was overshadowed by pines. It wouldn't do to get caught off guard with all the gold Numaga had entrusted to him. He yanked the pack mule in close. He sure wanted to start things off peaceably, seeing as how he meant to buy this timberland for the Paiutes. Good land it was, too. Clayton hoped he'd brought enough gold.

What was supposed to be the cry of a red-tailed hawk punctuated the air, and Clayton smiled. They needed to practice that one so it didn't come out like a sick owl. He could feel them closing in now. One up ahead where rocks came down to the trail and the other just behind.

Clayton walked forward very slowly, making damn sure he kept the horse between himself and the high side of the trail; he wanted to give the man in the rocks something to think about.

A dislodged pebble bounced down onto the trail just ahead and it spooked his wary horse. Clayton eased his coat back from the gun on his hip. He felt more confident with the buffalo rifle, but in close quarters like this forest, the handgun was better.

"Hey, you up there," he said, "I don't want—"

His words were drowned out by the wildest, most unearthly scream ever heard by man or beast. Clayton looked up as a crazed giant launched himself off the high overhead rocks from above, screaming all the way down.

Clayton's horse rolled the whites of its eyeballs and jumped sideways right under the wild man whose cry suddenly took on a much higher pitch as he lit on the saddle horn. Clayton cracked him across the forehead with his gun barrel and the man flipped over backward, howling in anguish as his twin brother charged through a stand of manzanita with a two-foot-long knife engulfed in his upraised fist.

Clayton spun around, yanking his terrified animals after him as the knife-wielding giant slashed and missed, falling against the pack mule, cutting the beast across the rump. The mule brayed in pain and its hoove lashed out fast and hard. It got the attacker pinned against a tree and unloaded twice on him, first in the stomach, then a pair of hooves in the face. The fight went out of wild man number two like he was a squished toad.

Clayton glanced at each of the brothers and figured it was plenty safe to leave his gun holstered while he led his frightened animals down the trail a piece and tied them up to settle down. He made a note to give them both some sugar when next he could.

"So," he said, returning, "you must be the Grubb boys."

No answer. They were still both in considerable discomfort. Clayton squatted down and lit his corncob pipe, wanting to give them a chance to recover while he studied on the unexpected way things had gone so far. One thing sure, the Grubbs were awesome men. At least six and a half feet tall and as well-muscled as a team of draft horses. Clayton shook his head in amazement. He'd been told that these two were more playful than smart. But they sure hadn't been playing when they'd attacked. He was lucky.

Both of them were as ugly as a pair of porcupines. Long snoots, little black eyes, beards like quills, no chins. Dirty, too. Their lard-stiff overalls would draw flies and their shirts carried evidence of every meal they'd eaten in years.

Clayton shook his head. He hoped old Cornelius was a little more civilized than his offspring. He finished his smoke and carefully removed their weapons, pinching his nose from the smell. Then he returned to his place and relit his pipe, listening to them groan, one holding his behind, the other his mouth. All in all, Clayton thought, these Grubbs were a sorry tribe at best. When they left this mountain, he thought they should go far north where not many men went. And they could buy another mountain. A bigger one, even, with all the gold he'd be willing to pay. Then they could spend their time whipping up on grizzly bears and such. It seemed like a good idea. One thing certain, though. Old Cornelius wasn't going to like the fact that his boys got so messed up.

The one he'd clobbered with the gun barrel had a knot on his forehead like a budding unicorn and was howling something ferocious. Maybe that's why Clayton didn't hear the footsteps which moved in behind until it was far too late.

The man's rifle cocked ominously behind him and Clayton threw up his hands and yelled, "I come in peace."

"Who are you and why'd you hurt my good boys? Speak up or git blown away!"

The pipe slipped from his teeth and fell into his lap, little ashes burning on leather. Clayton didn't notice, nor did he move to brush them away. Instead, he took a deep breath and growled.

"I'm blood brother to a Paiute chief and I was weaned off'n a grizzly bear."

"Oh, yeah, well, my name is Cornelius Grubb and you are dead meat."

"I came to buy your timber rights for gold."

"Dumb, mister. 'Cause I'll kill you then have the gold."

Clayton could feel the sweat popping out across his body. "My gold belongs to the Paiutes. Chief Numaga told me to buy you out."

"Don't believe you, stranger."

"Take my gold and the Paiutes take your scalps. Maybe then you'll believe."

"Turn around slow and let me see your eyes."

Clayton did as ordered and saw that Cornelius Grubb looked like a snowcapped mountain. Bigger and even uglier than his offspring. He wore bib overalls with legs on them bigger than most waist sizes. One of his ears was bitten off and part of his lower lip was gone, while the remainder was embedded with black gunpowder. It gave him a queer and sinister expression, and when he spoke it was out of one side of his off-balance face. When it came to showdown time at the ugliness contest, Cornelius Grubb had his boys whipped six ways to sundown.

"How much does the Injuns want to pay?" the towering old man demanded.

"Two thousand."

"Ha! Feller named Dade Taylor offered me twice that."

"I'll match his offer."

Grubb spit a monstrous wad of tobacco on Clayton's foot. "Hell, I wasn't interested then or now. Value goes up as long as miners go down."

It made sense, and Clayton frowned. Cornelius obviously had a leg up on his boys when it came to brains. "What you say is true enough today," he conceded, "but all mines go from bonanza to borrasca sooner or later. When that happens, this timber won't be worth spit. So if I were you—"

He never quite finished because the mule-kicked man suddenly attacked with a tree limb. Clayton tried to dodge, but lost his footing then and was knocked flying.

"Git 'em, Ernie!" he yelled as his brother with the knotted forehead snatched up a rock and drove in at him.

Clayton glanced at the father, who said, "Them boys love a

scrape. Go and give it to 'em so they won't pester me no more today."

"Thanks!" Clayton panted, ducking a swipe of the tree limb, then kicking out with his foot into the man's groin, doubling him up in pain.

The one with the rock closed with him, and Clayton managed to grab his upraised arm. For a moment he held it; then youth and sheer strength began to overcome resistance, and Clayton stepped close inside and threw unicorn-face with a hip-roll. Before the man could regain his footing, Clayton kicked him in the nose, and it cracked, then gushed redly.

"Damn you!" Cornelius roared, throwing the big fifty-caliber Hawken rifle to his shoulder and firing at near-point-blank range. Clayton tried to duck but didn't quite succeed as he felt something akin to the top of his skull being torn off. Then he felt nothing.

Glenn Donovan heard the gunshot and pitched off his horse with the Navy Colt hammered back to fire. The big retort echoed up and down the mountainside, and in the deep ravines where streams gurgled to the valley, flocks of grouse and quail blasted out of the cottonwoods. He waited until he was sure no one had him in his sights; then he holstered his gun.

It seemed a wise idea to go the rest of the way afoot, so he tethered his horse under cover, removed the saddlebags with every cent he owned plus a couple thousand of Bevis' money, checked his new Winchester rifle, and started uphill. It could be Clayton or the Grubbs. He hoped it was the former, because the warnings he'd been given made him half-believe the Grubbs were inhuman.

Glenn moved toward a gnarled, fire-scorched old stump which groped up at the sky with lightning-charred fingers. For a moment he hesitated, then vaulted over a log and continued upward until he saw them through the trees. He flattened behind a rock and saw Clayton being loaded like a shot deer across a saddle by three of the biggest men he'd ever laid eyes on.

They had to be the Grubbs. Glenn swore in anger, wondered if Clayton were alive or dead. There was no way to tell unless he followed them, and besides, if they'd killed Clayton, they'd have to be arrested and brought to trial. Glenn hunched down close as they passed on a trail a hundred yards above. What was he going to tell Julia if Clayton was dead? How could he possibly apprehend those three?

Glenn pushed the question out of his mind and followed the trio to their cabin. Only it wasn't a cabin—not really; more like a brush-and-mud hut dug out of a mountainside. It was big, though; big enough to swallow all of them and their animals too.

Once Glenn was certain there were no dogs to sound his arrival, he crept to within a hundred feet of their place and waited. If he charged the hut, he'd probably be killed, and that wouldn't do Clayton or himself any good. So he kept waiting. His patience was rewarded when they emerged supporting a wobbly Clayton James.

So, Glenn thought, now we have a chance!

The two younger ones threw Clayton down beside a big pond they'd dammed and ordered him to drink while the older one stood with his head thrown back, nose up, sniffing the wind like a wild thing. He seemed to catch the scent of danger, for all at once he bellowed an order to grab Clayton and get back to their hut.

Glenn knew he could not afford to wait another moment, because the old man was slowly revolving toward him.

"Freeze!" he yelled, leaping out of cover. The old one started to throw his big buffalo rifle up to his shoulder when Glenn fired a warning shot that buried itself in the rifle stock, shattering wood. "Next one is through your heart!"

Cornelius Grubb studied the shattered Hawken and his remaining lower half-lip quivered with black fury. Then he slammed the gun down and bellowed, "Ya ruint it!"

Such was his rage that Glenn thought sure he was actually going to charge. So he aimed the rifle at his chest and said, "I've got enough money to buy you a thousand more just like it if you're smart enough to stay put and listen."

"I'm listenin'. But I favored *that* rifle!"

"Then have it fixed, dammit! That man you've got is my friend. I want him, and I want to buy your timber rights."

"Oh, yeah!"

"Yeah."

Cornelius pulled up his bib overalls, then jerked his thumb at Clayton. "If this fella is your friend, how come *he* tried to buy our land?"

Clayton looked up. His face was tight with pain and his

color was poor but there was nothing wrong with his thinking. "We're partners," he rasped.

"Thought you were with the Paiutes," Cornelius said, "otherwise I'd a killed you back there."

"You would have at that." Clayton's fist clamped into a ball, and with blinding swiftness he struck. His punch drove in just under Cornelius' breastbone and the man's eyes seemed to distend from his face. Clayton grabbed him by the whiskers, then swung him into a half-circle and threw him into the water. The old man bellowed like a bear. "I cain't swim!"

"Get in there and help him!" Glenn yelled at the two younger ones.

"But—"

Glenn fired twice, each time close enough to cut whiskers, and they both went in fast after their father.

The water must have been ice cold, for they moved very fast and would have been out in an instant if Clayton hadn't yelled, "Not until you agree to sell the timber rights!"

"No!" Cornelius boomed.

"Then you'll freeze before I let you out of there. You'll stay in until ice covers your hides. I swear you will!"

"How much you offering!"

"Five thousand. That all right, Glenn? You and me and the Paiutes."

"Sure." It was just fine. Better than fine, because it would make it that much tougher for Dade to grab control.

"I already been offered five thousand by Dade Taylor. Turned him down."

"Not in water, you didn't."

The ugly old giant struggled to stand in the mud. He looked at his two blue-lipped youngsters and cursed for almost a full minute before he quit because his teeth were chattering so violently. "All right, damn you!"

"Hold it," Clayton said. "You don't get out until I see the papers."

"But how—?"

"Tell me!"

"Shit!" Cornelius screamed. "This is a torture!"

"The papers. Tell me where you hid the papers."

"Under the lard bucket!"

Clayton took off at a run. When he returned he had all sign their dripping X's and made them take the money and leave without any ammunition. "I'll throw in an extra five hundred dollars for your pelts and gear," he said.

"Can't we at least hang around by the fire?"

"Yeah. But someone else's. Not ours. You're on our land. Go buy your own. Five thousand dollars ought to get you half of Oregon. Mount up and ride out. All three of you."

"Yore a hard, hard man, mister."

"That's right. But you Grubbs got a lot to learn about making a stranger feel welcome when they come to call. Now, git off this mountain."

The next day they went down to see the lake. "You ever see water as clear as this, Glenn?"

"Nope."

Clayton shook his head. "I'll bet those rocks are fifty feet under and they look like you could reach out and touch them."

It was true, but right that moment Glenn wasn't of a mind to contemplate the purity of Lake Tahoe. "You know anything about logging?"

"A little. Drove mules and oxen up north one summer. But this country is too steep and rugged for that."

"Agreed. Are there any big rivers?"

"Not with enough water to float logs down, month in, month out."

"Then we'll build wooden flumes, Clayton."

"You know how?"

"I'll learn," Glenn said. "I'm told they'll carry logs with only a couple inches of headwater."

"Then we're in business, because there're plenty of good year-round streams we can trap." Clayton frowned. "How would you feel about working beside a couple of my Indian friends?"

"Safer. Why?"

Clayton laughed. "Pardner, you and me are going to get along just fine."

And on that they shook hands.

It took three back-breaking months of laboring from dawn to dusk before their flume was constructed. It was two miles long, ending beside a huge dam they'd built and which had slowly been filling while they'd worked. The idea was that the logs would shoot out the flume and drive into the water, thus keeping them from splintering to pieces. Or at least that's what they hoped.

Now, Glenn thought, everything was ready. He'd inspected every foot of flume from top to bottom and was finally satisfied it was as smooth and tight as human hands could make it.

"Open the valve."

Water seeped, then rushed into the dry wooden trough. "A little more."

The trickle became a healthy flood, laughing and dancing merrily around the first bend of the flume and out of sight. Four or five minutes later he saw it reemerge, glancing sunlight.

"Okay," he breathed, firing his pistol in a signal to Clayton below.

An Indian shoved a big log into the trough. For a moment it just lay there; then slowly the thing began to float down the chute, thumping and bumping the protesting wooden walls. It disappeared around the first curve, picking up speed like a train of railroad cars.

Glenn held his breath. Prayed until he saw it surge into view then fly across a long span he'd constructed over a ravine.

"Look at that thing move!" he whispered as his eyes tracked the racing log as it hurtled down its private runway. The thing gathered even more speed as it entered a straightaway. Then it soared out twenty feet over the pond before gravity seemed to snatch it down in a great showering cascade of water.

Clayton's gun rang out over the mountainside and Glenn fired his answer-back. "We've done it!"

They all clapped each other on the back, even the Paiutes. Clayton James rode up to join the celebration, and when some of the Indians made motions toward the chute, the big man laughed and jumped onto a floating log, to the great delight of the Paiutes.

"You'll kill yourself!" Glenn shouted.

But Clayton wasn't listening. His legs were up high on the log to keep them from getting crushed against the sides. His lips formed a wild yell that traveled with him as his log rocketed through the first curve, then shot across the ravine. Glenn heard him hollering down the straightaway, and as the log went spinning skyward, Clayton James whipped his pistol up and fired at the sun before he kicked away from the thing he rode and went falling end over end into the pond.

The small group of warriors laughed like children. One of

them stopped long enough to point down at the swimming figure, then make a circular motion beside his head.

"Yeah," Glenn whispered, "the man is crazy as a loon—but ain't he something!"

During the six months that followed, they built a sawmill and selectively logged ever higher into the mountains. By then, they were selling over a thousand board feet a day and going off in every direction across the mountainside. Most of the time, Glenn had to devise a different type of flume because of the lack of water. What he came up with was a smooth-sided crib made of split logs bolted and braced together to withstand tremendous interior pressures.

These dry cribs, some of them more than three miles long, were always very steep affairs, and when logs were thrown into them, the tree bark really flew. More than once they'd come barreling down the cribs with the intense friction creating a fire that sent smoke and sparks into the air. Because of the fire danger, Clayton placed buckets of sand along their entire length and kept men close enough to use them.

"We're really on our way," Glenn said one afternoon as another train of freight wagons rolled out of their sawmill toward Virginia City.

"Sure we are. That load going out now will earn us over a thousand dollars alone. But we're running out of timber." Clayton frowned. "We can't strip this mountain of young trees."

"We won't."

"Then we're about to go out of business. If we log another few months, then next spring when the snow melts, there won't be enough shade on this mountainside to keep everything from melting all at once. It'll flood out the valley."

"I know that," Glenn said quietly, his eyes scanning the far shores of Lake Tahoe.

"Then we find more timber," Clayton said.

"There's plenty over on the California side."

Clayton scoffed. "Yeah, and there's plenty back in Colorado too. But that doesn't help us."

"How far do you think it is to the other side?"

Clayton studied it for a long minute before answering. "Be a hell of a swim. Nine, ten miles at least."

"That's not so far." Glenn turned to his partner. "I think we should buy the rights to it."

"You mean try to cut a road and freight it all the way around to here? Why—"

"Huh-uh. I mean we'll float it across. I'll buy a couple of small steamboats and have them dismantled and freighted up here. We could figure out a system to tie all the logs together on the far side and tow them across."

"Wouldn't even have to do that," Clayton said, excitement showing in his eyes. "I worked logs on an Oregon river and we didn't have to fasten them together at all. All we'd need is to run a line of buoys around them and they'll follow."

"I don't understand," Glenn said. "What if the wind came up and the lake got rough like it usually does each afternoon?"

"The logs would still stick together. Don't ask me to explain why, but they would, just like you'll see little chips stick in bunches floating down a river. Wait and see if I'm not right."

"Well, I'll be!" Glenn said. "I have seen that before, and I'm sure you're right."

"So that means the tough part will be getting the steamboats up here."

"It can be done easier than you'd think," Glenn said. "Those California freighters have lots of experience hauling big pieces of mining equipment over these Sierras. Every piece of machinery on the Comstock was brought over that way. I know a couple companies who'd jump at the opportunity to bring the first steamboats up here."

"Then good luck."

"Thanks," Glenn said. "I'll be leaving in the morning. Watch out for Dade. One of these days he'll come after us."

"That will be the day he gets buried," Clayton said. "I mean it for a fact."

Glenn didn't doubt Clayton's sincerity, but nevertheless he left the next morning vowing to set a record pace in getting the boats up to Lake Tahoe.

So it was he rode a fast horse over to Sacramento and had no trouble finding two side-wheel steamers. He ordered them disassembled and loaded on wagons, then hired a freighter and his crew that he'd often used to haul steam engines to Virginia City during those first years.

Because he trusted the freighter and was so worried about being absent in case Dade Taylor decided to attack their logging operation, Glenn left the freighter and rode straight through the night and reached camp the following morning.

"All done? Hell," Clayton said, "you barely had time to get there and back."

"I had enough. Those boats will be up here within the month."

"Paid for?"

"Yes, but it left us almost broke. To get the western-shore timber rights we'll need, I'll have to borrow some money from Bevis York."

Clayton frowned. "Let's make sure they can get those boats up here first."

"You're worried, aren't you?"

"Damn right I am. I've freighted some in my time. But never something that big."

"You wait," Glenn promised. "They'll be here and you'll soon enough be handling them like canoes."

Clayton laughed outright, but he still looked a bit worried, and as the days passed, they both found themselves constantly gazing out at the south end of the lake, where delivery was to take place.

It took the Sacramento freighter only twelve days to haul the boats up, and just four more to reassemble the hulls and machinery. Glenn worked on the engines and boilers; his earlier experiences with the steam pumps and hoists now proved invaluable. Finally, exactly one month from the date they'd been purchased on the Sacramento River, the Tahoe steamers were launched.

"Some of the gaskets will have to be replaced before we can start work, but I can go to Virginia City and find them tomorrow," Glenn said. "I'll see Bevis at the same time for the loan we need."

"Maybe I'd better come too," Clayton argued. "There could be trouble."

"No there won't. I'll be in and out before Dade realizes. Don't worry, I'll be fine." Glenn looked away. "Someone I *could* see is Julia Tillman. Thought maybe you'd like me to pass on your regards. Tell her you're doing fine."

"Tell her nothing!" Clayton spit, his face suddenly a mask of hurt and anger. He stomped away, shouting, "Better yet, tell her I died."

"No," Glenn said quietly, "I'll tell her the truth—that she almost destroyed a very good man."

That evening Glenn took a long, solitary walk beside the

great expanse of lake nestled jewellike in the Sierras. He felt depressed and knew it was because of Clayton's reaction to Julia. Why, he wondered, did everything go so wrong when it came to matters of the heart? He'd tried to forget about Fay all these years by driving himself, first at his studies, now at this logging enterprise. Perhaps Clayton had made the same attempt to escape his tragic past and forget about Julia. None of it worked. One word, or some perverse trick by the memory, and all the heartache and longing came flooding back.

He'd read somewhere that time was the great healer. Glenn didn't believe that. Not unless they meant that if one survived long enough, he'd become senile and forgetful. Glenn thought if he lived to be one hundred and his brain reduced to childish daydreams, his very last memory would be of the very first time he'd held Fay Taylor through a long blizzard night.

Someone called him from the sawmill about a mechanical problem and Glenn went to attend to it, thinking that no matter what the cost, a person *had* to keep trying because if you gave up the fight—said the hell with it all, that it wasn't worth it—greedy, ruthless bastards like Dade Taylor would take over and rule the world.

25

Julia hummed softly to herself as she dried Jason and prepared to give his little twin sister a bath.

"You really are happy, aren't you, Julia?"

It was a statement and not a question. Julia turned, walked over to Holly, and placed the infant in her arms. "Yes, I am."

"Good," Holly exclaimed. "I don't know what I'd have done without your help. Really, you've spoiled me something terrible. I wish you'd rest a bit yourself."

"I'm fine. Honest." It was true, she thought as she began to bathe little Jessica Taylor. The baby liked the feel of water and splashed, waving her tiny arms with obvious delight and making happy gurgling sounds that made Julia feel good inside. There was something clean and innocent enough about a baby to renew her faith in the purpose of living. And often, like now, when she held Jessica, Julia wished she could protect her from the inevitable pain and disappointments which must surely enter her future.

"Julia?" Holly asked.

"Yes?"

"Do you ever think you'll remarry and have children of your own?"

She turned away so that Holly couldn't see her face and continued to wash Jessica. "I . . . I don't think so."

"You should. You'd make a wonderful mother and wife. Dade thinks so too, though he told me you'd probably remain single."

"What else did he say?" she asked, feeling the usual ball of fear knot up inside at the mention of his name.

"Oh, not much. He never does anymore except when he discovers I've contributed to charity or spoken in favor of the miners' union. Then he says plenty."

Julia imagined he did. It was common knowledge that Dade was notorious for his absolute lack of understanding and charity, while Holly was the very opposite. It was bound to cause violent arguments.

She finished toweling off the baby and dressed her for Holly, who still hadn't completely recovered from childbearing. Julia had decided to stay until Holly was strong and her color back to normal before leaving. Leaving where? she asked herself, realizing she had nowhere to go, no one to go to. Maybe that was why she'd been so glad to stay indefinitely. Actually, she knew she dreaded the day when Holly would no longer need her to care for the babies. It was just a matter of time before that happened and she would have to go away someplace.

Alone in her room at night, Julia often lay awake trying to think about her past and future. In her only happy dream she'd go away to find Clayton James, who'd love and protect her. Theirs would be a deep relationship, one where they'd be comfortable together even in silences. They'd live in mountains, away from people like Dade who stared at her, undressed her with their eyes. In her dream, Clayton would teach her about wildlife and nature. They'd swim in cold, clean streams and walk hand in hand . . .

Hand in hand. Julia stopped dreaming and sat up in her bed.

The doctor said she'd never regain the complete use of her fingers, but she meant to prove him wrong.

Julia's face tightened in pain so intense her eyes watered as she slowly flexed and bent each finger. The sensation was as though she was stretching her flesh until it ripped apart. But it never did, and after each finger was bent one time, the remainder of the exercises was bearable.

Even more important, they were working. Julia could flex her fingers a little more each month. She was never going to be able to play the piano, but neither would she constantly be dropping small objects. Besides, while her hands might someday regain their suppleness and strength, the scars would always remain. There were vivid red flames of tissue across the backs of her hands which made the skin puckered and ugly. Once they'd been graceful, with beautifully shaped fingers. Now, to avoid causing anyone to feel bad, she kept them gloved. Julia turned off her lamp. It was very late and the babies woke up early.

She didn't know how long she'd been asleep when the hand clamped over her mouth. Julia was shocked into wakefulness and knew in an instant that it was Dade. She smelled his whiskey breath as she struggled with an almost insane panic to throw his weight off. And as afraid as she was of him using her body again, Julia was terrified that Holly might discover them together. So she quit trying to yell and fought him with silent desperation. He was nothing more than a black weight, an animal trying to possess her.

Julia tried to twist on her mattress, throwing him off, but he used her motion to his advantage by yanking her nightgown up until it bunched about her waist.

His hand slipped from her mouth, tearing her lips as she hissed, "Dade, please don't. Not here."

"Yes, here!" he rasped hoarsely. "Just like I've been dreaming of doing every night since you came."

"Holly—"

"She'll never know if you shut up."

"Dade, please," she breathed, throwing her head from side to side. "Please don't do this! I—"

He clamped his palm over her cut lips and she knew there was nothing she could do to stop him from raping her. Julia relaxed, wanting him to take her in silence and go before—

"Dade!" Light from the doorway leaped across her dark bedroom.

He froze, his body hanging just above hers. She closed her eyes. Wanted to die of shame.

"Holly," he choked. "She lured me in here. I—"

Whatever excuse he'd been about to voice was forgotten as Julia buried her teeth into his hairy chest. She felt him beating at her, but she hung on like a bulldog until his scream filled her ears. Then she let go, tasting her blood and his.

Holly began to cry hysterically and was joined by the babies in their cribs.

"Damn you!" Dade roared, recoiling upward while slashing down with his closed fist. The punch caught Julia a glancing blow high on the right cheekbone, and she was grateful for the pain as Holly slammed the door and ran.

Dade dressed quickly. "It's all your fault. *You're* the one who came here knowing this would happen. Driving me half-crazy."

He staggered toward the door, hopping on one leg, as he tried to pull up his trousers, then flinging it open so hard its doorknob shattered. "Holly," he pleaded, "she kept taunting me. I had too much to drink and she came out and—"

"Liar!" Julia shrieked. "Liar!" as she crawled to her feet and ran into the hallway, where she stopped.

Inside their bedroom, Holly was backed against the far wall, her babies held in her arms. Her eyes were dilated with anguish and she yelled, "Get out of this house! Both of you. Get out."

"But, Holly! She made me."

"Liars! You're both nothing but a pair of dirty, two-timing liars. Get out!"

And then she whirled around and sobbed with great heaving jerks of her shoulders while Jason and Jessica cried as though their hearts would break.

Julia doubled over with self-disgust and loathing. She reeled down the beautifully carpeted hallway and clawed blindly at the front door. The cold night driven by a hard westerly wind flattened her nightgown to her chilled body and she raced into the darkness. She ran blindly, wanting only to escape the horrible vision she'd just seen in Holly's eyes. She ran and fell. Jumped erect and ran on into the sagebrush and rock until, finally, she collapsed into unconsciousness as overhead the cold wind blew the clouds around until just before sunrise.

An old miner found her on his claim. Fortunately he was a good man, gentle and definitely bewildered as he tried to get her to drink a cup of weak coffee. Over and over he kept asking her where she belonged.

Finally she told him. "Nicole's French Palace."

At the mention of the famous madam's name, a shadow of disappointment flickered across his lined old face, but also understanding.

"You're one of the Silver Girls," he told her in the way a judge would pass a hard sentence. "They love only for silver, and it comes outta the pockets of fools."

"That's right, mister," she whispered softly.

"You aren't so smart, though, and you let someone talk you into going out for a walk, then he took advantage right on my own claim."

Julia said nothing. His mind was set. Besides, he'd given her a purpose.

"Can you walk?"

"Yes."

"Good. I'll take you back. Then I got to get busy. Can't waste all morning on the likes of you."

They left his campfire, and it was sunrise. Already, miners were working, and not a few saw the old man leading the bedraggled woman clad only in a torn, dirty nightgown. They woke their friends, who stared until their sleep-swollen faces split into big knowing grins. The old man colored deeply as they skirted each mining claim and plodded doggedly onward. Julia didn't color at all. They saw her now, and she was going to the only place left. She'd become one of Nicole Barrie's girls.

Julia lifted her head. "Thank you, mister, but I can find my own way to Nicole's French Palace now. You did me a favor. Stop by and I'll return it."

He blushed, hurried off as men laughed at her boldness. Julia stood for a moment, her body outlined against the bloody red rising sun. She remembered Nicole saying that a real beauty in a popular brothel had only a year or two until she either retired or got hard used into an early grave.

Fine. She'd take the latter option and be done with this miserable world.

Julia threw her head back and tramped down Sun Mountain swinging her hips provocatively. They'd know she meant business.

On the afternoon that Glenn Donovan rode into Virginia City, he heard all about Julia's sunrise walk. Everyone was talking about the woman, and Glenn was told her actions caused a stampede on Nicole's French Palace. Glenn felt sick about it, and even worse when Bevis York informed him of what had transpired in the Taylor house less than twelve hours ago. Dade had vacated the house and moved into a hotel, leaving Holly a devastated woman alone with a pair of infants.

"The doctor is there and gave her a sedative. She's asleep now and I think she's going to be all right," Bevis said weakly. "She'll come to realize that Dade was nothing but scum from the beginning. Besides, she has the babies."

"What about Julia? She isn't—"

"Don't!" he shouted vehemently. "Don't *ever* mention her name to me again. As far as I'm concerned, she should have been working for Nicole Barrie all along."

Glenn said nothing, but made a mental note to see Julia as soon as he left this room with Bevis' letter of credit for their required operating capital. He understood Bevis' fury, yet he couldn't accept that Julia was responsible.

He was still thinking that way when he exited Bevis' office a short time later and met Dade Taylor coming up the street.

"What are you doing at our offices?" he demanded angrily, his clothes rumpled, his eyes bloodshot against the backdrop of his puffy unshaven cheeks.

"None of your business," Glenn said, cursing himself for not playing it safe and taking the back door.

"The hell, you say. We got *plenty* of business, starting with timber."

"It's not for sale."

Dade's eyes narrowed. "Don't play games with me. Set a price and I'll draw up the contract today. You've saved me a trip."

"Wrong again," Glenn said angrily. "You are the last one we'd sell out to. Now, step aside and let me pass."

Dade's lip curled and his fingers drifted toward his gunbelt. Glenn advanced a half-step, and Dade went for his gun. The gambler was faster on the draw and he had the start. Glenn had no choice but to throw himself forward, and as Dade's weapon came up, Glenn batted it aside and drove his fist into the gambler's belly.

What little color there'd been in Dade's pasty complexion evaporated as he jackknifed, gasping for air, as the gun clattered on the boardwalk.

Glenn kicked it into the street and waited for Dade to recover enough to attack.

But he did not. Instead, he slowly straightened upright, his lips white and cruelly shaped with hatred. "You're a dead man. You won't escape the Comstock alive. There is no place you can run or hide that my men won't find you."

Then he turned on his heel and headed back the way he'd come. Glenn didn't need to ask who he was going to see.

Glenn felt sweat pop out all across his body. People were staring at him as he retrieved Dade's pistol and jammed it into his belt. One extra gun probably wouldn't make much of a difference against a gang of hired professionals, but he'd use it anyway.

With long, quick strides, Glenn hurried toward the livery, remembering he'd paid the hostler to grain and rub down his horse. It'd be unsaddled, and that meant precious minutes lost.

When he reached Howard Street, he glanced back down Taylor and saw them—four men; two carried rifles. Glenn dashed out of sight and ran to the livery. "My horse! Where is it?"

"In the big pen with the others. All rubbed down and grained. You leaving already, Mr. Donovan?"

"I'm trying," he yelled, grabbing a bridle and sprinting toward the corral. His heart sank to his boots when he slipped between the rails and the horses spooked and began to circle.

"Hey, Mr. Donovan, that's the wrong bridle!"

Glenn jumped for a horse—any horse. He caught a skinny buckskin by the neck, jammed the bit into its mouth, then ripped the headstall over its ears. Glenn wrapped his fingers in the animal's mane and swung up bareback.

"Hey! What the devil's wrong with you! That ain't your horse."

"I'll trade you, then! Open the gate, man!"

"But—"

"Keep my saddle, too! But open it!"

The hostler jumped to action. A saddle was worth a month's board bill. He slid the lodge poles aside and Glenn pounded his heels into the buckskin's ribs as a volley of shots exploded across the livery yard.

The buckskin bolted for open space with Glenn lying flat on his back. The hostler cursed as he dived for cover and then wailed with lament as his entire pen of horses went streaming after the racing buckskin.

Glenn saw his pursuers running in at an angle to cut off his escape, and he reined the buckskin toward the first corner, where buildings would shield him from their bullets.

He didn't make it. A slug whacked through horseflesh, and the buckskin went down thrashing. Glenn tried to leap free but only succeeded in smashing headlong through a white picket fence. He rolled hard and felt his left shoulder take the impact. A dirty-faced kid standing on the porch yelled something unintelligible, and his ratty-looking terrier attacked ferociously, nipping him on the leg.

"Get inside boy!" Glenn shouted, kicking the dog in the face and jumping to his feet. He saw them coming and dropped to one knee as he aimed Dade's gun. Firing with cool deliberation, he shot the fastest runner through the coat front, and when his friends scattered, managed to wound a second one. Then he crammed the pistol into his coat pocket and lit out running. If there'd been any question of Dade's boys being motivated, it was gone now.

Darkness was still a few minutes off, and they'd be combing the streets, leaving no one or no place undisturbed in their quest. For gunfighters were a fraternity. If an outsider killed one of their members by luck or cunning, they all felt threatened. It was going to be worse than a witch hunt.

He was fast. And months of working on the logging crews had toughened his muscles as he dodged through an alley and their probing gunfire faded into the background.

There were only three ways out of Virginia City: Six Mile Canyon to Dayton, Geiger Grade to Reno, and Gold Hill Canyon down to Carson City.

They'd all be blocked in minutes.

He pounded on the back door of Nicole's French Palace. The chained door opened a crack and a voice he recognized as the madam's spoke sharply. "You know I don't answer this door."

"Listen," he gasped, fighting for breath. "I must see Julia Tillman."

"Go away, whoever you are! I'll tell you like the others. She will not take men. Now, I have plenty of other girls who—"

"That's not what I want! I'm her friend, but I need help."

There was a pause before Nicole answered. "She can help no one. Not even herself. Please, go away or I will summon help."

The door slammed shut, and he swore, then raced around to the front and knocked impatiently, his head swiveling from side to side as he expected company at any minute.

A big man, slightly past his prime and thickening at the waistline, opened the door and scrutinized his disheveled appearance. "Give me your weapons and show me your money," he ordered curtly.

Glenn didn't argue. The doorman had the look of a veteran fighter.

He handed both pistols over, and the man looked even more suspicious. "Are you an outlaw?"

"No. A friend. Really. I'm a friend."

"Very well, see you act like one or I'll tear down your meat house."

"Where are the girls?" he asked impatiently, thanking his good fortune to have money in his wallet.

"Take the first door to your right if you'd like to be served a drink and just look awhile first. If ya can't wait, go to the left."

Glenn nodded and hurried by, angling through the right-hand doorway and coming to a standstill. It was a palace, all right! A big splash of color. Red and pink everywhere, and velvet curtains from ceiling to floor. There were two pedestals upon which sat solid silver wolves howling at the moon or their misfortune at having cigar butts tossed down their smoky gullets. And overhead, Glenn had to admire the most beautiful crystal chandelier he'd ever seen.

The entire far side of the palace's main room consisted of a shining mahogany bar of epic proportions with polished brass footrails gleaming like gold. The bartender was dressed in a shirt and stiff collar and pouring casket-aged Kentucky whiskey to patrons who never counted their change.

On the left side of the room, a piano player knocked out a rousing melody, but nobody seemed to listen.

"Good evening, sir," a low French-accented voice purred. "Which one of my girls would you like to have entertain you this evening?"

Glenn turned to face Madame Barrie. She really was a good-looking woman.

"My name is Glenn Donovan. I'm on the run."

"How interesting," she said with a smile. "Then you will want quick service. Susie Pie!"

"No, no, wait! I'm the one who just spoke to you at the back door. I have to see Julia."

"*Sacre bleu!*" she cried. "You will see my doorman!"

He grabbed her arm. "Please, don't get him before I have a chance to explain. I'm a friend of Clayton James—his partner, in fact. Julia must have told you about Clayton."

"Yes. They have brought each other nothing but unhappiness. You must go now."

"I can't," he said simply. "Dade Taylor and his men are hunting outside for me. I've nowhere else to run."

At the mention of Dade's name the madam's face hardened. "Why does he want you?"

Glenn told her quickly. About the logging and his own refusal to either work for or sell out to the man. When he ended his story by saying he'd struck Dade and taken his pistol, Nicole actually smiled.

"Oh, if only I could have seen that!" she cried excitedly, making a small fist and brandishing it threateningly. "How I wish sometimes I were a man and could beat him to death!"

"If you were a man, we would all weep."

Her eyes widened. "Oh! You have a way!"

"Not really," he said, blushing, "but—"

There was a loud pounding at the door, followed by muffled voices. A moment later, the doorman hurried down to them.

"Madam, it's the sheriff and his deputy. They say they have to come in and search for a murderer."

"They're lying, Miss Barrie. I had to defend myself up near the livery from Dade's gunfighters."

She studied him for a moment. "All right, Glenn Donovan. You have an honest face. Even so, I must tell you that Sheriff Thompson owes Dade Taylor. That means he'll search every nook and cranny before he leaves."

"Then I'd better keep running," Glenn said. "Where's the back door?"

"Wait." She grabbed his arm and looked to her doorman. "Amos, could you recognize by voice which deputy he brought?"

"It's Monte."

Nicole brightened perceptibly. "We are in luck!"

"We are?"

"Of course! You see, this Monte thinks he is a ladies' man, and he has the torch for my Ruby Jane. She will see he is kept occupied."

"And the sheriff?"

"He is a fool who will never think to search for you in the laundry."

"Laundry?"

She shrugged with her palms turned up as if to say it was regrettable but necessary.

"All right," he conceded.

The doorman looked aggrieved. "You mean under the dirty bedsheets?"

Nicole stamped her foot. "Yes. Now, hurry! I will see to the door. Ruby Jane, come with me!"

A pretty young woman disengaged herself from the bar patrons and hurried over. Glenn didn't have a good look at her because Amos had him by the arm and going to the laundry room.

"There you go," he said, pointing to a great mound of sheets piled against the wall. "You're in luck, mister. The Chinese are picking 'em up tomorrow morning."

Glenn smiled weakly and took a deep breath, then burrowed into the pile.

It was the most humiliating moment of his life.

He sat across a small hand-carved table and watched the candlelight play across Julia's perfect features. "So that's about all I can tell you," he ended. "I did as you asked, and Clayton and I are now partners."

"Glenn, I wanted you to go *far* away! Not just up to the Sierras, where Dade can find you both."

"I know you did, Julia. But neither of us could run away from trouble. I don't know what happened between you and Clayton, because he wouldn't talk about it. All I know is that he had to help the Paiutes or he'd have destroyed himself. It was his only reason for living."

Glenn stood up. "There's something else."

She tensed, as though conditioned for hurt.

"Clayton still loves you, Julia."

She swallowed, blinked, and stared down at her gloves.

Glenn knelt beside her. "Look at me and say you don't love him too."

"I can't do that," she murmured softly. "You know how I've always felt about the man."

"Yeah," he heard himself say. "You always had a way of looking at him differently from other men. I saw it years ago."

"Then you know why I can't tell him. If he even suspected, I think he might come for me and be killed."

"Don't you think you ought to let him decide?"

"No!" She'd screamed it. "If he were killed on my account . . ." She couldn't finish.

"What happens to you now, Julia?"

"I'm not sure. Twenty-four hours ago I thought I was going to do something terrible enough to drown my guilt. Now . . ." She shrugged. "Now I'm not so certain."

"Julia, I wish you'd reconsider about Clayton. I know he'd understand."

"Maybe he would." She shook her head. "I think that's why I decided to live. Who knows? Perhaps Dade will fall down a mine shaft or something. Then we'd all live happily ever after."

"Stop it, Julia!"

"All right, I will," she said, her eyes coming up to meet his. "I won't wait for an accident to happen. I'll take care of Dade myself."

"You'd hang!"

"No," she said with finality. "But I will find a way to kill the man. If not for myself, then for Holly. He's managed to destroy her and her father, plus countless others. I think now he even had my late husband killed, though he hasn't exactly come out and said so."

She raised her head high. "You must return to Clayton. Make him stay up there until it's done."

"I . . . I can't let you do this!"

She smiled. "And you can't stop me. I've nothing to lose. Now, we must get you away from here! Nicole and I have decided on a plan."

"All right. But I'm coming back."

"We'll see. We must go now. The carriage will be outside and waiting."

It was. Glenn wedged himself in under the seat while Nicole and Julia packed blankets around him.

"Here we go," Nicole said, her breath making little puffs of steam in the night air. "If we can get past Devil's Gate Toll, it'll be all right."

Glenn tried to ease the cramped position he'd been forced into. It was a good enough place to hide from casual observation, but if Dade had set up a trap at Devil's Gate, he'd be caught hiding under the seat and as helpless as a baby.

And there was no way around Devil's Gate. It was a narrow defile in the rocks through which all traffic funneled. Day and night, sentries stood watch along both of its lips, and nothing got through without paying the toll.

Despite the chill of night, Glenn shuddered under the seat. His toll could be a bullet, and he didn't want to think about what would then happen to Nicole and Julia.

Even Dade Taylor couldn't allow them as witnesses to murder.

26

Julia sat stiffly upright as the buggy jolted over the divide and dropped down the sharp switchbacks toward Gold Hill. There was a three-quarter moon with a faint golden halo, and the stars twinkled brightly in the heavens. The unfamiliar and exotic smells of Chinatown reached Julia, and she saw their fires upon the hillside. Curious how the Chinese were the only foreigners banned from owning a claim or working in the Comstock mines. Perhaps it was because people still resented how they'd continued to pan gold out of California rivers long after most of the forty-niners quit or were starved out.

There were several hundred Chinese living just outside Virginia City, and Julia knew they had their own thriving community, with markets, gambling and opium dens, as well as a ceremonial joss house. The latter was said to be a beautiful structure where they worshiped their gods, possibly prayed for an easier existence than they'd found on the Comstock.

Julia felt a little sorry for the Chinese because they were so despised. Unable to earn miners' wages, they found whatever employment they could as cooks, servants, or laundry workers in the busy washhouses about town. A great many of them scratched out their living as wood peddlers. During summer, they scoured the barren hillsides digging up stumps to be sold in the winter for one dollar a donkey load.

Gold Hill came into view as they passed the big Liberty Engine Firehouse, then the Maynard Block, a collection of businesses which even included and proudly advertised a French hairdresser.

"So far, so good," Nicole whispered as they entered town and rolled silently past the weathered buildings.

What seemed a long time later, they saw the huge bonfire at Devil's Gate Toll where guards kept an around-the-clock vigil in order to collect their toll.

"It's the same as usual," Nicole said. "One guard down here on the road to collect money, two more posted on top with rifles. Better let me do the talking."

Julia didn't argue. She felt, rather than saw, the men up above on the high rock walls as they peered down into the firelight. Every month or two, someone tried to run Devil's Gate without paying. Maybe once in ten times they survived the rifle fire, which was poor odds to save a dollar.

"Well!" the guard exclaimed, rising from his haunches beside the fire and strolling toward them. "If it ain't a pair of ladies!"

"How much?" Nicole demanded abruptly, making it clear she wasn't interested in small talk.

The guard's wide smile turned sour as he squinted out of the firelight. "Is that you, Miss Barrie? Sure it is! Why, I been to your place before. Haven't been able to afford it since."

"How interesting. Now, would you state the toll so we can pass? It's cold out tonight."

"Hey, fellas! It's Madame Barrie!"

"Who's her friend?" a voice called down.

Dudley Harris gawked, and Julia drew her robe up around her face, but it didn't help.

"Why . . . why, you're Julia Tillman! God damn if this isn't my night for surprises. Hey, fellas—"

"Please!" Nicole swore. "We really would like to continue this, but Miss Tillman is ill and we're going to see the doctor in Carson City."

"I *am* sorry to hear that, and . . ." His voice trailed off. "Listen! Sounds like the United States cavalry on its way here."

Nicole shoved money at him and grabbed her buggy whip.

"Then we'd better get on through and out of their way. Good night."

They all tipped their hats, and Julia heard one yell for them to come back soon and the hope that she got well. Then the buggy was flying down the dark and dirty road.

"It'll be Dade and friends," Nicole gritted. "Can't be more than a mile or two behind."

Glenn squeezed his way out from under the seat and was so stiff and muscle-cramped that Julia had to half-drag him onto the bench between them as the buggy careened its way into Silver City.

Glenn took over the reins as they thundered by the collection of shacks and businesses, then passed the huge holding tanks which carried Silver City's water supply.

When they came to McCone's Foundry, Glenn pulled in the team. "End of the line for me," he said, jumping down to the road. "Listen."

Julia heard the hoofbeats drumming ever louder and gripped the seat, fighting back the unreasoning fear which Dade now caused her.

"We'd never outrun them," Glenn said, "and if they overtook us somewhere out of town, Dade might just have us all shot. That's why I'm leaving now."

"But how can you escape?" Julia asked. "It will be morning soon, and they'll see you. You'll never get away."

"I haven't quite figured that part out yet," he admitted. "This canyon isn't much of a place to hide. But I'll find a spot. There are probably lots of abandoned mine shafts."

"Glenn—"

"No," he said abruptly. "We haven't time to argue. Let the team run another mile, then pull them in if Dade hasn't overtaken you yet."

"All right," Julia said, knowing he was right. "But we had a fine chase, didn't we?"

"Yes. Very fine."

"Tell Clayton I love him."

"Sure," Glenn said. Then he slapped their horse across the rump and she saw him disappear, a tall, lonely figure standing in the road, glancing from side to side, trying to know which way to run.

Glenn waited that extra few seconds, trying to judge the distance between the buggy and the riders so close behind. They were very close, and as he jumped off the road and crouched behind a clump of brush, they emerged from the night. As they swept by, he counted at least a dozen riders. He could smell their horses' sweat, and the dust hung in the moonlight like a whispered cloud low on the ground.

He glanced up at the sides of the canyon and knew that he could scale them before daybreak. That would give him a good headstart on Dade, who'd have to ride miles around to cut him off.

Glenn's eyes left the canyon. He heard shouts on the road ahead. "The hell with this running," he growled as he started to walk toward the confrontation just ahead. Depending on how Dade treated Nicole and Julia, he'd plot his next course of action. But not until he was certain they were going to be safe.

When he reached them, Glenn slipped into the brush and stalked in close as Dade was saying, "You're both lying! She isn't sick and you were trying to help Donovan escape. Now, where did he get off!"

The question went unanswered. "One more time before I make it look as though you ladies had a real bad accident. Where's Donovan?"

"Right behind you. Freeze or you're a dead man."

Dade froze. Threw his hands skyward as Glenn yanked him out of the saddle. "Tell your friends to throw their pistols into the brush and dismount slow and easy," he ordered, wrapping a forearm around Dade's throat and jamming his gun against the man's spine.

"Do it!"

The guns began to sail into the brush, and then the men started climbing out of their saddles. Glenn felt a rush of confidence. Maybe he could get out of this mess alive, but he had to be sure no harm came to Nicole and Julia.

"Hear this," he shouted for everyone's benefit. "Dade and I are going away for a while."

"No," the man in his grip choked.

"Yes! And if anything, anything at all, happens to either one of these ladies, then you boys are out of work and your boss here is going into the ground without so much as a pine box."

"You bastard!" Dade wheezed. "There is no way you can do this to me!"

Glenn tightened his grip. "I've nothing to lose at this point. Keep remembering that . . . You men, start walking toward the east side of the canyon. Don't stop to talk it over." He looked up. "Miss Barrie, turn that rig around and go back to Virginia City. Those gunmen have nothing to gain by hurting either of you so long as I'm holding Dade."

"Take care of yourself," Julia whispered. "Watch him every minute."

"I won't forget this, Julia!" Dade growled. "When—"

Glenn pistol-whipped him. "Get out of here," he grunted, reaching an arm under Dade and hoisting him across the saddle.

As the buggy circled and then left, Glenn quickly unwound a lariat and strung all the horses together, then tied Dade in place before mounting. He felt good. Last night he'd been in Dade's stronghold being hounded like a rabbit. Not anymore. Now he was heading back to the mountains, where he and Clayton had a chance. No, better than a chance. Dade's gunnies wouldn't go running to the law, because if they did, too much of the truth would come to light. Nicole Barrie was not without powerful friends of her own. And doubtless those friends would feel very obligated to help.

He booted his horse forward, Dade and the other animals being trailed along behind. To the east, he could hear the swearing gunmen as they groped toward the canyon's wall. To the west, he had a friend waiting to help.

Glenn had a message for Clayton, a message he'd want to hear, from the woman he loved.

Glenn hadn't anticipated the explosive reaction he encountered when Clayton James recognized his captive. The big mountain man yanked Dade off his horse and might actually have strangled him on the pine needles if Glenn hadn't intervened.

"Give me one good reason why I shouldn't kill him!"

"Julia."

At the mention of her name, Clayton stiffened, but when he spoke, his voice was flinty. "That's the reason I want to kill him, Glenn. He used her. Made her love him."

"It was an act!" Dade cried. "I swear she did it to keep me from killing you that night."

Clayton's powerful hands released his neck. "You better not be lying again," he warned shakily.

"He's not," Glenn said gently. "I saw Julia. She and Madame Barrie saved my life. The last thing she asked me was to tell you she loved you."

Clayton rocked back. Looked bewildered, then seemed to come alive. "Then I've got to go to her! Get her outta Virginia City."

He started toward his horse.

"Clayton, you can't do that."

"Why not?" he challenged, reeling about.

"Because as long as we have Dade here, those women are safe. If you go to Virginia City, something might happen to you—or Julia. They'd be watching."

"They couldn't stop me."

Glenn knew he had to change Clayton's mind. If he went roaring into Virginia City, he'd never come out alive. "Maybe you'd escape. Maybe even get Julia out. But are you willing to risk her life—and Madame Barrie's? Those are *gunmen*, Clayton."

"Well, we can't just do nothing!" he raged in helpless anger.

"Of course not. I'll write a long letter to Bevis York telling him everything. We can send a man in with it today. After that, Bevis will start gathering evidence against—"

Dade's voice was vicious. "That old man won't lift a finger 'cause of Holly. I'm still her husband. Father of her kids!"

"Maybe," Glenn conceded. "But it's the only chance we've got. I'll bet enough could be dug up on you for a hanging."

"Sure, Donovan," he sneered. "But what kind of jury would convict me, knowing it would cause the stock market to fall? There ain't a miner on the lode that doesn't own some stock. And who'd take me into custody? The sheriff? Hell, I *own* him."

Glenn looked at Clayton. "We'll find a way," he promised. "Just give Bevis a chance before you ride."

Clayton started to say something, then appeared to change his mind. "All right," he said grudgingly. "I'll give him two weeks."

It wasn't much, but then, it was more time than he'd hoped for. And Bevis York was still a sharp old man. One other thing—he hated Dade Taylor.

They'd lashed him to a goddamn pine tree and gone off to work down by the steamboats again. They didn't tell him anything, but Dade had overheard enough conversation to realize they'd brought the boats up in pieces and had them reassembled.

There'd been some gasket trouble with the boilers, but now that was about taken care of and the vessels were ready for work.

Smart, Dade thought, the idea of using steamboats; and floating logs clear across the lake was damned smart. He'd do the same, once he escaped.

He'd caught wind that Glenn and Clayton were ready to cross the lake for the first time tomorrow. They'd have to return the following day with their first batch of California logs. Dade's mood soared as he watched them head down toward the cove below. He edged himself around the tree trunk so he could get a better view. The two steamboats both fired up as easy as could be, and Dade watched with genuine admiration. Today they'd be steamed out a small distance on the lake and tested for tomorrow's long run across Tahoe.

They were smaller than he'd expected or was used to observing ply the Sacramento River trade. But then, when Dade considered that they'd not be fighting any upriver currents and that dragging a pack of logs wasn't too rough, he could understand why Glenn had chosen the vessels.

But what interested him the most was how many loggers would go on the voyage. He found this out at once as he watched Glenn captain one boat, Clayton the other, and each take a half-dozen. That meant only five would remain at the sawmill to do work and play guard.

And one of them, he was certain, would betray the others for money. Dade heard the steam engines change pitch and saw their side-wheels begin to throw water as the boats sailed out of the U-shaped cove, which was well protected from the wind by two thin but high-rocked peninsulas.

The five left behind watched for a time, then started up the hillside toward Dade, who studied them intently. He was searching for weaknesses. Something or anything which might be the tip-off of a flawed character.

And as if in answer to his prayers, one of the five smiled grimly as he passed close. Then he knelt and pretended to tie his bootlaces. "Name's Cletus," he whispered, eyes never leaving the backs of his fellow workmen. "You got the biggest diamond ring I ever laid eyes on, mister."

Dade smiled. This was no time for subtleties. "Set me loose after they leave tomorrow morning and I'll give it to you."

Cletus swallowed nervously. "I know you. Big man on the Comstock. Someone's gonna come looking for you. Raise hell."

"That's right," Dade said easily. "Every last one of you might be sentenced to prison."

"That vest watch. Can't see it 'cept the chain. Solid gold, I suspect."

"Sure is. Worth six months of your wages. Diamond is worth ten times that."

Cletus' eyes widened. He was a hatchet-faced man in his forties and had the vein-busted nose of a heavy drinker. "I want 'em both."

Dade hesitated as though reluctant. Finally he said, "All right. When?"

"First chance. I . . . I could just take the things tonight . . . without letting you go."

Dade quelled the jolt of fear which attacked his insides. "I'd holler before you got close. They'd come running, and I'd tell 'em about us."

"Not if you was dead," Cletus said.

Dade felt sweat trickling down his shoulder blades. "Be smart, dammit!" he hissed. "Neither of us would get what we want."

Cletus finished tying his boot. "Yeah, I thought of that," he groused. "All right. We got a deal."

Dade sagged against his ropes, knowing he'd just run the biggest gamble of his life.

That evening after dinner, Clayton and Glenn came by. "We're leaving before daylight tomorrow morning," the engineer said. "I know you've been watching and have probably figured out that we intend to steam across the lake because we've run out of prime timber on this side."

"What a pity," Dade said cryptically. "Will you be gone long?"

"One night is all. But don't worry, you'll be well guarded until we return."

"We might be taking you down to the jail in Virginia City real soon," Clayton growled.

"Oh, yeah, on what charges?"

"How about the murder of their marshal?"

Dade laughed. "You can't pin that on me," he told them. They were fishing, and he knew it. "I never killed Tillman."

"Julia thinks you did," Glenn said flatly.

"Who cares what she thinks? Apparently you've both forgotten one very important fact of life in these parts."

"Which is?"

Dade knew he'd be better off to keep his mouth shut, since he was escaping anyway, making the whole conversation pointless. Yet it occurred to him that uninterest might cause suspicion, so he played along.

"Merely that in addition to what I told you already about my power—"

"Virginia City power," Clayton gritted, "not Carson City."

"You *think!*" he spit, feeling his temper getting the better of his judgment. "But I exert influence even in Carson City, while Julia Tillman will be exposed as nothing more or less than a high-priced whore."

Clayton rocked back on his heels, then slapped him in the face so hard he loosened teeth. "Either way, by man's hands or by rope, you'll die," he said, grinding out the words. "It's my promise."

"Have a nice voyage, gentlemen," Dade told them, "and watch out for rocks."

"Keep it up," Clayton warned ominously, "and you'll go to jail in a basket."

This time Dade shut his mouth.

Cletus was eager. The next morning, while everyone trailed down to the steamboats, he feigned a bellyache and stayed behind. When he could hear the steam engines, Cletus brought two horses around and cut the bonds from Dade's wrists.

"There," he said as Dade felt the blood rush into his hands and burn his nerve endings like hot needles. "I'll be taking your ring and watch now."

Dade rubbed his palms together, bidding for time and the numbness to drain away. He also noticed Cletus hadn't sheathed that long bone-handled knife of his.

"Sure," Dade said, "we made a deal."

The man's bony shoulders settled a fraction as he relaxed. Dade began to make a show of removing the big diamond ring.

"You going back to Virginia City with me? I protect my friends."

"Well, thanks for the offer, Mr. Taylor," he said, showing bad teeth. "But I guess not. My destination for tonight is west toward Hangtown."

Dade pulled the ring off and handed it to the man. "Worth over a thousand dollars," he said. "Want to sell it back?"

"Why . . . why, sure!"

Dade removed his wallet from inside the coat pocket and winked slyly. "Those fools didn't even check my money."

Cletus leaned in, craning his neck, but Dade shaded the money from view. "Yes, sir, you're in luck," he purred. "Guess I will buy that diamond right back."

"How about the watch? I'll sell it cheap!"

"Really?"

"Sure! How much you got altogether?"

"Take a peek, Cletus."

The man's greed overran his good sense, just as Dade had foreseen. When he reached for the wallet, Dade grabbed his wrist, doubled it up, and slammed the knife back and upward into his stomach.

Cletus shrieked and the wallet jumped from his suddenly rigid fingers.

Dade clamped his free hand over the gaping mouth. He didn't look into the horror-filled eyes as he twisted the knife.

Cletus seemed to lift off the ground as though he might somehow rise above the killing steel. He stretched to the very tips of his toes; then his throat filled with a death rattle and his body collapsed around Dade's bloody fist.

Dade pulled his hand away and let Cletus drop. He bent and quickly retrieved his diamond ring and nearly empty wallet. Studying the lake below, he saw the two little boats edging across the smooth mirrorlike surface. Then he replaced his ring, pocketed his wallet, and collected the reins of the two horses which Cletus had so thoughtfully saddled.

The nearest horse was jittery, and Dade wiped blood onto the back of Cletus' shirt.

"Easy, boy," he soothed, jamming his boot into the stirrup and swinging aboard. Then he reined east, pulling the second horse behind. He'd switch with someone on the other side of Carson City. The relay animal would take him home by nightfall. He'd gather his forces and return before Glenn Donovan and Clayton James completed their little voyage. He'd have a surprise ready for them.

And as for Julia? Dade whipped his galloping horse viciously as he remembered her betrayal. He'd settle with her and Nicole in the same way he'd treat anyone who'd turned on him. There would be plenty of time for him and his men to make a call on Nicole's French Palace.

He'd teach the lot of them how really hard life could be.

27

Julia knew without the slightest doubt that Dade Taylor would come hunting for her. Sooner or later he would return to the Comstock and punish her and Nicole Barrie for their role in helping Glenn escape.

Julia was no longer afraid. She'd gone through hell and back. It was Dade's fault; he'd deliberately ruined her chances for happiness. He'd probably murdered Bob Tillman and burned the Emporium, thus robbing her of any possible livelihood. Even more cruelly, he'd made her loathe herself because of Holly. Now these things were finished, and she realized guilt and shame had very nearly destroyed her life.

Julia had one thing left, and she meant to hang on to it—Clayton's love. No matter what else happened in her future, she vowed never to hurt or disappoint him again.

Her greatest fear was that Dade, having been thwarted and now taken prisoner, would exact a terrible vengeance. He was certainly capable of it.

Julia tried not to worry. She kept telling herself that Glenn Donovan must have known what he was doing, had some kind of plan. She only wished he'd told her what it was.

There was something else she wished, and that was that Glenn and Fay might have found happiness in each other. But they obviously hadn't, and she wondered why, because he still loved her. Sometimes, Julia thought, it seemed as though an evil plan existed which brought people together, then cruelly tore them apart. Julia knew this wasn't true, yet when she thought about her own life and about Glenn and Fay, she couldn't help but wonder why things never seemed to end happily. Even Holly, dear, innocent Holly, had been cheated by love. But at least despite all the deceptions and betrayals, Holly had the twins.

As evening settled over the Comstock, Julia forced her mind back to the danger she could almost feel approaching from the Sierra Nevadas. She just couldn't allow Dade to retaliate without at least putting up a good fight.

Nicole Barrie's voice interrupted her thoughts. "You're worried Dade is coming, aren't you?"

Julia nodded. "Glenn and Clayton would never injure Dade without provocation. So they'll try to hold him captive. But he'll find some way to escape."

"If this is true, you must go away!"

"I won't. No more running, Nicole." She tried to smile. "Besides, we needn't just give up in defeat."

"Defeat?" she scoffed. "Never defeat. All my girls, they know he comes, and have promised to help."

"That's the spirit!"

"But spirit is not enough," Nicole sadly admitted. "Not against his gunmen."

"Then we must trick him into giving us the advantage."

"Yes! But . . . but how do we do that?"

Julia frowned. "Can any of your Silver Girls shoot?"

"Of course! A couple are even pretty good shots."

"Are they willing to do this, Nicole? We are talking about taking on gunfighters. We could be killed."

"I know. They know. Now you know."

Julia was convinced. "All right, but perhaps we can figure out a plan so that no one gets shot."

"That would be very nice. I will leave you alone to think of such a plan. Until that time, I will find our guns."

"Good idea, Nicole. In the end, that might be the only plan we have."

An hour later, Julia still wasn't exactly sure what they could do, and the small pile of weapons on the floor was not on the level of an arsenal. In fact, about all they had was a modest collection of hideout guns. Mostly inaccurate little one-shot derringers with pretty handles.

"This won't do," Julia said. "We'll have to buy some bigger guns if we're to be taken seriously."

Nicole snapped her fingers. "Hold on a minute. I just remembered I have some."

"You do? Where?"

"In the basement under the coal chute. I forgot I used to

take them when someone couldn't pay. But one night it caused a hanging."

Julia was puzzled. "How?"

"My customer left his gun in payment, then went to a saloon, where he got into an argument. He drew, only too late remembering his holster was empty. He died for his forgetfulness."

Nicole was finished. Julia shook her head. "But you told me he was hung."

"Not *him*. The man who shot my unarmed customer. Who was an even *better* customer."

Julia raised her hands. "Please. Never mind. I see why you quit that practice. Let's find them and make sure they still operate. Any rifles?" she asked hopefully.

"One or two."

"Good! We probably won't need them, but it's nice just in case."

A few minutes later Nicole had all weapons dumped on the table. "Just one each, girls," she ordered her charges.

The shiniest ones went first. Ruby Jane showed them all how to load, aim, fire, and reload. She seemed to know quite a bit about pistols.

"My father was a Texas Ranger," she informed them. "But he died young."

"At least you know your father," Delia De Rose said, lighting one of her thin, black, crooked Mexican cigars. She was a pretty girl with red hair and green cat-shaped eyes. "Do we have a plan, or do we just face off here in the Palace and draw for it?"

"Don't be so waspy," Nicole said sharply. "Julia is working on a plan."

They all turned to look at her, and she could almost feel their relief. Julia knew she had to say something assuring. "Well, to begin with, we have the advantage of surprise. He won't be expecting a fight."

"Go on," Delia urged.

"Well," she admitted, "that's all I've been able to come up with so far. But surprise is very important."

"What if Dade catches *us* by surprise—like up in our rooms doing business—or are we going to lock the Palace?"

"We stay open," Nicole proclaimed. "I know several people who will—for future favors—stand a vigil night and day."

"*Stand* a vigil. I bet." the one called Susie Pie laughed nervously. "They'll want to hold the vigil in our rooms."

"I'll persuade them otherwise," Nicole said without humor.

"Remember," Julia said, "Dade will have to come over the divide and go to find his riders before he can even think of coming here. That will give us plenty of time to be ready."

"There's another thing, too," Nicole added. "As powerful as Dade is, he can't afford to come in here shooting. We also have friends."

"But what if he goes crazy? He's got that kind of reputation, you know."

Nicole studied the blond one named Kitty. "Well, I can't promise it won't happen. But if you're really scared, you'd better leave. There are other houses you could work, and I'd gladly recommend you."

Kitty glanced at the others. She saw only determination. "I'll stay. Besides, if he does anything, it'll be something sneaky like trying to burn up the French Palace. That's probably what he did to your place, Julia."

"I know."

"Let him try!" Delia De Rose hissed, blowing a stream of smoke at the ceiling. "This is the best place I've ever worked, and *no one* is torching it."

Her opinion was loudly seconded by all the girls, and it made Julia proud to be a Silver Girl. They weren't risking their lives just for the money now.

"If he comes, and he will," Julia said, "I'd like one of you to open the door and let him in."

Nicole said, "My doorman sure picked a bad time to go to Sacramento. Ruby Jane, if Dade arrives before Amos returns, you fill in."

"Yes, ma'am."

"Pretend you're delighted to see the business," Julia told her. "Then lead them into the saloon, where we'll all be hiding. Once they're in, we jump up and surround them with drawn guns."

"Oh, Gawd," Susie Pie muttered, "I think we've just heard the plan."

Julia couldn't help but note the cynicism or blame the girl. It really wasn't much of a plan. "If any of you come up with something better," she said evenly, "don't wait for someone to ask. Speak out."

"What about these guns? We . . . we can't hide 'em under our dresses. That's the first place anyone would look."

Several of them giggled. Nicole frowned. "Put them under your mattresses."

Kitty whispered something about that to Ruby Jane, who laughed aloud.

"Tell us the joke, too," Nicole ordered, trying to look stern but failing.

Ruby Jane was a small young woman with black hair and the most contagious smile Julia had ever seen.

"Well," Ruby began, "it really wasn't all that funny. Kitty just whispered something about how maybe under our mattress wasn't the best place for a gun because it might go off and—"

Delia burst out in wild guffaws, and even Susie Pie forgot she was scared and laughed.

Nicole and Julia looked at each other and smiled. If they could laugh about Dade's coming, they'd be able to face up to anything. Maybe there was a chance.

If any of the longtime citizens of Virginia City has been asked what they thought about the old man named Elmer Pulley, they'd have said he was lucky to be alive and was some kind of medical miracle.

And they'd be right. Two years before, he'd been a down-and-out alcoholic. He'd swamped saloons and cleaned spittoons for whiskey, and when the work was slow and his appetite for drink raged, he'd bark like a dog and swim on the floor like a fish if someone paid for another round. Elmer was fifty-three, looked seventy-three, and felt even older. He'd wanted to die two years back. But to die took courage, and his courage came in quart bottles, so Elmer stole four of 'em from the back room of Casey O'Grady's Saloon one December night after sweeping the place.

He'd only had a few drinks, but there was fresh snow flying horizontal to the ground, hard like it did when a blizzard raced off the Sierras. Elmer didn't care. He was going to blissfully drink himself to death right at a special place near where the road passed over the divide. He'd pass on through his own great divide, he'd told himself, and it was damn sure none too soon.

He'd settled in against the hillside and put his bottles down in a row and they'd melted little holes in the snow, and that seemed pretty nice as he drank the first one very quickly.

He could see how a snowstorm came in gusts instead of just always solid like he'd thought all these years. Funny how a fella could live his whole life and never see the difference of something that important. Into the second bottle, he'd gotten the notion that maybe he ought to stay alive and pass on this great secret before he froze.

Elmer actually tried to get up, He'd giggled when he'd risen halfway, then crashed facefirst in the deepening snow. I'll tell them in hell, he'd decided.

Maybe he would have. If Nicole Barrie hadn't spotted him as her driver curved and fretted his team of horses up from Gold Hill.

Nicole kept him from freezing, though his hands and feet were frostbitten and partially destroyed. Then she gave him a home and some respect. Enough respect to quit drinking and live again. He'd stayed at the French Palace for eighteen months before deciding to leave.

Now he was coming back. From the divide. In the dead of night. Half-crippled, but striving with the courage of a bare-knuckle fighter because he *had* to give the warning.

Dade had passed by the divide!

Nicole caught the old man in her arms. Supported him. "Take it easy, Elmer. He's here?"

"Yes, ma'am. Went to get his men."

She reached into her purse and gave him a handful of silver coins.

"Oh, no," he said, shaking his head vigorously. "Not from you."

"Take them, you old devil," she said, dropping them into his coat. "Save 'em for my wedding."

It was their private joke, but this time he didn't laugh.

"I want to stay."

"No."

"Please!"

"I'm sorry."

"Then I'll hide across the street. Dade comes here, tries to leave after hurting you, I'll blow him apart with my shotgun."

"Elmer, listen—"

"No!" he'd cried like a defiant child. "You can't stop me. I won't let him hurt you."

Then he'd turned and run in his jarring, half-footed shamble off into the night to get his shotgun. Maybe, Nicole thought, she could have made it a big issue, but that would have destroyed that well-earned respect.

A voice called down the stairway, and Julia took her place behind the couch while Nicole and her girls marched to their own hiding spots.

"Open up!" It was Dade's voice. Angry. Vicious. "Open up in there or we'll bust the door in."

"Here goes," Ruby Jane said nervously. "Just wait until our gawddamn doorman returns. I'll kill him."

"Just relax," Julia prompted. "You'll do fine. Give them a big smile and lead them all back here."

"I'll try," Ruby Jane whispered, "but I wish we had an even better plan."

"Go!" Nicole hissed as the banging grew even louder.

"Cock your weapons," Julia ordered, ducking down low and hearing the metallic click of hammers circle the saloon. "Here they come!"

Rough voices flooded into the hallway, and Julia heard Ruby Jane's high, nervous laughter, then assurances.

"Right this way, Mr. Taylor. What an unexpected surprise!"

"Like hell it is! Where are they?"

"This way. In the saloon. I'll find them."

Julia shifted uncomfortably, felt her heart racing. She heard the heavy boots leave hallway carpet and pound into the saloon.

"Where are they? Ruby—"

Julia stood up, shoved the gun out with both hands and yelled, "Hands up!"

The men swiveled around, guns jumping into their hands.

"Drop 'em!" Nicole yelled, popping up from behind the bar with Delia alongside, the Mexican cigar clenched between her full lips.

There was one instant of confusion when it might have gone either way if Ruby Jane hadn't cocked two pistols and covered them from the door. "Move and we'll riddle you."

Dade's eyes, wild and frantic, darted around in the confines of the saloon. He saw six women with cocked pistols surrounding them. For a split second he almost went for broke; then the wildness died. "Do as they say," he gritted. "No sense in a massacre."

His hired gunfighters twisted in every direction, and knowing their backs were still exposed, were happy to comply.

"Now," Julia said quietly, "what in the hell do you want this time? A bullet?"

He gaped at her and then visibly gathered himself under control in a way that was somehow more frightening than his rages. "So you've been expecting me."

"Yes."

"And now you probably think you've finally gotten the better of Dade Taylor. Shown him a lesson, so to speak, and it's over."

"No," Julia whispered. "It will never be over until you're dead."

"You can't do it." He took a step forward.

Julia began to squeeze the trigger. He saw it and threw his hands up. "Don't!" he begged.

"Get out of here. Never come back. If you raise a hand against Miss Barrie or these girls, I'll make a formal charge against you for the murder of my late husband."

"You've no proof."

"Yes, I have," she lied, realizing the only way to beat this man, make him worry, was to play by his rules. "But either way, you can't afford the loss of public confidence. Your stocks would plummet, costing you millions."

He visibly blanched. "How do you know about such things?"

"Because," she replied coldly, "you made me listen all these years. And sometimes you said things after too much whiskey that would make fine reading in the *Territorial Enterprise*."

"Damn you, woman!" he stormed. "I'd deny everything."

Julia began to taste victory. He was right in that she had no proof, yet she knew by the tone of his voice that Dade was rattled. "Of course you would," she heard herself say in a calm and reasonable tone. "But I know how you've manipulated the stock market by paying hirelings to start rumors. And isn't it true about the assay reports?"

He actually went pale! Julia had just been fishing, yet suspected he might use the most common method of mining trickery. I've struck a nerve, she thought. "Of course it's true. You've told me the names of some of your 'friends.' If one talks, they all must."

"I *own* judges!" he raged.

"Not all of them," she countered. "You've even boasted of which ones. Ought to make a great story."

"All right," he said with reluctance. "I think it's obvious

we've got a standoff here. I'll allow you and Nicole to run this whorehouse as long as you want, in exchange for silence."

"Not quite," Julia told him. "There is one other thing."

"What?"

"You must leave Glenn Donovan and Clayton James alone."

Dade's eyes bugged. Blood infused his complexion as if he were choking on a bone. But after a great struggle he managed to nod his head.

"Good," she whispered, feeling light-headed with her sudden and unexpectedly easy victory. He'd agreed to *everything*!

"But know this, Julia. Break the deal and you'll wind up begging me for a quick death."

He whirled around, slamming into one of his employees and cursing at the man for not getting out of the way fast enough.

When the front door banged, Nicole let out a whoop and Julia wanted to cry for happiness.

"Wooo-wee!" Delia De Rose shouted as Ruby Jane danced about in an impromptu victory celebration.

"Did you see his face?" Nicole exclaimed. "He . . . he looked like a man who'd swallowed an entire chili pepper!"

Julia laughed until tears filled her eyes, and she realized Nicole was staring. "What's wrong?" she managed to ask.

The madam's eyes glistened. "Nothing, really, it's . . . it's just that this is the first time I've really heard you laugh, Julia."

Julia bowed her head for a moment, trying to control her emotions. Then she looked at each of the Silver Girls and Nicole before saying, "I've never felt this free before. And I owe it all to you."

There was an awkward silence; then Nicole swallowed noisily and smiled. "This calls for a celebration! Lock the front door and I'll bring out the champagne. I'm declaring a holiday!"

It was to be a party. A good one! Susie Pie hung the "CLOSED" sign out front and had to argue with a disgruntled customer while Nicole and Julia brought out the champagne. Ruby Jane and Kitty found the lead-crystal goblets. Delia De Rose, always a trifle bossy, smoked her Mexican cigar and directed traffic.

They filled their goblets, then looked to Julia, who blushed. "All right," she conceded, "to Nicole's French Palace and all those who live under her roof, I wish happiness, marriage, and freedom from—"

A loud banging on the front door was instantly followed by

Elmer's high-pitched voice. "Madame Barrie! Madame Barrie! Open up!"

Julia and Nicole lowered their goblets of champagne without touching them to their lips. They and every other girl in the room guessed what had occurred—Dade Taylor had broken the agreement. Death rode a high horse.

"Tell it slow," Nicole urged as they grouped around Elmer, who was panting from his exertions.

"Ain't much to say," he gasped. "Dade and his boys left here and went to the saloon. I followed outta curiosity. Next thing I know, they all came barreling out of the back room and I heard one of 'em swear they'd blow 'em the hell outta the water."

"What do you mean?" Julia asked.

"I *don't* know. Honest. All I *do* know is that they yanked old Harland Raney out of bed and made him open the Silver Exchange Mercantile. I couldn't rightly tell for certain, but they toted out a box of dynamite, and a hell of a lot of ammunition, then mounted up and galloped toward the divide."

Julia's mouth went dry. "He's heading toward Lake Tahoe to blow up the sawmill and kill Glenn and Clayton."

"If he does that," Nicole said, thinking aloud, "he'll be coming back here to finish us off. He can't go halfway now."

Julia spun around and was partway down the hall before Nicole yelled, "Where are you going!"

She stopped, turned, and looked at them clustered by the doorway. "This is all my fault and I've put you in danger. So I'm leaving. I'll take a gun and a rifle, borrow a horse, and trail them up to Clayton. Maybe . . ." She bit her lip, realizing the futility of trying, yet knowing she had no choice. "Maybe I can warn them in time. Give them some chance!"

"I'm going too," Nicole said, coming after her.

"We all are," Ruby Jane called. "Me and Delia, Kitty and Susie Pie. We're in this together."

Julia rubbed at the corners of her eyes. "Thank you," she whispered.

"Elmer," Nicole yelled, "race over to the livery and have the man hitch up his lightest wagon to his fastest team. Tell him I'll pay him in silver dollars. A hundred if he's ready in five minutes!"

"I'll tell him fifty and we'll split the money. Don't worry, we'll be fast!"

Nicole looked into each of her girls' faces. "Girls, this won't be as easy. Up in those mountains we won't have any help. But if we can stop those men from destroying Julia's friends and then coming back to finish us off, well, I'll give you each an equal share of all my future profits, because you deserve it."

She waited for their excited voices to quiet. "You'll deserve it, because our chances of returning alive aren't good."

"Nicole is telling you the truth," Julia said evenly. "If we arrive too late . . ." She had to force herself to push on, even though the thoughts of failure seemed too horrible to bear. ". . . then we'd still be witnesses and Dade couldn't permit us to leave—ever. He'd have to kill to ensure silence."

"Now," Delia said, breaking a protracted silence, "if school is out, I suggest we all put on everything we own, 'cause it's going to be colder than . . ." She smiled, blew a cloud of smoke at the chandelier. "Well, seeing as how I don't want to be fined for bad language again, it'll be *real* cold."

They went to get their coats.

In remarkably short order, the liveryman hauled up a dancing team of sorrels before the French Palace, yelling, "Sorry, but this is all I had in running order."

"An ambulance!" Nicole shouted with exasperation.

"Yes, ma'am! Ain't got anything else in running order big enough to carry six passengers."

Julia studied the thing, feeling her heart drop. The ambulance wagon had side doors with a hanging iron step plate so the injured were easily lifted onto one of the front traverse seats or laid out on a padded stretcher along the back end. It had a black canvas roof and screens hanging to the wooden floors. The front was an open affair with only a dashboard between the driver's seat and team. To Julia it appeared to be a converted hearse.

"Don't let the looks fool you, Miss Barrie. This here Dougherty ambulance is light and fast. Tough as hell, and hard to roll over."

"Very well," Nicole shouted. "Get in, girls, and drop the tarp all around. There is no reason why you should eat dust. Thanks, Mr. Kinlaw."

"Don't wreck her, Miss Barrie. And don't kill my horses! Fifty dollars won't near pay the damages."

Julia hopped up beside Nicole on the driver's seat. "Even if this thing is fast, we'll never catch Dade. All we can hope is that he's forced to wait in ambush."

Nicole laid the buggy whip smartly across the team's rumps and they bolted like a pair of jackrabbits. Julia was nearly bowled over and the girls in back yelped as the ambulance slewed onto C Street headed west.

"He was right," Nicole yelled. "This devil is the fastest thing I've ever been in!"

Julia gripped the seat bars and hung on for dear life as they crested the divide and skidded on down into Gold Hill, riding mostly on two wheels from curve to curve.

The night air was shockingly cold and the sorrels liked to run. At this rate, if the wagon held together and Nicole stayed on the road, they might even overtake Dade and his gunslingers.

It seemed a frightening possibility.

28

Julia and Nicole thundered into Carson City just before dawn and paid a groggy hostler twice what his fresh team of horses was worth. The air was very cold, the stars dying one by one when they stiffly climbed back into the ambulance. As they swept south out of the sleepy town, Julia began to see the faint outline of the mountains towering off to her right. The last plaintive howls of coyotes rebounded across the Carson Valley as they passed through Mormon Station and swung up into the Sierras, where little creeks and aspen-clustered springs joined to become the east fork of the Carson River.

"Not much farther to the top!" Nicole yelled.

Julia hoped not. This was a brutal grade out of the valley, and their second team of horses was already badly winded.

Behind them, the sun escaped from the horizon and bathed the morning with a fresh wash of its rosy glow. They topped the basin, and Nicole, weariness etched in every line of her face, pulled the horses in for a breather.

"Everyone get out and stretch your legs," she ordered.

The disheveled girls tumbled from the wagon. By the looks of their eyes, it seemed obvious none of them had even attempted sleep. Julia figured she probably appeared every bit as weary.

"My heavens,"—Susie Pie blinked, pushing the tangle of blond locks away from her forehead—"I haven't seen a sunrise since I was about twelve years old."

"That long, huh?" Delia quipped nastily.

Susie Pie shot her a go-to-hell look that went unnoticed as Julia pointed down toward Lake Tahoe. As weary and battered as they all felt, it was hard not to feel awed by how the rising sun danced across it on patterns of red and gold, then suddenly erased the color to leave it a clean and shining blue.

They rolled the tarp curtains up all the way around and then stood about hesitantly, because they were not outdoor women, and the size of the land, its majesty and beauty, made them timid. Perhaps, as with Julia, each of the women realized this day might be their last and how beautiful the world was and why hadn't they ever noticed it until now?

Julia forced herself to climb up into a nearby pillar of rocks where she could view the entire lake, shoreline to shoreline, though the distances were so great she could barely distinguish the north end.

"Do you see anything?" Nicole asked, climbing up to join her and panting heavily in the thin air.

"No . . . yes! Look there!" she cried, pointing across the lake.

"I see them," Nicole answered. "We're in time. They're coming right this way."

"Yes, and both have a big catch of logs in tow." Julia's eyes dropped to the shore below and began to trace its every curve. "Do you see where they'll dock? My guess is that cove a few miles to the south."

"I think you're right. It's the only good harbor at this end."

Julia agreed. The cove was a natural harbor because of a fingerlike peninsula of rock that cupped a sandy beach protecting it from the hard afternoon winds. It had . . . She drew a sharp breath. "I see them!"

"Dade's men? Where?"

"On that peninsula. Almost to the tip."

"I see them. But . . ."

She didn't finish and Julia didn't need to ask why. It was obvious why they were hiding out there. The peninsula itself reached less than a hundred yards from shore, yet was situated so that Glenn and Clayton would have to steam by its tip in order to enter the sheltered cove. At that point they would be at the complete mercy of Dade's guns—and dynamite.

"Let's go!" Julia said quickly. "We've got to move in behind them. Perhaps get them in a crossfire."

"We can try," Nicole said, "but from the shoreline, they'll almost be out of pistol range."

"Maybe all we can do is warn the boats." She looked at the boats again. "They're moving across the water faster than I'd thought."

That was chillingly evident as Julia and Nicole scrambled off their perch and went down to the wagon. In a few terse words they explained the situation and that they'd have to go on foot straight through forest to have any chance of reaching the lake in time. The girls were almost relieved not to get back into the ambulance.

But not for long. The brush was thick, and though Julia tried to choose the easiest path, there just weren't any. Manzanita ripped their dresses and tore angry scratches across their legs. The slope was very steep and a blanket of dead pine needles made the footing treacherous. Even so, they went downhill at a wild scramble, now and again catching a glimpse of the shining water through the trees.

Three hundred yards above the cove, Julia stopped. Her lungs were on fire, burning for oxygen, and she and the other girls bent at the waist for a moment, fighting for breath. At last she straightened. "We'll have to be careful from here on. They might hear us."

So they crept forward, and now Julia could hear the hammering steam engines beating their side-wheel paddles into the water. Closer and louder they became, until finally the girls arrived at the edge of the lake and spied a big fallen pine tree to hide behind.

Delia De Rose tripped on a loose rock, and it tumbled off the bank and splashed loudly into the water. Everyone flattened behind the tree.

It was a long time before Julia felt her heartbeat slow. They'd escaped detection because of the loud steamboats. Julia counted at least six men hidden in the rocks, but the thing that really scared her was when the two steamboats disappeared behind the peninsula. Now she could only guess how many minutes would pass before either Clayton or Glenn unsuspectingly navigated into the cove beyond their view.

"What are they doing?" Nicole whispered.

"They're opening a box of dynamite. Look, there's Dade! He's passing it around."

Julia resisted the urge to fire because she knew she'd miss—and also she reminded herself that she must wait. Wait until Clayton and Glenn were still far enough from danger, yet close enough to help once the fighting began.

The next minutes that passed were the longest Julia had ever known. Because the steamboats were hidden from view as they approached, she didn't know exactly how close they were except by trying to guess from sound.

A thousand doubts assailed her in those anxious moments. Would she be able to warn Clayton and still expect help once Dade's men recovered enough to counterattack? Because if he couldn't, the girls would be overwhelmed by Dade's professionals, no matter how valiantly they fought.

"How much longer!" Ruby Jane cried. "They've got to be on top of those boats!"

The steam engines were thunderingly loud by now, and Julia knew she couldn't risk waiting another second. So she lifted her pistol, cocked the hammer back, then glanced to each side. They were ready. Tight-faced, scared, but determined as hell.

Julia squeezed the trigger. The pistol bucked in her hands and the explosion was deafening. Gunsmoke erupted from the barrel and completely obliterated the scene. Julia chased the smoke away as guns discharged all around her. She fired again and again as Dade and his men whirled around in surprise and began shooting.

When her pistol clicked on an empty shell, Julia remembered to duck, then swing the reloading cylinder open and extract the spent cartridges.

Susie Pie moaned, and Julia saw her slump forward with a bullet hole through the forehead.

"Bastards!" Nicole shrieked, firing in blind fury. Julia grabbed her and pulled her behind cover as bullets ripped into wood all around them. She'd dropped several cartridges into the dirt, then scooped them up and jammed them into the cylinder, wondering if their dirtiness would cause them to misfire or explode in the gun.

"Got one!" Delia yelled.

Julia fired methodically now; her eyes stung from smoke, and a chunk of bark splintered off a tree and a piece of it cut her cheek. Then she saw Dade yelling and gesturing wildly toward the cove, and an instant later, two sticks of dynamite sailed end over end through a high arc against the pale blue sky.

The explosion seemed to rock the very mountains themselves, and Julia had a vision of the little steamboats disintegrating in a shower of wood, iron, and smoke. Clayton and Glenn would be torn apart by fragments of flying boiler and engine and left to die in the cold mountain lake. She saw Dade Taylor shouting at the top of his lungs, exorting his men to hurl more dynamite at the boats and forget about the ineffective shooting at their backs.

Julia couldn't stand it. She jumped up and charged the peninsula. She *had* to divert their attention.

"Julia!" Nicole shrieked as Dade pivoted around.

He saw her coming through the rocks. Very deliberately he raised the Winchester to his shoulder and tracked her through the maze of boulders.

Julia tripped as he fired. She went sprawling into the rocks as his rifle slug ate granite and whined meanly into space.

"Julia!"

She twisted around and saw Nicole Barrie, a gun in her hand, running from cover. The woman charged into view. Dade grinned. Then his rifle swung in an eighty-degree circle. That's when Julia, elbows ground into rock, braced the big Navy Colt pistol in both hands and squeezed the trigger.

Her shot and Dade's were like a single roll of thunder. One ending where the second began.

Julia heard Nicole's cry of pain at the same instant that Dade staggered and almost dropped his rifle, then cursed and raised it again. Julia cocked back the hammer with her thumb, pointed the barrel at the place where his big gold pocket watch and chain met, and fired.

Dade's rifle seemed to disintegrate in his hands as he felt himself rising on his toes, saw, through a watery sheen of pain, the body of Nicole Barrie, the form of Julia. Then a white flower blossomed where she was and he felt himself being driven backward once more.

He suddenly knew he was dying, perhaps even dead. It was all wrong. The rifle in his hands went stone-heavy and he let it clatter to his feet. He spoke her name, yet heard only a loud, very shrill noise which gained force in his head. And just before something dark and thunderous blotted the world from his eyes, he saw the white flower open again and felt the gentle touch of something punching him over backward.

At the very final moment of his life, Dade remembered Holly.

Glenn had been in the lead boat when Julia and the girls opened fire. One moment they'd been chugging peacefully across the smooth lake surface; the next thing, all hell broke loose. He'd been just inside the cove and Clayton almost to the tip of the peninsula when the first sticks of dynamite were thrown. Fortunately they died in the water before exploding. But as he yelled to reverse the engine and the paddles stopped, then began to change direction, he saw another stick of dynamite being lobbed into the sky. He knew at a glance this one wouldn't miss. It seemed to hang up above their vessel, then fall directly down.

"Jump!" he yelled, throwing himself into a low dive. The explosion went off a dozen feet over the deck and Glenn saw the boiler jump skyward like a big kicked can as the entire cabin disappeared. He didn't know how many of his crew had time to react, but he thought most of them had gotten into the water as bullets searched for them among the logs.

Clayton's steamboat was farther out but took a blast right off the port side. The big side paddle actually lifted above the surface and churned crazily across the debris-strewn waters before disintegrating like a smoking Fourth of July pinwheel.

Glenn bellowed Clayton's name, but the explosions cut his voice off at water level.

Maybe Clayton and his men had reacted in time. He just didn't know. Glenn heaved his body half out of the water and called again. A hail of bullets drove him under the numbingly cold water. He surfaced a moment later to hang on to a log and try to keep his head down. His chances of survival were impossibly slim given that Dade's men kept lobbing dynamite into the wreckage. Sooner or later one of them was going to blow him to eternity.

He felt bitter helplessness as he heard the cries of wounded men. All they could do was to swim out into deeper water and hope the cold didn't cramp up their limbs and leave them to drown.

Glenn heard a barely audible cry for help. He picked his way between the logs until he reached one of his crew and saw the man's bloodied face as he fought to keep it above water. Glenn saved him from going under for the last time, knowing they couldn't survive for long. Maybe another fifteen or twenty minutes.

"Hang on," he urged the wounded man at his side, realizing that unless something changed, and fast, a few more minutes would not alter the final outcome. If these logs were smaller, or there'd been more survivors, perhaps they could have ferried them ahead as shields and gained the beach. But then what? Dade's hirelings were marksmen who'd enjoy nothing better than picking their quarry off as they hobbled across the beach.

Still, there was no choice. Anything beat hanging on to the logs and being blown to shreds. He had to try. If only, he thought, Clayton James had survived. Maybe together they'd have been able to formulate some kind of desperate plan. Glenn fumbled to unhook his belt and use it to tie the man afloat. But his fingers were so numb, it was taking forever.

Clayton had a plan, and it was pathetically simple. When he'd seen Glenn's steamboat fly apart under that first blast of dynamite, and caught a glimpse of Dade and his men tucked away up in the overhead rocks, he'd known their fate was sealed. With a yell split by the explosion he'd told them to dive and swim for safety if they could. Then he'd promptly taken his own advice as he saw the dynamite sticks falling. Clayton had driven his powerful body deep into the water. Even so, when the dynamite exploded, he felt as though a mountain had fallen in on him as a violent underwater upheaval twisted him and punched the air from his lungs. An explosion at surface level blew one of his eardrums out and he felt as though a river of lava had been poured through a funnel into his brain.

He convulsed. Thrashed wildly until something lanced through ten feet of water and sliced across his hip. Clayton's vision went black and then he groped at the projectile, and suddenly his head cleared the surface as bullets began to probe the water.

One kicked a tiny fountain into his eyes, and Clayton took a long gulp of air and dived. There are few lakes in the world as pure and with greater visibility than Lake Tahoe, and he could see at least seventy feet ahead as his powerful arms and legs worked like pistons driving him into deeper water.

He could also see the water churn as explosion after explosion sent objects skyward. Some of the debris was large, and he had the impression of how a frog in a pond might feel in its attempt to escape being speared. He circled the log flotilla, surfacing twice behind their cover before rounding the peninsula and angling back toward its outer edge. If Dade was tracking his progress, Clayton knew he was finished as soon as he touched beach. But he thought he might have a chance because of the debris and confusion.

With his lungs stretched to bursting, Clayton surfaced among the rocks, gasping for air.

He expected to see Dade or one of his gunmen crouched overhead with a bullet marked for his brain. Instead, he saw Julia desperately trying to drag a woman to cover, while just beyond, three other girls were shooting as though lead and powder were free.

"Julia!" he gasped, leaping out of the water and running on numb legs like a man gone wild. The distance was about sixty feet, and he covered it in seconds. With a dip of his shoulders he scooped Nicole Barrie off the rocky ground with one arm while his other encircled Julia's waist and propelled her along with sheer momentum.

He felt a bullet slice the muscle over his ribs, then ricochet across bone. Clayton took the last few strides, then dived over a rotting log as lead punched into soft decaying wood.

Julia threw her arms around his neck and he felt her tears for a moment before she broke free and looked at him in a way that he'd never forget. "I *knew* you'd come. That it would be *you.*"

"I'm just sorry I couldn't get here quicker."

"You'll do," Nicole Barrie gritted, holding a blood-soaked silk handkerchief to her head. "Got any idea how to get us out of here alive?"

"How badly are you hit?"

"I'll make it. Just a scalp wound. Not half what you got wrong. Even so, don't be expecting me to run up to the wagon."

"Wouldn't think of it." He peered over the log. "We need a rifle."

"You got one," Ruby Jane said. "I forgot how to reload the damned thing after I emptied it."

Clayton took the rifle and quickly reloaded. Now, he thought, we've got a chance!

He squeezed Julia's hand, feeling self-conscious because of the other women huddled around. "I'd better go now."

Julia's fingers gripped his own tightly. "Can't you stay here?"

"No. If I started firing, I'd hit a few but they'd retreat off those rocks to shore, then circle back around on us. We'd be driven into the lake and shot like ducks on a pond. Besides," he added, "Glenn and some of the others might still be alive down in the cove. But they can't hang on much longer."

"Dade is finished."

He stared at her.

"I killed him. And . . . and I lied to you, because I never loved him at all. I swear it!"

"For hell sake!" Delia swore. "Can't you two work that out later?"

Clayton laughed. Then he kissed Julia good-bye for what he hoped would be the last time. "It needed sayin'," he told her. "Win or lose. I needed to know."

"Here they come!" Ruby Jane cried.

Clayton whirled around to see a half-dozen or so men flitting from rock to rock as they headed for shore. He jammed the rifle against his shoulder, took a deep breath, and held it waiting for the first man to break from the rocks and sprint across an open space to the trees.

One bolted, and Clayton knocked him spinning into the water as the rest answered with a murderous volley.

"Get down!" he yelled, trying to watch and knowing, this time, they'd all break like a covey of quail.

They did. He sent a bullet among them. A runner yelped and went down thrashing. Clayton levered another bullet, and just as he started to fire, he saw one man moving strangely—and knew he carried the dynamite. Clayton had to kill one to open a line of fire; then he took dead aim and sent hot lead streaking into the dynamite.

None of them were prepared for the blast that leveled everything, including the trees and rocks for thirty yards in every direction. It seemed the entire world obliterated before their eyes. Clayton grabbed Julia and pushed her back under the log as rock and timber began to shower down.

It was a miracle none of them were killed by falling objects, and when they finally dared to look back down, what had been a peninsula was now just a long, skinny island.

29

Julia sat beside Clayton as he drove the wounded and dead into Virginia City. This was a day she'd never forget—its victory and its cost.

As they rolled up C Street toward the hospital, a crowd gathered to follow, and the news of their arrival brought the townsfolk in droves. Dan De Quille and Mark Twain were running beside the wagons with notebooks in their hands. Here was a story!

Julia saw Bevis York rush out of his office as Glenn Donovan rode over to tell the old man that Dade's power was broken and that now he intended to leave the Comstock to work on the Central Pacific Railroad. She understood why. Virginia City reminded Glenn too much of Fay Taylor. Even Clayton hadn't been able to talk him into staying with their logging operation.

Just up the street, Julia saw Holly's place. Julia said, "Please rein in the team. Someone's got to tell Holly she's a widow, and since I killed Dade, it should be me."

Clayton pulled the horses to a stop and motioned one of the crowd to change places and drive on in, saying to Julia, "I'm coming too."

"All right. But I know her better than you. And I should like to tell her alone."

"Fine. I'll wait outside," he replied, helping her down, then taking her arm.

Julia was grateful for his quiet strength, for it steeled her against the dread she felt inside as they approached the memory-filled house.

"You look like we're headed for the gallows," Clayton observed.

Julia tried to smile. "It's almost that bad. All these years I've been dreading this moment of truth, and now, on top of everything else, I have to tell Holly that I killed Dade and made her a widow."

"He deserved to die," Clayton reminded her gently. "Holly wanted a good-looking man back then and wasn't thinking too clearly, or she'd have known Taylor was rotten inside."

"I know, but she's got his children. Children need a father."

Clayton took her hand. "The woman will find a better man in time. One who'll love her for herself and not just money."

"The saying is easy, though you are right." She started for the door. "I may be inside quite awhile. I couldn't leave her crying."

"I got nowhere to go without you, Julia. I'll be here."

She wished she could tell Clayton how much she loved him. But she couldn't. Not until she'd faced Holly and begged her forgiveness. So Julia walked up slowly and knocked on her door, not knowing what she'd say or even if she could speak.

Holly swung the door open and almost dropped her son. "What do you want?"

"I have to talk to you," Julia whispered in a voice that threatened to break from strain.

"If it's about my husband, I already know," Holly said, her voice thick with emotion.

"You do?"

"Yes."

"I'm sorry. More than I could ever tell you."

Julia felt the tears, big wet ones, roll down her cheeks but she stood like some kind of dummy, unable to say any more, or even to run while Holly and Clayton watched.

"Come inside," Holly finally said, taking her arm and leading her through the doorway and to a chair. "You know, Julia, I'm not as naive as you thought."

"I . . . I don't understand."

"It's simple enough. From the first moment Dade met us up in the Sierras the time we were nearly stranded in the blizzard, he had his heart set on possessing you. What happened later is as much my fault as your own, because our marriage gave him the power to take what he desired. You, Julia. You were always the woman he desired, and I realized it even on our wedding night."

Julia squeezed her eyes shut. "All this time you knew?"

"Yes."

Julia dared not speak, as Holly continued. "I stuck it out with Dade this last year knowing what he'd become—and done—to you, my father, to everything good in Virginia City. I did it because of the babies. Stupid, really, to think they'd transform the man. After that terrible night when I found him in your room, I realized my mistake and made him leave. This is my house, bought and paid for by me."

Jessica began to cry and Julia rushed to pick her up without thinking until it was too late.

"It's all right," Holly said. "Look, already she's starting to quiet. She still remembers you. Anyway, I desperately wanted my babies to have a father, no matter what kind of man he was. After that night, I changed my mind. I won't ever take him back."

Julia peered into the woman's eyes. Made herself say, "You can't, Holly. Dade tried to ambush Glenn and Clayton up at the lake. I . . . I shot him."

Holly blinked, and one hand flew to her lips. Then she fainted.

"Are you going to be all right?"

Holly smiled wanly. "Yes. I've never done that before. Once I recover from the shock, I'll be fine. The babies will keep me company. And with my . . . with Dade gone," she corrected herself with slow deliberation, "I'll be able to become more actively involved in the hospital and school. They are badly understaffed and financed."

"You may want to remarry someday," Julia said, trying to make her feel better.

"Anything can happen."

"There are good men, Holly. You'll find one. Until then, it's obvious your life will be full. The people of Virginia City adore you. They have for years."

"Thank you." Holly took the baby. "I've never touched your room. It's still yours if you'd like to live with us again."

Julia glanced out the window. Saw Clayton out by the front gate smoking his pipe and waiting. "I can't. But I'll want to visit often."

"Of course." Holly stood up. "Well, take care, Julia. Tell Glenn Donovan—"

"Holly," she blurted. "For Glenn's sake, I need a favor."

"Ask it."

"You probably have guessed that Glenn has always loved Fay."

"Yes, he's talked to my father about her many times."

"Could you please write Fay? Tell her that Glenn still loves her and is leaving the Comstock."

Holly shook her head. "It wouldn't change things. Fay intends to marry some European."

"Oh." Julia was suddenly at a loss for words and glanced away, feeling terribly disappointed by the news, yet unable to accept it as final. "If you don't mind, I'd still like her address. I should write to say what happened to Dade."

"I'd appreciate that." Holly located the address somewhere in a giant rolltop desk. "Your best chance is to write her in Vienna, where she may be staying with her old friend and manager, Rosie Raye."

"I will. Thank you."

"Good-bye," Holly told her softly. "If ever I've met a woman with a right to some happiness on earth, you're the one. Clayton is a fine man."

Julia squeezed Holly and rushed away.

Now that she'd faced up to it and received Holly's forgiveness, Julia felt wonderful. She tugged playfully on Clayton's beard. "I have to say that if you ever wanted to shave, it would be fine with me."

He grinned through the heavy growth. "You don't like it? We aren't even married yet and you're trying to change me around."

"Oh, no!" she protested with alarm. "I like you fine. Only I know you . . ." It was difficult to say.

"Speak up," he ordered gently.

"I know about the bear-claw scars. And I just wanted you to realize they wouldn't matter, even a little."

Clayton shook his head. Glanced away for a minute. "You coming with me to the mountain?"

"Yes."

He engulfed her hands in his own. "You always wear these gloves, Julia?"

A river of unreasoning panic swept through her body, and

she involuntarily tried to pull them away. But he gripped her wrist and removed the gloves to study the slash of scar tissue. Then he raised them up to his lips and said, "Julia, you're too damn beautiful for a man like me, but I'm going to marry you anyhow."

A deep well of happiness bubbled up inside, and Julia kissed him in a way that she'd never kissed any man.

For the rest of her life, she knew everything was going to be just fine.

Fay reread only the last few paragraphs of the letter she'd just received from Julia James.

> Holly will be fine and I'll visit her often. Soon the babies will be crawling, and then her real work will begin.
>
> I can't describe how sorry I am that your brother had to end as he did. Perhaps you blame me in part, and I can only ask your forgiveness. But as I've already said, it is Glenn Donovan who loves you. I had to tell you this in the slim hope you haven't already married.
>
> Glenn departed yesterday to work on the Central Pacific Railroad, which has now left Auburn, California.
>
> You could find him, if you were lonely. Perhaps I am just being a fool because a woman in love wants all others to feel the same. Wish us healthy children. Either boys strong like Clayton or girls with your courage and talent.
>
> I have made terrible mistakes in my lifetime, but marrying Clayton has erased them all. Because of this, I now realize this one truth:
>
> In this world, love matters above everything.
>
> Sincerely,
> Julia James

Rosie dropped her pen and rubbed her aching fingers. "Honestly, Fay, if we ever complete all these wedding invitations, it will be a miracle. Did André have to invite every theatrical family and ownership in Europe?"

Fay stared at Julia's letter. "He said it was a wonderful

opportunity to publicize my upcoming tour. Our wedding is sure to be the social event of the year.''

Rosie frowned. ''But you look so tired, Fay. Can't you and André at least set aside a month for yourselves?''

''He says not.''

''What do *you* say?''

She shrugged. Wanted to change the subject. ''Are you curious about the news I've just received from Virginia City?''

''Should I be?''

''Not really. It's just that my brother died.''

''I'm sorry,'' Rosie offered, coming over quickly.

''He was shot.'' Fay looked away. ''Dade was no good, Rosie. It took me years to accept that fact. The woman who killed him says Glenn Donovan still loves me.''

''Donovan. Donovan.'' She frowned with concentration. ''Is he that wild man who tried to kidnap you in New York City? The one you jumped into the filthy ocean and received such terrific send-off publicity with?''

Fay closed her eyes, and the scene almost came to life. ''Yes, only it wasn't for publicity. It was . . . oh, you may think this silly, but when that happened, it was almost like the day we met, when he rescued me from drowning in the American River. Just us two.''

''Sounds like you and he enjoyed being in the water together a lot,'' Rosie grumbled. ''First the river, then the Atlantic Ocean. What else did you enjoy?''

''Not much. Mostly just each other. We were each mighty dreamers in those days.''

''And they came true, Fay. He's now an engineer and you've become world-famous.''

Fay couldn't get the letter out of her mind. ''But he isn't happy, Rosie. So . . . so what good is a dream come true that leaves you hollow inside?''

Rosie knelt down beside her. ''Can you say that right before your own wedding?''

''I've never lied to you, Rosie, and I won't now. Yes, I can't help it, but that is exactly how I feel.''

The older woman's expression grew troubled and pensive. ''Do you love him?''

''Very, very much.''

''Then I don't understand,'' Rosie said in a discouraged voice. ''You have your dream and the man you love. What—?''

''Not André,'' Fay quickly declared. ''I still love Glenn.''

Rosie took a deep breath and stood up, then walked over to her desk. Almost ceremoniously, she lifted her first stack of carefully written wedding invitations and dropped them in the waste container beside her desk. "You'll be giving up your career. All you've worked for."

"I know," Fay said, her heart beginning to pound faster.

"Will you leave soon?"

"Yes," she whispered. "As soon as I write a letter for André asking for his forgiveness and breaking our engagement."

Rosie shook her head; a trace of amusement tugged at her lips. "And where is this wild young engineer of yours? Will you rejoin him in some river or stream?"

"No." She laughed, a feeling of joy making her want to sing. "I'll find him in those magnificent Sierras where we first met. And I'll be there when he builds a great railroad."

Fay Taylor's eyes focused on a single line of Julia's letter, and she knew it to be the truest thing she would ever learn:

In this world, love matters above everything.